"A dead hostage is of no value,"

she said, repeating the words she had uttered so many times in the past week. It was her only defense.

"I'm thinking this *live* one is of no value." It was said lightly, yet there was something terribly wistful in the words themselves that caused a streak of anguish to run through her.

"It seems a waste, my lady, to save my arm, and my life, only to hang me later," he continued.

"Mayhap it will make better sport," she replied, but her eyes were warmer than he'd ever seen them.

"And this?" he asked, his gaze sweeping the comfortable room. "Temporary, I fear?"

"Aye."

"Back to my bare cell?" The potion was working; his mind was growing sluggish. But he didn't want to close his eyes, didn't want to lose sight of the face he was so foolishly growing to cherish.

"Aye," she said reluctantly.

His eyes began to close, long black lashes sweeping over the dark, cryptic gray, and he looked terribly like a tired young boy. Elsbeth continued to watch him as he slept, a single tear falling down her cheek.

bringing you a new historical romance from
Lynda Trent, *The Black Hawk.* Forced by
circumstances into marrying an enigmatic sea
captain, Lady Bianca Stanford has no inkling of the
intrigue that will soon threaten her life and the lives
of those around her.

Patricia Potter fans will be delighted by
The Abduction, a tale of double kidnapping that
pits an English nobleman and a Scottish woman,
who is the leader of her clan, against their
collective enemies.

In *The Loving Swords,* by Marjorie Burrows,
Clemma Wells finds inner strength and love in the
untamed territories of the American northwest. And
Peggy Bechko's *Cloud Dancer* captures the
tenderness and power of the love between a young
Pueblo maiden and a seasoned Apache warrior.

Once again, join us for four historical romances
from the line that always brings you your favorite
authors: Harlequin Historicals.

Yours,

Tracy Farrell
Senior Editor

PATRICIA POTTER

is a former journalist with a passion for history and books. While working at the *Atlanta Journal* she met and reported on three presidents and covered southern news stories as varied as the space launches and the civil rights movement.

A resident of Atlanta, Georgia, Patricia has her own public relations and advertising agency. Her interests in animals and travel are not especially compatible, but she does manage to fit them both into her schedule, along with her reading, which runs the gamut from biographies to espionage. She is a past president of the Georgia Romance Writers and is now busy winning awards for her historical romances.

Prologue

Scottish-English border, 1552

Tension slithered in the air between the two men—enemies and allies both.

And because they knew each other, neither trusted the other beyond this one transaction. They were opportunists, and recognized the treachery in each other. In a month, a year, they would probably meet in battle.

But now they had a common objective: to rid themselves of relatives who kept them from title, land and power. And they could achieve all three by pitting their two obstacles against each other.

This night both were dressed in black, and rode without retainers or servants. They knew, without doubt, that if they were discovered, their families would kill them.

Each considered the prize worth the risk.

In the dark of the march, where the mist hung like a curtain, the two cloaked men were almost invisible; though each man knew his companion was heavily armed.

"I fulfilled my part," one of the men said. "Now I expect deeds from you, not words."

"I can do nothing without her consent," the other said stiffly.

"Then get her consent, plague take you!"

"She has a mind of her own."

"Perhaps," the other voice said slyly, "you are not man enough for her. Perhaps I should take her. Show her a true man—"

"You! She would as soon plunge her dagger in your heart. In the heart of any Carey."

"Well, we'll just have to provide one for her, won't we?"

The taller man looked at his companion with distaste. "If any harm comes to her, there'll be no place for ye to hide."

"Nor you, my Scots friend, if anyone discovers you're dealing with me."

"That goes for you, too. Even if your brother was gone for eight years, he's now earl, and the lord, and commands his people's loyalty."

"He's weak," the younger man spit out. "All he talks about since he returned is peace. And cutting the rents. God's blood, peace on the borders?" There was a smirk in his voice as he continued. "That won't suit you any more than it does me."

"No," the other man agreed slowly. He had gotten wealthy in the past five years by stealing from the English, just as the man opposite him had increased his wealth by raiding the Scots. "Let's get to the business at hand, then. Where is the best place to take Huntington?"

"At the pool. He bathes there every morning just after sunrise. Alone."

A heavy eyebrow rose in surprise. "'Tis a wonder he hasn't already died of the ague."

"Worse luck. He seems to thrive on it. A habit he picked up on the Continent, he says."

"Every morning?" The taller man wanted reassurance. It wasn't wise for Kers to ride the marches during the day. It might be risked once, but more than that was foolhardy.

"Every morning," came the assurance.

"I don't know if she's ready. She's still in mourning."

"I'll make sure she is," the other man said. "We'll burn out some of her crofters tomorrow night."

There was a pause, a hesitancy, but finally the cloaked man agreed reluctantly. "'Twill be done."

"Done," was the satisfied reply.

Chapter One

Elsbeth Ker threw the pewter goblet across the room with all her strength. It went skittering noiselessly across the rich carpet until it hit the stone wall with an unholy clash.

The two men, who were sprawled in velvet-covered chairs, sat up suddenly, amusement in the eyes of one, wariness in the other.

"God's blood!" Elsbeth cursed. "How dare they?" Her voice lowered into a sound of absolute rage. "How dare they?" she repeated.

"The Careys," Ian Ker said, "dare anything. They have the warden's ear, and they think ye are vulnerable now. There is no chief."

"I am head of the clan," Elsbeth replied. "And by God's truth they will not get away with this."

Ian leaned back and looked at his cousin. Her auburn hair with its vivid streaks of copper was loose and flowed to her waist. Her hazel eyes were shot with golden sparks, and her chin rose higher and higher with pride.

She was lovely, this cousin of his, and both he and Patrick, another by-blow cousin, were among a host of suitors for her hand—her hand and the title, for both would go to her husband.

Elsbeth, even as a child, had been full of fire. Fire and enthusiasm and sometimes foolish bravery. She rode like the wind, and had learned the rudiments of swordsmanship, although she could not handle the large two-handed sword he and Patrick used. Instead they had presented her with a light slender blade at which she had become most adept, and her quickness and determination substituted for strength.

But though she worked at men's games, Ian and Patrick both worried about her capacity to carry on as nominal chief of this particular branch of the Ker family.

Now her eyes showed the old combative fervor.

Ian looked over at his cousin. Patrick was dark haired where his own coloring was light, his cousin's eyes unemotional where his own were usually laughing. But now Patrick's dark onyx eyes were regarding Elsbeth with interested approval. They had grown up together, the three of them, although Elsbeth was legitimate—and the heir—whereas they were bastards and lived on tolerance.

Ian had learned to accept his lot years ago. Patrick never had.

But they had become the right and left arms of the old laird, Robert Ker, who had been killed six months earlier during a Carey raid.

And now the Careys had struck again, burning out the crofters who depended on Elsbeth for protection.

Many among the Ker clansmen had wanted to strike back immediately after the death of the old laird. But Elsbeth, in mourning for her father, had hesitated. She heard that the earl of Huntington and his oldest son had died of a mysterious fever, and it seemed God had, indeed, smitten the wicked. But this new outrage proclaimed that nothing had changed, and Elsbeth knew that if she did nothing, her clan would no longer respect her authority. Both Ian and Patrick had told her there were already rumblings, and she knew there was strong feeling that she should marry and pass the title and leadership to a man. But on this point she was adamant. She had seen her parents' unhappy marriage, and she would not marry except for love, although the queen regent herself, wanting stability on the border, had urged it.

Elsbeth knew that both her cousins desired marriage with her, but they were more like brothers than suitors, and she could not imagine a marriage bed with either of them, although each was attractive in his individual way: Ian with his laughter and good nature, and Patrick with his dark brooding intensity. She loved them and trusted them with her life and those of her clansmen. But marriage?

No, she would wait. And she would show her clan that she was both strong and determined, and that she could protect it.

"The new earl is back?" she questioned now.

"So we have heard," Ian answered carelessly.

"He, then, is responsible for this newest outrage?"

"I expect so."

She turned to Patrick. "What do you think of this man?"

Patrick shrugged. "We donna know much about him. He used to go on border raids years ago. Then he disappeared. He was believed dead."

"His brother, John, couldn't have been pleased when he turned up alive," Elsbeth said thoughtfully.

"No," Ian replied with quiet amusement. "He thought Huntington and the title his."

"And a greedier man never existed," Elsbeth said. "Except perhaps for others in his clan."

"The new earl has Northumberland's ear, I understand," Ian said, naming the most powerful man in England, John Dudley, Lord Protector of the boy king, Edward VI.

"English dogs," Elsbeth said, not caring that her language was not quite appropriate for the lady she was. As the only living child of a border chief, she had early learned independence and to hold her own with the rough-speaking borderers. "I think it's time we taught this new lord—all the Careys—a lesson they'll not forget," Elsbeth added heatedly.

She blamed herself for not attacking the Careys earlier, but she had hoped for peace when the old earl died, an end to what had become a blood feud, knowing it would, sooner or later, hurt the hundreds of crofters—tenants—and lay waste the land desperately needed to feed her people. She had tried to ignore the fact that when the Careys killed her father, they had moved from the traditional raiding that plagued the border by violating one of the principal tenets of border warfare: one did not kill, especially not in ambush. Now the Scot borderers believed any response was justified, including a few killings of their own. The devil take a warden who tried to keep peace in such a circumstance.

"Aye," Elsbeth repeated, almost to herself. "I think we must teach the Careys a lesson they won't soon forget, and particularly this new English whoreson who calls himself earl."

Patrick frowned at the use of the word *whoreson,* but Ian merely grinned. This was the Elsbeth he remembered from childhood, not the quiet uncertain girl who had recently mourned her father with such sorrow.

"We hear the new earl has some very peculiar habits," Ian said. "He bathes in the pool close to the border each morning soon after sunrise."

"Without guards?" Elsbeth asked.

Ian shrugged. "'Tis what I heard."

"He must be a fool."

Patrick interrupted for the first time. "He's no' a fool, I think. Nor a coward. I met him once eight years ago on a raid, and he's as wily as they come. And skilled."

Elsbeth stared at the wine trickling down the stone wall, thinking of her choices. Patrick and Ian would carry out any orders she gave. She could have the new earl killed, but then she would have to cope with John Carey.

But if they held Lord Huntington hostage and demanded ransom?

She could humiliate and chasten him, while obtaining Carey funds to recompense the burned-out crofters. It would be good to have a Carey under her thumb, perhaps relieve some of the anger that had been boiling inside her since her father's murder.

She knew the new earl hadn't been directly responsible for her father's death. The old laird was killed nearly six months ago, and Alexander Carey had returned to Huntington less than a month ago. But it mattered not. He was a Carey, now the Carey lord, and the attack on her people last night proved he was no different from the others of his name.

"We'll take him hostage," she said abruptly.

Ian raised an eyebrow, and Patrick glowered. "It would be better to kill him," the latter said. He had loved the old laird, Robert Ker, who had treated him roughly but fairly.

"We need the money," Elsbeth said. "And we'll make his stay nae a pleasurable one. He'll learn about the Kers."

"It might be difficult taking him alive," Ian warned.

"Aye," Patrick added in rare agreement, and with a glint in his dark eyes that Elsbeth didn't miss.

"I shall go with you," she pronounced.

"You will not," the two cousins said in unison.

"The Careys would dearly like their hands on you, cousin," warned Ian.

"They would probably rape you," Patrick added darkly.

"They would take everything we own as ransom," Ian continued.

"Great God above, but 'tis a foolhardy thing to do. You will endanger all of us," Patrick reasoned.

But she would not be dissuaded. As much as she loved her cousins, she didn't quite trust them not to kill the earl of Huntington. They had their own grievances against the Carey family.

"You know I can ride as well as either of you," she said. "And use my dagger. Fa taught me well."

"In games, dear cousin. In games. This is nae sport."

Her eyes twinkled. "But it is, Patrick. It will be great sport to catch a Carey. And I intend to be in on the kill."

Ian sighed. It was useless to argue. "Let us plan well, then," he said.

He refilled their goblets with wine, and the three of them sat companionably as they plotted a kidnapping. Now they had decided on a course of action, they did not consider the possibility of failure. Instead, they discussed how they would hold the new earl once they had him. There were no dungeons in the peel tower that was both their home and their fortress.

The custom, Elsbeth knew, in holding captives for ransom was merely to accept the hostage's word that he would behave. But there had been too much treachery over the years ever to take a Carey's pledge.

"I'll have the blacksmith bar the upper tower room," Elsbeth said.

"I'm not sure I like a Carey in the tower," Ian said thoughtfully. "He can see and hear too much—our defenses, our strengths and weaknesses."

Elsbeth had to agree. But there was no other place. No place safe or secure enough. "We'll blindfold him when he's not in the tower room."

Patrick grunted. "All that trouble for an English cur, and a Carey at that. I still think we should kill him."

"We will do as we planned," she said. "As soon as the tower room is prepared."

Alexander Carey was in a cold fury as he faced his younger brother. "You knew I ordered no more raids!"

"They had taken some of our cattle," John answered furiously. "We had to retaliate."

"And now they will burn out our tenants. God's blood, John, when will it ever end?"

"It won't," John said. "The Kers have been our enemies for centuries."

Alex carefully measured his words as he slowly delivered them from a mouth frowning with displeasure. "You will never—do you hear me, John—never again take out my men without my consent."

John, three inches shorter than his brother and slighter in build, tensed with an anger of his own. "They were *my* men two months ago. You haven't been a part of this family for eight years." He wanted to say more, but he held his tongue. If all went well, his brother would be a short-lived annoyance.

Alex took a long deep breath as he regarded his younger brother. He had felt John's simmering resentment ever since he arrived, and it disturbed him deeply. They were all that were left of a father and three sons.

He thought for a moment of Nadine, gentle Nadine, who had taught him so much about courage and sacrifice, and he could barely tolerate his brother's selfish concerns.

In the galleys where he had labored as a slave for long endless years, he had thought of little else than his home, the free green forests of Huntington. He had no more than reached London and regained his strength when he learned that his father and older brother were dead of fever, and that his younger brother, John, believing Alex dead, had assumed the title.

When Alex arrived at Huntington, he discovered his brother was distinctly displeased to see him. Although disappointed, Alex was not altogether surprised. His mother had died years ago, and his father had been a cold, even cruel man who had set son against son. It was one of the reasons Alex had left Huntington years ago to seek his fortune, perhaps in marriage. But his time abroad and the years of hell in French galley ships had misted over the ugliness of his youth. He had remembered the cold crisp air, the blue streams and the vivid green of the marches, and little of the old aching pain of rejection.

Now he was the earl, and he had not liked what he saw when he arrived. John was overtaxing the tenants to the point of starvation, and the fields had been neglected while John, and previously his father, used all the men to raid along the border. He was particularly angered to learn that his father had killed Robert Ker and fueled an already bitter feud.

Alex was tired of adventuring, of captivity, and he wanted, above all, peace. He wanted a prosperous contented estate; he wanted a gentle wife and healthy children. Instead he found a furious brother, angry tenants and a private war he did not start.

It was not that he avoided danger or conflict. Indeed, he had known his share, both as a boy and a young man on border raids, and then later, when he took up the cause of the Protestants in France and helped them escape persecution. On his last such attempt, he himself was caught and sent to the French galleys. He had thought himself condemned forever to the dark damp bottom of a galley until John Knox, the Scottish firebrand minister and his fellow slave, was freed thanks to pressure by the English, and told John Dudley, duke of Northumberland and Lord Protector, that Alexander Carey was alive....

Home, in those dark months, had represented light—the sun high in the sky, the sun glinting against the blue water of a mountain pool, the sun hitting the fresh tender leaves of a tree.

And freedom. The greatest light of all.

Alex had tried, since his return, to work with John, to ease the younger man's jealousy. He had even thought about leaving, and rejoining King Edward's court, but he felt the estate grossly mismanaged. He owed something to the tenants, although they remained suspicious of him. He had been gone too long, and they had already suffered under his father and brothers.

And he had little desire to return to court. Since the death of Henry VIII, London had become a hotbed of intrigue and conspiracy as the nobles sought to control the sickly boy king, Henry's only son. It was dangerous to one's health to be a part of that hotbed, even if one had highly placed friends....

The quiet pain of loneliness, which he had tried to smother, rose again and struck him like a bolt of lightning as he listened to John's explanations about the latest raids on Ker land.

"I'll hear no more," Alex roared suddenly, surprising his brother. "Like it or not, I am earl of Huntington. There will be no more raids." With those last angry words, he left the room, fighting to keep his temper, struggling to keep the hurt within him from showing.

He strode to the stables, ordering his black stallion, Demon, saddled. He wished there were one man in his household to trust, but he knew few of them well enough to do so. They were his father's men, and then his brother's, and they had benefited from the frequent raids across the border into Scotland. They were all, he knew, resentful of the new restrictions he had imposed.

Only one, whom he had played with as a boy, seemed to view him with any understanding—a lieutenant now with the Carey army. David Garrick had not been at Huntington when Alex first arrived, for he had been on loan to another lord; Garrick had become a superb trainer of fighting men, Alex was told, and was often loaned out for substantial sums, most of which had gone to Huntington rather than Garrick. He had returned only yesterday, and Alex had had but a brief glimpse of him.

Discouraged, tired and still angry, Alex decided to seek him out. He hoped Davey would not have changed so much since they were lads together. He had already asked the location of Garrick's cottage, and he rode directly to it, dismounted easily and tied the reins of his horse to a nearby tree. After hesitating a moment, he knocked on the heavy oak door.

Davey's appearance had changed little over the years. His body was muscled but lean, his sandy hair short but thick and thoroughly mussed. His blue eyes were as clear as Alex remembered, but his face was harder. There was a startled look on it now, but then the lips widened with a smile Alex knew well. "M'lord," Garrick said simply. "It's well you've come home at last."

Alex looked inside and saw a woman rise quickly from a table. "Davey," he said softly, "I should not be interrupting."

David's grin grew wider. "But you are not," he replied. "Please enter. I want you to meet my wife, Judith."

The woman was slender and blond with a sweet countenance and a sweeter smile. Alex just barely remembered a child named Judith, a tenant's daughter. "Millie's daughter?" he asked, and noted her delight at being remembered.

David nodded, putting his arm around the woman.

"You are a very fortunate man, Davey."

The nickname dissolved what little tension remained. There had been few differences between them as children, and that time was now remembered.

"Would you sup with us, my lord?" Judith said in a small shy voice. "It is but a simple stew."

"I can think of nothing I would like better," Alex replied, taking his cloak from his shoulder.

David Garrick stood awkwardly until Alex sat and motioned him down. "I have been an earl a very short time," Alex said with twisting lips that held a hint of self-mockery. "I am not accustomed to such deference," he added as his mind flicked back to the galleys, where the only attentions given him were curses and the whip.

"We all thought you dead, m'lord."

"Obviously," Alex replied shortly, thinking of John's usurpation of the title.

"You were gone for years without word."

"I was serving the French," Alex said, his mouth once more twisting ironically in anything but a smile.

Garrick was warned by the expression and by the cloudy gray eyes that defied him to ask more questions. He knew that France and Scotland were allies against England, and he also sensed Alex's short explanation was no explanation at all. But, God's blood, he wouldn't be the one to question the new lord.

The supper, served on wooden trenchers, was simple but hearty and tasty, and Alex ate with more appetite than he had since he left London. He had grown to hate the tense formal meals with his glowering brother.

The meal was over all too soon, and he saw the looks cast between David Garrick and his Judith. He felt very much the outsider, and reluctantly he took his leave.

David accompanied him to the door. "I am glad you've returned, m'lord."

"You make a sum of one," Alex said dryly.

"There will be others," David said. "Reducing the rents helped, but after years of mistreatment, trust doesn't come easily." He suddenly realized what he had said, and so did Judith. Her face paled.

"My lord, he did not mean that."

"He did," Alex said. "And I'll not punish a man for speaking the truth. I could do nothing before, which is why I left, but I can now. And I will make changes, Davey."

A wide grin crossed Garrick's hard face. "It will be my honor to serve you, m'lord."

"And one to have you at my side once more. Tomorrow morn, we shall have a long talk."

"Yes, m'lord."

"I was Alex to you once, Davey."

"That was a long time ago."

"Aye. A million years," Alex said. "But I'll always be Alex to you."

David could not force the word. But he nodded as he watched Lord Huntington mount his horse and ride away. As he turned back inside, he wondered if he would ever forget that note of yearning in the earl's voice.

Alex strode upstairs to his room, his mind impatiently sorting through a multitude of problems facing him. He had not yet taken the master chamber, but kept the one he had used as a young man. There was already so much resentment on John's part that Alex had not, as yet, demanded it as his right, and John had not offered it.

The candles were lit, but the chamber was dim and as plain as Alex's clothes. A simple bedstead was made comfortable by a thin mattress; after three years on a wooden bench he could bear little else. There was a table and a basin newly filled with water. An embroidered chair and a rich rug provided the only traces of rank and color.

He discarded his unfashionably simple jerkin and doublet, then his soft Spanish boots, one of the few luxuries in which he indulged. He stripped off the breeches with the long tailored hose stitched to them.

Completely naked, he strode to the window and looked out over the keep below. His now. It was still difficult to fathom after the past bitter years. His to hold. His to protect. He sighed, knowing none of it would be easy. He had never expected to inherit, not with an older brother who was married. But his brother's wife had borne two dead babes and had later died, along with the child, in her third attempt to produce an heir. Now the English crown expected him to protect his part of the border and to quiet the incessant raiding that was so much a part of life here.

The Scottish monarchy had tried to control the raiding, too, even to the point of hanging one of the most popular Scottish chieftains, Johnny Armstrong. But neither England nor Scotland had been able to control the border nobles and their families.

Alex had been charged by the Lord Protector, who had arranged his release from the French, to try and put a stop to some of the lawlessness. And then he had discovered his own family was one of the chief offenders—even after he'd returned.

The Kers would be furious at the latest raid, and could be expected to retaliate. He wondered about the daughter who had inherited after his father had killed hers. He himself was not guiltless; God knew that he had, many years ago, played a role in the centuries-old feud. As a boy, he had wholeheartedly taken part in the hit-and-run raids on the Ker lands, just as the Kers had on this side of the border. But eventually he had come to question a practice that enriched the lords and impoverished the tenants, who saw their homes and lands burned repeatedly. His stumbling questions to his father were met with contempt, and he was banished to the English court. There he met Nadine and her father, French Huguenots, who had come to plead the Protestant case. His idealism and sense of adventure eventually took him to France, where he sided with the persecuted Huguenots in leaving the country—until he and Nadine were caught. Because he was English, he escaped death and was enslaved on the galleys. Nadine and her father were condemned to the fire.

His idealism faded on the galley, worked and sweated out of him, until he met John Knox, a preacher, who had been stolen out of Scotland and also enslaved. They kept each other alive, until Knox was freed and in turn helped to free Alex.

Although he was intrigued by John Knox's passion, he never really shared the man's beliefs. He disliked fanaticism in any form, and in the past years he had found that religion, any religion, too often took that form. It sickened him that Catholics killed Protestants, and Protestants Catholics, in the name of God. His efforts in France had been for individuals, not for religion.

Still, out of necessity, he and Knox had become friends. Hunger and pain and misery were a common bond, and on the days the wind blew heavy and the oars remained still, they passed the dark hours in argument and conversation. Knox challenged Alex in a way he had never been challenged before, and created in him a hunger for knowledge and ideas, a hunger that continued after his freedom was restored.

But now he faced more immediate problems. He thought about possible ways of approaching the Kers, mayhap making reparations. But then he might lose the loyalty of his own people. The feud had become a blood one now, no quarter asked or given. And he knew he had to show strength to keep what was his.

He lay down, stretching his tall lean frame across the hard mattress. Tomorrow. He would talk to Garrick and some other men Garrick thought might be trusted, and see what could be done to quiet the hate and violence between Scot and English.

Alex closed his eyes, thinking of the future.

Chapter Two

Elsbeth accepted Ian's help in mounting, seized the pommel and swung her leg around it, then settled her gown modestly around her legs. She wore a heavy cloak against the night mist, and a dagger was fitted into a special sash of the Ker green-and-red plaid.

Both Ian and Patrick had made last-minute attempts to discourage her from coming, but she remained adamant. It was her clan, her retribution. And she wanted to be a part of it.

They traveled slowly through the dense marches, over trails that only the Kers knew. The moon was full, which made the way easier. Patrick, who had the eyes of an eagle, led the way for the twenty men and one woman. He was dour as usual, but Elsbeth caught a hint of suppressed excitement. Like all borderers he enjoyed the adventure of night riding, the promise of danger that made all the senses alive and tingling.

It was not so with Elsbeth. While she knew what she was doing was necessary to protect the Kers from further raids, she wondered about the ultimate outcome.

There was a void in Scotland now, just as there was in England. Scotland had a girl queen, and England a boy king. Both were in the hands of ambitious relatives fighting to retain control while the kingdoms lay divided by religion and internal feuds. There was little, if any, order.

No one would stop a full war between the Kers and Careys, and Elsbeth shuddered at the bloodshed that could result, the cottages burned, the land destroyed. She was not fainthearted, but such a prospect could not be ignored. It would be her people who would suffer.

It was cool this morning, and she wondered about a man who would bathe each day in such weather. She was fastidious, but used only water warmed by fires and poured in her wood tub. The thought of bathing in an icy pool was more than she could comprehend.

She tried to remember him, the new earl of Huntington, knowing that as a girl she must have seen him at one of the Truce Days, a time of settling disputes. But she could not. She had seen his brothers, John and the late William, who possessed neither good looks nor character. Elsbeth thought this middle brother must be much the same, although Patrick had warned he could be a man to be heeded.

'Twas no matter. She would be rid of the treacherous dolt quickly. In the meantime, he would be locked tight in her tower.

The thought lightened her mood, and she spurred her horse to ride alongside Ian, whose eyes were also bright with anticipation. He wore a leather jacket with iron reinforcement and a steel bonnet, and carried a heavy two-handed sword as well as a pistol. Some of the other men carried spears, which they held carefully as they wended through the heavy foliage of sycamore, beech, oak and elm and crossed fast-running streams.

They should reach the dale, where Carey was said to go each morning, several hours before sunrise. She looked at Ian, who grinned back. Perhaps it would be a fine adventure after all, this hunting of Careys.

When they approached the pool, situated well on Carey land, they dispersed quickly through the trees, several climbing agilely into their branches, others taking positions around the perimeter and several more leading the horses out of hearing and sight.

Since they had decided to hold back their attack until the earl was in the water—and stripped of weapons as well as clothes—Elsbeth reluctantly retreated with the horses, warning all her clansmen that the Englishman must be taken alive. At the first shout she would join them, as it was up to them to have the man decently clad.

The waiting was difficult. The night seemed longer than ever before to Elsbeth as she remained behind with the horses and one disgruntled clansman who fretted at missing the fun. The first faint glimmers of light snaked through the heavy trees, and she heard the first sweet song of birds. She wanted to be with Patrick and Ian; she wanted to experience the Englishman's humiliation. She thought about returning to the pool, but propriety demanded otherwise, and she did not wish to expose her whole clan to possible dishonor. So she waited, passing time by quietly asking her companion about his family and whispering gently to her mare. As the sky grew lighter she heard a flock of pheasant taking wing, and she knew the Englishman would be approaching.

Quiet and tense, she remounted her horse. Sensing her mistress's anxiety, the horse sidestepped until Elsbeth soothed her with a long stroke of her hand. Finally she heard a shout, the battle cry of the Kers, and she spurred the mare forward.

Alex was distracted by his thoughts. In the two months since he'd come home, he'd traveled to several estates that were now part of his holdings and he knew he was a very wealthy man. Yet wealth in itself meant little to him now; it couldn't buy the peace he wanted or ease the growing loneliness in him. John would eventually have to be dealt with—he was learning that more with each day—and the prospect did nothing to cheer him. Nor did the possibility of war with the Kers.

He neglected his usual caution as such thoughts bedeviled him. He felt safe enough here. He had told no one of his early-morning swims, although the gate sentries were aware, of course, that he went riding each morn. But he doubted if anyone except John, whom he had taken there several times as a boy, knew exactly where he went or what he did. The pool lay in a small clearing in a heavily forested area seldom used by any but hunters, and he knew there would be no hunting parties out now. He had also dismissed any suspicion of a Ker raid. The Kers never raided during daylight hours.

Alex looked forward to his morning exercise. On a hot summer day it was refreshing, but on a cool spring morning like today it brought every fiber of his being alive. When he was on the galley, filthy and sweat-stained, he had promised himself a bath each day. It was like a renewal, a rewakening.

Alex stretched out in long strokes, ignoring the cold and taking pleasure in the response of his muscles as he thought of the day ahead. When he finally tired, and his body had adjusted to the chill of the water, he turned over, closing his eyes and relaxing in the water for several minutes, once more thinking of the day ahead. At last he slowly walked from the water to where his clothes lay, and instantly noted that something was wrong. They were not folded neatly as before, and his weapons were gone. His eyes scanned the woods, but saw nothing. He hastily pulled on his breeches, wondering whether someone was playing a joke on him. His brother? God's blood, he thought, why had he not been more cautious?

There was a movement among the trees, and a man stepped out, and then another, until he was surrounded by a circle of swords. He realized immediately the men were wearing the Ker plaid, and he knew what a fool he had been to come here alone. His hand automatically went to his side where a dagger usually lay, but he grasped only the empty scabbard. He heard a shout, but no one moved, and he realized he would probably die if he himself did anything but stand still. One tall darkhaired man stepped forward and placed the point of his blade against Alex's bare chest, pricking it and sending a small trail of blood downward.

And then he saw several heads turn, and his eyes turned with them. A woman, sitting tall and proud in the saddle, was emerging from the trees on a midnight-black mare. She approached until she was a few yards from where he stood.

If he had been still before, he was as a statue now. She was, quite simply, one of the most striking women he had ever seen. Her hair glowed fire red in the new-morning sun, and her eyes were a combination of colors, mostly gold. Her figure was hidden in the folds of a cloak but he could tell much from the grace and ease with which she sat the horse.

He watched her eyes sweep over him. He thought there was surprise there, but then they filled with undisguised anger. "Take him," she said.

With lightning speed that surprised his captors, Alex spun away from the sword touching him and aimed his shoulders at the stomach of one of the nearest Scots. The man went down, toppling the two on his left and leaving a hole through which Alex darted. But as he ran through the woods to his horse, a man swung down from a tree, causing him to stumble and slow. Suddenly there were others wrestling him to the ground, pinning him there, tying his hands together behind him before he was roughly heaved to his feet.

He shook off the restraining arms angrily and stood straight, his eyes going back to the woman, who was watching him now with profound interest.

With as much dignity as he could muster under the circumstances, he declined his head slightly in acknowledgment.

"Mistress Ker?"

"Huntington," she returned, acknowledging his title.

"I'm apparently at your service," he observed with a small ironic smile.

Elsbeth struggled to withhold a smile at his impudence. The words were said easily and with a sardonic courtesy that both intrigued and annoyed her. Even more irritating was the fact she couldn't take her eyes from his face. He was a striking man with thick black hair, cropped short, and stormy gray eyes, and he was far handsomer than the other Careys she had seen. He was also clean shaven, unlike many of the nobility who, like his brother, now wore beards and mustaches. But his outward looks, pleasing as they might be, probably hid a heart blacker than those of his brothers.

"Blindfold him and put him on a horse," she said, nodding at the tall dark-haired clansman who had pricked Alex with his sword. The tall man was noticeable in that most of the others had sandy or red hair. And the set of his mouth was even grimmer than the rest, which was saying a great deal.

Alex unconsciously stepped back. He did not like the idea of being blindfolded, of once more losing all control over his life and future.

But his arms were clasped and he was made to stand still while a black scarf was tied over his eyes. He was then shoved along for several steps until he was tossed like a bag of oats across a saddle and tied securely there.

He was perched uncomfortably with the horse's spine at his stomach, and his head hanging toward the ground, as were his feet. If the Ker tower was his destination, it was going to be an infernally uncomfortable ride, and he suspected it was meant to be.

Alex had learned long ago to endure discomfort and pain, and to do so with a surface indifference, although the old anger had already started simmering deep inside him. He had been a fool, well enough, to travel alone near the border, but it had been a long time since a Ker raid, and he had not altogether accustomed himself to the constant danger here.

He tried to move slightly, but the motion only caused the ropes around his wrists, waist and feet to tighten. His captors had, in some way, connected them, and he realized he would not fall although every step seemed to promise such an ignoble fate.

They apparently planned to hold him as prisoner, for ransom, or else they would have killed him immediately. And the fact that they did not offer to take his word as a hostage meant he would not be treated much more kindly at the Ker tower than he was now.

If he weren't so uncomfortable, he could almost laugh at the misjudgment. If the Kers expected ransom in return for him, they would have a rude surprise. John would be only too delighted to be rid of his "long lost" brother. And the Kers had enough grievances that he had little doubt he would die if a ransom demand was not met.

Unless he could escape.

His mind, seldom idle, shunned the physical discomfort by concentrating on that particular option. And his greatest hope, he realized, was the woman.

It was an area in which he was experienced . . . and skillful. Prior to his three years in the galleys, he had been uncommonly successful with the ladies of both the English and French courts. After Nadine, however, brief affairs had held little appeal. He had been very aware when he returned to London that his reserve only whetted interest rather than dampened it.

The Ker woman was his best chance. But he would have to control his temper, which was growing increasingly warm, and try to revive that old easy charm he had once perfected.

The thought of seducing the lady was unexpectedly attractive as he recalled the golden fire in her eyes. He wondered if she were as cold as the few words he had heard her say. And what it would be like to warm her.

Elsbeth's mind was more on their prisoner than on the dangerous ride back.

Everything had gone according to plan except her reaction to him—and she still couldn't fathom that.

His eyes had been the gray of a thunderous sky, and his hair as black as a moonless night. The water had set it curling slightly around a lean strong face that held its own secrets, and his naked chest, its dark fur beaded with drops of water, had been annoyingly attractive in its raw masculine power. Even more distracting, however, had been *his* odd reactions. He had shown little anger at the ambush, and she had admired the quickness with which he tried to escape.

He was nothing like John Carey, whose cold blue eyes held more than a hint of cruelty, whose mouth was weak and whose clothing was that of a fop, albeit a dangerous one.

She knew the ride must be agonizing for the English earl, and she felt a twinge of guilt that they had intended it so. They could have tied him upright to the saddle, but they had planned this additional humiliation to cow him.

He's a Carey. Nothing that can be done to him is bad enough, she told herself. He had burned out innocent crofters, killed one in the doing, and deserved no mercy. It was, indeed, a mercy they did not kill him outright.

But still there was something about him, something proud and indomitable, when he had met her eyes and held them, when he had stiffened his back as he was being so roughly handled.

Elsbeth also knew, from those brief moments in the clearing, that they had taken a prisoner far more dangerous than they had anticipated. She wondered if even the tower room would hold him long.

And she wondered how long it would take to ransom him. She prayed it would be no more than a few days. She would send one of her men immediately with the ransom demand, and make sure that it was delivered in the presence of others so John Carey would be forced to act. Not even a Carey could get away with allowing an earl to die, especially one in favor with the court.

Elsbeth felt a shiver of apprehension. If anything went wrong, if the ransom were not paid, her clan would demand his death in exchange for her father's. She turned and looked back at the trussed-up form, which bounced with every movement of the horse, and she knew the man must be cold with only his breeches for warmth. She had ordered his other clothes to be taken with them, and planned to return them once he was safely ensconced in the tower. It could get very cold there, and she wanted a live Carey, not a dead one.

A branch alongside the path brushed the Englishman's bare back, and she saw his muscles tense in pained reaction. But there was no word of complaint, no plea. She suddenly felt a strange desolation over the purposeful act of cruelty she was permitting.

Yet she knew her clan well, and knew she could show no sign of weakness. Her hold on their loyalty depended on it.

She straightened her shoulders and told Patrick to increase their pace.

It seemed forever before they arrived at the peel tower, and they trotted through the barnikins—enclosures of stone—before entering the stable area within. Elsbeth watched impassively as the ropes tying the prisoner to the horse were cut and he was allowed to fall, much to the snickers of several of her clansmen. He lay on the ground for a moment, his hands still tied behind his back and his eyes still blindfolded, before he rose stiffly to his knees and then to his feet.

She could not see those piercing eyes, but the dark hair fell over his forehead in curling clumps, and his mouth was grimly set.

She let him stand there while she looked at him closely. There was a rough ragged scar on his shoulder, and the wide shoulders and muscled chest narrowed to a lean hard stomach. His legs, covered by tight-fitting hose, were strong and muscular, and strangely relaxed as he stood. Instantly she realized he sensed he was being scrutinized, and her face flushed with the knowledge.

"Take him up," she ordered, forcing a note of contempt in her voice.

She saw him tense as he waited for the hands to seize him again, but he turned willingly enough when they did so. Then he stopped suddenly, so suddenly he shook off the hands holding him. He turned quickly in the direction of her voice, bowing as gracefully as any lord at court.

"My lady," he said in a low mocking voice, and then he was jerked away toward the tower entrance, leaving Elsbeth with a most disquieting flush of heat running down her spine as she watched him being shoved through the two doors protecting the tower.

I'm just tired, she told herself. She wearily dismounted, not waiting for assistance. She knew the small sturdy horses would be well handled. She turned toward the prisoner's horse, which they had found hitched to a tree. It was black as the earl's hair. And his heart, she noted as an afterthought. The stallion would make a fine addition to their stable.

She walked inside, feeling all the effects of a night in the saddle and two days without sleep. Annie, the housekeeper, was hovering near the door, her eyes full of lively interest.

"When we heard ye coming, my lady, I ordered yer bath with water kept aboiling. And there's some pheasant and wine ready."

Elsbeth smiled. Annie kenned her all too well. She nodded.

"I saw the lord taken up the steps," the housekeeper said with undisguised curiosity. "He's fair 'andsome."

"For a Carey," Elsbeth said, her voice uncommonly harsh.

Annie regarded her mistress quizzically. She had been friend as well as servant to Elsbeth through the years, and she had no fear of her. But when she saw the stubborn set of Elsbeth's chin, she knew to keep her silence. "D'ye take a bath, then?"

Elsbeth grinned, knowing exactly what Annie was thinking. "Aye, but first I must send a message. I don't wish a guest any longer than necessary."

Annie frowned. "I'm thinking that one wouldna be so dull."

"The very reason I want him returned and the Kers richer."

"Ah lovey," Annie said, reverting to her old pet name for her mistress. "Was it so hard?"

"No," Elsbeth answered. "I'm just very tired."

"Of course, ye are." Annie wanted to add that it was because she needed a husband, but that, she knew, would meet with the same blank stare it always did. "Yer bath will be ready."

Elsbeth met with Patrick and Ian when they came in the main apartment downstairs. Patrick had seen to the lodging of Carey, and Ian had doubled the guard around the tower.

"I want to send the demand immediately."

"I wouldna do that," Patrick disagreed. "'Tis better to let them yarp a while."

"For once, my cousin is right," Ian agreed.

Elsbeth looked at Patrick. "Did you have any trouble?"

Patrick's eyes grew blacker, colder. "He didna ha' much choice." He started to say something more, but stopped.

Elsbeth looked at him questioningly.

"He asked to talk with ye. Insolent bastard."

Elsbeth had to agree. She had no desire to see the Englishman again until he left. "Guards?"

"One at all times. And he'd have to go down five flights of stairs and through the whole clan to escape."

"His clothes?"

Patrick gave her another dour look. "As ye ordered, Elsbeth, but I'd as soon see him naked."

"A dead hostage would do us no good."

"It would do me good," Patrick stated matter-of-factly.

"Bloodthirsty, aren't you, cousin?" Ian interjected.

"He's a Carey," Patrick retorted, as if that explained everything.

Elsbeth looked at both cousins. Patrick was striding impatiently across the floor, and Ian was sprawled in a comfortable chair. How glad she was to have them both. They were so different, yet so dependable, and she wondered what she would do without them.

"When?" she questioned, her thoughts still on the immediate problem.

"Two days will be soon enough," Ian said. "We took care in hiding the tracks."

Elsbeth nodded slowly. They needed time to strengthen their defenses in the event the Careys decided to attack. "So be it." She smiled, part triumph, part weariness, part apprehension. The deed was done now. They could only await the results.

Upstairs in her chamber, the wooden tub was full and blissfully hot. Elsbeth sank into it, thinking of the lord imprisoned four floors above her in a chamber made bare of comforts. She had had the high window securely barred, knowing he could see little but forest from it. A hole had been made in the door, also barred, so he could be watched.

She felt the same shiver run down her spine as the first time she had seen him. And she felt a compulsion to see him again, to see if those eyes were as turbulent as she remembered, and the face as secretive. She wished he had blustered or raged, rather than met his fate with charming mockery.

Elsbeth reluctantly rose from the bath and ate a lonely meal of beef, bread and wine. Annie came in, but one look at her mistress's preoccupied face sent her away again.

Elsbeth finally lay in the soft feather bed, thinking she would be asleep in moments. But minutes and hours passed, and she felt a restlessness new to her.

Dear God, but she wished she could wrestle the man from her thoughts.

God's truth, but he needed to think.

Alex lay on the thin pallet that was the only comfort in the room besides several rough blankets. The fireplace went unlit, and there were no chairs. Only a chamber pot was a possible weapon, and he found that even that possibility had been considered; it was scarcely heavy enough to down a chicken, much less the stout men who had taken him in the clearing.

He had seen little else since he'd arrived here.

The blindfold had not been taken off until he was in the room. He still felt the bruises on his arms where two men had half pushed, half guided him up an endless series of steps.

When they finally stopped, he was pushed into a room and the rope around his wrists cut. As he reached to take off the blindfold he heard a door shut, and a bolt slam tightly.

It had all been very efficient.

His eyes took several seconds to adjust to the light, which was filtering through a barred window above him. As his eyes swept the room, he quickly found the door and took measure of the small hole cut in it. It had been so designed with metal overlaps that he could not stick so much as two fingers through it. But he could see out, and worse, his captors could see in.

One of the men who had faced him in the clearing stood outside, watching him as he took note of his surroundings. He was the dark one with the murderous eyes.

"Comfortable, my lord?" It was said in a low taunting tone, as a dog might growl at a bearbaiting.

"I've seen better," Alex said carelessly. "And worse." And he had. Much worse. But they wouldn't know that.

The man's slight smile disappeared. "Carey whoreson," he spit.

Alex forced himself to relax, as he had done so many times before when insults were hurled at him. He had learned to bide his time.

"Your lady. I would like to speak with her."

It was more an order than a request, and Patrick knew it. "D'ye think she would see a Carey?"

Alex's eyes locked on him, and his voice was very soft when he spoke again. "It is for her well-being as well as mine."

"Brave talk for one in your position, my lord."

"And what position is that?"

"Have you no' guessed yet? 'Tis to see what you're worth to Johnny."

Alex grinned sardonically and shrugged. "The message," Alex prompted. "I would be grateful."

"I've no' need of gratitude from an Englishman or a Carey," the Scot said curtly and turned to leave.

"Some water, at least."

Patrick hesitated. Elsbeth had said the prisoner was to have food and water, as well as blankets, if little else. "Aye," he said grudgingly. "If you keep your English mouth silent."

Alex watched as Patrick quickly issued orders to the two men with him. Patrick and one other stayed while the third disappeared down the steep steps. So he was right. The dark man was one of the leaders.

He took measure of the man. He was tall, but not as tall as Alex, and solidly built. He looked as dangerous as a Scot could be…and that, Alex knew, was dangerous indeed. His eyes were elusive, almost black but very private.

Alex leaned casually against the door. "Your name?"

Again, it was more order than question, and Patrick bridled. "It's Ker. Ye donna need to know more."

Alex wondered. He had heard that Lady Elsbeth Ker had not married, nor was she betrothed. This could not be a brother, or she would not have inherited the title. Just what was this man to her? A retainer? A suitor? He was surprised at how important the answer suddenly seemed.

And yet he knew he would get nothing else at the moment. The brief glimmer of tolerance had gone from the man's face, and Alex understood he had asked one question too many. He would be fortunate to get his water.

When it came, Alex knew they were taking no chances with him. He was told to face the far wall. He heard the door open, and the sound of wood hitting the stone floor of his chamber, and he heard the door close again and the bolt fastened.

He went back to the door. The Scot was starting down the stairs, and another man, dressed roughly, stood like a statue across from his door.

Alex picked up the wooden cup and took it to the pallet. Until he savored the first cool taste, he had not realized how thirsty he was, how much the long uncomfortable ride had drained him. He sipped the water slowly, saving most of it, for he did not know when he would have more. It was a habit he had developed from his time on the galley.

He carefully reviewed everything that had happened, and one idea stuck in his mind. The Kers had obviously known he would be at the pool. Few people at Huntington knew where he disappeared each morning, since he usually left before much of the castle stirred. One of those who did know was his brother.

Ransom? He laughed low and bitterly. He wondered if he was even meant to have been taken alive. Mayhap an afterthought?

If the ransom wasn't paid, he didn't hold much hope for his future. The hate in this tower was palpable, and he had little to bargain with.

There *was* Garrick.

And the Lord Protector, if he could get word to him. But how? If he knew John, his brother would ignore any ransom demand and blame his murder on the Kers. It would be reason for yet another assault on the beleaguered clan.

God's blood, but the woman had to listen!

The light finally faded from his small austere room, and he knew it was evening. He wondered if Davey Garrick had looked for him, or if he thought Alex had just disappeared again.

The door to his room opened just wide enough for a trencher of food to be pushed in. He ate hungrily, knowing he needed his strength. It was salt meat and cheese with a chunk of stale bread, plain fare but better than he had expected after all the other discomforts of the day. With it came the rest of his clothes, and he dressed except for his boots. The evening was already cold, and he thought about a warm fire dancing in his fireplace at Huntington.

There were no candles within the room and only a glimmer of light from a torch on the wall outside. As he had so many times before, he forced himself to sleep, burying the aches in his body and the questions in his mind.

He would try again tomorrow to speak with the Lady Ker.

Chapter Three

The two men once more stood in the mist of the marches, hostility radiating from both. One kept his hand on the sword at his side; the other had his on a dagger.

"He was to be killed," the shorter man spit out.

"The lady wouldna have it. I couldna convince her. She sees the ransom as a way to help the crofters." The words became a sneer. "It seems ye did your job too well."

"There will be no ransom."

"And if the English court hears ye refused one of its favorites?"

The Englishman glared at the Scot through the darkness. "If you have been playing with me, you'll pay dearly."

"Not as dearly as ye, my would-be lord."

They were snarling now, both of them caught in a trap of their own making. The plan had always been to kill the new earl. His kidnapping presented a whole new range of problems.

The Scot knew he had been walking on shaky ground since his alliance with the English bastard. But he deserved the leadership of the clan, by blood if not by legitimacy, and by God's blood he would get it, and Elsbeth as well. He felt some guilt at his complicity in the old laird's death, but he had been sure it would hurry a marriage with the daughter, and he knew he would make a strong laird, a strong leader of the clan. The old laird had become soft and weak, wanting peace. Peace had no place on the borders. Raiding the English was a favorite and time-honored tradition. It kept the clan strong for the next time the bloody English tried to invade Scottish soil.

And he would make the clan strong again, if he had to treat with the devil to do it.

The Englishman had been quiet for several minutes. "The court must never know, my retainers must never know, that there was a ransom demand. They must believe he was killed before a ransom could be paid."

"So you have an excuse to wipe out the Kers?" the Scot mocked as suspicion and distrust permeated the air like an evil disease.

"One day I will," the other man retorted, "but right now we have common interest."

"And I should trust a man who would betray his own brother?"

"As you betrayed your laird?"

Their hands clasped their weapons more tightly, violence barely suppressed. It was the Englishman who relaxed first. He had too much to lose should he give in to anger and slice this impertinent Scot to shreds.

"Back to the problem of my . . . brother."

The Scot said nothing.

"If he escaped . . ."

"And was killed by another borderer . . ." The Scot picked up the thought.

"Or foundered in a stream where his body was found!"

"He willna be easy to kill. You didna warn me how wily he was."

The Englishman shrugged. "I have not seen him in battle for more than eight years. But there are always ways. I know the path he would be using. I could ambush him. It would be up to you to see he escapes."

"You?"

"There's one other man. Between us we can down him."

"The messengers conveying the ransom demand?"

"They must be killed."

"They're my clansmen!"

The silence was heavy between them. Finally the Scot nodded reluctantly.

"When the ransom is not paid and your captive escapes, your clansmen should get very impatient, perhaps demand that the lady take a husband," the Englishman said as an added incentive. "Since you can't do it yourself," he added with a slight jeer he couldn't quite resist. Despite his words, he would use Alex's abduction as a call to arms against the Kers; he could probably get help from the crown. He would just have to make sure this particular Scot didn't live to tell tales.

The Scot knew exactly what John Carey was thinking, and he had his own plans. The English didn't know he knew their path through the march. After John ambushed his brother, then he would ambush the bloody Englishman, destroying forever any evidence of his alliance.

"So be it," he agreed.

"A pact," the Englishman said.

They didn't shake hands but walked cautiously to their horses and mounted.

The plague take it.

Elsbeth strode across her apartment, worry etched in her face. The second messenger sent with ransom demands had not returned, and two days had passed.

There could be only one explanation. The Careys had taken them. Which meant they had no intention of paying a ransom.

It also left her with an unwanted hostage of little value, and a clan that would happily see to his demise. There was already talk of hanging him in retaliation for her father's death. The Carey's had started the blood feud, and now it was permissible by unwritten border law to avenge the death in kind. The thought was unexpectedly painful, and it was that pain that bothered her most. She could not believe she cared what happened to a Carey.

But she could not erase those gray eyes from her mind.

He had been a prisoner nearly a week, and he had made several requests to see her. But each time she had refused, frightened at the impact he had made on her. She had heard her friends and women relatives giggle and talk of the marriage bed, but they had made little impression. *She* had never felt the warmth they talked about, or the sweetness they sang of. She had only seen the mating of horses, heard the screams of the mare, and thought the act must be totally loathsome. She did not want to be controlled that way, or any way.

Until now, when little darts of heat settled someplace deep inside her when she thought of the English earl, igniting an insatiable craving for something she didn't understand. It tormented her day and night, particularly night, when sleep eluded her and her body trembled with a need she had never felt before.

And now she was left with the problem of dispensing with him.

Patrick, not surprisingly, thought he should be killed. Ian cautioned patience.

Both were gone this evening; Patrick was hunting, and Ian had said he was checking the guards. The rest of the household had retired, a fact that had given her this time to think. In addition to Annie and two maids, there were two other women in residence—Patrick's mother, Joan, and a shy cousin, Louisa, who was, like Elsbeth, an orphan. She liked Louisa, but disliked Patrick's ambitious mother intensely.

She tried to read one of her fathers books; unlike so many lords and barons who concentrated their skills on arms and hunting and were illiterate, he had learned Latin as a boy and had taught her when she indicated an interest. He had collected a small library, including some books painstakingly penned by hand and others acquired since 1501 when printing came to Scotland. But the words blurred in front of her, and a hard-lined face appeared where ideas had rested.

Elsbeth knew she had to make some kind of decision soon. Even she could hear the muttering about wasting food on a Carey and an Englishman. Curiosity about his request to see her hammered at her. She owed him the right to speak before she decided his fate.

She was pleased neither Ian nor Patrick was in the tower; she knew they would demand to be present, and she didn't want to argue with them. Elsbeth wondered how best to handle the situation, for she had sensed in that first contact with Huntington that he could be a dangerous man. She could go to the upper tower room, or have him brought down here. There were no windows in this room, and she could station men outside the heavy oak door.

What if he attempted to grab her and exchange her life for his own? She would put nothing past an Englishman, particularly a Carey. Yet she didn't want to talk to him through the tiny window, or with a guard present. She wanted to know more about him, what kind of a man he was, and she could only do that alone, in her own way. She didn't allow herself to think there was any more to her desire to see him than basic fairness.

But she didn't trust him and she had to protect herself. There was always a number of armed clansmen in the lower apartments for protection, and she sent for two, ordering them to bind and blindfold the English prisoner, and bring him to the withdrawing room she used to entertain visitors and conduct business.

She paced nervously, not entirely sure what she intended to accomplish but seized by the need to see Carey again, to discover more about him. Perhaps she would realize readily enough that he was the despicable villain she believed him to be, and she could dismiss him from her mind and conscience, turning him over to Patrick without another thought.

Elsbeth heard the tread of boots on the stone floor outside, and stopped pacing, turning toward the door as the Englishman and his guards entered. Once again, she was struck by her prisoner's poise, even when unseeing and bound by ropes. His magnificent shoulders and chest were now covered, clothed in a plain doublet and leather jerkin that did nothing to hide the strength beneath. She had expected richer clothes and was surprised at his modest appearance.

"You can take off his blindfold now," she told the guards, "and wait outside."

"D'ye think . . . ?"

"Outside," she said again, this time in a tone she had learned from her father. Their faces creased with apprehension, the two men scowled and did as they were told, but not without a mutter that "Patrick was no' going to like this."

Alexander Carey blinked several times, and Elsbeth knew it must be difficult accustoming himself to the candlelight and the bright flames flickering in the huge fireplace. But then his eyes cleared and found her. They were cautious as they scanned the richness of the room, the books in a corner, wine on the table.

He bowed, as he had before, but now the motion held tension that had not been there before. He had grown angrier over the days, his temper barely held in check as his requests to see Lady Ker had gone ignored and unacknowledged. He had been told nothing of the ransom, but knew his guards were growing surlier. He could only surmise that his brother had refused to pay a ransom, an eventuality that did not surprise him although he did feel a certain sadness that such was so.

"You wished to see me?" he said after waiting several minutes for her to speak. The words were arrogantly spoken, and Elsbeth's own temper flared as she saw the simmering anger in his eyes.

"No," she replied sharply. "I did not wish to see an English dog. You requested an audience, and I thought it only fair before you hang."

"There was no ransom then," he said softly, a certain coldness creeping into his eyes and turning them from smoke to the color of cold steel.

"Your kinsmen apparently hold you in no greater regard than I."

The corner of his mouth twisted upward in a half smile, and Elsbeth felt her heart lurch. There was no arrogance in his face now, only a brief look of wry sorrow that twisted her insides. But it was gone as fast as it had come, and she wondered if she'd imagined it. She didn't imagine its lingering effects, though. Nor the sudden overwhelming need to touch him.

He's a Carey. His family killed her father. He burned out people who depended on her.

But as she looked at him, it was difficult to believe him a brute, even with the bristles that now darkened his face like an outlaw's. His mouth was firm but not cruel, his eyes angry and clouded, but not evil, his face secretive but not ruthless. He was not like his brother. She didn't know how she knew it, but she did.

She went to the table and poured herself a glass of wine, knowing his eyes never left her. He was standing easily, but there was so much suppressed power, so much restrained anger in his stance that she could feel it.

And yet he didn't speak except with his eyes, challenging her to make the first move. She could feel the sudden hot breath of air between them, a spray of sparks that burned them both. She saw the surprised awareness in his eyes, and knew that he felt the same glowing sensations that were assaulting her.

"Why did you ask to see me?" she whispered, using every bit of will she could to stay where she was, to keep away from him.

"To warn you, my lady." His voice was low, intense and almost a caress.

Her eyes narrowed as she struggled to think clearly, to maintain her dignity. What trick was he playing? "Warn? There's naught to warn me of except the Careys." The reminder stiffened her spine.

"Do you not think my brother would welcome my capture? He would cry no tears for me, and it would be the very excuse he needs to arouse his neighbours—even the crown—against you."

"And what care you about the Kers?"

He fastened his eyes on her with intensity, and he felt a muscle throb in his cheek. She wouldn't believe him whatever he said. But he had nothing to lose by trying. "The crown wants peace on the border."

She laughed, a bitter unamused laugh. "So much that you burned our land a week ago, killed one of our crofters."

His mouth set. It would do little good to lay the blame on John. And it was not in him to beg. "You cannot win this battle," he said, trying another approach. "My brother will not pay the ransom, and if I am killed England will send troops and level this land."

"You are so important, my lord?" she mocked.

"No," he said slowly, his eyes holding hers. "Not I. But Northumberland means to see this border pacified. My death would be an excuse for him to invade, just as Somerset did."

"Then the Scots will fight."

"And many will die. Is that what you want?"

"I want the Careys to pay for my father's death."

She stood there, proud and defiant and beautiful, and Alex yearned to touch her. He cursed his bound hands, wanting to struggle against the ropes but reluctant to allow her to see how she affected him.

"They will not pay as long as you hold me," he said bluntly.

"Mayhap not in money, but in blood," she retorted.

"And then more Ker blood. Do you wish the feud never to end?"

Some of his weariness and frustration was reflected in his voice, and she stared at him. "I wouldna believe a Carey if my life depended on it," she said finally. "And in a fair fight, we can defeat anyone."

"Do you think my brother fights fair? He must needs only call the English warden, who would summon enough men to raze this tower and hang everyone in it."

"And what do you propose, my lord?" she said mockingly. "Let you go free and earn the Kers the contempt of every borderer?"

"Allow me to escape," he said easily, as if he were suggesting a pleasant outing.

Elsbeth looked at him in amazement. "You're daft! Even for an Englishman." She took another sip of wine, and Alex regarded it thirstily.

"I don't suppose you would cut me loose if I swear not to try to escape?"

She was bewildered by his sudden change in topic, and she wondered immediately if that was his purpose. "You're more than daft."

"Mayhap." He grinned. "I'm also bloody thirsty."

Elsbeth stepped back at the impact of his rare smile. If the room had not already been warmed by the fire, she was sure it would have been by the force of his charm.

Dismayed by her reaction, she started for the door. "If that was all you had to say—"

"My lady, that is not all." The voice had hardened and demanded her attention.

Elsbeth turned back to him and saw the smile was gone, that the life that had danced in his eyes for an instant was swallowed in the same threatening thunderclouds she had seen there at the pool. She wondered how he had seized control so easily. She tipped up her chin, determined not to let him best her.

"What message did my brother send?"

"He has sent none. Two of my best men have not returned. If they were killed, it's even more reason for your death," she added coldly.

"Perhaps they never arrived," he said softly.

She looked at him in surprise, wondering at the remark but holding her silence, waiting for him to continue.

"Does anyone other than your clan know you have taken me?"

She eyed him suspiciously, wondering what trap he was springing now.

"Do they?" It was a sharp question, demanding an answer.

"I doubt so," she admitted finally, after considering the matter. She could not see how it mattered.

"So," he said softly, "no one would ever know that my brother refused ransom...if the messengers didn't reach Huntington."

Her eyes widened at the implication. No one knew about the messengers except her clansmen. If the messenger had not reached Huntington, then one of her own people had prevented them.

"No," she whispered.

He strode across the room until he faced her. "I can assure you, my lady, that the crown would not look fondly on my brother if he refused my ransom. He might have killed one of your messengers, but two...before they reached anyone? I doubt it."

"I don't ken your meaning," she said.

"I think you do, my lady."

"We have no traitor here."

"Any more than my brother would betray me?"

"You're English," she said as if that explained everything.

Once more he allowed himself a small smile at the pure simplicity of her charge. "And there is no betrayal amongst the Scots? Look at your history, my lady, and think about it. That's all I ask."

"You ask much more," she retorted.

"I want peace," he said intently, and his face was suddenly immeasurably weary. "I want fat cattle and rich fields and happy tenants."

"You want Ker cattle, and Ker fields, and dead Scots," she said, trying to shrug off the compelling magic of his words, of his eyes, of his face. She had had enough of his lies.

She went to the door and opened it to the guards. "You can take this English dog back to his chamber."

But he stepped deftly away from them. "Could this English dog have a small light in his kennel?" His mouth held a hint of a smile, and she knew it was not humility in his voice, but a challenge.

"Perhaps a book, too," she said sarcastically. She knew few of the nobility, English or Scots, could read.

But he surprised her with a serious intent look. "I would be grateful."

"I should think you would have prayers to make."

"According to you, they would be a waste of time."

The teasing, mocking lights were back in his eyes, and she wondered if they appeared often. They greatly eased the hardness of his face.

"You read, then?"

"Aye, my lady. And I also breathe. And sorrow. And even laugh on occasion."

Elsbeth bit her lip. He was mocking her again, and it was devilishly difficult to take offense, for he was also mocking himself. Yet she sensed an undercurrent of seriousness in his voice, a true desire hid only slightly by light surface words.

"I will consider it," she said, partly against her will.

"It will keep me from mischief," he urged, and this time she had to smile. He lacked neither arrogance nor wit. But honor? That was an entirely different matter.

She nodded to the guards, who came to his side and lifted the blindfold back to his eyes.

"And mayhap some wine," he goaded further, seeing her trace of a smile before the cloth once more darkened his vision.

"Return him," Elsbeth said, "before I hang him myself."

* * *

God's truth, but she was a beauty.

He had wondered in his week here whether she was really as pretty as he remembered. He had had only a quick look between his attempted escape and the blindfold, but his thoughts had dwelt on the hair brushed with red and the golden eyes. He'd thought he magnified the beauty during his isolation, but he had not.

She had been even prettier when she had tried to hide her smile and look severe.

He rubbed his wrists as they were untied, and went to his small window. It was high in the wall, and he had to reach up and seize the iron and pull himself up to see out. Even then he could see little but bonfires flickering in the forest, encampments of Ker clansmen. He could tell nothing about their strength, nor could he see the rest of the tower fortifications. They had chosen his pen well.

There was a slice of moon in the sky, nothing more, and even that disappeared behind the lace network of clouds. He slowly lowered himself and sat on the pallet, thinking about the recent conversation ... and the woman who so intrigued him.

He had been right about her form, which had been cloaked that morning in the dale. It was quite enticingly shaped. She had worn a green damask dress with the Ker red-and-green plaid as a sash. The bodice had been well fitted and trimmed with pearls, and the skirt long and flowing, displaying her slender frame to perfection. Her hair had not been hidden by a hood, but had tumbled unrestrained down her back in glorious abandon.

But it was her eyes that fascinated him, hazel and gold, and alive with intelligence and spirit.

And she was quick. She caught his meanings immediately, although he knew she didn't believe them. But they would nag at her, and make her aware, and that was more than he had expected.

Alex had learned patience, had learned to husband his anger and use it to his advantage, although it was always there, smoldering and ready to explode at the right moment. And his target would be his traitorous brother...not the Kers, who had a measure of justice on their side.

If only he could get free.

As he had done before, he dismissed minor considerations—discomfort, anger, the lingering ache of bruises from the painful ride—to concentrate on the immediate problem facing him. They were taking no chances with him. There were always at least two huge guards whenever his door was open, and when being led down the narrow steep stairs, he had heard considerable movement of heavy boots. Although he could see nothing, he knew the tower was filled with angry Ker clansmen.

Yet he had to try. He was only too aware of Lady Elsbeth's dilemma if his ransom was not paid. Despite her fierce words, he had known almost instantly she would not order his death, but he wondered exactly how much control she had over the unruly and vengeful clansmen. He recalled too easily the hate in the eyes of the man who first brought him to the tower room.

For the moment, he could only hope the seed he had planted in Lady Elsbeth's mind would grow, that she would realize there might be treachery in her hall as well as his. That thought brought back haunting reminders—the scent of roses, the hint of a smile at his impudence, the saucy tilt of her head, the angry fire in her eyes.

She was the first woman who had attracted him since Nadine, Nadine with her quiet beauty and resolute courage. He had respected her above all others, had thought he loved her, and had long mourned her death. Now, for the first time in many years, he felt excitement in his blood, an ache in his loins and the awakening of feelings he had thought dead forever.

He laughed at himself. He had always fought against the tide, tried to conquer the unconquerable. Yet this was probably the greatest folly of all, this undeniable fascination with the one person in the world most forbidden to him.

Lady Elsbeth Ker was the head of the clan sworn to destroy him and his, the person who could never forget the shed blood between them and one who held his life in her hands.

God help him.

* * *

Elsbeth stood in front of the fire in her bedchamber, watching the flames flickering.

Alexander Carey, earl of Huntington, was a riddle she didn't understand. And she had always been very, very good at riddles.

His change of moods, of ideas, of requests, left her head spinning. The daft notion that she help him escape had been casually mentioned and quickly dismissed, as well as the suggestion that one of her people was betraying the clan.

They were, she realized now, just enough to whet her curiosity without giving her a chance to reject the thoughts out of hand, enough to tantalize and worry her.

She uttered an oath she knew would annoy Patrick and amuse Ian. The English lord was far more clever than she had thought, the plague take him.

He had looked more brigand than lord with his plain clothes, dark unruly hair and unshaved cheeks. Yet he had acted every inch the earl. And she was afraid he was far more charming than she had imagined possible.

She thought of his crooked self-mocking smile when he mentioned the candle for his "kennel," and the unabashed request for wine. There was no end of arrogance in this English borderer, and yet there was something else, too. There had been a peculiar longing in his voice, a momentary vulnerability in his eyes, when he mentioned peace, and yet he did not defend himself against her charge that he himself had recently raided Ker lands.

He was like the marches, dangerous and unfathomable, and deceptive to those who didn't know the way. What looked like sound ground often proved deadly.

But there was something in his eyes that reached out to her, and she feared it had taken root. She didn't understand what, or why, but she felt an overwhelming desolation that she had started something she couldn't stop, and that nothing would ever be the same again.

Chapter Four

Elsbeth did not forget her captive's requests. But the more she thought about the implied accusations the angrier she became. Let him sit alone in the tower room with only his wicked thoughts as company. Her clan was loyal to her, as it had been to her father.

Patrick and Ian quickly learned of the meeting when they returned, and neither was pleased. They were only slightly mollified by the precautions she had taken.

"Why in the devil—"

Elsbeth had learned the art of arrogance herself, but she seldom used it. "I wanted to see a Carey face-to-face," she said, her eyebrow arched challengingly, almost daring another comment.

"Was that wise?" Ian said mildly.

"He was blindfolded."

"Aye," Patrick said, "but if he needs killing it might be the harder for ye."

She drew back her shoulders. "I can do what is needed."

Ian grinned. "I have no doubt of that, fair cousin. And what do ye think of your guest?"

She didn't have a ready answer. She really didn't know what she thought of Alexander Carey, earl of Huntington. So she shrugged. "He appears like the others, well versed in treachery." The words, however, didn't ring entirely true in her heart.

Elsbeth changed the subject. "We've still heard nothing of the messengers?"

Ian's grin faded. "Nothing, and there's none more reliable than Robin and Will."

Patrick growled his assent. "I donna know how to tell young Cara, though I'm sure she suspects by now."

Elsbeth bit her lip. Cara was Robin's daughter, and a prettier, sweeter lass didn't exist.

"She will be welcome here, of course," she said. "Annie can always use more help, although the wages would be small."

Patrick frowned, his eyes clouding. "That willna be enough. Someone must pay."

Elsbeth looked at him directly. "Someone will pay," she said softly.

"Our English earl?" Patrick queried.

"Perhaps," she said. "I'd rather find the true murderer."

"Just look in yon direction," Ian said with unusual bitterness, nodding his head to the south toward Huntington.

"What of Lord Huntington?" Patrick queried. "We canna keep him forever."

"No?" Elsbeth said with a gleam in her eyes. "I don't know why not."

Patrick permitted himself a rare scowl. "He's a danger as long as he's here. It's plain enough now tha' his brother doesn't want him."

"That's exactly why we should keep him," Elsbeth said. "It keeps the earl helpless in our tower and John Carey uncertain. He cannot move until he knows his brother is dead. Why give him that gift?"

Both cousins stared at Elsbeth, Ian with a growing smile and Patrick with furrowed brow. "We canna keep him forever," Patrick repeated in a growl, but his eyes held a question that had not been there before.

"He cannot escape," Elsbeth said, heartening to her subject.

Ian chuckled. "John Carey will be none too pleased."

"He can't claim the title," Patrick observed.

"Nor raise his men," Ian said.

"Unless they know Alexander Carey is dead," Patrick added thoughtfully.

They both looked at Elsbeth with new respect.

* * *

Alex counted the days religiously. He had nothing to mark them, and little with which to pass them. It was, he knew, a fortnight since his ignominious capture. He still winced when he thought about it and swore he would never be quite so careless again.

It had been the freedom, the freedom that he had so relished that had led him back into captivity. He had so much appreciated those moments in the woods alone, the freshness of the pool, that he had forgotten how dangerous the border could be.

It had been so for more history that he could remember: The Scots raiding the English and the English the Scots. The feuding was madness when they had so much in common, a love of the border land, of sport, of hearty laughter and a good jest.

He paced his austere prison like a caged wolf, knowing all the time the pacing only made him more restless. At least on the galleys the pain of ceaseless labor had made for dreamless sleep. Now he could not sleep at all as he tried to puzzle a way out of his trap.

It was that—possibilities of escape—as well as intrusive thoughts of the lady below, which occupied his mind. It was more than a week since his meeting with her, and it apparently had yielded little. Despite her words that she would consider a few more comforts, there had been none. He was left completely alone with his thoughts, except for Spartan meals twice a day and his guards' occasional quick look at him through the barred window.

To see if he was still there? His mouth turned up in the slightest of smiles. Ah, but to be a bird.

He went over to his window, looking toward the sky. At least he had that. In his three years in the galley, he had seen the sky three times, each when one of his fellow prisoners had died and he carried the man topside to be dumped without ceremony in the ocean.

Alex tried not to remember those years; after he was released he had banished them, because they were too painful to live with. It was better not to think of them. Even his scars were fading, those around his ankles where he wore his chains, and those on his back from when he had attacked a guard who was beating a man too weak to row.

And Nadine. Why was it that she, too, was fading?

He heard a noise at the door, and felt eyes on him. He hated that—the total lack of privacy. And then the door opened slowly, and the woman was standing there.

Perhaps it was the way the sun angled into the room, or perhaps he was just so infernally bored and empty, but she looked even more glorious than before.

He watched her with wary eyes although his mouth relaxed into a smile alive with charm as he noted that her hands were full. Alex moved quickly, taking the items from her hands—a candle and flint, a book and a leather container that appeared full of liquid. He placed them on the floor and stood straight once more.

"My lady. I thank you . . . or is this only a boon for a condemned man?"

Her eyes focused on him, and he was fascinated by the currents so alive within them. They were full of curiosity—and not a little hostility. They were also very direct. The one thing that was missing was fear.

She dared much by coming in here alone with him unbound. He could grab her and threaten a broken neck to gain his release.

He knew she knew what he was thinking, and her mouth trembled slightly before steadying in a grave line. His admiration grew as she turned toward the still-open door and the guards. "Wait outside," she said. He was amazed that they obeyed, although they obviously did so unwillingly.

"You're not afraid of me?"

"Should I be?"

"You seemed so at our last meeting. My hands were bound."

She shrugged. "The guards have orders. If you take me, they are to kill you. Even if they kill me in doing so."

"You value your life so little?"

"Honor is not a small thing."

"No," he agreed softly.

"And what would a Carey know about honor?"

"And why would a Ker ask, since you obviously feel you know the answer?"

"Curiosity," she said frankly.

"About the English dog?"

She flushed, remembering their last conversation. "Mayhap," she admitted.

He leaned against the wall, appearing relaxed although every nerve was as taut as a bowstring. He did not want to startle her or give her reason to leave.

"And have you decided my fate yet?"

"You will stay here a little longer."

"Ah, a period of grace?"

"I did not think of that," she said, and her mouth turned up in a small enchanting grin despite herself.

"Because the English have no grace?" he questioned with an ironic twitch of his lips.

One of her eyebrows arched meaningfully.

As if to dispute that, he bowed low, still careful to keep his movements nonthreatening. "If it's grace you desire," he said, "I will attempt to provide it. Please allow me to welcome you to my humble abode." There was just a touch of sardonic humor in his courtesy.

Elsbeth looked around the bare, bleak walls, the cold stone floor and the rough pallet, and felt chagrin. What must it be like to be locked in here? She didn't think she could abide it, not for a day. Her hazel eyes clouded and met his directly.

She wished she could read them. But they were a gray mystery, revealing nothing other than what he wanted them to reveal. There was not the obvious anger she had expected, nor even the arrogance of the other day, only a challenge that asked much of her.

How could he affect her like this. He was *her* prisoner, and yet at the moment it was almost the other way around. She could not think around him, because she feared every thought was so easily known to him.

As if reinforcing that thought and respecting it, he moved his eyes away from her and down toward the gifts she had brought. With lazy ease, he leaned down and picked up the book, opening it and discovering with pleasure it was a Latin translation of Homer's *Iliad*.

Alex was stunned that she had even brought it. Books were priceless throughout England and Scotland, particularly in this rough border country. He had been amazed when he saw the small collection below, and despite their conversation a week earlier he had never expected to be granted this privilege.

He looked at her with something akin to wonder. Few in Scotland or England were able to read and write, although the Scottish parliament fifty years earlier had ordered that all eldest sons and heirs of barons and freeholders learn Latin and study law. Still, many borderers had seemed to evade this edict. That this isolated peel tower of a minor lord should contain such treasures was astounding. That the lady would share them with one whom she thought her greatest enemy was even more astounding.

Alex's own family scorned learning, and neither his father nor his brothers had learned to read. Neither had he until he met Nadine and her father, both passionate scholars, who had painstakingly taught him to read and write.

The mask slipped from his eyes and they gleamed with a certain pleasure. "My thanks," he said softly.

Once again, Elsbeth felt assaulted by conflicting emotions. He was not feigning his interest, and part of her was surprised. She had picked up the book as an afterthought, remembering his retort of the other day. Perhaps she had wondered if he really did read, if he really were interested in what many thought frivolity. Her father had taught her to read when she repeatedly harried him about it, but neither Ian nor Patrick had shown any interest, nor had any of the other clansmen shared her obsession with written words and the thoughts they conveyed.

No one but an Englishman and a Carey. It was a dismaying discovery.

Elsbeth knew she should leave, but she could not. It was as if she herself were chained to the floor. She watched a lock of dark hair fall over his forehead and his brows furrow together as he studied the precious object in his hand. In two weeks his beard had grown so that it covered most of his lower face, and it served only to enhance his rugged attractiveness. His doublet was open, and she could see the dark soft hair on his chest; she remembered once more how powerful he had appeared at the pool. He still did. The fact that he was obviously restraining that power, impatience and strength only served to make them all the more evident.

His hands were caressing the book, and for one heart-stopping moment she imagined them on her. She suddenly wished she had brought him every book she had, if only to see that brief flash of open pleasure in his face and to hear his soft word of appreciation. Elsbeth had read about the Sirens whose songs lured sailors to their deaths, and now thought she knew how it could actually happen. His voice had been seductively suggestive, and she could hear her own heart thump in reluctant response.

She despised herself for feeling that way. She despised him for making her feel that way.

She turned to go, but his voice once again caught her more securely than a hand ever could.

"Have you thought any more of what I said?"

Elsbeth turned around and faced him again, thankful that her trembling legs were hidden by her dress. "You said a great deal, my lord, most of it nonsense."

"You credit it, then, that some was not?"

"Aye," she said. "That your brother would most readily betray you."

"Nothing more?"

"Inventions of your mind, my lord, to trick me."

He said nothing, but once more his eyes were challenging her, willing her to consider what he had to say.

"I must go," she said, wondering why she even hesitated, but she did.

"I have another request."

"You have a great number of requests for one in your position."

He grinned, but there was little humor in his face, more a wry acceptance of her observation. "It seems I have little to lose."

"Time, perhaps," she replied, "if you continue to annoy me."

"Then I owe my continued existence to you?"

"My clansmen don't have my patience, but I warn you even that is running short."

He strode over to her, and Elsbeth required every ounce of courage she possessed to continue looking at him. He was overpowering: taller than any other man she knew and, though he was no broader than some of her burly clansmen, she suspected he was just as strong. But it was his eyes that frightened her more than his physical strength. Not that they were threatening; it was, instead, their intensity that made her want to believe him, to do anything he asked. And that was more frightening than any physical attack.

"You would do us both a boon if you consider what I ask."

She looked at him with disbelief. "How so?"

"You want my ransom more than my death?"

"Aye," she said slowly. "The Careys have created much hardship among my clan. It would help restore what you have stolen."

A muscle moved slightly in his cheek, the only sign that he was under any strain, and again she had the impression of tightly controlled emotions.

"There's a man at Huntington, David Garrick. If my brother is keeping this silent, David can be trusted to get word to the crown. John wouldn't dare ignore the ransom if the Lord Protector were aware of the demand."

Elsbeth nodded. They, after all, wanted the same thing. He wanted his freedom, and she wanted to be rid of him.

All the same it galled her that he so easily seemed to be in charge. "Anything else, my lord?" she asked sarcastically.

"Give the message to a man you can trust without question—and tell no one else."

She flushed angrily. Once more he was blackening the loyalty of her clan. "I do not like your suggestion that the Kers, like the Careys, deal in treachery."

"Then," he said softly, "you shouldn't mind showing me how wrong I am."

"I don't need to show you anything. You forget yourself, that you are *my* prisoner and subject to *my* will."

"Oh no, my lady," he purred softly, but it was more like the noise from a tiger than a kitten. "I forget nothing—not where I am, nor why I'm here."

"Be cautious with your tongue then."

"My tongue is my only weapon at the moment."

"Or your greatest weakness."

"And what is yours, my lady... Elsbeth? Refusal to believe that which is evident?"

"I gave you no permission to use my name."

"You avoid the question."

"I trust my people, Lord Huntington. I need not test them."

He leaned against the wall, deep gray eyes probing her every thought, and once more she thought of a sleek forest animal, patiently awaiting its prey, forcing itself to restrain the powerful muscles and strength. Her lips trembled; she could not help it even as she despised herself for showing weakness.

"I only ask," he said, "that you tell no one other than your messenger."

"And if he, too, is killed, if your man is not as loyal as you may think?"

"I'm willing to wager my life. Are you?"

"It's not mine, it's his, and yours is already somewhat ... in doubt, shall we say?"

"You want the ransom, my lady. You have to take some risks."

It was a challenge. She looked up at his face, and knew that he understood her well. It was the one tack she could not resist.

"I shall consider it," she said slowly, not wanting to give him a victory.

Alex had to withhold a smile. He had achieved what he wanted. If someone reached David, he could report back that no message, no ransom demand, had been received at Huntington. Mayhap that information would crack her solid faith.

But Elsbeth had to have the final word. "It was the Careys who killed my men," she said stubbornly. "They are known for their murdering ways."

Again, the muscle in his cheek moved slightly as he sought to control his impatience. If only she would listen to possibilities he had already decided were probabilities. He took a step toward her. He did not mean to touch her, or even approach her closely. But his tremendous need to reach her, to dispel some of her suspicion drew him near. That and something else.

She was lovely with her face flushed, her eyes fiery, her chin set with determination, even if it was determination to disbelieve him. He ached to reach out and take her in his arms, to bring those lips to his. He was surprised to discover how much.

He saw her tremble slightly, and realized she was not altogether indifferent to him. Their eyes met in an instant of recognition, of joint need, before she stepped back.

Watching the cloud of dismay filling those expressive eyes, he turned around and strode back to the wall, once more leaning against it. He moved his hands behind his back, not wanting her to see the knotted fists that he knew were probably turning white with pressure, but his eyes didn't move from her.

The flush in her cheeks had grown deeper, and her eyes were now full of confusion. Her hands moved compulsively, tightening around each other, and he was reminded of a rabbit frozen in fear. But she was no rabbit. Not with that spirit.

"Tell me how your father died," he said in a low compelling voice.

It was a risk, that question. He knew it. Yet he had to know. He had to know everything.

She was still for a moment, and he was afraid she would bolt, perhaps even change her mind about keeping him alive a while longer.

"He was hunting," Elsbeth finally said to her own surprise. "He was ambushed and killed. It wasn't even a raid. Only one of his four men escaped, and he only by playing dead. He died later, after telling us what happened."

"Ambush?" Alex questioned, his mind running over the possibilities.

"Twenty men against five," she said bitterly.

"How would—" he could not bear to name his father "—the Careys know where to find the laird?"

Her eyes grew wide again as she kenned his meaning. He was doing it again, trying to cast suspicion on her clan when his own were the murderers.

He saw that he had gone too far as she moved toward the door once more. "Pray wait," he said, but it was more order than request.

Again she seemed to have little choice. Her legs would not move.

He went to the door and looked out. Both guards were several feet away, apparently at her orders. He doubted they could hear when he spoke softly. "Just consider it, mistress." And his eyes willed her to so.

Then as suddenly as he had during their first interview, he abruptly changed the subject. He had planted another tiny seed and now he must wait to see if it rooted. He could not water it overmuch for fear of drowning it before it had a chance to sprout.

"How does my horse fare?"

"It is no longer your horse."

"Demon tolerates few riders." Alex had named the horse himself. He had relished training the difficult nervous stallion after his years away from horses. Before his enslavement, he had been a superb horseman, and the training of Demon had, by necessity, quickly reawakened all his old skills. He had taken great pleasure in taming the horse, but it was still half-wild with anyone else, even grooms.

"Patrick can ride anything."

"Patrick—is he the dark-haired one?" It was a matter of reason. The dark-haired Ker had appeared to be the leader the day of his capture. Alex's isolation had prevented him from discovering any of the relationships or leadership, and he supposed that was on purpose.

She nodded, wondering why she was staying, why she was answering his questions.

Alex wanted to ask more, whether the man was anything to her.

"Patrick is my cousin," she said, seeing the question in his eyes and unable to keep from answering it.

"He is the . . . leader?"

"He and Ian lead the men," she replied, once more chastising herself as she answered his questions.

"Ian?"

"Another cousin."

Alex saw a momentary softening in her eyes, and he felt a stab of jealousy. "And what do they wish to do with me?"

"It makes little difference," she said, stiffening her resistance to him. "I make the decisions."

"Tell me about your father."

The question surprised her and she answered almost without thinking. "He was a scholar. A kind man, yet a brave warrior all the same."

"You loved him?"

"Aye, most dearly," Elsbeth said softly, drawn by the insistent intensity in his eyes. Insects do this, she realized suddenly. They fly toward brightness, only to find it deadly.

Defensively, she summoned her old anger. The knave was doing it again. Throwing her off balance. Her anger swelled as she thought that this man's family was responsible for her loss of her father, and she was mortified to realize that tears were welling in her eyes. She never cried.

As she turned once again, most assuredly for the twentieth time she thought with self-accusation, she heard his low deep voice pulling her back. "Don't go."

There was a plea in his voice that had not been there before, and it stopped her. It was difficult not to heed it, and something inside melted at the pure need she found in the two simple words.

She half expected mockery again when she turned, but there was none. His stance had changed from lazy to tense, and she could almost feel the need in him to touch her. For she had the same need, even while she didn't understand it. She wanted to wipe away the furrow around his eyes, and ease the pain lines jutting from his mouth. She wanted to touch the dark hair that framed the face and even feel the bristles on his chin.

When his eyes drew hers once more, she thought for a second she understood.

There was something in his face, an anguish that was so deep she wanted to cry, a loneliness that had no strictures. She recognized it for, since her father's death, she too had been lonely. But she knew instantly her loneliness did not compare to the English earl's. Hers was the pain of losing someone she loved, but there were also warm thoughts and happy remembrances. His was, she realized instinctively, of another sort, the pain of someone who had not known much happiness or love. Something had cast a deep shadow over him despite his attempts to hide it.

But even as she considered such things, she called herself a fool, for his mouth quirked up in that same mocking smile and his eyes became unfathomable; she knew she must have imagined anything vulnerable in him.

He was, after all, English. A treacherous Carey, and probably well versed in seduction. She supposed in her most bitter of bitter thoughts that he was probably very good at it. He probably had bastards throughout the countryside, and that was why they had seen and heard so little of him. He had been too busy at the business of seduction and whoring.

She turned once more, now for the twenty-first—and last—time, toward the door and called for her men to open it. It opened and closed with a heavy groan, and the grating noise of the lock being secured seemed even louder. She flinched at the sound, thinking of him. It was then she remembered that he had said nothing else after that one longing "don't go," nor had she, and the ache inside her grew deeper.

Elsbeth knew she had saved his life for the time being. She had gained time. But she didn't know how much longer she could control her clansmen, who wanted his head in return for her father's.

How much longer?

Chapter Five

Sweet Jesu. What had made him say that?

He had meant to disarm her. He had not meant to betray himself, the part of himself that was so vulnerable.

Don't go. What foolish words when he was the prisoner. They had come rushing without thought, and he immediately regretted them, particularly when he saw her eyes shutter against him.

But he was so infernally lonely.

The past few days had made clear exactly how alone he was.

After eight years, especially the three nightmarish ones, he had hoped that he might have been just a little welcome at Huntington. He had quickly realized how absurd the thought was. His brother hated him, the men-at-arms were suspicious, the tenants bitter. Yet he had had plans, and those had sustained him and filled his life.

Now he had to accept that his brother wanted him dead, and probably no one on his estate would raise a finger to help him, except possibly Davey. Even that was questionable. Garrick had his own future to consider.

It was a desolate thought to know that no one really cared whether he lived or died. An unbearably lonely one.

Which was why those few moments with Elsbeth Ker seemed like great riches to him.

She cared. Despite herself, she cared. He didn't know whether it was simply because she disliked killing or because she felt something of the same attraction he did.

When their eyes met, he could not mistake the current that flowed between them, something that defied the centuries of feuding between their families. It had taken all his strength not to touch her, and he had seen the same need in her. He knew it would have scared her away, and he could not do that. Not now. Not for several reasons. And so he had restrained himself. Again. Always again. Always holding back a part of himself. Even with Nadine, for he knew she had not loved him as he had thought he loved her. It seemed now he had always played roles, roles in plays written by someone else and over which he had little control.

He remembered, only too well, how he had reined his anger on the galley as curses were thrown at him, as food was denied, or when they were forced to row beyond any normal endurance. Then he was restrained by chains, and defiance injured not only him but his fellow prisoners.

And he remembered his restraint with Nadine. It had not been difficult because her father, whom he respected greatly, had usually been with them. And Nadine, who had said she loved him, never really showed any human passion, not in her eyes, in her touch or in her words. All her passion had been directed toward her cause, toward saving those loyal to their religion, and there seemed little left over for baser desires. There had never been the spark he saw in the Scots lass, the flare of desire he had glimpsed more than once, and that had warmed him more than he wanted to admit. He wondered now if his love for Nadine had been more admiration, or even a terrible craving for belonging, than heart's love.

By the devil's own hand, but he had too much time for thinking. He must not forget his objective, his goal, which was freedom and his own retribution. He was tired of being the pawn of others, and he must consider Lady Elsbeth Ker as another chess piece to be taken. Nothing more. She could never be anything else to him, nor he to her with all the spilled blood between them.

He stopped pacing and went to his pallet where he had placed the book. He reached for it. Reading should demand all his attention, take it from changeable eyes with their golden light. He opened the soft leather cover and studied the woodblock drawing, and wondered how Elsbeth Ker would appear in Helen of Troy's flowing graceful gown.

God's blood, but he needed to quit this place before his mind went completely addled.

On the day after Alexander Carey's visit, David Garrick had waited for the promised summons. By nightfall, he knew something had happened.

Although he had seen little of the new lord since they were young men together, he had, last eve, recognized many of the qualities he had come to admire so in their youth.

Alex had never been like the other nobility he had met. He had little of the arrogance and much more of the compassion. David's father had been a mercenary in service to the old lord, a step above many of the tenants but far below the children of the castle. William, the oldest Carey son, had usually lorded it over all the other children and bullied them unmercifully. When David had once struck back and hit the young heir, he himself was publicly whipped by the earl for daring to touch his son. The incident had made Garrick wary of the other two Carey sons.

When his father died, there was little food left for his mother and himself and one other child; the small cottage had been in payment of his father's services, but they had no other support. One day when he was poaching rabbits to feed his family, he stumbled into Alex, who was hunting. David knew he could well hang for the offense, and dived at the young lord. He didn't quite know what he would do then, for attacking an earl's son was even more serious than poaching. But self-preservation made some action necessary.

Alex was younger than he, and smaller, but David quickly realized that Alex's speed and reflexes more than compensated for strength. He soon found himself fighting for his life—not only his but his mother's and younger brother's, because they were completely dependent on him.

He never knew how long the fight went on, but they pummeled each other for what seemed like half the day, until they were both bloodied and nearly prostrate with exhaustion. Still, David would not surrender, and Alex fought for his life.

Until they could fight no longer. Neither of them.

Finally Alex stirred, sitting up painfully and looking at David. A small grin split his battered face. "You fight like the very demons."

David had looked at him with perplexity. He had expected curses and threats of punishment. "'Twas necessary when fighting a demon," he allowed.

"Why did you attack me?" the young nobleman asked.

David just looked at him with puzzlement. He was too exhausted to defend himself any longer. "I had taken one of your rabbits," he said slowly, knowing that the evidence was there to be seen.

Alex just shrugged. "There are many rabbits. I don't think one less is that important."

David stared. Alex's father had already hanged several tenants for poaching. It had not endeared him to his tenants, particularly when the rents were so high.

Alex returned the stare steadily. "I am not my father," he said, and David soon found the truth of it.

They had helped each other rise that day, and walked slowly back to the village with the rabbit.

The next day David was summoned to the castle and, trembling, he obeyed. He had little choice. He remembered how he prayed, both for his mother and brother, and for himself. He was eleven years old.

Alex was standing next to his father, and David would never forget the cold eyes of the old earl. Yet the expected pronouncement never came. Instead the eyes swept over him carefully.

"You are Eric Garrick's son?"

David bowed, praying his trembling legs wouldn't betray him. "Aye, my lord."

"He was a good warrior."

David was silent, not knowing why he was here or how he should respond.

"My son said you, too, have the makings of a fighter."

David's eyes went to Alex and saw only a small grin there.

"He wishes you as a companion, a servant. You will be taught the necessary skills of war with him."

A servant. David had no wish to be a servant, but he did have the wish to be a soldier like his father. And to be anything more than an archer he needed the promised skills . . . and the sponsorship. "My mother and brother?"

"You will receive a small subsistence," the earl said and waved him away. David was unable to believe his sudden turn of fortune. All for attacking a young nobleman. Only later did he learn that he was a servant in title only, for he was treated by Alex as an equal. He also discovered that Alex had paid a price for his own good fortune. David learned quickly of the strain between Alex and his father, and in the next seven years understood how Alex hated to ask his father for anything. When he did, it was usually on behalf of a servant or a tenant fallen on hard times, and the request was usually refused.

Alex went on the border raids, as expected, and always acquitted himself well, but he was usually quiet and brooding on the return, and David could say little to hearten him. Their relationship had never been that of master and servant, but more of friends, especially as David's skills sharpened and he became as skilled a warrior as any of the men of Huntington.

After one especially violent raid, when several women were taken and raped, he learned Alex and his father had engaged in a loud bitter argument and Alex had been sent to London. David, who was in the employ of the earl, was ordered to stay.

And he did, first because his mother and brother needed him, and neither he nor Alex had the money to take them with him. They would suffer under the earl's rule if David left. And then he fell in love with a girl whose family was bound to the land. He had missed Alex over the years and had wondered frequently what had happened to him. There had been no news for a long time, not even when the old earl and William died, not until several months ago when Alex unexpectedly appeared as if from the dead.

David had not been at Huntington then, but "loaned" to another border lord to help train his men. When he got back several days ago, he found Alex had returned. He had considered calling on the new lord, but he hesitated to take advantage of their earlier friendship, and he knew naught of the man who had returned.

Until Alex Carey, the new Lord Huntington, stopped by his cottage, and David learned that little had changed in the man except, perhaps, he was harder in his determination. And there was an aloneness about him that had cried out to David in some silent way.

And then he had disappeared.

David knew he was probably the only one who cared. Nearly all the men at arms now with Huntington had been employed within the past eight years. Few stayed long, since the Careys inspired little loyalty and were tight with their funds. Any additional income came from raiding, and Alex had openly pledged to put an end to that. Neither had he received any support from tenants. Squeezed and starved for years, they had no greater expectations of the newest Carey.

And John. John cared less than any about his brother. And David did not like the small smile that had hovered around his mouth the few times he had seen John Carey's face this day.

David knew a deep apprehension. There had been no more dependable friend than Alex Carey, no more determined man. He knew Alex would not have left Huntington without word, not after their talk last eve. Something had happened to him, and he would wager all he had that John Carey was behind it.

He made a pledge of his own. If Alex Carey were not dead, he would find him.

If he were not dead . . .

A man you can trust . . . and tell no one else.

Why did the words haunt her so?

Was he merely trying to trick her as she first thought?

But how? What would he have to gain if she merely sent a ransom demand through another source? Delay, mayhap. Delay of dying. Delay until he could escape?

'Twas possible, of course. Anything was likely when a Carey was involved. She would put nothing beyond them . . . not the worst of deeds or greatest of lies. Yet the more Elsbeth turned over his suggestion, the greater it gained in strength.

They had wanted to keep the abduction secret until the ransom was paid. They did not want to inflame both the Scottish and English wardens, the two people charged with maintain-

ing peace on the border, until all was done. Now she wondered
at the wisdom of this.

But she had little faith in either of the men appointed to keep
peace. They had their own interests at heart, and the English
warden, after all, had done nothing when the Kers had made
charges concerning her father's murder. He claimed there was
no proof of ambush and purposeful murder, except the word
of the one Scot who had escaped and later died. He had refused to charge the Careys. And the Scot warden, though he
had uttered threats, had little influence on the English side and
was not going to risk a confrontation.

By kidnapping the earl, the Kers risked censure from the
Scottish warden, and mayhap orders to release him. They
would then have to fight battles on two fronts. At the same
time, the other clans, knowing the background of the feud,
would expect the Kers to kill their hostage if no ransom was
paid. It would be a matter of honor, a matter of proper retribution for the death of the old laird. The Kers would lose all
support and respect if they did otherwise.

She was, quite simply, placed in a trap as secure as that
holding the earl.

Elsbeth, not for the first time today, wondered what her
prisoner was thinking. It had been a night and morn since she
had seen him, yet it seemed a lifetime. She sensed the helpless-
ness he must be feeling because she now also felt it.

She suddenly made up her mind.

She could not tell Patrick or Ian, for neither would understand or believe. And there was one man she would trust above
all others, a man who had been completely loyal to her father,
but who had now passed his sword to younger men. Hugh.

He was an Armstrong, who had married into the Ker family
and then returned to Armstrong lands. But after King James
had hanged Johnny Armstrong, along with other of his clansmen, Hugh was declared an outlaw, and he brought his wife
back to her home. He was protected by Elsbeth's father, and
became one of his most trusted counselors. He still rode on
occasion, but old wounds had made riding painful, and now he
mostly stayed in a cottage he shared with his wife and three
younger children. Three older ones already had rejoined the

Armstrong clan, and two more had been killed in battles between the English and the Scots.

She disliked to burden him with requests, but she knew he was loyal and wily, and she wished his advice.

Elsbeth asked that her mare be saddled, and she accepted a hand up. Hugh's cottage was not far distant, and she declined an escort, feeling safe enough this close to the peel tower.

She enjoyed the privacy, the rush of fresh air against her skin. Only once did she look back, up to the tower with its barred window. She shook her head, ridding it of the image.

Hugh was sitting in a chair, his leg propped up in front of a fire, his wife preparing bread. Both Armstrongs wished her good-day, and then Hugh nodded to his wife, silently bidding her to leave them alone.

"What is it, lass?"

"We've heard naught from Robin or Will. Or from John Carey."

He was silent. She was the chief. She had to make her own decisions.

"Would John Carey dare sentence his brother to death?"

"Aye," Hugh said. "Wi'out a thought."

"But his people?"

"The new lord has been gone a long while."

"It was a mistake taking him."

"If it were revenge you were wanting, nay. Ransom, aye."

"Revenge doesn't rebuild or put food in Ker mouths."

She paced nervously as she waited for a response. She should have come here first, when they first considered the kidnapping, but she had wanted to prove herself, and she had had the support of Patrick and Ian.

He was looking at her with sympathy. "He's a braw-looking man."

"You know him?"

"I've seen the lad on Truce Days, watched him in contests, before he left. He wa' the best of them."

Elsbeth fell silent, considering his words. Then her mind jumped back to her prisoner's words, his implications, the ideas he had planted in her head. "What do you know of my father's death?" she asked suddenly.

"It wouldna have happened if I'd been at his side," Hugh said sadly.

"Do you think one of our people betrayed him?"

There was a long silence, and Hugh's gnarled hand moved compulsively across the arm of his chair. "'Tis possible," he said at length. "I oft wondered how they knew he would be there."

"You don't believe then that the Careys found them by chance and took advantage?"

"It was a well-planned ambush, lass."

"But why?"

"Some thought the laird wanted peace. Some dinna care much for tha'."

A pain, deep and aching, settled in Elsbeth's stomach. Her people. Her friends. Her father's friends. "I don't believe it."

His hard mouth softened. "'Tis hard, lass, I know, but ye should be aware, and on guard."

"Why haven't you said anything before?"

"Ye wouldna have believed it," he said quietly.

"But who?"

"If I knew, he would be dead," Hugh said. "Wha' put the thought in yer head?"

Elsbeth was silent for a moment. She was loath to admit it was Alexander Carey, but Hugh was the only one she could talk to. "The prisoner," she said finally.

Hugh's brows furrowed together. "He's cannier than I thought."

"He says he knows his brother won't pay the ransom."

"And why should he when he can get the Kers to do wha' he wants the most?"

"Oh, Hugh, I don't know what to do. I don't want him killed. There's been enough killing."

"Aye, there has that." He was quiet a moment. "Does the Carey offer anything?"

She stared at him. "How do you know?"

"Because he never woulda put that other idea in yer head unless he did."

"He asked me to send a message to one of his men. He said that man would take it to London. He doesn't think his brother would dare defy the Lord Protector."

"That might be too late," Hugh said thoughtfully.

"He also..." Elsbeth hesitated.

Hugh waited, but his expression encouraged her to continue.

"Suggested I help him escape."

A smile tugged at Hugh's mouth. "God's tooth, but I ken I could like that Carey were he of another name."

"An Englishman?" Elsbeth said, astonished.

"In fifty years of life, lass, I've learned there be good an' bad on each side of the border."

It was a new idea for Elsbeth who had always thought right was on the Scottish side. Disbelief was written all over her face.

"Aye, lass," he said, "'tis true. I'll never forget the day of James's treachery. A Scottish king, aye, a royal Scot, hanging the laird of Gilnockie and his men who rode to greet him unarmed. All because they had done no more than raid the English as the English raided us."

Elsbeth had heard the tale dozens of times. The infamy of the deed, more than twenty years past now, had lived in border legend. Johnny Armstrong, the most popular laird along the border, had been foully taken by his own king. At receiving the sentence of death, the laird had faced the king who condemned him without trial and said it was "folly to ask grace of a graceless face."

"But our own clan—"

"There's always the jealous and the greedy, lass. 'Tis better ye learn it now."

She nodded slowly, the hurt spreading. Clan loyalty was so much a part of her. Here on the borderlands, where death rode daily, it meant everything. To even consider that one of her own clan could plot his laird's death was inconceivable.

"I will take yer Carey's message to his man at Huntington," Hugh said.

"But your leg—"

"Needs a bit of a change," he finished.

"I could not bear to lose you."

"Wha' Carey would take aught of an old peddler?" he re-assured her. "Talk to your Carey, lass, and bring me the message tonight. I'll be back in three days, no more."

"He's not *my* Carey. I'll be pleased never to set eyes on him again."

"He's yourn for the time," Hugh said with a smirk. There was a new light in Elsbeth's eyes, a new awareness, and he had not seen it there until the Englishman came. There was also a lilt in her voice every time she referred to the Carey hostage.

"You will be careful?"

"Aye, lass. There's a few more bairns I want yet to make."

She couldn't help but smile. He was notorious for the number of his "bairns," both legitimate and bastard.

"'Tis unhappy I would be," she sallied back, "were I to limit the population."

"'Tis most unlikely," he agreed seriously. "Now off with ye, lass, while I reason with my wife."

"Thank you, Hugh."

He merely nodded, the smile fading as she turned away. She was a brave lassie, but she needed a man. A strong canny man.

Elsbeth suffered through the midday meal with difficulty. It was always the largest meal, several courses, served with wine, and the table held all the Kers who were present at the time. She always sat at its head, usually with Patrick and Ian, unless there was nobility from some other clan present. Joan and Louisa sat below them, and then the other clansmen, each according to his rank.

Elsbeth used to love the formal meal when her father was alive, but now it had become a chore, mainly because of Joan Ker, a distant cousin of another Ker family who bore Patrick by Elsbeth's uncle. She was a bitter, unhappy woman who thought Patrick should be laird, and who took the slightest comment as an affront.

She started this day complaining about the prisoner. "I donna ken why he's still alive."

Elsbeth ignored the comment, as she often did. She did not enjoy the arguments that a defense usually caused.

"He's a bonny man, I hear," the woman continued. She was dark haired, like Patrick, but her face was narrow and pinched, and Elsbeth had often wondered why her uncle, known for his taste in women, had ever chosen her as mistress.

"If you like Englishmen and Careys," Elsbeth retorted, her own tongue waspish. She didn't like herself this way, but Joan brought out the worst in her. She could not ask her to leave the tower, however, since she was Patrick's mother.

Joan, who was forever intimating that Elsbeth should accept Patrick's standing offer of marriage, looked at her slyly. "Perhaps you no longer feel so strongly against the Careys."

She said it loud enough that every person at the table could hear, and silence descended over the room. The clan was evenly divided over the fate of the Englishman—whether he should die immediately or whether another attempt should be made for ransom.

Elsbeth looked at the waiting faces, and her speech lapsed into the border tongue. "'Tis na mon here with mair reason to hate the Careys."

The thirty men at the table nodded.

"Or see judgment done."

Again the nods.

"Do any here doubt tha'?" It was a challenge, direct and simple, and none accepted it. Even Joan was still.

"The Careys will no' escape our vengeance . . . they will pay dearly. This I swear to ye."

There was no more mention of the Englishman upstairs, although Ian flashed a quick approving grin at her. Patrick's face was shuttered and unreadable.

Both men joined her after the meal.

"What are ye going to do?" Patrick questioned.

For the first time in her life, Elsbeth eyed her two childhood companions with suspicion. Was there a traitor? And if so, was it one of these two men?

The thought was too painful to consider. She loved them both as brothers, Ian who made her smile, and Patrick who grumbled much but was always there when needed. They had both loved her father and served him well. She wanted desperately to voice her questions, but she could not. If she did, and one was a traitor, he would be that much more careful.

Could it be both?

She doubted that. The cousins worked well together because each had qualities the other lacked. And while they seldom fought, neither did they voluntarily choose each other's company. Part of that, she had once thought, was their competition for her hand, but now she wondered.

Elsbeth directed her question at Ian. "Your contacts on the border. Have they heard anything?"

Patrick shook his head. "Only tha' the earl has disappeared."

"Ian?"

The taller man shrugged. "'Tis apparent now no ransom will be paid. Ye must consider wha' is to be done."

"He is not the one who killed my father."

Ian studied her with his clear blue eyes. "But he's the son, and honor demands a life for a life."

Elsbeth stood and walked around the room. Patrick had been the one to first counsel killing the man; now he seemed willing to wait. Ian, on the other hand, had counseled patience and now was urging death. Did this change mean anything? She knew only that she needed to get rid of them for a few days.

"Ian, I wish you to deliver a message to the Clan Douglas, and Patrick, to the Homes."

Ian raised an eyebrow. "You are going to tell them?"

"Only that we might ask their assistance against the English. Not why."

Patrick's mouth tightened. "I donna think both of us should be gone at the same time. Wha' if the Careys attack?"

"Hugh is here," she said, "and two more men would not make that much difference. But the support of the Douglases and Homes would."

"Wha' if they want to know why?"

"They know of our troubles with the Careys. 'Tis to their benefit to see justice done and the border quieted."

"When do ye want us to leave?" Patrick asked without more argument.

"Today," Elsbeth said. "That should bring you back in four days."

Ian started to protest, but Elsbeth cut him off. "Today," she said again. "You best get started."

Chapter Six

The light dimmed in Alex's bleak chamber, and he realized it was late afternoon. He knew his chamber faced the east, for his greatest light came in the morning. When the sun crossed the tower to the west, the light started gradually to fade. He had the candle, of course, but he used that sparingly. And he had the leather container of wine. He took a swallow now.

He had whiled away some time today with the book, trying to keep from going mad and wondering if it were possible. How he wished to feel the thrust of the wind as he rode his horse, or to hear the ripple of a stream. Instead, his only distraction was the grating of the lock or the groaning of the door as meals of oatmeal and salted meat were set on his floor.

God's blood, but he was ready to do something reckless. He had hoped to get through to Elsbeth Ker, but it was becoming increasingly evident he had not accomplished that. The fact that she had not returned in two days did not bode well for him.

Yet part of him understood. There were years, even centuries, of hate between their families. Why should she trust him? He had tried to will her into doing so. Apparently he had failed.

He would have to rely on himself—even if it meant killing more Kers, although the thought sickened him. But he would not, could not, sit still and be led like a lamb to the slaughter.

Alex wished he could blank out his thoughts of Lady Elsbeth, of the fierce hatred in her eyes, and the contempt around her mouth. Both would grow deeper with more blood between them.

But he had vowed he would never again be another man's slave, another man's pawn, and he had a score of his own to settle with his brother.

God's truth, but he had little to work with: the fragile chamber pot, a half-burned candle, a skin partly filled with wine and a book. The book was the heaviest object.

And the dearest.

It made him think of the evenings with Henri and Nadine, before their arrest. He was twenty-three when he made his first trip to France, and he had longed to do something worthy with his life after years of empty English court life. He had been sent to London after a particularly strong argument with his father following a raid during which his father's men had raped several Scottish lasses. Alex had protested the action bitterly and, in turn, was branded a coward by his father. He was ordered to London to choose a rich wife, and therefore make himself of use to his family, but the noble ladies of London bored him, and their scant morals disinclined him toward marriage. He was in no hurry to bind himself to a wife he didn't love.

He quickly grew tired of the intrigues at court, but a common interest in fine horseflesh drew him into an unlikely friendship with the powerful John Dudley, the earl of Warwick, who was charming and bold, and an uncompromising Protestant.

Alex's own family was Protestant. It had been unwise to be anything else in Henry VIII's England, but unlike Warwick, he had little interest in religion. He observed cynically that Henry's decision to break away from the Catholic church stemmed more from lust than from belief.

Until Nadine.

It had been Warwick's reputation as a strong and loyal Protestant that brought Nadine Marchand to him.

Alex would never forget that day. He felt like a lad when he first saw her with her bright and shining hair of gold, and blue eyes full of fervor. He and Warwick had been hunting together and arrived back at Warwick's castle to find the visitors.

The soft sound of her accent charmed him and her fragile beauty bewitched him. Even the worldly, older Warwick seemed smitten and promised her help when she told him of the cruel and bloody repression of her friends and family in France. She needed money to smuggle them out and help them begin a new life in England.

Within days she had a goodly sum, including a few coins from the tightfisted King Henry, who could never resist a pretty face or an opportunity to bedevil the French. Alex had offered to escort her and her father home to France. By the time he reached its shores, he was determined to assist the Marchands. Posing as an English Catholic, he was accepted at court and soon learned how to ferret out information as to which Huguenots were to be arrested. He then helped the Marchands smuggle them to England, often securing an English ship to take them aboard along some lonely shore. It was adventurous and exciting and the happiest time of his life. A fool's happiness, he knew now.

When he could get away, he would stay with Nadine and Henri Marchand, and there, for the first time, he felt the warmth of a family. He cared deeply for Nadine in a gentle way, a giving way. They walked together, and shared books and ideas and hopes. Since it was the first affection he had known, he believed it love. And he relished it.

And, God help him, he enjoyed the danger. He believed himself clever and invulnerable, especially after he had the wits to survive a brief English invasion in which the small French port of Boulogne was seized. While other Englishmen disappeared, his charm saved him.

His luck lasted another year. It collapsed suddenly when he was visiting the Marchands, who held a small Protestant service. An informer told French troops, and the small comfortable house of Henri Marchand, merchant, was surrounded and all its occupants charged with heresy.

Alex would never forget Nadine's white, yet calm, face when she was taken. "Have faith in God," she whispered as she was roughly jerked from his arms. He charged headlong at the two men holding her, but there were too many soldiers, and he was knocked unconscious. When he woke he was in a foul-smelling cell. He never saw her again....

Now he heard a noise at the door, and quickly rose from his pallet. It would be his meal, he supposed, but he felt no hunger. He had been fed little in the galleys, and in the five months of his freedom, he had not been able to indulge in the huge meals so common among the nobility. The offerings here, as meager and tasteless as they were, more than satisfied a stomach accustomed to much less.

The decision was made instantly. Alex would no longer sit here and wait. He had noted in the past days that his guards were not nearly as wary as they had been at first. He had lulled them with his seeming docility, and they no longer required him to face the stone wall when they entered. Their expressions were often contemptuous, and he knew they thought him cowardly. Which suited him well.

He relaxed against the stone wall, his face blank. Only his eyes betrayed any tension, and the guards did not look closely at those in the dim light.

As one of the men was setting a trencher on the floor, along with a wooden mug of water, Alex decided it was time to move.

He had lost weight in the galleys, but his shoulders, arms and chest had been made granite hard during years of rowing, and he was deceptively strong. Alex propelled his upper body into the kneeling guard, who then tumbled into the guard behind him. His fist went into the jaw of the first man, and Alex heard the thud as the burly Scotsman hit the floor. As the other man was struggling to his feet, Alex grabbed the sword from the first guard, who now lay still, and he fixed its tip at the throat of the rising Scot. Alex's hand held the weight easily and left no doubt of intent.

"You will do as I say," he said softly, menace in every syllable.

"Ye'll no' get away—"

"Mayhap, but neither will you live through this day if you don't back into the room, and drag your companion with you."

The guard hesitated, weighing the Englishman he now knew he had badly misjudged. He felt a pain in his neck and the trickle of blood. "Aye," he said finally, and the sword moved slightly away from his neck, but close enough to strike efficiently if need be.

The Ker clansman moved back in the room, dragging his companion with him. When they were well inside, Alex ordered his captive to turn around, as he had been ordered so many times in the past days. Once more the man hesitated, and Alex knew he was weighing his chances of surviving a sword thrust.

"Do not even think about it. Turn around," he said again, and the softness in his voice was more convincing than a curse would have been.

The clansman did as ordered, partly expecting the bite of the sword in his back. There was a brief blinding pain in his head, then darkness.

Alex looked at the two men on the floor. Both were bleeding but lived. They would feel none too well, however, on the morrow.

He took the jack, a leather jacket with iron reinforcement, from one unconscious man along with his plaid, which was also used as a cloak. He quickly donned both garments, then buckled on the man's sword belt. Perhaps he could blend in with the clansmen. His hair, he realized, was a problem. Most of the Kers were red-haired; only the man named Patrick had his own match. And there was his new beard. Most of the Ker men he had seen were either clean-shaven or sported full beards of a reddish color.

Alex stooped once more, and relieved the two unconscious men of their dirks. He dragged one body over to his pallet and covered him with a blanket. The other one was stretched against a wall, out of range of a brief look from outside the barred window in the door. Alex quickly weighed his chances. He had to find a room and remove his beard, before he tried to leave the tower. If it were like other strongholds on the border, the keep would have stout outer walls and a well-guarded gate. His only chance was guile. And that was slim.

He left the tower chamber, locking it behind him, and slipped down the stairs quickly, grateful that the soft Spanish leather of his boots made little sound. He had been blindfolded each time he had been taken up or down the steps, and now he tried to remember how many flights there were. Five, he believed, which meant five levels below him, each with its own chambers. He encountered no one on the first stairway, but heard voices below. He ducked into one of the chambers, hoping it would be empty.

God's grace was with him. The room, located on the west and still alight with the late sun, obviously housed one of the lesser family members. It was plain, much like his at Huntington, but held several weapons, several pieces of armor, a plaid and a bonnet. There was a piece of polished steel evidently used for a mirror, and Alex allowed himself a small satisfied grin. His smile broadened as he found water, cold and dirty, in a bowl. He dampened his face and took one of the dirks from his belt, deftly scraping the bristles from his cheeks and chin. He then put on the bonnet, wishing it hid more of his face, though it covered most of his dark hair.

Alex decided to wait until it was dark, and hoped to slip past while most of the household was at the evening meal. He had surprise on his side; no one would look closely at one dressed like the others, and if this household were like his own there were often strangers coming and going.

He tried to keep his eagerness at bay as the chamber darkened. He occasionally heard voices, and he tensed. But no one came to the chamber where he was waiting, and finally there was quiet. He slipped from the room, listening intently, and quickly but carefully he descended one level and then another. He saw a servant come from a room and he averted his face. He held his breath as the girl paid him little heed but moved past him with a tin flagon in her hand. The tight knot in his stomach relaxed, and he descended yet another set of stairs.

Alex heard an increased volume of noise down and to the right. It must be from the hall where the Kers ate. He would have to get past it.

Servants moved quickly in and out of the room from which issued the sound of voices. Again he averted his face, but the servants were absorbed in their tasks. The pace of his steps increased, and he reached the door of the tower, quickly unlatching it and finding a second door. He opened it deftly and slid outside, his eyes meeting the soft dusk of evening.

He took a deep breath of air, and looked around, seeking the stables. Perhaps he could even steal back his horse. He warned himself against taking chances but, God's truth, that horse meant much to him.

Alex reached the stables without incident, and found there only a young lad whose eyes widened as he recognized the English lord.

Alex saw the realization in the boy's face as well as the movement of his mouth. It two strides he was in front of the lad, his hand on the boy's mouth, a threat in his eyes. The boy could be no more than five and ten, and Alex didn't wish to hurt him, yet neither could he allow him to sound an alarm. He cursed softly as he saw the terror in his captive's eyes, but he had few choices. If he let go long enough to gag and tie him, there could be time for the stableboy to shout a warning.

He twisted the boy around until the lad's back was pressed against Alex's chest. With one hand still on the boy's mouth despite the frantic movement of the young wiry body, Alex reluctantly used his other hand to hit his captive on the side of the head. He caught the boy's body as it went slack, and he gently eased him to a pile of hay. He leaned down to hear the boy's soft breathing, then stood.

And went completely still.

Framed in the doorway were two men, one dark and one blond, both dressed for travel and both heavily armed. Alex swiftly recognized Patrick, sizing him up instantly as the more dangerous. A sword was already in the Scot's hand, and a broad challenging smile on his lips.

Alex was surprised to realize that the clan leader was waiting for him to draw the sword he had appropriated. So it would be a fair fight. Alex felt excitement rise inside him. He had been battered, bruised, humiliated and imprisoned by these Scots and, by God's blood, he now had a chance to fight back.

"English whoreson," the dark-haired man taunted, and Alex knew he was being goaded purposely. His glance darted over to the other man, whose hand remained on his buckled sword, but who leaned against the wall with an amused air that told Alex he faced a superb opponent.

Patrick's sword went up and Alex's met it, the sound of metal against metal echoing through the dark stables. The eyes of the two antagonists never left each other. Each man measured the other as the swords separated and met again, probing and testing.

Alex knew he was at a disadvantage. He had once been an excellent swordsman, but sword fighting was a skill he had not exercised in years, other than a few friendly matches with Warwick when he had returned to England. Yet he was in superior physical condition, and he knew he could outlast most men. If nothing else, he thought wryly, the French had developed his endurance.

Patrick tried an experimental thrust, and Alex parried it, moving backward until he felt a stall blocking further motion in that direction. He heard the nervous, frantic movements of the horse within the stall, and moved gracefully to the side as he feinted and lunged.

The dark Scot defended against the attack easily enough, but Alex saw the surprise on the Scot's face. It was obvious Patrick Ker had expected to win easily and quickly. The surprise changed to wary determination.

The stable was dark and crowded, and Patrick moved back through the door into the courtyard. His steps were cautious, his eyes intense, and the smile gone from his face.

There was a shout from the tower, and Alex knew his chance for escape was gone. The red and green plaid of the Kers was everywhere, and he and Patrick were now fighting within a circle of watching men. Alex wondered briefly if Elsbeth were among them, but he dared not look. Patrick Ker was much too fine a swordsman.

Alex tried a riposte, and it forced Patrick back, but only for a second before the Scot lunged at him. Alex sidestepped but not quite quickly enough. Patrick's blade caught the edge of his arm, and Alex felt the trickle of blood mix with his sweat.

Again their swords clashed and disengaged as the dusk moved into evening, and their breath became labored, their steps slowing. The next moments were grueling, Alex meeting Patrick's onslaughts with skill but unable to find an opening in the Scot's defense. Only Alex's deftness and endurance enabled him to survive Patrick's attacks, but Alex knew the Scot was the better swordsman, and one small mistake would mean his own death. He could see the hate in the Scot's eyes, the determination in the tight mouth. There was a blood lust there that Alex recognized.

It was a duel of life and death, grueling and without mercy. Alex thought he saw an opening and thrust once more, but Patrick easily met it and lunged forward, knocking Alex's sword from his hand. Alex dived after it, rolling on the ground to avoid the Scot's blade as he grabbed the handle of his own and sprang to his feet, hardly aware of the exclamation of surprised admiration that traveled among the Scots.

Patrick was breathing heavily, and Alex knew the wisest thing was to exhaust his opponent. He could not win by direct attack; it was too long since he had practiced swordsmanship. He moved sideways, his feet light as he kept barely out of Patrick's reach.

Angered at his elusive opponent, the Scot attacked viciously. Alex defended himself well, restraining himself from attacking. He knew he couldn't afford another fall, and he saw that Patrick Ker was tiring, his breath coming in short gasps. Alex also knew the Scot had decided he must finish the battle quickly.

Patrick feinted and lunged as Alex moved, once more dancing backward, taunting and teasing his opponent. When he thought the Scot was angered enough to make a misjudgment, Alex sprang forward suddenly, his sword driving toward Patrick's heart. In the last second it swerved, going toward the sword arm instead.

But the moment's hesitation was a serious mistake.

Patrick had caught the indecision in his opponent's eyes, and whirled, that one split second giving him the time he needed. He wielded the blade as if it were a part of him, knocking the now unprotected sword from Alex's hand. In just as quick a movement, the tip of his blade rested at Alex's heart, and Alex read the deadly intent in his eyes. He stood silently. Waiting.

"No!"

Alex heard her cry, but his eyes never left Patrick's. He knew Patrick wanted to kill him, that the dark Scot was considering disobeying that quick sharp desperate order. He was tense with the need, with the intent.

"No," Elsbeth said again, and the word was like a shot in the quiet evening. "I will not have it."

Slowly Patrick lowered his sword and sheathed it, his eyes telling Alex that only his lady's word had held his sword. His eyes raked Alex's, promising another opportunity, before he turned away.

Alex leaned against the stone wall of the stable, his heart thudding against his ribs. The pounding beat, he knew, was from both exertion and that one moment when he thought he would die.

There was silence in the courtyard, broken only by the rasping breath of the two combatants. Then one man moved, the blond one who had entered the stables with Patrick. He leaned down and picked up Alex's sword. The smile was back on his face. "Fair for an Englishman," he observed dryly. "No' so many can hold their own with my cousin."

Alex was too spent to answer. Nor was there an answer. He had achieved nothing this day except to put his captors more on guard.

Sweat drenched his jacket and hose, and dripped from his face. He looked down at his arm, which was only now beginning to pain him, and he saw streams of blood run down his arm and hand. His other hand went to the wound to stanch the flow.

When he looked up, he saw the clusters of Ker clansmen, their faces curious. His eyes sought and found Elsbeth Ker. He grinned weakly and shrugged, seeing the anger ignite and flame in her eyes.

"Take him back to the tower room," she said, and turned away abruptly, moving toward Patrick.

Alex felt a new stab of pain as she looked up at Patrick, her eyes concerned. He felt arms on him, and he jerked away from them. God's blood, but he was sick of being manhandled, and for a moment he really didn't care what happened to him. Everything appeared so bloody hopeless. But then he caught the inquisitive look of the other Ker, the blond one, and Alex resolved he would not admit defeat. He never had. He never would.

He stiffened his shoulders, ignoring the fatigue and pain, and turned toward the peel tower. Pride in every inch of his body, he led the way back inside, strode to the stone steps and mounted them to his erstwhile prison.

The door was still locked, and the key was gone.

The blond Ker had escorted him to the room. His eyes were dancing with amusement as he peered through the window and saw one of his clansmen inside. The man had shrugged away the blanket and was trying to rise.

Ian tried the door, and arched an eyebrow when he found it locked. He turned to Alex. "The key?"

Alex shrugged. He had no special wish to return.

"Ye enjoy living dangerously, Englishman."

"I don't enjoy it at all," Alex replied coldly. "But neither do I particularly enjoy your hospitality."

"Be grateful ye're not in chains. 'Tis only by my sweet cousin's wish that ye are not," the Scot said. "But I suggest ye not try her patience further. She can be . . . short tempered."

There was an affection in the man's face when he spoke of his cousin that Alex did not like. "You're Ian Ker?"

The man bowed, but his eyes went suddenly hard. "The key. I ha' no more time to waste. I could call the blacksmith, but then I might well ask him to do a wee bit more work for us."

Alex caught his meaning well enough. Chains. He had had enough of those. He pulled off one of his boots and tipped it upside down. He heard the loud clank of a key as it landed heavily on stone.

Ian picked it up, a half smile on his face as he opened the door and looked at the guards, both of whom were stirring now. "I should leave them in here with ye," he said with disgust at the two red-faced Scots. "An Englishman and a Carey besting two Kers. 'Tis a sad day." He waited, however, for the two men to lumber out, both casting malevolent stares at Alex.

Alex expected Ian Ker to follow them but he did not. Instead he leaned against the wall, his hand playing with the key, watching Alex's eyes blaze with new fury as he thought he was being played with.

"Nay," Ian said softly. "I ha' no reason to mock. Ye surprise me, Englishman."

"And why is that?" Alex said coldly, his arm burning like hellfire.

"Why did ye spare Patrick?"

"Is that what I did?"

"You ha' him for a second."

Alex turned away from him, walked to the pallet and sat.

"Huntington?" The Scot's voice was like a pistol shot.

Alex's mouth twisted into a grim smile. "I wouldn't have been any better off, would I?"

"Satisfaction, mayhap?"

"A man's death is precious little comfort to me," Alex observed wryly.

"Yours would ha' been to Patrick."

"And you?"

"Mayhap to us all."

"I apologize then for being so unaccommodating as not to offer it freely."

Ian grinned. "I think I could like ye, Huntington."

Alex looked at him sourly.

"I'll have some water sent up."

Alex merely nodded, wanting desperately to be rid of the man, to be rid of everyone.

Ian gave him one last wry searching look and went out the door, closing it behind him. Alex heard the lock turn, then the man giving orders to the two guards who had accompanied him.

Alex leaned back against the wall. The plague take it, but his arm hurt. Yet he welcomed the pain for it took his mind from his failure, from the fact that he was worse off than before. He had lost his advantage, and knew his guards would be particularly careful henceforth.

And he had been so close. So very close.

Chapter Seven

Patrick and Ian rode off an hour later, Patrick to the Homes, and Ian to the Douglases. But before they left and while Ian was seeing to the captive earl, Patrick washed the sweat from his face at a trough in the courtyard and delivered a lecture to Elsbeth.

It was not one that Elsbeth appreciated.

"Stay away from him, Elsbeth. He's more dangerous than we thought. Tha' room willna hold him long."

Elsbeth merely looked at him stubbornly.

He shook his head. "I wish we'd never taken him."

"Aye," she agreed. "But now it appears we're trapped along with him."

Patrick eyed her carefully. "He's seen the whole of the peel tower now. 'Twould not be wise to let him go."

"There's many who've seen it," Elsbeth answered sharply. "I would have preferred it otherwise, but 'tis nothing the Careys could not have learned elsewhere with some effort."

"I donna like going and leaving him here wi' ye."

"There's more than a hundred Kers here," Elsbeth soothed. "I don't think even Lord Huntington can go through all of them."

Patrick shook his head. "I think ye should put him in irons."

The thought was abhorrent to Elsbeth, although she didn't quite fathom why. She couldn't have cared less about the earl of Huntington—the arch-enemy of her clan—or his comfort.

He had, after all, just tried to kill Patrick.

Or had he?

Had she imagined that brief hesitation when he had the advantage?

She saw his face again at that moment, the sweat beading his forehead, his eyes the color of a stormy Scottish sea as his arm moved ever so slightly in the first mistake she had seen during the tense battle. Her mind's eye then went to his arm, and the blood pouring down it, and finally the proud way he had shaken off the hands that seized him. Her heart lurched in a peculiarly hurtful way as she realized she admired the man ... admired his courage, his spirit, his pride.

And he was, God's truth, a Carey! She should have no feelings for him. None but hate. Certainly not the racing of the blood, the quickening of the heart when she thought of him.

She looked up at her cousin's curious gaze. "I'll think on it," she said abruptly. "You'd best be on your way."

Patrick regarded her dourly. "Aye, Elsbeth, but take care," he said with just a trace of reluctant surrender in his voice. His hand reached out and touched her cheek with gentleness. "Take care," he repeated with more feeling than he usually allowed to show.

Elsbeth softened. It was always so. Patrick was infinitely dear to her, especially when his serious shell cracked to reveal a softer core. She often wondered if it was Joan who had created the solemn hard man that most saw, Joan who maneuvered and manipulated and complained, Joan who seemed to spread poison wherever she went.

But her thoughts were interrupted by Ian's arrival. He flashed his wide grin.

"He is all right?" Elsbeth asked about their prisoner.

"Arrogant as ever, my dear cousin. 'Tis a quality the English seem to perfect." He bowed and took her hand to his lips with an impish smile. "I'll miss ye."

Despite her worries, Elsbeth smiled back. Ian's charm never failed, and could usually jolt her from a dark mood. He could have nearly any woman he wanted, Elsbeth knew, but he insisted she was the only one he would marry. If he had liaisons with others, he had kept them secret.

Patrick, on the other hand, was famous for his dalliances. His proposal of marriage between them had been based on his ability to protect her and the clan. There had been no lavish protestations of love, although he and she shared a strong affection born of childhood friendship.

How could either be a traitor?

If there was one in the clan, it must be someone other than her cousins.

She smiled at both of them. "God go with you."

"I'll be back quickly," Ian said.

"Remember wha' I said," Patrick added. "Be cautious."

Ian gave her one last look, and turned on his heel, mounting a horse that had been saddled along with Patrick's while Elsbeth and her cousins talked. She waited patiently as Patrick, his eyes dark and secretive again, hesitated as if he wanted to say more.

"You are refreshed enough to travel?" Elsbeth asked belatedly.

"'Twould take more than a Carey to delay me," he replied brusquely."

"Aye," she agreed, studying him. Patrick was unsurpassed in battle. She often wondered if it were that dour single-mindedness that made it so. He didn't allow anything or anyone to distract him.

"By your leave?" he said now, and Elsbeth once more felt waves of guilt at allowing even a tiny shred of suspicion to touch him.

As she nodded, he turned abruptly and left her. Elsbeth watched affectionately as he swung easily into the saddle, and, with Ian beside him, spurred his horse to a fast pace. It was a bright moonlit night, the time often favored for travel by borderers. Elsbeth knew the cousins would travel together for some five miles, and then go in different directions.

She felt a sudden desolation. Ian and Patrick had become indispensable to her during the months since her father's death. They had been constantly at her side for support and comfort, and now both were gone, partly, she knew, because of the doubt planted in her mind by their hostage.

He was wrong! It was nothing but trickery. She would no longer allow him to affect her so. She thought of his bleeding arm, and considered tending it, but discarded the notion. The wound had not seemed severe, and Ian had dismissed it casually. Lord Huntington would only spread more of his poisoned words.

And then she remembered Hugh, Hugh who was waiting for instructions. Huntington's escape and sword fight had all but erased her original purpose from her mind, the real reason she had sent Ian and Patrick away. Curse him, but she would have to see Huntington tonight after all, learn again the name of the man Hugh should contact.

She might as well see to his wound at the same time, she conceded to herself, unwilling to admit there was any other reason.

Elsbeth went back into the peel tower, only to be met by Louisa, who hovered nervously in the dark hall that was lit by torches and candles. Elsbeth stopped suddenly, seeing the distress on the girl's face.

"Is Patrick safe? I heard he fought the Englishman."

The note of concern penetrated Elsbeth's thoughts. She looked at Louisa, and saw a face openly adoring. Why, Elsbeth wondered, had she not noticed before?

"He was untouched," she replied gently, taking measure of the relief in the girl's face.

"I—I—" Louisa had started, but she couldn't finish. Her face flamed red, and she turned and fled, leaving the surprised Elsbeth in her wake.

Elsbeth stared after her. Louisa had been with them two years, brought here by Elsbeth's father, who took the young girl as his ward after her father, a knight, was killed. She was bonny, her hair light brown with the familiar red streaks of the Kers, yet she was painfully shy. Elsbeth had tried to befriend her, but even after many attempts she received little more than short nervous responses.

Elsbeth thought now she should have tried harder. But in the year before her father's murder, Elsbeth had been absorbed with clan responsibilities and had traveled with him to visit other border families and even to Edinburgh several times. She'd left Louisa with Patrick's mother to learn womanly arts. Then in the months since her father died, she had worked hard at assuming his responsibilities, trying to assure the clan that she could, and would, provide the strong leadership they needed.

In doing so, she now realized, she had neglected her obligation toward Louisa. So many depended on her, and she felt woefully inadequate to meet their needs, to provide the protection that was their right and due.

Perhaps everyone was right. Perhaps she should marry. Ian? Patrick? One of the many other suitors who had asked for her hand in the past year? An alliance with another clan, perhaps, to strengthen her own?

But when she tried to think of each prospective husband, she could see only steel-gray eyes and unruly black hair and a twisted, mocking half smile.

She wanted to scream in denial, but she could not. Elsbeth suddenly felt as helpless as a bird sighted by a hawk. Yet the pull to Alexander Carey, earl of Huntington, was irresistible, even though she knew how completely deadly it was.

Her only hope, she realized, was to rid herself of him as quickly as possible and then choose a husband. No matter how distasteful the thought, she was beginning to realize she owed it to her clan.

She called one of the two maidservants who, with Annie, did most of the domestic work in the household. There was little money for more help except on special occasions. She asked that water be heated and brought to the tower room, and she herself found some clean linen. She told herself she was going to the Carey only because a dead hostage was of no value, and because she had to extract information for Hugh. But she couldn't slow the speed of her heartbeat, or dismiss the reluctant anticipation she felt.

There were new guards outside the prisoner's chamber, both with grim determined looks on their faces. When she asked them to open the door, they regarded her unhappily but did as she asked, drawing their weapons before unlocking the door.

"Annie will be along in a moment," she told one. "You will both wait outside until she comes."

"Mistress . . ." One of them ventured a mild protest but was quelled by her look.

She took one of the torches from a wall bracket in the corridor and entered. She quickly found a bracket inside and placed it there, her eyes seeking the English lord. He was rising and she saw his eyes blink at the light, then lighten as he recognized her before they went blank again.

He was no longer wearing the jack, although he was wearing his own breeches. Despite the chill in the chamber, his upper body was naked, a piece of blanket tied tightly around his arm. She could not help but notice that it was darkly stained and wet, nor could she miss the lines of pain etched on his face.

"Impatient to leave, my lord?" she queried.

His eyes captured hers. "I thought to relieve you of a burden."

"You almost succeeded, my lord. Completely."

The corner of his mouth turned up. "Is that disappointment that I'm not dead, or that I didn't escape?"

Elsbeth was tired of the jousting. "I want the ransom. Nothing more, English."

He moved to see her better in the dim light, but he stumbled on his doublet, and instinctively threw out his injured arm to balance himself. A lightning bolt of agony swept him, and a low moan involuntarily escaped his lips as the wound reopened. He stepped back and leaned against the wall, his eyes closing against continuous waves of pain.

"Sit down, my lord, and I'll tend that."

Her voice was unexpectedly gentle, and Alex slid down the wall to the pallet. He opened his eyes, relishing the concern in her face, the softness of her hands as they started to unwrap the piece of blanket he had used to stanch the bleeding.

He forced his gaze from her when he heard the door opening again. A woman entered with a large bowl. Her eyes widened at the sight of her mistress kneeling beside the Carey and tending him.

"I'll do that, my lady," she said formally, because the Englishman was there.

"Just leave the water here, Annie," Elsbeth said.

Annie's eyes filled with silent disapproval, and Alex couldn't resist a grin, despite the burning in his arm. The Lady Ker could be formidable.

Her voice softened as she turned once more to the woman. "Please, Annie," she said. "Prepare a bath for me. I'll be there soon."

Alex saw the curiosity in the woman's face and the stiffness of her back as she retreated, but his attention quickly returned to Elsbeth, who was regarding him solemnly. What, he wondered, was she thinking? For once, he could not tell.

With a brief flurry of panic, Elsbeth wanted to call back Annie and flee. She simply did not understand what was happening to her, nor why nothing was working the way it should...not her heart, not her hands, not her speech. She was struck anew with the handsome symmetry of the man's face now that the rough beard was gone. The mouth was wide and sensual, the nose straight and well formed, the chin strong and resolute. But it was the eyes, as always, that melted her soul. They were like crystals, prisms, that never stayed the same but held the constant of mystery.

"Why did you not kill Patrick when you had the chance?"

The question was totally unexpected. That moment during the sword fight had come and gone so fast even Alex wondered if it had been a conscious decision. But Ian Ker had seen it, and so had the Lady Elsbeth. She had a fine eye for sword fighting.

"*He* would have killed *you,*" she said, prodding him.

"I know."

"Then why?"

He shrugged, watching her hands as they tugged at the strip of cloth. "It would have done me little good."

"You would not have died for it. We Scots favor a fair fight."

He wanted to tell her that he was sick of bloodshed, of hate and useless violence. But she would not believe him. He was a Carey, and to her all Careys burned and ambushed and raped. So he remained silent, and watched as she washed his wound with water and bound it carefully with clean linen.

She finished, and looked at her effort with satisfaction. Her eyes then moved to the scar on his chest. It was relatively new, and strange looking—not a clean thrust, nor a pistol wound. She was familiar with both.

Her hand touched it, and his body visibly flinched, his eyes, warm a moment earlier, turning cold.

"What . . . ?" She stopped the question when she saw his expression. Forbidding. It was so intense that she moved back from him, unwilling to be caught in the ferocious gray thundercloud of his eyes.

For a moment, she was suspended there, unable to draw her eyes from his, until slowly he relaxed, his taut muscles easing, and a slight ironic smile came back to his face. "Thank you, my lady, for your succor." But although there was mischief in his eyes again, there was also a darkness that Elsbeth didn't understand.

"You fight well," she said finally.

"I've had little practice of late."

"Patrick's never been bested."

He smiled at that. "I believe it."

She eyed him curiously. She still didn't understand why he hadn't killed Patrick when he had the chance. Any other man she knew would have under similar circumstances. She didn't understand him at all.

Elsbeth looked around her. His doublet was tossed carelessly on the floor, and the wine pouch she had brought him was near where he had been sitting. She could tell it was empty or nearly so.

"Patrick believes you should be placed in chains."

Once again she saw the darkness invade his eyes, and she wondered at the depth of it.

Alex said nothing, unable to beg, although part of him wanted to do so. He didn't know if he could take irons again without going mad. It took all his will to raise an eyebrow in pretended indifference.

"And my lady, what does she think?" Only a muscle flickering in his cheek betrayed any tension.

"I don't think you will take the guards so easily again."

"'Twas not so easy the first time," he retorted, and once more Elsbeth felt the full force of his presence. It swept over her with the strength of a Scottish spring storm. She balled her fist to keep from touching him.

But he had no such scruples. He saw the sudden flame in her eyes, the way she flushed so prettily. He reached out and touched her hand, his thumb running over the balled fist until she opened her hand, and then he turned it over and traced leaf-light patterns in her palm with his thumb.

She trembled from the resulting waves of sensation that swept over her, the heat that started where he touched, that galloped through her body in a maddened chase of an elusive quarry. Each movement made her want something more, but she didn't know what. She just knew it had everything to do with Alexander Carey, English lord, freebooter and destroyer. She jerked her hand away.

"Mayhap you *do* belong in chains."

He stiffened and his eyes turned icy. "I beg your sufferance, my lady, but you are a lovely woman...and more than enough to make one lose his wits."

It was contemptuously said, without real apology or plea, and Elsbeth immediately regretted her thrust. She suspected that in some way she had asked for the caress. She had to leave now, before she made more of a fool of herself.

She rose. "The man you spoke of—the man at Huntington. His name?"

For a moment, he didn't understand, and then his hard eyes relaxed. "David Garrick."

She nodded and started for the door.

"Lady Ker."

She turned, and saw him tug something off his finger. He rose unsteadily and approached her, taking her hand and putting the object in it.

Elsbeth lifted it up. It was a heavy ring, a large ruby set in the Huntington crest.

"Send this. He'll know it's from me," Alex said. "And ask him to pass it to the duke of Northumberland. He will pay any ransom you ask."

Her eyes opened wide. "You have fine friends, my lord." She knew that John Dudley, earl of Warwick, had been recently named duke of Northumberland as well as Lord Protector. Ian had told her that Huntington had friends at court and the ear of Northumberland; they must be even closer than Ian thought if Huntington believed the duke would guarantee a large ransom. . . .

"But not many," her hostage noted wryly.

"He'll see the ransom paid?"

"I believe so."

She hesitated. This kidnapping was turning more complicated by the moment. If Huntington was truly a close friend of Northumberland, she had placed her clan in more danger than she'd first believed. Neither the Kers nor their neighbors could withstand the might of an English army.

Alex saw her hesitation and surmised its cause. He cursed himself briefly. He should have trusted David alone. He had just given her good cause not to contact David, and to dispose of her prisoner quickly and quietly. He knew she was considering all the consequences of his words.

"I wish I had never seen you, English," she said suddenly, frustration and anger in every word.

Alex watched the door open and close and heard the grate of the key once more. He stood silently, swaying a bit with weakness, before he sat. As if in mockery, the torch, still in the bracket in his wall, flamed merrily, throwing dancing shadows across the now too familiar chamber. He wondered what in the furies Lady Ker was going to do.

Lady Ker was wondering the same thing.

Every direction she turned seemed more dangerous.

She wished she could stop thinking about her prisoner long enough to make sense of the whole mess.

Her father, she thought bitterly, would never have kidnapped someone no one wanted.

Except, perhaps, a very powerful lord who could destroy them all.

And, said a small voice deep inside, herself.

But how could that be? She had learned to hate the Careys since she was old enough to talk. They were the devil incarnate, each one of them, and the only good one was a dead one.

Why hadn't he killed Patrick?

And did Patrick realize what had happened? He had to have realized. He was too fine a swordsman not to recognize that hesitation. And yet he had been ready, nay, eager to kill the Englishman.

Could Patrick be the traitor? Was there indeed one among them?

Her head was spinning, and the only person to whom she could turn was Hugh. She put on a dark cloak and slipped out the tower's main door. There were guards there now, too. Another precaution against the wily Englishman. It galled her that it was necessary that she could not leave her own home without identifying herself.

Hugh's cottage was not far outside the gates, and Elsbeth accepted help in mounting her horse but again refused escort. The cottage looked comforting to her tired eyes as she approached it, the smoke from its chimney friendly and the light in the window welcoming.

Even more easing, however, was Hugh Armstrong's rugged familiar face. He rose from the chair, where he was surrounded by his wife and children, and limped toward her, bowing his head in courtesy. He walked with her outside, away from other ears.

"I heard o' the fight. This Carey must be the best o' the lot."

"There is no best," Elsbeth said sourly, still feeling humiliated by her response to the Englishman's brief caress.

"Ah, lass. Ye must learn to take the measure of a mon for himself, no' fer his country or clan."

Elsbeth set her chin stubbornly, and Hugh sighed. "Tell me wha' he said."

"The man at Huntington is called David Garrick."

"I know of him," Hugh said slowly. "'Tis said he's a good fighter. He's hired out to train others along the border."

Elsbeth hesitated, then showed Hugh the ring she had pinned in her riding skirt. "He said to give this to Garrick so he'll know it comes from him."

Hugh nodded, taking the ring and turning it over in his hands.

"He said something else."

Hugh watched her in the darkness. He had no trouble in recognizing the worry on her face. "Wha' is it, lass?"

"The...earl asked that this Garrick relay the information to John Dudley."

"Northumberland?"

"Aye."

Hugh let a low whistle escape his lips. "I'd heard he ha' friends at court, but no' they were tha' high."

"It could start a war."

"Aye," Hugh said. He remembered two years ago, when Northumberland's predecessor as protector to young Edward VI, Lord Somerset, sent an army of three thousand men to the border. A blood war had resulted. Several Scots, taken as hostages, were hanged out of hand, and the border was once more steeped in blood.

Hugh was thoughtful for a moment. "'Tis no' so hard now to ken why his brother wants him dead, and it blamed on the Kers wi' no' suspicions in his direction."

"Why then didn't John just set men on Lord Huntington, and blame it on us?"

"Too risky, lass. Too many know of John Carey's greed. He would be suspect if his brother disappeared. Involving the whole Ker clan warranted tha' it would no' remain secret."

"And one of ours helped?"

"I donna ken he knew of the Carey's connections... tha' it could bring down the whole clan. And the earl was probably meant to die right off. They would no' ha' kenned you would stop it."

Elsbeth remembered the night they had first planned the kidnapping and how opposed both Ian and Patrick had been to her going. She'd had a strange feeling then that one or both of her cousins would not worry overmuch if the earl were killed.

She should have abandoned the idea of the kidnapping then. If she had been wise, she would have. But she, like the other clansmen, had felt a terrible need for justice, for revenge. She had started a whirlwind, and now she didn't know how to end it before it destroyed everything, and everyone, she loved.

"What should I do, Hugh?" she asked in a low voice.

"Wha' we planned," Hugh said. "I shall take a message to this Garrick, but I willna tell him about Northumberland. No' yet."

"What if he's in league with John Carey?"

"I donna think your Carey would make tha' mistake," Hugh said slowly.

Elsbeth looked at him questioningly. "You respect him, don't you?"

"I donna know him," Hugh said, "but of all I've heard he seems a braw mon, and the fact his brother wants him dead says more of him."

"And you still believe one of our clan is betraying us?" she pleaded, wanting him to say nay.

"'Tis possible," he admitted reluctantly.

"Patrick would have killed the Englishman today."

"Patrick is hotheaded and hard t' stop once he's in battle."

"Is there no end to this?" Elsbeth cried out in sudden despair. In the past several days, her whole world had been shaken. She no longer could believe in anything—not herself, not her clan, not even the total evilness of the Careys. All the absolutes in her life were gone.

"Aye," Hugh said gently.

With that Elsbeth had to be satisfied. She wished Hugh Godspeed, and accepted his assistance in mounting her horse. She would pray for Hugh tonight. She would pray for them all.

The two horsemen came from different directions. They didn't bother to dismount this night. They were in a hurry, and dispensed with any civilities.

The Ker clansman was very late. It had been luck, pure luck, that this was the night they had established to meet. Approximately a week at one hour past midnight. It was safer than trying to transmit messages. The day of the week changed according to a specified schedule, so as not to reveal a pattern.

John Carey regarded his heavily cloaked companion with fury. "You are late."

"Ye're fortunate I arrived at all," the other horseman said. "I was sent north to see if the other clans will join us in a border fight. I'll have to ride all night now."

"My brother?"

"Still unhappily locked in the tower."

"They will not kill him?"

"Elsbeth will not allow it. She still hopes to get the ransom."

"Then he has to escape as we planned."

"When I return."

"Every day he lives is dangerous to both of us."

"Aye, an' no one kens that better than myself," the other man replied wryly.

"When do you return?"

"In no more than four days' time."

"Then on the fifth night . . ."

There was silence, then reluctant consent. "Aye, it will be done."

"And I shall be waiting for him."

No more words were needed. They spurred their horses in different directions, neither of them aware of a third figure, which had edged up close enough to hear the voices.

When he was sure both men were gone, David Garrick left the safety of the huge oak tree. He slowly walked to where he had tied his horse after following John Carey much of the night. Thoughtfully, he mounted.

So that was what had happened to his lord. The Kers had taken him with the connivance of John Carey. And by some miracle, Alexander Carey was still alive. But not for long, if John had anything to do with it.

David cursed John Carey, searching his mind for the worst possible profanity. Like many mercenaries, he had few scruples about killing in battle. But he valued loyalty and courage and detested treachery. He could never forget what Lord Huntington had done for him; he would quite willingly die for him.

Five days. He wondered what John Carey had planned. Carey could not involve many others; it would be too dangerous. So it must be an ambush. Carey was good at ambushes, but this time there would be a surprise awaiting Alexander's brother.

And the Scotsman? What part did he play in all this?

The questions kept pounding at David as he rode back to Huntington. Five days to try to find some answers.

Chapter Eight

Elsbeth tried desperately to dismiss the rogue earl from her mind the next day.

She went to visit Cara, the twelve-year-old daughter of one of the messengers who had been sent to Huntington ten days ago and had not returned. The girl was staying at a neighboring cottage.

Elsbeth found Cara bravely trying to hold back tears as she looked up hopefully. But Elsbeth had no hope to give her, and once more walled her heart against the Careys. Yet she could not escape a terrible sense of guilt herself. She had been responsible for kidnapping the earl of Huntington, and it was also her responsibility that three of her clansmen were probably dead after trying to deliver ransom demands.

For one of the few times in her life, she felt inadequate to her position and guilt-ridden over the consequences of a decision. The kidnapping of Huntington had had far more implications and effects than she had ever believed possible, not only to her clan but to herself. The fact that Ian and Patrick had concurred did nothing to soften her growing apprehension over what she had put in motion.

The bloodletting had started, and she knew it had not yet ended. How many more lives would be forfeit because of an act of revenge?

But she tried not to let the troubling thoughts show as she comforted Cara, who she feared was now an orphan, her mother having died two years earlier in childbirth.

"Would you like to come live at the tower?" Elsbeth asked. "You can help Annie."

Cara's face brightened slightly. It was an honor to work at the tower, for Lady Elsbeth was known for her kindness and patience. Otherwise, the girl knew, she would be given to another family that probably already had too many mouths to feed and would resent yet another. "Aye," she said quietly.

Elsbeth put her arms around the girl and hugged her tight. "Everything will be all right, Cara. It will." And she knew she was trying to convince herself as well as the girl.

It did not take long to move Cara and her few belongings to a snug room in the peel. She instructed Annie to teach her to sew, but still hesitated to leave her alone. The girl's eyes held a world of sorrow. In a fit of inspiration, she asked Louisa to look after her, and was delighted at the sudden flash of happiness in Louisa's eyes.

Perhaps that was what Louisa had required—to feel wanted and needed. Some of the shyness, the reserve, disappeared from Louisa's eyes as she took Cara's hand in her own and squeezed it tightly.

Patrick's mother, Joan, had no such feelings of charity. She grumbled about the lack of a proper maid, proper servants, and proper food.

When an irritated Elsbeth said there was no money for these things, Patrick's mother spit waspishly, "There's enough to feed a Carey. Wasted food it is. Ye should kill him. The whole clan believes so. Weakness is wha' it is, letting him live, eating our food, bringing ruin on us."

Her words would not have bothered Elsbeth overmuch, except Joan was not the only Ker to express such an opinion. Elsbeth was hearing it more often each day. *Kill the Englishman. Hang the Englishman.*

And Joan fed the hatred. She had not liked the fact that the earl of Huntington had almost outmatched her son, and she sensed that he could be an obstacle to her plans for Patrick and Elsbeth to marry. How, or even why, she did not know. She just knew he was.

Elsbeth had heard Joan's whispers, her challenges to the others. The Englishman would bring them all grief, she told everyone who would listen—and there were more than a few of those. Every man jack of the Ker clan had a score to settle with the Careys. Not one family had gone without a death, or theft, or burning by their English neighbors.

The patience of the Kers was running out.

Elsbeth was well aware of the guarded eyes and bitter expressions. She wondered how long she could control the members of the clan, particularly without Patrick or Ian. Or were they, like Joan, part of the problem?

Elsbeth kept herself busy for the rest of the morning, settling a dispute over a cow and reducing rents for two of the families burned out by the recent Carey raid. Her own funds were low, and she prayed for Huntington's ransom to be paid, so that she could replenish stolen stock and help rebuild. But deep inside she knew that payment was unlikely. Instead of collecting ransom, they might well have a major war on their hands.

The plague take Alexander Carey.

She was feeling quite proud of herself until late in the day when the insidious need to see him returned. The more she busied herself, the more she felt the compulsive need to see him. Instead, she ordered her horse saddled, taking an escort since she planned to be gone most of the afternoon, visiting the outlying crofters. She would urge them to move under the protection of the peel tower until the matter was solved. It would make conditions very crowded, but Elsbeth felt she had no choice.

It was late afternoon when she and her escort of five men returned, with one family that had decided to come in with them that day. Others would arrive over the next few days.

She was met at the entrance by a tall clansman who was one of Lord Huntington's guards. "He's ill, my lady," he told her. "The wound is poisoned."

Elsbeth's heart stopped, then resumed at an erratic pace. "Have you sent for Magdalene?"

"We were waiting for you."

"Then do it immediately." Magdalene was the healer among them, midwife and grower of herbs. "Tell her to bring what she needs for a poisoned wound and fever."

She gave her horse to a groom and hastened up the steps to the tower room. One of the guards unlocked the door, and she hurried in. The room was dim, but she saw the man on the pallet, and once more her heart stilled. His face was pale and bathed in sweat, and his eyes were open but unseeing. He moved restlessly, his breath coming in small labored gasps.

Elsbeth turned to one of the guards. "Water and clean linens."

She turned back, her hand touching his face and feeling the intense heat of his skin. She touched a lock of the damp dark hair, and whispered to him, "Lord Huntington," but there was no response.

Elsbeth looked around the dingy room, saw the dirty pallet and blankets and remembered how he had wrapped a soiled strip around his wound yesterday before she had replaced it with clean linen.

"Take him to Patrick's chamber," she said suddenly, knowing she had to move him from this place.

"My lady?"

"He won't get well here, and a dead hostage is of no value," she said sharply.

The guards obeyed her. She followed them down two flights of stairs and into a chamber with several windows. They lowered the earl onto the feather bed, and looked for further orders as a third man brought in the ordered water and linen.

As if he knew something had changed, he had closed his eyes, long black lashes giving him an air of innocence and youth. He moved and groaned slightly.

Where was Magdalene? Elsbeth wondered.

Sometime during the previous night or that day, he had pulled his doublet on, but now it was wet from the fever sweat. Elsbeth bent down and pulled off the garment to reveal the linen cloth on his arm. She gently removed it, noticing the redness around the wound.

With water and cloth she wiped away the beads of sweat from his face, and then from his chest. She was afraid to touch his arm; it looked raw and painful.

"My lord," she tried again, and his unfocused eyes opened slightly.

"Nadine?"

Elsbeth didn't expect the sudden agony that assaulted her when she heard the name, nor the emptiness she subsequently felt.

"Nadine," he repeated, this time pain in his voice. Terrible pain.

She leaned down, her hand trying to soothe him, but it seemed only to disturb him further. He struggled against it, and she drew back, her heart thundering with fear for him, with pain for his pain.

"I'm here," she said softly. "Nadine's here." They were the right words. He stopped thrashing and lay quietly, bearing her ministrations as she resumed washing him. She wondered where his mind was, who Nadine was, what had happened to cause him so much hurt—hurt that she knew didn't come from his injury alone.

She steeled herself against the sadness in him, the longing of the cry when he called another woman's name. Her chest was like a fist, curling and tightening until there was no air left inside. It was her fault, all of it. She should never have brought him here. She should never have so lightly dismissed his wound.

"You will be well," she told him. "You will."

It seemed like half a day before Magdalene finally appeared, carrying a basket of herbs and powders.

Elsbeth watched intently as the woman made a salve with the powders and rubbed it into the wound, then mixed another powder with water and bade Elsbeth to hold the Carey's head while she forced it in his mouth, a drop at a time.

Unconsciously, Elsbeth ran her hands through the dark curling hair, feeling its thickness, watching the damp wayward strands wrap around her fingers. He was so warm, so frighteningly warm. So quiet and removed from the vibrant, sometimes mischievous, sometimes arrogant lord with whom she had matched wits.

Dear God, protect him.

"M'lady." Magdalene was staring at her.

Elsbeth took her eyes from Alex. "He will survive?"

"With care."

"He will have that."

"I can see tha', m'lady," Magdalene observed with a small smile hovering around her mouth.

"No ransom will be paid for a dead hostage," Elsbeth said defensively.

"No, m'lady," the woman agreed. She was a healer and had seen much, and judged little. Elsbeth had always been kind to her, and had made sure that she had all she needed. Magdalene, like the other Kers, feared and distrusted the Careys, but she doubted whether her mistress could care about one with no heart. "Give him this powder with water tonight and in the morning. And rub the salve into the wound in the morning. I will come back in the afternoon."

"There's nothing else?"

"What ye are doing, Lady Elsbeth. Keep him quiet and soothed." With those few words, she left, wondering about the man she had just tended. The Ker clan had been waiting for their lady to select a husband. Was it possible that she had lost her heart to a Carey? If so, Magdalene knew, there could be a war to end all border wars. A war of both the heart and the clans.

Elsbeth did not leave Lord Huntington that evening nor during the night. Annie often brought more water to cool the feverish earl and urged her mistress to rest. The guards remained, but more to help Elsbeth than to act against any possible danger from the prisoner.

In time, the earl's frantic movements eased along with his labored breathing, and Elsbeth credited the change to Magdalene's powders. She continued to bathe him with cool water, for his skin remained warm. He still muttered, but she understood little of what he said. Much concerned "Henri" and "Nadine," but there were curses, too, and cries of pain as if he were reliving something terrible. It was then her heart would break a bit, even though she knew how unwise it was to feel that way about the man he was. She thought how vulnerable he looked now, how . . . handsome. And she thought about the half smile that so intrigued her, and the mischief in his eyes when there should have been none—given his situation.

She would have given most anything if he were aught but a Carey.

But there was no changing that, and she must think of him as a hostage, nothing else. Yet when her hands touched him, they tingled and yearned to touch more. And every time she saw that scar, she longed to learn more of him, and discover what had made him the contradictory man he seemed to be. She wanted to know everything. Yet she instinctively knew that the more she learned, the more she would want. And how could she bear wanting more than she already did?

Alex regained consciousness, his eyes opening slowly as they carefully focused on his new surroundings. The room was ablaze with light. A fire roared in the large stone fireplace, and torches lined the walls.

His head ached, his arm felt as if it had been laid in a fire, he was infernally hot, and he felt as weak as a mewling kitten.

He wondered briefly where he was, and discovered he didn't care. Not when he saw two hazel eyes studying him with such warm concern. His pain was swallowed in that gaze.

Her hand reached out with a cloth, and he felt her touch, deft but gentle. It was a very long time since he had known tenderness, and something in him snatched at the human warmth offered and held it closely in his heart.

Even as he knew how foolish it was. Nothing had changed. He was still a prisoner, one more likely to die than not, and these moments were temporary. He knew he was to be kept alive only as long as he might be useful, and he knew he should judge his current treatment in that fashion. There could never be more, not given the centuries of feuding between the lady's family and his.

His eyes still on her, the gray flashing silver like a sun-kissed ocean, he attempted a feeble grin. "I should have tried getting wounded earlier."

Elsbeth was stricken silent. How could he still make her feel this way? There was always so much hidden meaning behind his light words that she never knew how to respond.

"'Twould be nothing I'd advise," she said finally. "We could decide you're too much trouble."

"Am I?" he replied, his eyes reaching into her soul.

"Aye," she said. "By much."

"And yet you're here. Like a bright angel."

"To combat the devil."

He chuckled then, disregarding the wave of pain that resulted. "Good versus evil... you're certain then how it will end."

"How it *must* end," she replied grimly.

"I'm not your enemy," Alex said softly.

"Every Carey is my enemy."

"That could change."

She shook her head in denial, and forced her eyes away from his magnetic ones. What power was it he had over her? He surely *must* be the devil.

As if aware of her confusion, he moved his eyes once more to look around the room. "Where am I?"

"Patrick's chamber."

He grinned again, this time with real amusement. "And what does the good Patrick think of that?"

"He's not here."

Alex raised an eyebrow and tried to sit up, but weakness put that effort to a quick end, and he started to fall back, his head full of discordant hammering like a blacksmith's shop.

Before she could help herself, Elsbeth leaned over and put a gentle hand on his shoulder, easing him all the way down, and looked into a face both weary and pained.

"You should not talk." She went to a table and measured more of the powder mixture, then brought it to him, one hand lifting his head slightly. "Drink this."

His eyes questioned hers, considering the order, then he obediently sipped from the proffered cup. He needed his strength. "Was I very ill?"

"Aye," she said. "Your arm was poisoned."

He looked down at the bandaged area. It still hurt like the furies. "Thank you," he said quietly.

"It was Magdalene."

"Magdalene?"

"A healer."

"My thanks for fetching her then."

She could scarcely bear his soft words, nor the obvious sincerity behind them. She wished he was angry and vile and hostile.

"A dead hostage is of no value," she said, repeating the words she had said so many times in the past week and especially this day. It was her only defense.

"I'm thinking this live one is of no value." It was said lightly, yet there was something terribly wistful in the words themselves that caused a streak of anguish to run through her.

As if he were embarrassed that he had let her see something he would rather have kept private, his mouth twisted into the old ironic half smile. "It seems a waste, my lady, to save my arm, and my life, only to hang me later."

"Mayhap it will make more sport," she replied. But her eyes were warmer than he had ever seen them, and he knew she didn't mean the words.

"And this?" he asked, his gaze sweeping the room. "Temporary, I fear?"

"Aye."

"Back to my bare cell?" The potion was working, he realized. His mind was growing sluggish. But he didn't want to close his eyes, didn't want to lose sight of the face he was so foolishly growing to cherish.

She couldn't force the word of agreement. She did not want him to go back there. She didn't want him to go anyplace, but his eyes demanded a reply.

"Aye," she said reluctantly.

His eyes closed halfway, long black lashes sweeping over the dark cryptic gray, and he looked like a tired young boy.

"You are so devilishly pretty," he said in a sleepy lazy voice that drifted into silence as his eyes closed all the way, and his breathing became soft and regular.

Elsbeth continued to watch him, a single tear falling down her cheek as she thought silently how very bonny *he* was.

She stayed by Alex's side during the night, sleeping only occasionally. Each time she woke she put a hand to his forehead, and each time it felt cooler, although a trace of the fever was still evident. Magdalene's magic had worked again. The nightmares also seemed gone, and he rested easily, a small smile on his lips, the same one he had when he called her pretty.

Pretty? She had never particularly thought of herself that way, perhaps because so many other things seemed more important to her, such as horsemanship, challenging her cousins, managing the property. She had had many offers for her hand, but marriage in Scotland—as in England—was usually a loveless matter and had little to do with appearance. It was a means to add wealth, to increase power, to satisfy debts, or end feuds.

End feuds! There had been many such matches between clans, particularly between Scottish families; there had been fewer between Scottish and English borderers. The bitterness and hatred between Scots and English, especially on the border, was usually far too deep to be neutralized through a marriage alliance.

Even as she knew how absurd her thoughts were, she couldn't help but wonder how his lips would feel against hers, and the very thought set her afire. Just as watching the rise and fall of his chest made her want to touch him. He must be a sorcerer to affect her this way.

A Carey sorcerer.

With a lump in her throat, and a knot of sick emptiness in her stomach, she knew he would be soon gone, taking his strange sorcery with him. No matter what happened, she would not, could not, permit his death. If this last attempt for ransom proved futile, she would help him escape herself after extracting a promise that there would be no reprisal.

And then she would never see him again. She would marry— Patrick or Ian, probably, because they were both dear friends and one of them as husband was to be preferred over a stranger. She still could not believe that Ian or Patrick was a traitor.

The thought was a cold one, a joyless one. But she feared she could no longer hold her clan together. This misadventure with the Carey proved it. The fact that she felt she could not openly release him confirmed it. Her clan wanted ruthlessness, and she was finding she did not have it. She was a woman, with a woman's heart, and although she once thought she could be more, she knew now she could not.

If she were entirely truthful, she knew that the reason she had not ordered an immediate raid on Carey lands after the slaying of her father was not the mourning period she had claimed. She simply had not been willing to prolong a feud that caused so much misery, not even for the honor of the Kers.

She bowed her head in sorrow, and the tears she had not shed at her father's death, nor at the loss of friends, nor at the rape of her lands, freed themselves and tumbled down her cheeks in tortured streams.

Alex didn't know what woke him, what brought him slowly from a faraway misty place to a room bright with candles and torches.

His eyes opened slowly, blinded by the sudden light, and he tensed as he heard the quiet sobs next to him. He swallowed, his heart in his throat as his eyes finally focused on Lady Elsbeth Ker and the grief so evident in her face. Without thinking, he held out a hand, and without hesitation she placed her own in his.

Time stilled as she looked up from her hand clenched in his strong warm fist and met his searching compassionate eyes. His hand moved slightly, bringing her closer and she was suddenly on the bed, her hand being drawn to his mouth and caressed with so much tenderness that her tears started again.

"Come to me," he whispered, and she had no choice. He took her hand from his lips, his fingers continuing the soft seduction of her senses, the magic that seemed to bind their very souls.

She could no more deny him, or herself, than stop breathing.

Her head bent toward him, and she could feel his lips touch her wet face, his tongue licking away the tears in gentle healing. She was embraced by warmth, sympathy and understanding such as she had never known, and she wondered if she could ever relinquish it.

Their lips met in sweet exploration, yet there was fiercely demanding passion simmering below each sensitive movement. They needed this first—this rare sharing and giving of self—as flowers need the sun. He touched, and she touched, both with a wonder that defied all there was between them. It was as if there were no one else in the world, that life was theirs alone in a glowing golden hue that blessed them.

Elsbeth opened eyes that had closed with the first wondrous touch of his mouth. His eyes smiled at her, more expressive and open than she had ever seen them.

His lips moved slowly, sensuously, across her face, awakening sensations both gentle and fierce, until once more they met her lips and coaxed them into opening. Even then, he controlled his growing passion, wanting, instead, to give comfort, to see the bleakness in her eyes disappear.

He had thought he loved before. But he had never felt like this. Elsbeth Ker had reached inside him and found sources of feeling and emotions he had not known were there. He almost shook from the intensity of them, from the need to feel her gentleness with its underlying passion, to hold the glow in those golden eyes, to see the small curving wondering smile on her face.

Alex ignored the pain in his arm as he put it around her, clasping her tightly to him, willing her to understand he would move heaven and earth for her, that he would sacrifice anything to keep her with him.

"Elsbeth," he whispered. "Trust me."

The words ate into Elsbeth's soul. She wanted to. She wanted to follow the lure of his soft promise. Her hand touched his face, exploring each hard plane, each curve, each small line, tracing invisible words of love on it.

But that was all she could do. The words would always be unspoken, always elusive, for there could never be more. No matter how much her body and heart and soul demanded it. He was a Carey, he wanted his freedom, and a terrible voice murmured inside that she could never trust a Carey... never trust a Carey... never trust a Carey.

His hands stilled as if he heard the refrain, and his eyes suddenly reflected a sorrow that stabbed her to the core of her being. He took his mouth from her lips, and simply held her, the hand of his good arm stroking her, and part of her rejoiced in it while another part trembled with need... and fear.

Elsbeth wasn't sure how long they stayed thus, nor could she identify the complicated feelings that racked her. She knew she could not do as he asked: trust him. But she relished the warmth of his body, and the honeyed touch of his hands, and the whisper of his warm breath against her hair. She treasured the spicy masculine smell of him, and etched forever in her memory the feel of his body against hers. For she could never allow it to happen again.

Yet she didn't have the will to move.

It wasn't until she heard a stirring outside, the changing of the guards, probably, that she forced herself from his arms. Even then his hand caught hers and held it for a fraction of time before releasing it.

"I'll never hurt you, Elsbeth," he said achingly. "I know you don't believe it. Not now. Perhaps not ever. But mayhap—"

He never finished. There was a knock on the door, and the woman he now knew was the housekeeper bustled in, carrying a bowl. Her eyes were disapproving as she saw Elsbeth's tired face.

"Lady Elsbeth, ye must get some rest, or I'll be tending ye, too." She threw a look of dislike toward the Englishman.

Elsbeth nodded. She was infinitely tired. And she knew she had to escape the steady demanding gaze of his eyes.

"He looks some better," Annie acknowledged reluctantly, her tone suggesting it would have been preferable for all of them if he did not.

Elsbeth caught Lord Huntington's fleeting wry glance. "You can rub the salve on him," she ordered, wondering if Annie would be caught up in the man's infernal charm.

Behind Annie, Alex winced, and Elsbeth threw him an impish smile.

"He be ready to go back soon?" Annie asked with the impertinence of a servant with a special relationship to the mistress. "Patrick is no' going to like his chamber used thus."

"When Magdalene agrees," Elsbeth replied shortly.

"It best be done soon," Annie grumbled. "Patrick's no' going to like this, and I donna, either. Treating a Carey like a guest."

Elsbeth was weary of repeating her reasoning. And she was tired. "Annie!" she said, more sharply than she ever had before, and felt new guilt when Annie turned a pained face toward her.

But Elsbeth said nothing more and left the room, her mind whirling with all that had happened, all the strange new feelings she was experiencing. She merely nodded to the two guards outside, then escaped to her room where she could think, and remember, and consider.

Consider what?

That the devil of the Englishman could look at her and make her forget her clan, her obligation, her position. That his smooth tongue could make her forget the cowardly murder of her father.

Trust me.

She would sooner trust a viper.

And then she remembered the pain in his eyes as she denied his trust, the comfort of his arms when she felt so alone.

The comfort of a Carey.

She had to hate him. She had to mistrust him. She had to suspect his every motive, for he had everything to gain and nothing to lose by seducing her.

She undressed, and pulled on a chemise. She started to lie down, but she knew she was too restless to sleep. Elsbeth went to the window and looked over the rich green hills that separated the Kers from the Careys. How great the distance, how absolute the divisions.

Elsbeth remembered the first beacon fires she had seen as a child, the first that warned of an attack. She still remembered the horror of watching the fields and the crofters' simple huts burn. She still heard the curses and cries of revenge, the wailing of widows and the grief of children.

Nothing had changed.

She would order Lord Huntington back to the tower room as soon as he was well enough. That simple act, more than anything, would reinforce the line between them.

Scot and English.

Ker and Carey.

Captor and captive.

Enemy and enemy.

No warm gray eyes or comforting arms could bridge that.

Elsbeth left the window and lay down on the bed. But she knew she wouldn't sleep. She wondered if she would ever sleep peacefully again.

Chapter Nine

Aided by Magdalene's potion, Alex slept on and off throughout the day. By nightfall the fever had left him, and he felt some of his strength returning.

He took a sip of the wine that had been left by his bed and wondered whether Lady Elsbeth would visit before dispatching him to his former mean chamber. That she would do exactly that, he had no doubt.

He should have asked her, that morning, whether she had sent a message to David, but he had become distracted. Very distracted.

When he saw the tears in Lady Elsbeth's eyes, nothing had been important except stemming them. She had felt so...right in his arms, as if she belonged there—when nothing was farther from the truth.

And then she was gone with one last fetching look of mischief. He had soon learned why. The housekeeper had been none too gentle when she applied the salve, nor had her attitude given him much comfort. If all the Kers felt as that one did, he had little hope of mercy.

Food came. Heartier than before. Soup and a stew, good bread and cheese. But the fever, along with the hopelessness of his situation, had suppressed his appetite.

He studied the chamber, hoping it would reveal something of its usual occupant. But it did not. It was much like his own at Huntington, plain and utilitarian, with little decoration. There was armor in a corner, several garments, all plain; and a mirror of polished steel. Nothing more. The feather bed, with its soft blankets, was the only visible comfort.

An old woman whom he guessed to be Magdalene came in later in the day, alone except for a sturdy Ker clansman who stood at her side.

Alex was at his charming best for her, grateful and pleasant, and he was rewarded by an absence of the usual hate he saw in the faces around the Ker stronghold.

She shook her head as she looked at his arm.

"That poor?" Alex questioned. "I thought it much improved."

"Oh, 'tis, m'lord. I've no' seen a mon heal faster."

He frowned slightly, trying to understand.

"M'lady told me ye're to leave this chamber when well enough."

"And am I?"

She grinned, showing great gaps between her teeth. Her eyes were a lively brown and he knew she must have been winsome as a girl. "Nay," she said. "Ye need the light."

Alex looked up at the guard, who had moved away toward the window. He smiled slightly. "Even a Carey?"

"Aye," she said. "Most of all the Careys."

Alex sighed, and his eyes turned bleak. At the moment he would have given all he possessed to claim a different name. It had caused him nothing but grief since he was but a boy. And now, among a brave people he respected, he was considered no better than his father and brothers.

Perhaps he wasn't.

"Nay," the old woman said. "Ye aren't the same."

He looked up sharply, wondering at how accurately she had read his mind.

"Ye don't have the cruel eyes," she continued.

"You've seen them?"

"Aye. Yer father killed my Johnny."

God's blood, did it never end? "Your son?"

"My husband. Six and twenty years ago. They burned the crofters on the edge of the border. They left me for dead."

Alex couldn't reply. If they had left her for dead, he well knew what had preceded their departure. He didn't understand how she could have doctored him, or why she was so kind now.

"The old laird was a good mon, but the one before him was a devil, just like your father. It's part his blame there be so much hatred 'twixt us."

Alex's mouth tightened. Since a lad, he had heard stories of the Ker atrocities. It was why he'd gone on the first raids with such enthusiasm. But the excitement had soon died when he saw that most of those killed were the innocents....

"I would dear like it to end," he said. He half expected her to laugh, but she did not.

"Did ye tell m'lady that?"

"To no purpose," he replied. "She will believe nothing good of my family."

"She will," the old woman said. "Have patience."

"Do I have time for patience?"

"Aye, young Carey. I think we ha' been waiting for ye a long time."

Alex stared at her. Her eyes were calm and serene despite all she had seen and experienced, and there was a peace and certainty about her that gave him hope.

"What do you know about the man whose room this is?"

"Patrick Ker? He is something like ye . . . he has mysteries in him."

"And Ian Ker?"

"He spreads laughter. All like him, and follow him gladly."

"They have been here long?"

"All their lives. They were nephews of the laird, and he made them his wards when his brother died."

"Has either married?"

"Each would like m'lady as his bride."

"And my lady?"

"She waits." Magdalene's dark eyes bored through to his soul. Alex could have sworn she saw everything dwelling there.

The old woman rose, looking well satisfied. "I must go. There's a babe to be born. I will check yer wound again on the morrow."

He didn't know how to convey his gratitude. It was, at the moment, too deep to express. Not only because she might have saved his life, but because she recognized him for what he was—not what his family was, or had been. Such insight was a rare quality in the Kers, yet he could blame them little.

But he didn't have to say anything. Her expressive eyes told him she understood.

When she left, he felt more hopeful than at any time since his capture.

David Garrick was biding his time.

He had followed John Carey for days before discovering the meeting with the Ker clansman. He had heard enough then to begin making plans. He had continued to watch the younger Carey during the next two days, and noted John's meeting with Simon, a man known for a particular viciousness.

Everything started to come together.

David wondered who among the Scottish clan was the man who met John Carey, but the rider had been heavily cloaked, and the darkness of the night had shielded his features.

He also wondered about those who had taken his lord and friend, and how Alexander Carey fended. David had little optimism, knowing as he did the bitter conflict between the families. He had gone on many of the raids on Ker lands, and had also defended Huntington against the Scottish clan's raids. Fighting was his profession, and he thought little of the consequent destruction and death. It was border life, and if there were no conflict, there would be no livelihood for him.

It had bothered him little, therefore, when crofter huts burned and men died. It was the natural way of things.

But he was enraged at John Carey's duplicity and determined that the right man would hold the title of earl of Huntington.

But he needed assistance, and he didn't know whom he could trust. He was only a lieutenant in the Carey force. The yeomen and archers had all been employed and paid by John Carey, who commanded their allegiance if not their hearts. Alexander had not been home long enough to change that. David was also aware that John Carey would pay well for David's death if he knew of his snooping.

David could send word to the English court, but he had no proof of John Carey's treachery. There was only his word against a noble's. He had little faith that he would be the one believed. He would, more likely, die on the gibbet or in the wood some dark night.

No, the only solution was to be present at the ambush. The problem was the Scots. He didn't know their intentions, particularly those of the man who met with John Carey.

David had a direct mind. He did not like complicated plans, or trickery, or ambushes. He was a man who attacked directly, who asked no quarter nor gave any. His loyalty was absolute, his beliefs unchanging, his prejudices firm. He disliked the Scots because all English disliked the barbarian neighbors to the north, and in a lifetime of fighting he had found little reason to change that attitude. He distrusted everyone but himself . . . and the one man who had made possible the respected position he now held, the boy who had held his life in his hands and given it back to him.

But he wished he were not so completely alone in this affair. If anything went wrong, his lord's life was at stake as well as his own. Yet he could find no other solution. There was no way of warning Alex Carey, Lord Huntington, in advance.

Three more days . . .

David was training some of Huntington's tenants in the use of the two-handed sword when a young boy found him.

A peddler was asking for him, the lad said. He had said the stranger had a most unusual knife, and had heard that a warrior named Garrick might be interested.

Another weapon was the last thing David needed. He started to say nay, and then pondered the message. Where would a peddler get his name? He had no wealth. His curiosity aroused, he instructed the tenants to continue practicing, and headed for his cottage.

The peddler's wagon was poor, and carried few goods. The man standing next to it was rough-hewn, his hair a mixture of gray and red. He looked familiar in some way, but David couldn't immediately place him.

The peddler's eyes were wary, but his mouth held the good-natured smile of a merchant hoping for business.

"Good sir," the man greeted him. "I was told ye may be interested in a certain article." He extended his hand, which held an object wrapped in cloth.

David took it and unwrapped the hard item he felt inside. He stared at the heavy Carey ring with its falcon crest. "Where did you get this?" he grated.

The peddler looked around, his eyes still cautious, his expression fawning, in case curious onlookers became suspicious. "Lord Huntington sent it by me. He asked that ye be told he's being held for ransom."

David straightened. "Why come to me? Why not to his brother?"

"Three messages were sent to Huntington. None was answered, nor have the men returned."

"You're a Ker?" David's tone was hostile.

"An Armstrong," the man replied, the fawning gone, replaced by a defiant pride. "But I fight with the Kers."

David studied him carefully. The man had courage. He had walked into the enemy's camp with only guile as a weapon. David turned the ring over in his hands. "How do I know Lord Huntington's alive?"

"He said to come to ye. No one else." Hugh's voice was suddenly harsh. He disliked being supplicant to an Englishman, a Carey lackey.

"Lord Huntington is well?"

Hugh shrugged. "He's alive."

David didn't particularly like the emphasis on the last word. The two men stared at each other, measuring, judging.

It was Garrick who broke the silence. "What does he wish me to do?"

"He wonders if his brother received the ransom demand."

Garrick's mouth twisted. "If so, he has said nothing." He could have said more, but he wasn't ready. Not yet. This could be a Ker trick.

Once again, the silence stretched out, neither man ready to trust the other.

David was the first to break it. "God's blood, but why did you Kers expect the lordship's brother to pay a ransom? He wants nothing more than to rid himself of the rightful heir."

"We didna think he'd have a choice."

"There's a traitor among you," Garrick said suddenly, hoping to surprise a reaction from the older man.

"We both have curs among us," Hugh replied with a snarl. "'Tis time to expose them if ye'd have the stomach for it."

David unexpectedly grinned, his doubts gone. A trickster would have sought to lull him. "Come," he said. "Let's walk."

Several hours later David Garrick, dressed in dark clothing, was riding beside one whom he had considered an enemy. And who would probably be an enemy again.

Neither had liked what the other said.

The Englishman had confirmed the Scot's fears, that a Ker was treating with the English. Hugh wanted to kill the traitor with his bare hands.

But more needed to be done. When the two had reluctantly shared their information, Hugh knew it was essential that Lord Huntington have certain information, and that he be allowed to escape. He also questioned whether the English lord would believe what a member of the Ker family told him.

David had insisted on going with Hugh to help convince Alex. He would pose as an Armstrong cousin of Hugh's and hope that no one would remember his face. He had seldom attended Truce Days, and usually wore a mask when raiding, so he felt secure. There was no problem with speech. Both English and Scottish borderers had much the same tongue.

Despite the temporary alliance, however, there was deep distrust between the two men, and they rode in silence, broken only by the sound of hooves against fallen rocks.

It was an all-night journey, as they travelled east toward Armstrong land. Hugh finally stopped just before dawn, and told David to wait for him. Edgy and uncomfortable at being alone on Scottish borderland, David prepared and ate a portion of oatmeal he had carried with him. Unable to sleep, he leaned against a tree and rested, aware of every rustle of the leaves, every scampering of a rabbit. He wondered whether he was a complete fool to trust a Scotsman.

The sun was arcing upward in the sky when David heard the neighing of a horse. He took out his pistol and held it at the ready, but a soft call told him the person approaching was Hugh. Still, he kept the pistol aimed in the direction of the sound.

The Scotsman smiled grimly as he saw the aimed pistol, but he merely rode toward the Englishman and threw a plaid at him. "'Tis Armstrong," he said, "and it wounds me sorely to see an Englishman dishonor it."

Garrick pursed his lips. "'Tis no less dishonor for me in wearing it," he replied bitterly, but he took it and fitted it over his shoulder.

"'Tis a sorry-looking Scotsman ye be making," Hugh grumbled. David's eyes grew colder, wishing he could use the pistol at his side. But his lord was more important now than his own desires.

It was noon when they arrived at Hugh's cottage. David Garrick was introduced as a man who claimed to be a distant Armstrong cousin, who, like Hugh, was outlawed and seeking sanctuary. Hugh was careful to emphasize he had no previous acquaintance with the man, to protect himself in the event David's true identity was discovered.

David was left at the cottage with Hugh's wife and many children. David and his wife had had one stillborn child and no more, so he was not used to youngsters, particularly ones who climbed all over him. He winced as a chubby girl climbed insistently onto his lap, and two boys fired questions at him.

God's eyes, he thought, but he'd rather be in battle, knocking heads.

But then he felt small fat arms twine around his neck, and wondered for the first time in his violent life whether the Scots were the devils he'd always believed them to be. Slowly, reluctantly, almost without conscious will, his own arms went around the tiny enemy.

Elsbeth could not stay away. No matter how hard she tried, she simply could not remain distant from the Englishman. She tried to think of him that way, as the Englishman. Not Alexander Carey, not Lord Huntington, simply the Englishman. It was easier to build barricades against an Englishman than a man named Alexander. Alexander...

She heeded Magdalene's advice to leave the English lord in Patrick's chamber, grateful to have the decision not to move Lord Huntington made for her. The healer said he should not yet be moved. Elsbeth had the excuse she needed to combat the growing complaints and grumbling, which Joan abetted, especially when she learned the Carey was in *her* son's chamber.

An outrage, Joan had protested during a particularly acrimonious meeting with Elsbeth. Patrick would never condone it. It was an insult to him. Who cared whether the hostage died anyway? Except, mayhap, she added with malicious slyness, Lady Elsbeth.

Elsbeth said something she had held back for a year. "You are free to go wherever you wish, madam," she said, "but as long as you stay here you will respect my wishes." She then turned and left, knowing she had made an implacable enemy and had probably created a deep rift between her and Patrick.

Patrick. Her father and she had depended on him for so many years. Patrick and Ian and herself. She could not let the Englishman divide them. Yet she was doing exactly that. She was believing his insinuations, his taunts. She hated him for making her do that.

Yet she couldn't stay away from him.

It was almost as if her mind and feet had different masters. Her feet went in the direction of Patrick's room, and wouldn't stop even as her mind directed otherwise.

Alex was sitting up, his arm bandaged and held stiffly next to him. His chest was bare, and once more she thought how fine it was, and wondered about the scar that was its only blemish. An arrow of dark hair, curling slightly, ran down the middle and disappeared under the blanket. She forced her eyes upward to his face. His expression was blank, as if he were mesmerized by some object or scene she could not see. His eyes, usually so quick and wary, took a moment to focus, giving her the first image of uncertainty she had seen in them.

But the slight cloud quickly vanished, and the gray was as deep and powerful as always. His stern mouth curved into a smile both charming and expectant. Only a slight tensing of his facial muscles showed an apprehension.

"Lady Elsbeth . . . I was thinking of you."

She wanted to ask what he had been thinking, then told herself it was no matter. He would probably lie.

"Magdalene says you are improving."

He cocked his head at an angle, questioning. She was unsmiling, her mouth grim and her eyes hesitant. He wondered if he had dreamed the moments when she had, however briefly, allowed herself to relax with him, to give so much to him. There had been warmth and sharing and something more. But it was gone now, and hostility was back.

"Your Magdalene is a magician," Alex said cautiously.

"Aye," Elsbeth agreed, "and some are none too happy about it."

"And you, Lady Elsbeth?"

She turned away from him, unable to bear his piercing scrutiny. "I care only about your ransom."

He wanted to challenge her, taunt her into admitting there was more. But he did not want to scare her away. So he waited. She had come to him.

"There will be no ransom," he said softly. "Not from my brother." He had to know whether she had sent a message to David Garrick.

"I cannot wait much longer," she replied in a distant voice. "My clansmen are growing impatient."

"A head for a head?" Alex said wryly. "You kidnapped the wrong Carey. If you had taken John, I would have paid."

She turned, surprise etched on her face. "Even if he wouldn't?"

"I'm not my brother," he said, repeating words he had said once before. He wondered how many times he would have to say them to be believed.

She turned back to face him, studying every crease on his face, every hard line. Even they, however, were tempered with a compassion she had tried not to see, didn't want to recognize.

"You are a Carey," she said simply, and the statement was damning in its simplicity.

"And you are a Ker, but that doesn't make you the same as every other Ker," he replied gently. "I remember hearing some of the things your grandfather did. I would not blame his deeds on you or believe you share his blood lust."

"Mayhap you are wrong. Mayhap I am exactly like him."

"Is that why you stayed with me all night when I was ill?"

"You are worth something to us."

"Did you send the message to David Garrick?"

The question came as a surprise to Elsbeth. She had been so intent on the personal duel between them. "Aye," she said. "I did. But I've not heard anything yet."

Alex relaxed slightly. He had not seen David Garrick for a period of many years, but that one visit to his cottage was enough to convince him his old friend had not changed. But still Alex did not underestimate his own danger, despite the other evening with Lady Elsbeth. He was probably safe enough with both Ian and Patrick gone, for he had come to understand they were the leaders to whom the clansmen turned. But once they came back, his life was at risk. Patrick had been ready to kill him that day in the courtyard, and Alex wasn't misled by Ian's pleasant manners. There had been something equally dangerous in that cousin.

"When will your cousins return?"

"On the morrow." she replied shortly. She, too, realized his danger once they arrived. When would Hugh come back?

"Elsbeth." The word came softly, like a song on the wind, and Elsbeth couldn't withstand its call. She moved toward him as if in a trance, all the frantic denials and rejections dying in her mind as he held out his hand and she knelt and let him take hers.

He wanted to say something, to say that they were both bound by something stronger than anger and hate and revenge, that her hand in his calmed the world and made it gentle. He wanted to say that together they could start to heal wounds. But he couldn't say any of it, not from his position of weakness.

So he said nothing, letting the feelings flow from one to the other, knowing she still doubted his sincerity but pleased that she did not jerk away, or leave the room as she had done several times before.

The brief peace was interrupted by a harsh, impatient knocking on the door. Elsbeth moved away quickly from him, as if burned, went to the door and opened it.

"Hugh!"

"Aye," the Scot said as he strode inside, looking curiously at the hostage whom he had not yet seen but of whom he had heard much. The man had stiffened at his appearance, but not in fear, only in a certain wariness. One of his arms was swathed in bandages. The English lord was a fine figure of a man, Hugh admitted privately, and his face held no signs of the self-indulgent weaknesses he had seen in other Careys.

He saw in the face, in the steady eyes, what he had wanted to see. He turned to Elsbeth. "Mistress, may we have words?"

Elsbeth nodded, relieved to be interrupted, yet regretful, a contradiction that was becoming all too familiar.

They left the room without backward looks at Alex Carey.

It was obvious to Elsbeth that Hugh did not wish to talk within the tower. They went down to the courtyard where his horse stood waiting, and she ordered her mount saddled. They then trotted past the gates and through the fields.

"David Garrick is wi' me," Hugh stated flatly.

Elsbeth stared at him as if he were mad. "I asked you to have him send a message to London."

"There is no time, mistress. Garrick had news ye willna like."

Elsbeth turned large hazel eyes on him.

"Yon Englishman was right about Garrick. The mon is loyal to him. Garrick followed John Carey for days, seeking a clue to the earl's whereabouts."

"And?"

"He saw him meet one night wi' a Scotsman . . . a Ker. They were plotting. The Scot said he did away wi' the three messengers, but still ye refused to kill the earl. It was suggested that the Englishman be allowed to escape. Tomorrow night. John Carey be waiting for him. The earl's to disappear, but no doubt it'll be blamed on the Kers, and the English warden will raise the whole border against us.''

"One of ours?'' Despite all of the Englishman's warnings and her own growing suspicions, she had not been able to completely believe that a Ker could be a traitor.

"Aye,'' Hugh said grimly. "And apparently he had a role in yer fa's death.''

"Who, Hugh? Who?''

"The mon was wearing a dark cloak, his head covered. No names were said. But Garrick said he had the sound of authority.''

"When?''

"Three nights ago.''

Elsbeth's face paled. "Both Ian and Patrick left that eve,'' she said. "Before Patrick left, the Englishman escaped and Patrick found him. They fought and Patrick would have killed him, had I not stopped him.''

"Both Patrick and Ian ha' something to gain,'' Hugh said thoughtfully. "Or think they might. Wi' yer father dead, and yer clan wi'out a strong leader, ye'd be forced to marry, and 'tis likely ye'd choose one of them. Even if ye didna, yer clan could turn to either Patrick or Ian, especially if the English march on us.''

"Which one would they choose?''

Hugh shrugged. "Patrick's the better soldier. Ian's the more liked.''

"I cannot bear the thought one of them is guilty,'' Elsbeth said.

"Ye can and ye must.''

"What can we do?''

"If Lord Huntington dies at our hands, or wha' the English believe is our hands, we'll have no chance. We'll be hunted like rabbits. The traitor must know tha' too, and ha' plans of his own to blame the earl's death on his brother. 'Tis a risk, but one he apparently is willing to take.''

"But we are not,'' Elsbeth said with more determination and spirit.

Hugh looked at her with approval. "Tha's my lass.''

Her eyes now intense, Elsbeth stared into the woods in front of her. "If the traitor, whoever he is, is going to help Lord Huntington escape, we must do it first."

Hugh grinned. "Aye, lass."

Elsbeth looked at him suspiciously. "Is that why you brought the English soldier here?"

"I thought the earl might be lacking a bit of trust."

A smile finally broke through Elsbeth's grim countenance. "I doubt that. He'll dare anything."

Satisfied, Hugh nodded. "Still, Garrick could be useful."

"I'll not let any of my clan be hurt," Elsbeth said bitterly. "Not for him."

"There could be a great many more hurt if he's killed," Hugh said. "A ransom is one thing, the murder of a court favorite another."

"Then we shall have to plan well, Hugh. Very well. Where's your Englishman?"

Chapter Ten

Elsbeth waited until after midnight, until the tower was near full asleep.

She knew she could do nothing openly to help Lord Huntington without losing the complete loyalty of her clan. She must in no way be implicated in the escape. Neither must Hugh, or he would face the wrath of the Kers.

Even if she explained to the clan members the consequences of Alex Carey's death, they would take little heed. Vengeance and honor were at stake. Nothing else mattered, not the repercussions, nor the destruction of her clan, nor the forfeiture of lands.

Alex Carey, unfortunately, represented everything that her clan despised—every death, every burning, every theft perpetrated during the past thirty years. Her clan wanted money or blood. Nothing less would do.

Her head hurt. Her heart hurt. She had longed to prove herself to the clan and so had led them into an impossible situation. As she had led herself.

With the assistance of a traitor.

Nothing, she had finally realized, was as it seemed. Black was white, and white was black. Right was wrong, and wrong right. Enemies were suddenly allies, and allies enemies.

And she wondered if she would ever trust her instincts again.

Even now she wondered. Was she doing the right thing by releasing the arch-enemy of her people?

But the decision had been made. That afternoon, she and Hugh and David Garrick had made it together.

She did not like David Garrick, for all she recognized his competence. Or mayhap because of his competence. This man had led raids against her people, and though they were forced to join together this evening, she hoped never to see him again.

Or Alexander Carey, she told herself over and over again.

When the Englishman left, he would take his wizardry with him, and she would find the Ker traitor in her own way, in her own time. And she would marry and forget those bottomless gray eyes, the wry smile and impudent charm.

The first problem was removal of the guards. She thanked heaven that Lord Huntington was still in Patrick's chamber, for it meant fewer stairs, less exposure.

After Annie and the other servants retired, Elsbeth went to the kitchen. It had always been her favorite place in the tower, filled as it was with the smells of spices, roasted meat and fresh breads. A huge fireplace dominated the room, and a great iron caldron hung over dead ashes.

A cask of ale rested in one corner. She knew the guards who would soon take their post outside Lord Huntington's room would eat and drink a cup of ale before relieving the men they would spell. She carried the cask to a drain and poured out most of its contents. She then added to the ale the sleeping potion Magdalene had given her for Lord Huntington, and returned the cask to its place.

When she had completed the task, she went to her room. In two hours, if everything happened as planned, the guards would be asleep, and no one the wiser. She fingered the Armstrong plaid Hugh had given her. Lord Huntington would have to don it, and pretend to be Hugh's newly arrived Armstrong kin in order to get through the gates. With an armored bonnet pulled low on his face, he might well pass.

It was a dangerous plan, particularly for Hugh. It all hinged on the Kers believing that Hugh's "cousin" had misled him as well as all of them. To make that plausible, Hugh would have to be wounded and left unconscious.

Once Garrick and Lord Huntington were gone, Elsbeth was determined she would somehow discover who was the traitor. She didn't know how, but she would. Even then she didn't know what she would do. She knew she could order neither Patrick's nor Ian's death, no matter what they had done.

A tear trickled down her cheek. The future looked uncommonly bleak. She felt a terrible emptiness when she thought of the Englishman, and that he would soon be gone. An even worse ache swept through her as she thought of the betrayal by her clansman.

Minutes seemed like hours. She changed into her simplest dark gown, and waited, watching as the moon seemed to float across the sky, impervious to all the plotting below. Her fingers clenched and unclenched, playing nervously with a handkerchief as she urged the time to pass more quickly.

When she believed the hour was nigh, she made her way silently up the stairs to Patrick's chamber. The silence was absolute, signaling to her that the sleeping potion had worked. The two guards were, indeed, slumped against the stone walls, and now that she was nearer she could hear their gentle snoring.

The door had no lock, a fact that had been acceptable due to the Englishman's weakened condition and the two guards outside. Elsbeth opened the door slowly, wincing at the slight creak of its hinges. A candle, almost gone now, spluttered in one of the wall brackets, casting shadows over the sleeping form in the bed.

Elsbeth touched his shoulder gently. He reacted quickly, as if trained to do so. She put a finger on his lip, and saw him frown slightly in surprise and puzzlement. But his eyes cleared quickly, and he nodded, understanding she was asking for silence.

He sat up, searching the room for others before looking at her with a silent question.

Elsbeth met his eyes directly, then turned her head toward the door where Alex could see a man's legs sprawled out. A small grin started, then stopped as he saw the grim expression on her face.

He took the pile of clothes she offered, and his mouth quirked as he started to emerge from the covers before realizing that he was naked. He had grown heartily disgusted at the filth-caked hose he'd worn for weeks in the tower upstairs.

She looked at him impatiently, and he shrugged, rising slowly from the bed, watching her carefully as her eyes widened; even in the dim light he could see the flush start and grow on her face.

Despite the danger, he couldn't help but feel satisfaction as her gaze seemed unwilling to leave him; it traveled slowly from his chest to his lean waist and hips to where his manhood had begun to swell in response to her stare.

When her eyes returned upward, Alex saw the despair in them, and he felt shame and guilt. She was trying to help him, and he was acting the stallion. He reached for the armful of clothes she was holding, knowing instinctively they were for him, then turned his back to her. He awkwardly donned the rough woolen trews and cotton shirt, his movements stiff, for his arm still hurt each time he moved. He painfully placed the armored leather helmet over his head, knowing it hid his features well, then turned and nodded to Elsbeth.

Her face still fiery red from the magnificent sight of a body supremely muscled, she swiftly led the way downstairs, staying in the shadows and passing under the flickering torches on the walls. They gained the door and slipped outside, Elsbeth moving toward the stable more quickly than he would have believed possible. He knew from the last time he had tried to escape that the well-worn path was out of sight of the guards at the massive wooden gates.

Beside Elsbeth, he slipped into the stable, and felt someone grab his shoulder. He whirled around, only to find the rugged face of Davey Garrick grinning at him. His hand clasped David's heartily as a smile spread over his countenance.

"God's blood, man, how did you get here?"

"You don't want to know—not now," David replied. "'Tis time to get out of here."

Alex looked up. Two horses, including his own black stallion, were saddled. His eyes went back to Garrick. He, too, was dressed in Armstrong plaid, a helmet in his hands. His body seemed burlier than usual, and when Alex's gaze moved to a third man he knew why. The two men were now almost exactly the same size. Wrappings, he supposed.

He addressed the man he now remembered from that afternoon. "I'm Alex Carey," he said, disregarding his title. "I believe I owe you my thanks."

Hugh was surprised. From what Elsbeth had told him, he had expected arrogance. There was none here. Only gratitude.

"I did it no' for ye, my lord."

Alex grinned, the same self-mocking grin that had so fascinated Elsbeth before. "I know that well. Yet the result is the same, and I am grateful. I will not forget it."

"There will be no Carey raid?"

"Not against you or your clan," Alex said, and his voice was grim and implacable. In that moment, Hugh knew he would not like to be this man's enemy.

"Godspeed ye, then," Hugh said.

Alex nodded, then turned to Elsbeth. His eyes bored into her. "And you, my lady? Why did you risk all?"

"I will not be responsible for the death of my clan."

"Is that all?" he teased, his eyes holding hers like a vise.

"I am also ridding this tower of a Carey. That is reason enough."

The smile left Alex's mouth. He turned to David. "What news have you?"

"John, along with a Ker clansman, plotted to kill you. You were meant to die, not be kidnapped. 'Twas only luck that the lady decided otherwise."

"Who among the Kers?"

"We do not know. I followed John one night and overheard them, but I could not identify the other man."

Alex knew he should tarry no longer. Time was essential. Yet he couldn't leave Lady Elsbeth here with an unknown traitor. And if her part in his escape should ever be suspected . . .

He winced at the thought. Still another problem flitted through his mind. Both Careys and Kers had traitors in their midst, and he could see no way of proving it at the moment. He knew there would never be peace between the families until both traitors were found and their duplicity proved. A trap would have to be set.

But first he had to safeguard Lady Ker, and the only way he could do that at the moment was take her with him. At least that was what he told himself. He didn't let himself think that he just couldn't bring himself to leave her, that he couldn't bear not to see her again. Much within him rebelled at the thought of taking her against her will, but another part, a heart long denied, gave him no choice. He simply could not let her go. It was not reason speaking, but a need so strong and deep he could not withstand it.

His eyes moved to her face. Her eyes were golden in the dim light, her face tense as she waited for him to mount.

"You must go, my lord," she said.

"Go with me," he said suddenly.

Her eyes widened. "You *are* daft."

"You're not safe here." His voice was urgent.

"And I would be safer with you, a Carey?"

"Aye," he said, his dark eyes wary. "I reason so."

"Then you reason poorly. 'Twas not I who was taken so easily."

The self-mocking smile returned. "It was a lesson I learned well, my lady," he said.

"Then you'd better be on your way before you find yourself captive again."

"What if your clan discovers you've aided my escape?"

Her lips tightened. She well knew the consequences of her actions. She would certainly be reviled, perhaps worse. "It's not your care."

Alex knew he could argue no longer. Dawn was not far away. His eyes went to Davey's, and he knew the man read his thoughts. He nodded slightly.

David and Hugh had already agreed that Hugh had to be disabled, so as not to be suspected of involvement in the escape. But in that instant, as silent messages passed between the Englishmen, Hugh understood them . . . and balked. No one would take his lady if she did not wish it.

His sword came up and Davey's met it, as Alex stepped back, pulling the struggling Elsbeth with him. One of his large hands captured both of hers behind her and, tearing a piece of cloth from his plaid, he quickly bound them, fastening another piece around her mouth. He winced at the rage in her eyes as he finished, and turned to look at Davey and the Scot.

The clash of swords was loud in the stable, and he knew they could afford neither the time nor the noise. What made the situation even more difficult was that the Scot was seeking to kill while David was doing his best to avoid it. Alex knew he had to interfere, although his sense of fairness objected.

As Hugh backed up, Alex caught him from behind and delivered a heavy blow to the side of his head. David dropped his weapon and caught the Scot as he toppled forward.

"Tie him," Alex ordered curtly, avoiding Elsbeth's eyes. He disliked intensely what he had to do next, but there was no other course. They had to get through the gates, and they had to make it plain that Lady Ker had been kidnapped against her will.

He went over to her, seeing her eyes narrow as they saw something in his.

Alex put his hand gently against her cheek, drew her close to him, feeling her body stiffen in apprehension. "You must go as I came," he said softly. He turned toward David, who was finishing tying Hugh. "Find me a blanket."

Elsbeth struggled against him, a sudden panic taking her. She could not go with him. She would not.

"I want your word you will not move or make a noise."

She shook her head violently, biting helplessly into the gag. She couldn't believe he was doing this after she had helped him. He *was* a Carey. As despicable as any of them. Worse. Rage filled her as she struggled even more violently against him.

Elsbeth was so angry she didn't see the great pain in his eyes as he raised his hand and, as with Hugh, rendered her unconscious.

Alex didn't waste time on regrets. He and David worked quickly, wrapping her securely in the blanket, rags filling in curves, and each end tied with rope. Alex mounted and David handed the bundle up to him. Alex carefully laid her across the front of the saddle. Davey mounted beside him, and they trotted toward the main gate.

Davey led, his bulk under the armored jacket and helmet making him look much like the burly Scot inside the stable.

He merely nodded to the two sleepy guards who opened the gates and glanced only briefly at the man whom they had seen accompany Hugh in earlier.

One nodded at Alex's bundle, and he tensed, a knot forming in his stomach.

"Yer lady—" he imitated the heavy border accent "—gi' me wife and children blankets an' food. Whoreson English burned us oout."

The guard smiled sympathetically. It was like Lady Elsbeth to help. He turned away to close the gates, and David and Alex spurred their horses into a fast trot.

They traveled until well out of earshot of the tower before David finally slowed his horse and turned to Alex. "Do we go to Huntington?"

"Not yet," Alex said thoughtfully. "Tell me everything you heard between my brother and the other man."

David recounted the conversation, omitting nothing. "I thought about going to London but feared no one would accept my word over your brother's."

"So the Scot had a hand in Lord Ker's death?"

"So it appears."

"Lady Elsbeth will never believe it."

"Nay," David agreed. "I could scarce credit it myself."

"Unless it's proved. To both families."

"What do you plan?"

"Make our conspirators very worried for a while, Davey. I'll disappear, as will Lady Elsbeth. It will force them together again."

David grinned. "I've missed you, my lord."

"And I you, Davey. Now let us see about the well-being of our lady."

They stopped the horses, and Alex dismounted with agility. He had enjoyed feeling his horse beneath him again, pleased that Patrick had not taken him. He carefully lowered the bundle that was Elsbeth and quickly sliced the ropes wrapped around the blanket with a dagger he had taken from Hugh.

She was still unconscious. Alex untied the gag and the binding around her wrists, knowing she could do little against his own strength. "Elsbeth," he said in a low voice, then a more urgent one.

David kneeled down beside him, handing him a leather flagon of wine.

Alex poured a couple of drops into her mouth, and saw her lips move and then her eyes flutter open. They were confused at first, trying to focus, but then they fastened on him and he met their accusing stare directly.

"My pardon, Lady Elsbeth," he said softly, "but it had to be done." Even as he said the words, he knew they were not entirely true, no matter how much he wanted them to be. He needed her, and he thought she needed him, but there might have been another way to trap his brother and the Ker traitor. There might have been. But he hadn't wanted to look for it.

Her voice was full of loathing as she replied. "You lie, like all Careys. And so now you have your revenge. I am your prisoner, as you were mine."

His lips tightened, and his eyes pierced her, demanding she understand. "Not a prisoner," he answered.

"Then let me go back."

"No."

She turned her head away from him as if she could no longer stand the sight of him, and he felt a streak of agony stab through him that was worse than the bite of any sword.

"We must go," he murmured, offering her his hand.

But she refused it, her teeth biting her lip as she used a hand against the ground to steady herself. She rose slowly, stiffly, and stood proudly before him.

"Where are you taking me?"

"Someplace where we can talk."

Elsbeth's glare drilled into him. "I don't want to go with you."

"I know." His gaze softened at the proud defiance in her face.

"I thought you were different." The ache in her voice did what a blow couldn't, and his lips tightened at its condemnation.

"Come, my lady."

"I should rather ride with him," she said, nodding her head at David. "Or walk."

"It would be a long walk."

"I don't care," she protested, her chin tipping dangerously upward.

"Enough," he said suddenly, realizing that every additional moment meant danger. "You gave me few choices. Now I give you fewer still. You will ride with me."

His hand took her arm, and it was like a band of steel. He led her to the horse and, taking the reins firmly in one hand, helped her mount with the other. He then swung up behind her, moving to the back of the saddle. Neither of them would have a comfortable ride this night.

David led the way, along hidden trails Elsbeth hadn't known existed. She tried to hold herself stiff, leaning forward to avoid contact with Lord Huntington. She was still too furious, and she wanted to show him, in every way, that she detested him for what he was doing.

Yet his arms were warm around her and each touch tentative yet gentle. Just his nearness was compelling, as it had been since the beginning, and that awareness frightened her more than an army of English soldiers.

It was a long ride, and she was very, very tired. Sometime during the night her defiance and will bent to need, and her back fell against his chest, her head against his heart, and she heard the strong, rhythmic heartbeat.

She did not want to go with him.

She didn't.

He was treacherous. He had just proved it. She hated everything he was.

And yet she had never felt safer.

She didn't understand the riddle. She didn't want to. She only knew she had to escape, to return home where there was safety of another kind.

But was there?

She had never felt so alone. Yet she knew she could never let this man make it different. There was too much between them. There would always be too much.

Elsbeth wanted to look up, to search the face that had so turned her life upside down. But she dared not do it. There was something about that mouth—teasing, thoughtful, mocking—that made her indifferent to everything else. And she had to escape him. She had to.

Alex felt her body finally relax against him, and fought against cradling her as he wanted to. It was enough, for the moment, to feel her head against his chest, to have her body meld softly into his.

When he heard her soft breathing and knew she was asleep, his lips touched the top of her hair, tasting the sweetness of it. His arms tightened around her possessively, something he had been wanting to do, yet knew she would reject while awake.

He would have her alone for days . . . days during which he could earn her trust. He wanted her to look at him with something other than hate in her eyes, as she had that one night in Patrick's bedchamber. He had felt things then he had not felt before. And he wanted to feel them again.

He wanted it more than Huntington, more than a much overdue meeting with his brother. At the moment, nothing else mattered.

They stopped at the first crack of dawn. They were heading toward a hunting cabin he and Davey had once found. It had at one time belonged to a poacher, they thought, for it was well away from traveled paths and designed to blend into the woods. Neither of them believed anyone else knew about it.

The cabin would be rough, with few comforts, Alex mused as he thought ahead. Davey could bring them some fur skins for warmth. Although the weather was pleasant during the day, the nights could be damp and cool. It was not an ideal place for paying suit to a woman, but he had few choices at the moment.

If he returned to Huntington now, and could prove nothing, he would never know a peaceful moment. He would put nothing past his brother.

They stopped briefly to rest the horses. Elsbeth woke and slid easily off the back of the horse; she became once more rigid and hostile.

Ice slivered into her soul as she looked at him. The helmet was gone, cast aside hours ago, and black hair tumbled over his forehead, making him look young and reckless. Only his guarded eyes showed he was not as he seemed at that moment.

In the past hours, she had seen a hardness to him that he had not previously allowed her to see. He had been charming and pleasant and . . . deceiving. And she had been a fool, so completely a fool.

She thought of his accusations that there was a traitor among the Kers. She had started to believe him, but now she wondered. He had sown a crop of distrust, slowly, carefully. Hugh, to be sure, had also believed there was a traitor and that it was probably one of her cousins, but now Hugh lay unconscious, trussed like a goat, in her stable. Had it all been some grand elaborate plot of some sort, an intricate web, to take her? She could not dismiss the thought.

She looked away from Alex, unable to bear the sense of betrayal she felt. She didn't want him to see the mist of tears forming in her eyes.

But he would not let her. His hand took her chin and forced her to look up at him. "I said I would never hurt you," Alex said, his intense voice willing her to believe. "I meant it."

"You already have, my lord," she replied, this time her tone mocking, "and I now know the worth of any Carey's word."

"We need each other at the moment."

"You may need me, my lord, but I don't need you. I need only to see the last of you. And that, my lord, is a very great need. I should have known better than to trust a Carey." She jerked away from his hands, and he did not try to hold her.

"May I have some privacy?" she said in a haughty tone.

Alex gave her a long considered look. She had no place to flee . . . not without a horse. He nodded to the trees to the left.

With as much dignity as she could muster, Elsbeth walked slowly to a clump of oaks. When she felt well out of sight, she leaned against one, and let the hovering tears loose. She didn't know if they were caused by the deep disappointment she felt in Alex Carey, the thought of being captive when she'd been so recently captor or the terrible loneliness she felt at the moment.

There was no longer anyone to trust. She wondered if she would ever trust again. And she knew not what she faced. She had thought Alex Carey one kind of man; he had proved to be another. And she was the victim of her own trust. It was a mistake she wouldn't make again.

What did he want? That was the question. Was she to be held for ransom, as he was? Or was she to be made hostage against retaliation? If so, how long could he keep her?

Quickly she took care of her personal needs, not knowing how much time he would allow her. When she had finished, she moved toward the clearing. Perhaps she could grab one of the horses. She knew she could never make her escape on foot, not when she wasn't familiar with this particular trail. It was so dim as to disappear in places and she was aware of how dangerous these bogs could be.

But as she saw the outline of the horses, she saw that the man named Garrick was holding tightly to both sets of reins as he and Lord Huntington talked. She also saw Lord Huntington's head move as if he were searching among the trees for her.

She did not know this trail, and she doubted her kinsmen would. In any event, once they found she was missing they would wait for Ian and Patrick to return before striking back.

Both of her cousins were expected this day. What would they think? Unconsciously her hands combed the sides of her gown nervously. Would they think she went willingly? That she had betrayed her clan for a Carey? The thought was devastating.

When she returned to the Englishman, her face was full of despair, and she avoided his eyes. He offered his hand, but she refused it and grabbed the pommel of his horse, awkwardly mounting, wishing she had her sidesaddle. She felt his warmth and strength as he mounted easily behind her, and she stiffened as once more his arms went around her.

"It won't be long, my lady, before you can rest." His voice was gentle, deceptively gentle, she knew. He didn't really care if she were tired, or near despair. He didn't care that she really didn't want to stop because then she would be alone with him, and she didn't think she could bear that.

Her back hit his chest, and one of his arms circled her waist as if to buffer her. Its warmth was stinging, its protectiveness unwanted. She squirmed as if to rid herself of a burden and was relieved when the arm retreated and rested easily on the pommel of the saddle.

Elsbeth could tell he was a superb horseman by the ease with which he guided the spirited animal. Then she rid herself of the thought. He was the worst kind of scoundrel . . . a liar, a deceiver, a Carey. She would not, could not, believe anything favorable about him. He had used her. He had used Hugh. And she had put her clan in danger.

Now she must extricate herself. Even if she had to be just as great a liar, just as accomplished a deceiver.

She *would* escape and see that Alexander Carey, earl of Huntington, was paid back in just measure.

Chapter Eleven

Ian Ker was exhausted beyond all description. It seemed as if he had been riding forever.

But his errand had been successful. The Douglas, chief of that clan, had been all too eager to offer his support as needed. Not only did Douglas have his own grudge against the Careys, but the lord was jockeying for power in the Scottish court and could use the Ker support.

Ian was eager now to reach the tower, to see Elsbeth and to put an end to the problem of Huntington. The farce had gone on far too long, and decisions had to be made.

Ian had not missed the new brightness in Elsbeth's eyes. He knew her too well. The Carey was well formed, he had to admit, and he grudgingly admired the man's courage. He had fought well against Patrick.

But the welfare and honor of the clan was at stake. And Ian's own future.

He had loved Elsbeth as long as he could remember. She was everything bright and beautiful. They had played and tussled with each other, and one day as they wrestled in the grass he discovered she was more than a mere playmate. He was convinced that one day she would recognize his feelings and share them because they had too much in common for it to be otherwise.

They could laugh together, and tease, and race their mounts for meager wagers. And they would rule well together, for they both had the touch of ease in their relations with others. That the tower and lands would come with her were added benefits.

He knew he could strengthen the clan, weakened these past years by a soft laird and then a compassionate girl. Neither was suited for these times. Strength, and strength alone, meant survival on the border. It had always been so, and would always be so.

He knew Patrick had hopes of his own, but he felt his cousin's ambition was more for leadership than true love of Elsbeth. Patrick had a passion for the ladies, while Ian had been mostly celibate these past years, not wanting any scandal or gossip to reach Elsbeth's ears. Patrick, it seemed, could not have cared less about gossip, and in no way let it inhibit his amorous adventures. If God's truth were told, Ian believed that Patrick's suit for Elsbeth came mainly from his mother's carping and little from the man's own desires.

For those reasons, he had not taken Patrick seriously as a rival, but neither did he dismiss him completely. The goal of Elsbeth's hand had created a rift between the two men, though they had never truly been close; they were too competitive for that. Both wards, both bastards, they had sought to find their own place in different ways: Patrick through skill in arms, and Ian through charm. They had both succeeded masterfully.

Ian had bided his time, unwilling to press his suit too closely until he felt sure of success. But now, he felt, the time was nigh. The whole affair with Carey, and Elsbeth's apparent indecision, had caused grumbling throughout the clan. They felt they needed a strong leader with rank, and Lady Ker's marriage was the only way to achieve that.

He knew he was favored by the other clansmen, who were loath to see an outsider become laird and adopt the Ker name. The clan would not be unhappy with Patrick, either, but Ian did not intend that to happen.

Ian looked down at the Ker lands from the hill, and thought once more how much this green land meant to him. Michaelmas had passed, and cattle—those that remained after the Carey raids—had been allowed to enter the harvested fields and graze on the stubble. Plowing and harrowing had begun on previously fallow fields. Soon slaughter time would come, and the smell of smoked meat would replace the tangy scent of earth being worked.

Raids would resume, too. The mourning period for the old laird had ended, and he and Patrick, together and separately, would raid their English neighbors in time-honored tradition. Except for the blood feud with the Careys, the raiding was good sport and, if properly led, conducted without bloodshed.

It was only the Careys, the hated Careys, who made the border run red.

His heel dug into the side of his horse. They would be home by supper. God's blood, but he looked forward to it.

Patrick paced the main hall of the tower. He had arrived three hours earlier, his mood dark and his spirits blacker. He had raged at Hugh, sworn at the Almighty and generally chased everyone out of his shouting range.

How could everything have gone so wrong?

The hostage gone. Elsbeth missing. Hugh wounded and sheepish.

The cursed Englishman had turned the tables on them, and Patrick didn't like it. Not one bit.

He had already been in poor humor as he approached the Ker tower. The Homes had not been so ready to pledge their support. It was time for peace, they said. Both the English and Scottish governments were seeking to calm the borders. Even after Patrick had recited the long list of wrongs committed against his clan, the Homes only half-heartedly lent him support. Patrick knew he could count on few men-at-arms from them. He hoped Ian was meeting more sympathetic ears.

When he arrived, the tower was in an uproar. His mother was worse than them all. She had planned a marriage between him and Elsbeth for more years than he could remember. It had become so familiar a refrain that even he had started to believe its inevitability. It would be, he knew, a strengthening union for the clan. A union badly needed.

He and Ian had often talked about the need for stronger leadership. Strength—that was the only thing that counted on the border. Not education, or compassion, or justice. Just raw strength.

His mother, Joan, met him before he reached the stable. "He's stolen Lady Ker!"

Patrick's horse pranced nervously beside the screaming woman. "Elsbeth? Who stole her?"

"Lord Huntington."

"Huntington! How could he—"

"I know not. He escaped and kidnapped my lady. Hugh tried to stop them and was nearly killed."

Patrick's eyes narrowed. "Hugh? Where was he?"

"He was at the stable. His . . . cousin is gone."

The devil's blazes, Patrick thought, but his mother made no sense. A groom came out of the stables to take his horse, and Patrick leapt to the ground. "Where's Hugh?" he asked, thinking to get the right of this tale.

"In the tower, waiting for you and Ian."

"When did this happen?"

"Last eve."

Patrick swore again. It was too late to follow, and they could not attack Huntington Castle. It was far too well fortified against any force he could summon. But perhaps the kidnapping of a young lass would unify the border Scots as no other event could.

Perhaps the Careys, all the Careys, had played right into Ker hands.

But his fists tightened into knots as he thought of Elsbeth in Carey hands. He could only hope that even Careys wouldn't risk harming a lady of Elsbeth's rank and reputation.

But devil take their souls for the outrage.

The devil particularly claim the damned soul of the earl of Huntington.

Patrick knew he should have killed the English earl when he had a chance. He would have, had it not been for Elsbeth. Regret, hot and angry, boiled inside him. The whole affair showed how much the clan needed a strong leader.

His mother's strident voice broke into his bitter thoughts. "What do ye plan?"

"I can do naught until we know where she is, and what the Careys want. I willna risk her."

"If only ye had been more insistent in your suit."

Patrick clenched his teeth to stop a retort. He had presented his suit because he believed the clan needed a man at its helm.

And he liked Elsbeth, even loved her in a way. But he could not force her into marriage.

"Insistence, my dear mother, would only have driven her away."

"Ye could have kidnapped her, forced her into marriage."

"Ye do not win loyalty, or love, tha' way, Mother," Patrick said, his temper beginning to boil.

"Well, what do ye have now?"

Again Patrick bit back an angry reply. Sometimes he envied Ian, whose mother had died after giving birth to him. And then he felt a twinge of guilt. His mother was bitter, but then she had a certain right to be bitter. The old laird's brother had promised her marriage, and had never given it. She had been used and discarded, was barely tolerated now. His marriage would give Joan status, something she had always wanted. He understood her, although he oft tired of her carping.

"'Tis not the time to speak of such," he said abruptly.

"Do ye know she gave the Englishman your chamber while ye were away?"

He had started to leave, but now he spun around. "My chamber?"

"The wound ye gave him festered. She ha' him moved to your bed." Her tone was sly now. "She tended him herself."

Patrick's mouth grew grim. "What are ye saying, madam?"

"Perhaps she wasn't kidnapped. Perhaps she went willingly...."

Patrick's dark eyes grew blacker. "Ye'll keep such traitorous thoughts to yourself. I know Elsbeth's heart. It is tender. Far too tender to let a man die untended. But she has more reason than any of us to hate the Careys."

"She is a woman," Joan said determinedly. "And the earl is a handsome mon for all he is a Carey."

"I'll hear no more!" Patrick roared. He turned, moving in long strides toward the peel tower. He would seek Hugh and discover the truth of things. God's blood, but he wished he had killed the Englishman.

Patrick was still questioning Hugh when Ian arrived and hurried to the weapons room, which was occasionally also used as a sickroom. Knowing Patrick and Ian would wish words with him, Hugh had decided to stay there, rather than return to his cottage.

There was a deep gash on Hugh's head, and it hurt damnably. His chin was supported by one large beefy hand, anchored by an arm set firmly on his knee.

He did not have to feign his anger. He felt tricked and played false by the two Englishmen, and he was consumed with worry over Elsbeth. He had obviously misjudged and underestimated both the English earl and his lieutenant. They could, he thought now, even do harm to his lady. Yet he still suspected one of the two men before him now was a traitor, and he could not reveal his true role in the Carey's escape.

"Who was this kinsman you brought here?" Patrick asked.

"I donna know," Hugh said wearily. "I was visiting one of my cousins, and this man came by, asking for sustenance, saying that he had been outlawed. I ha' been away many years and didna recognize him, but he wore the Armstrong plaid. I told him ye might be in need of additional men."

"An English spy," Patrick spit.

"Aye," Hugh said. "He must ha' been, for when I went looking for him, he and the Carey prisoner were in the stable with the lady. She was bound. I went for my sword, and tha' was the last I knew."

"Bound, ye say?" Patrick queried.

"Aye, and spitting like a wildcat." That was true enough, Hugh comforted himself.

"How did he get away from the guards?"

"When I came to, I went to yer chamber. They were asleep—drugged, I think."

Ian's voice, when he spoke, was taut with anger. "Do ye think they will harm her?"

"Nay," Hugh said slowly. "I think she was their protection."

"Then mayhap they will release her?" Ian's voice was hopeful.

But Patrick broke in, his tone mocking. "A Carey, dear cousin? They will find some way to use her."

Ian stared at him. "I shall make them pay for this, every one of them."

"Both of us shall, cousin," Patrick replied, for a moment in complete harmony with Ian.

Hugh studied the two men. Their faces were taut, their mouths grim, their eyes filled with common vengeance.

"We shall send a spy to Huntington," Ian said.

"They wouldn't dare take her there," Patrick said. "The English warden would have no choice but to demand her release."

"But our man might overhear something. . . ."

"All right, cousin. Send someone. I'll do some searching of my own."

The cousins met with more than a hundred clansmen who had gathered outside the tower for word. Presenting a united front, they urged caution until they received a ransom demand or heard some word of Lady Ker's whereabouts. It took half the eve to prevent the crowd from riding directly to Huntington. Heated curses and shouts of revenge pierced the cold night air, and Patrick vowed they would have retribution in due time. Their lady's safety was of more importance now. With no small amount of muttering, the clansmen finally dispersed to the barracks or to the fires surrounding the peel tower.

Patrick and Ian ate a quick supper and ordered fresh mounts saddled. Ian would meet with a huntsman who had previously been to Huntington, to ask whether he would act as spy. The man claimed allegiance to neither the English nor the Scots, but Elsbeth had been kind to him on several occasions. Patrick would ride to all the outlying crofters and tell them what had happened, advising them once more to come to the tower fortress for protection; Huntington might strike back in revenge for his kidnapping. With a curt nod to each other, the two men disappeared into the night.

John Carey was growing restless. He and Simon had been hidden in these bushes half the night, and still no sight of his brother.

He had been foolish to trust the Scot, but he had little choice now. His brother had to die, and die in such a way that he, John, would never be suspected.

Why did the whoreson have to return from the dead?

After Alex disappeared years ago, John had carefully planned to hasten his own father's and eldest brother's demise. There was little affection among them; they shared only one thing—greed. And John had been an adept pupil in ruthlessness.

As the youngest son, he had been of little import to his father, ignored and neglected, cuffed when he did not perform to his father's satisfaction, which was most of the time. He hated his two older brothers, who were natural horsemen and adept swordsmen; he was neither, no matter how hard he tried, and envy started to poison his soul.

When his brother William was gone, it seemed the youngest son would have all he'd ever wanted—until Alex returned. And John lost everything. Again.

But he would regain it. He would show them all. He would make Huntington the wealthiest and most powerful holding in all of northern England. No one would dare question him, or accuse him.

There would be no more inquiries about the untimely deaths of his father and brother.

Where was Alexander? he wondered now. The Scot had sworn he would see him released tonight. But then you could never trust a Scot. When Alex was dead, he would then see to the death of the Scot. It was a satisfying thought. He hated him. He hated them all, and particularly this one who thought he was using John. The bastard would soon find out differently.

John checked his pistol again. He was near enough the trail that he could not miss with the one ball. If the shot was not fatal, Simon was ready to finish the deed. A river was nearby, one that ran downstream into the English countryside. Alex's body would be dumped there, to be carried down to a village where all would immediately assume it came from the Ker stronghold.

It was a perfect plan. But God's blood, where was his brother!

He heard the faint call of a bird, and he tensed. It was the Scot's signal. Something was wrong.

John returned the signal, but stayed in hiding until the horseman approached in the shadows. Cautiously, he went to meet the man.

"Where's Alexander?"

There was a mirthless chuckle. "Ye are a wee bit late, my would-be lord. He escaped last eve."

John's hand went for his sword. "You . . . betrayed me."

"Nay. I had naught to do with it. He did it on his own, or with the help of someone we don't know about."

John stood there, visibly stunned.

The Scot, for his part, had had several of his own questions answered. The moment he had seen John Carey waiting at the ambush spot, he knew Huntington had not returned to his holding. He continued speaking now. "He took my lady with him."

"Lady Ker?"

"Aye, and I want her back. Unharmed."

John tried to absorb the information, and what it meant. "They haven't returned to Huntington."

"He must know he's in danger there."

"He's no fool," John growled. "**He** knows no ransom was paid."

"Where might he ha' gone?"

John stared at him, the full import of the news falling on him. "We have to find him," he whispered.

"And get the lady back with her no wiser of our . . . arrangement."

"That's not my concern."

"It ha' better be, English, or I'll slice that greedy body in slivers."

John felt a cold wave sweep over him. He did not doubt the Scot's words, nor did he underestimate his own danger if the English court discovered what he had done. Men had been drawn and quartered for lesser offenses.

"Do ye heed me?" the Scot insisted.

"He has to die," John said in a strangled voice.

"Aye, he has to die. But not my lady."

"How do we find them?"

"He has to be hiding along the border. I'll start searching. Ye might try to discover who among your men would help him. There was a second man involved, and not one of ours.''

John considered the possibilities. It was more than eight years since Alex had left. All Huntington's men-at-arms were either tenants bound to the land or mercenaries hired by his father or himself. Alex had not been back long enough to hire any of his own men or to establish any personal loyalty. John also knew that he himself received little loyalty from servants, and did not credit his brother with inspiring more. He vaguely remember that David Garrick had once served his brother, but Garrick had been away, hired out to another border lord. Besides, Garrick was a mercenary, paid well, and John knew the breed had few more scruples than he himself. No, it wouldn't be Garrick.

"Why do you believe he took Lady Ker?" John asked, thoughtful.

The Scot shrugged, but his mouth tightened. "Revenge...ransom...protection...'' He didn't continue, but still another reason ate like acid in him. The English, particularly the Careys, had raped their share of Scottish women.

"If anything happens to her,'' he said through clenched teeth, "not a Carey alive will ever be safe again.''

Once more, John felt an icy coldness. He nodded, but his eyes wandered over to where Simon still lay. His hand holding the pistol rose slightly. Perhaps it would be wise to dispose of the Scot now.

He turned to Simon to signal him when a sword tip reached his throat.

"I wouldn't, English. Tell your man to come out.''

John couldn't speak for a moment as he felt blood running from his throat.

"Tell him!'' The sword cut deeper.

"Simon.''

The large man rose slowly, reluctantly, from the shadows.

"Such trust among comrades,'' the Scot said mockingly. "'Tis great regret I feel I canna puncture ye a bit deeper. But I want my lady. She must be on your land and, for the moment, I still need ye.''

John's hand went to his throat and felt the warm oozing blood. "Scot bastard."

The Scot's mouth tightened as he fought not to plunge his sword into the English breast. "Remember, 'tis your neck—" he paused for effect as he looked farther down Carey's anatomy "—or more at stake. Meet me at the old place in two nights' time."

The Scot jerked the reins of his horse and disappeared through the dark woods.

Chapter Twelve

David Garrick separated from Alex and Elsbeth just after dawn, first pledging to meet them at their destination as soon as possible. He would bring quill and parchment for a message...and news.

Elsbeth watched him ride away with little knots of fear forming in her chest. It was not that she feared physical violence from the man now her captor. But she greatly feared her own reactions to him.

His arms had encircled her again, and she could feel the restrained strength, the inherent gentleness in them. With every new slight pressure—which were many with the movement of the horse—something in her yearned to lean back against the hard power of him. Her skin seemed to burn, then melt wherever he touched until she had little will left of her own.

But she forced herself to angle forward, to hold herself from him. She must fight him, for it was his very gentleness that was her greatest enemy. She tried to recite every reason she had to hate him, particularly now that he had used her to escape, then taken her against her will. But nothing had the force of his presence, of the strange magic that always seemed to float between them when they were together.

A Carey trick.

It was naught but a Carey trick that could draw her clan into a death trap.

She was tired, so very, very tired and once more she found her body falling toward him, only to catch herself in time. That would be surrendering, and no Ker would surrender to a Carey. The thought stiffened her spine. She knew he could feel the withdrawal when his hands loosened around her.

"It will not be long now, my lady," he said softly.

"Where?"

"A small poacher's hut. It is crude but offers shelter."

Like his chamber in the Ker tower, Elsbeth thought. She was being paid back in like measure.

"I would offer better if I could," he said, as if he read her thoughts. It was another reminder of how often he had done that. She hated the violation.

"With your presence, a king's castle would be naught but a punishment," she retorted.

"I'm sorry it offends you so, Elsbeth," he said, making her name a caress on his tongue, "but we, you and I, have much to speak of."

"I have nothing to speak of with you."

"Well, then, you will listen."

"No," she said stubbornly, again calling on her willpower to move away from him, from the touch that made her weak.

One hand moved up the sleeve of her dress, sending ripples of sensation through her.

"You will stay with me until you do. I will not object if it takes weeks, or longer."

The pronouncement was mild but implacable, and it stirred the hot coals of anger in her.

"Treacherous English. I should have let Patrick skewer you."

His tone was mildly amused when he answered. "'Tis too late now, madam. Mayhap we will have another go at it, your Patrick and I."

"I wager you will," she said. "He will not let this pass. And he's a better swordsman than you," she retorted defiantly.

"But he's also more reckless, my lady, and that's a fatal flaw."

"He does not have a wounded arm."

Again came the warm chuckle that infuriated her. "Mayhap I wanted your tender care," he answered mildly, maddeningly reminding her of those brief moments of closeness they had shared.

She was glad he couldn't see the flush she knew was reddening her face. "It was no more than I would give a wounded dog."

"No?"

Elsbeth could see in her mind's eye the cocked eyebrow and mocking grin, and she hated him for reminding her of her weakness. "I loathe and despise you," she said in a low intense voice.

In answer, his arms tightened around her. "I will have to do something, then, to change that unfortunate opinion."

"You can release me."

"Anything but that, Elsbeth."

Once again his voice was like warm honey, singing its siren song. But she would not be lured by it again. She jerked away from his hold. "I wish to walk."

"But I don't wish it," he said silkily, with only the slightest hint of amused chagrin at her obvious rejection, "and for the moment you will do as I command."

Once again he had reminded her of their changed positions. She remembered how she had had him tied like a bag of oats to the saddle, and the bare cell she had given him. Her hands tightened against the pommel of the saddle. Had she so misjudged him? She had come to think of him as a decent man . . . decent, anyway, for a Carey. But just now there had been a definite threat in his voice.

Alex felt her new tension, and his voice softened. He should not have allowed her words to wound him as they had. She had every reason to suspect his motives and intentions. He felt every league of the gulf between them. "You will not be hurt, Elsbeth. In any way. I wish only to reason with you."

"By kidnapping me?"

"As you did me," he reminded her.

"*I* did not wish to reason with you."

"Aye," he replied wryly. "You made that most clear."

"What do you want?" The cry was desperate.

Alex did not answer, for his own motives were not entirely clear to him. He had told himself it was to escape the wall of the peel tower, to trap his brother and the Ker who apparently wished the feud to continue. He had told himself it was the only way to end the bloodletting between their families. He had told himself many things. He realized now they were only excuses for what he really wanted: Elsbeth. Yet to say that would give her a weapon against him. And it was something she was not ready to hear.

Instead, he ignored her question, and spurred his horse so the wind, blowing like a damp breath in the foggy dawn, would prevent any more speech between them.

It was noon when they left the path and rode through thickets that slowed their progress while the branches scratched their skin. Elsbeth thought they would never stop. Finally, when they reached a particularly difficult passage, Alex halted and dismounted. He shook his head as Elsbeth started to follow. Instead he took the reins and led the horse, and Elsbeth, into what seemed to be impenetrable forest, with vines and undergrowth blurring an old path. Still he continued farther into the maze, feeling the scrape of brush against his face and arms, realizing that Elsbeth must be similarly cut. He hated the thought of her suffering, and knew there would be little more comfort when they reached their destination.

When they came to the rough dwelling, he went to help Elsbeth dismount but, as before, she scorned his hand and slid down easily on her own, all the time eyeing the hut warily. It was a look that became more pronounced as the door creaked open and the dim interior was revealed.

The hut was even barer than he remembered. Mayhap as a boy he had cared less for comfort. Or it could be that time had carved chinks between the dried mud and cow dung that held the rotting pieces of wood and straw together. The floor was only earth, and time had taken toll of the few rushes that covered it. It was obvious that animals, other than humans, had taken advantage of the shelter.

'Twas not the way to win a maiden's heart, Alex thought regretfully as he looked inside, nor was it much of a place in which to reason, but at the moment he could think of no other sanctuary. He could only hope that David might bring a few robes and rugs to make the hut more habitable.

Elsbeth surveyed the room with dismay. It was humbler than the meanest of crofters' huts. Her gold-flecked eyes went to Alex's. "I am to stay here?"

Alex knew only too well what she was thinking. She had given him poor accommodation; he was exacting revenge in good measure.

"Just a short while, Elsbeth."

She wanted to hit him, but she suspected that even with his wounded arm he would be much too fast for her, and she was loath to give him satisfaction. "I gave no permission for you to use my name," she said haughtily, making her voice as cold as a loch on a sunless January morn.

His curious half smile returned, and once more she wondered at the hint of sadness that always seemed to haunt it. Sometimes mocking, sometimes almost sweet, his lips always had a curious turn to them that set him apart from other men— as if he were an interested onlooker at an amusement.

She leaned against the rough door of the hut, suddenly exhausted. She realized she had had very little sleep in the past three days. A bitter laugh escaped her as she thought why. One night nursing the Englishman, the second helping him to escape and the third his prisoner. Dolt. Her hand went to her face, and she closed her eyes, wishing to make some sense of the past fortnight.

Elsbeth felt his hand on her shoulder and she jerked away. "Don't touch me," she said, all the time wanting him to. She heard him move around the hut, and she stayed huddled near the door. When she finally looked up, he had gathered many of the rushes and was taking them out the door.

"Where—"

"To air these," he said.

Elsbeth stared at him in stunned silence. Never had she heard of a man doing such work. And a lord? An earl?

He smiled again at her expression, a truly engaging smile that finally lit his eyes. It was the first time she had seen both eyes and mouth work together in concert. She closed her eyes once more against the devastating impact.

She heard his boots rustle the leaves outside and felt safe enough to regard the world again. She opened her eyes and

peered outside, watching him shake the rushes and lay them out
in what little sunlight filtered through the trees. He could have
ordered her to do it. Blood pounded in her chest and heart as
she saw him kneel, his handsome face in silhouette, the mouth
firmly lined in concentration. The Armstrong plaid outlined his
broad chest and muscular arms, his lean hard waist and hips.
A lock of dark hair fell over his forehead, and his cheeks were
dark with new beard. There was so much grace and power in
each movement that Elsbeth felt pleasure in just watching him
in motion.

Dear God above, but she must be ill to think thus. She should
be praying for deliverance. She reluctantly turned her eyes away
and again surveyed the room. There was an open hearth and a
smoke vent in the thatched roof. The only furniture was two
roughly made stools.

A number of dirty rushes still littered the earth floor, and she
leaned down and picked up a pile herself. If he, an earl, could
stoop to such a lowly task, then she, Elsbeth Ker, could also. If
she had to stay here, she would make the best of it. Until she
could escape.

Until . . .

He looked at her in surprise as she brought out her load, and
his subsequent approving smile made her steps lighter, her
burden less cumbersome. But she forced a frown on her lips as
she did what he had done—shake out the rushes and lay them
in the slivers of sunlight.

When she straightened, she saw that much of the dirt clung
to her dress, which was already stained from the night's ride.
She had lost the hood covering her hair, and now curls tumbled down the front of her dress in reckless abandon. She
turned away, knowing she must look like the most shameless of
maids. For one of the few times in her life, she felt terribly uncertain and shy.

"You look lovely, Lady Elsbeth."

Elsbeth trembled, not only at his words, but at the sweet
compassion, the soft regret behind them. He had done it again,
read her mind and said the one thing that would soothe her. He
was a sorcerer. Once more she was consumed with the need to
go to him, to feel his hand on her, but something else, some-

thing even stronger, told her to stay her distance. Her eyes darted around the tiny clearing, looking for his horse. It was not visible.

Alex Carey stood. "He's well hidden, my lady, and I would advise you not to wander away. You can get lost here, and there are wild boars and other dangerous beasts in these woods."

"Like you?" she retorted. "I think I would prefer their company to yours."

"Ah, sweet Elsbeth, but *I* swear not to eat you."

"And why should I believe you?"

He eyed her speculatively. "You do look . . . tasty," he said with a small grin. "But I'm a bit tired, and I assure you that you are quite safe from this particular beast right now."

"I will not stay here with you," she cried out desperately.

"You will if I have to bind you," he said, "though I would much prefer not to." He looked at her with that smile that was no longer true, but mocking again. "I will take your word not to escape."

"Even if I would not take yours?"

"I must have more faith in my fellow human creatures than you," he said, his smile even more sardonic, as if every word offered a greater jest.

"My lord—"

"Alex," he said. "I much prefer Alex."

"I do not," she replied.

"You have not answered me," he continued as if she had not spoken.

She was confused, but then he always confused her.

"Your word. I would accept your word." He looked, for the moment, insufferably patient, as if dealing with an addled child.

"No!"

"Then I shall have to bind you to me while I sleep," he explained pleasantly.

She looked at him with horror. Little shots of heat already ran up and down her body, even as she remained at this distance from him. The thought of lying against him for any time was unbearable. "Knave. You wouldn't dare."

He arched an eyebrow, and she knew he was thinking of the night in Patrick's chamber.

"You were ill," she said defensively.

"And you were very kind," he said, suddenly gentle once more. Again his change of mood caught her unaware and dug into the well of vulnerability in her that he had so expertly exploited.

His statement required no answer, and she gave him none. She was ashamed of the way she had succumbed to him several nights earlier... even as she remembered the sweetness of their contact, the comfort of his arms. She shook her head to rid herself of the compelling images and feelings.

Alex's hand touched her cheek. "You, too, must be very weary," he continued softly.

Elsbeth regarded him suspiciously. He was like Proteus, the all-knowing Greek sea god who could assume any form to escape those wishing to capture him and learn his secrets. She could trust none of his moods, especially his most disarming one.

Without giving her a chance to answer, he disappeared into the woods, returning shortly with the blanket from the horse and a contrite expression. He gave her a small smile as he saw her look in the direction from which he had come.

"Do not look for Demon there," he said with the twisted smile. But then his lips pressed together tightly as he observed her speculative expression. "Don't try to ride him, Elsbeth. He can be dangerous."

"He could be no more dangerous than you."

"I told you. I will not harm you, and he well could."

Her hand went to the side of her head, which still ached slightly from his blow at the stable. His eyes followed the movement, the challenging light in them dimming.

He touched the discolored skin, feeling the small rise of the bruise. "I regret what was necessary."

"You regret much, my lord, but it seems not to deter you," she retorted.

His eyes, shaded now and charcoal colored, rested on her. She wished she could read them, but she had discovered that few could hide their feelings as well as this disturbing Englishman. She wanted to turn from his steady gaze, yet she could not. Why did she always feel so . . . helpless, so powerless with him?

His hand was incredibly gentle as it moved over the soreness, his touch soothing and healing. "I have never done anything more difficult."

She wished she could disbelieve him. She wanted to revile him, hate him, despise him, yet when he touched her like that, with so much tenderness, she could not doubt his sincerity. And her mind kept recalling to her everything she had done to him— the humiliating ambush, the painful ride to her land, the bare, lonely imprisonment. She swallowed, trying to dissolve the hard lump in her throat, the aching pain in her chest.

Elsbeth turned away, and Alex, thinking her move rejection, dropped his hand to his side. He watched bleakly as she moved away from him and sank beneath a tree, turning her face from him.

He wanted to go to her, but he could not. He had done enough. His right fist knotted as he wondered now how she would ever trust him. She had helped him, and he had rewarded her by hitting her, dragging her all night across the marchlands and bringing her to this mean place, which made his cell at the Ker tower seem a palace. That she should hate him was only natural. But it hurt. Great God above, it hurt in places he had long thought dead.

He had once believed the deaths of Nadine and Henri Marchand, combined with the cruel years on the galley, had armored him against his own tender feelings. Yet he had felt pain at his brother's betrayal, and now agony at Elsbeth's denial.

Emptiness, deep and racking, yawned wide within him as he considered a future that offered no warmth, no solace, but only hatred, distrust and constant warring. He had thought to grab some peace, to change a way of life that had ruled the borders for centuries, and he had only deepened the schism.

He didn't know how to bridge it. He had hoped, when alone with Elsbeth, that they might come to an understanding. But he had seen the fear in her eyes, the rejection in the proud lift of her head, and was sore afraid she would not listen.

He only knew he couldn't bear to watch her thus, to see the accusing eyes. The sardonic mask he showed to the world was but skin-deep, and never had he realized it so thoroughly before. He was as open to hurt now as he had been as a callow youth. Mayhap more so, he realized suddenly, for he seemed to need love... and belonging... more than ever. So much of his life had passed without love, he was now unbearably greedy for its light.

Fool!

He could not force Elsbeth Ker to listen, or trust or understand. As she so well observed, his very actions made a mockery of his words. He should release her; it was the only way to convince her of his sincerity—if anything would now. Yet something inside told him to wait a while longer, to keep her with him a day, and mayhap...

Mayhap she would look at him as she did that night in Patrick's chamber. It was only a very thin thread of hope, a dream. Yet he could not dismiss the thought. The need in him was too great for it to be otherwise.

Alex looked back to the tree. Lady Elsbeth Ker was still there, but now her eyes were closed, and she looked young and vulnerable with a smudge of dirt across her nose while wayward auburn tresses fell over the stained dress. Her determined mouth had softened, and great dark lashes shielded the golden eyes. He thought how lovely she was, how strong, how defiant. And how alive she made him feel. He walked over to her and knelt on one knee, his hand catching a curl and caressing it.

She caught his scent first, the smell of leather and horse and earth, for he had been silent in his approach. She forced herself to remain still as she felt his hand on her hair, and then its light touch as it moved, ever so caressingly, to the bruised place on her head and hesitated there.

"Sleep well, mistress," he whispered. "Sleep well, lovely lady."

As if from a distance, the words penetrated Elsbeth's hazy world. She had turned her face toward the woods and closed her eyes to shield herself from him and the unwanted feelings he always stirred in her. But she had not needed to pretend long.

She was nearly exhausted, and the sun warmed her as little else could at the moment.

Elsbeth heard his words, the infinite sadness in them, and her heart melted. He was not pretending now. There was no reason for him to, since he believed her asleep. His voice was low and deep and gentle and . . . wistful. A sense of drowsy contentment filled her, the anger seeping away and something warm replacing it. Knowing he was near, she slipped into an easy sleep cushioned by images of a slight ironic smile and warm gray eyes that belied it.

When she woke, he was nowhere to be seen. Quietly, she rose and checked the hut. It was empty.

Elsbeth looked up at the sky. It was cloudy and near dusk. Silence surrounded her like a shroud, and she felt a hesitancy in the air...a kind of suspension that sent bumps up her arms.

Where was Alex Carey? Had he left her alone here?

Suddenly, she realized she was free, even as the thought struck her that she might not want to be free.

But she wouldn't think about that now. She had to leave, to escape her growing dependency on him, the confusing feelings that had made her life a nightmare of contradictions.

And this might be her only chance to escape. To escape him!

Surely there would be search parties for her. She knew, from the setting sun, the general direction north. If she headed that way, she should eventually come upon someone. She remembered Lord Huntington's warning, and she hesitated. Then she recalled his impact on her. That was more dangerous than anything she might find in the woods. She had to get away from him before she betrayed everything she loved and understood.

It was that last thought that gave her courage. She slipped through the trees, hoping to put a fair distance between herself and the hut before deep night.

She was still tired, but forced her mind to think, her legs to walk. The forest was dense, but she was convinced that if she could find a deer trail heading north, she would eventually discover a trail she knew. She placed one foot in front of the other, trying to think of nothing else. One step. Another. And another.

The woods became darker, and more threatening. Elsbeth had never been a timid person. One did not survive life on the border with timidity. Her rough play with her cousins had made her adventuresome and bold, and she had become lost several times as a child, but she'd always known she would be found.

As the darkness closed in around her, she felt the first terrible clawings of fear. She had always liked the hooting of owls but now one startled her, and the fear deepened. It was such a lonely sound.

Dear God, what had she done? She heard the rustle of underbrush nearby, and her heart stopped before she saw the bright surprised eyes of a hare. Like two statues, they stilled, their stares fixed on each other before the small animal turned and darted away. Her legs felt weak, and she leaned against a tree, staring upward through dark branches. There were only small pieces of sky visible, and no stars, but she could see great dark clouds moving quickly now.

She wanted to go back. She was already chilled, and the clouds portended rain. But as she turned around she had no idea which way was back and which forward. There were no stars to tell her, no moon to give direction. There was simply darkness. She could see only shadows dancing in a growing wind.

Cold. She was getting so cold. And hungry. And tired. She leaned against a tree, afraid to go on with no more light than she had. She wondered how far she had come. And she thought, once more, of what a fool she was.

Alexander Carey, Lord Huntington. Of all her clansmen, of all her friends, he was the one she wanted most!

She rested as well as she could, but the damp cold seeped into her skin and then her bones. She knew she had to move to keep warm. Reluctantly she rose and started stiffly to move once more, trusting to instinct about direction, although she knew even the best woodsmen became confused in these heavy forests.

A sprinkling of rain started, and her misery deepened. Why had she been so certain she could find a path? There was none, only dense underbrush that scratched her ankles and arms and face until blood trickled from a dozen cuts. She took another step and mud caught at her ankle, pulling her down. As she sought to pull it free, she lost her balance and fell, her entire body sliding into a bog. Her hands frantically grabbed a branch as something tried to pull her down.

Panic, raw and overwhelming, seized her as the branch bent under her weight and the muck pulled her deeper and deeper into the bog.

She screamed. And screamed and screamed.

Chapter Thirteen

Alex had been convinced that Elsbeth would sleep through the afternoon, and had decided to set snares around the hut with cord supplied by David. David had given him some little pouches of oatmeal and some bread. It wasn't much, but it would relieve their hunger until David brought more food or the snares produced fresh meat.

Placing the snares had taken him longer than he'd anticipated, for he wanted them well out of the way of any searching parties. When he completed the second one, he returned to the hut, a lift in his step at the thought of seeing Elsbeth again.

But when he arrived at the small clearing in front of the hut, it was empty, as was the interior of the rough shelter. First apprehension, then a sickening fear, started building within him.

Surely she hadn't left on her own. Not after his warning.

Great God above! He had made light of the dangers, understated them. He had been convinced that she knew the perils of these borderlands. It was painful to believe that she feared him or despised him enough to risk her safety.

He hurried to Demon but didn't wait to saddle him. Taking the mane in his hands, he leaped to the back of the stallion.

But where had she gone? Where?

She would head north. Of that he was sure. He would go in that direction, and hope. And pray... although he realized he was not well practiced at that particular endeavor.

Evening shadows turned into stark blackness. He doubted whether she could go far in the thick woods and dark night, and he traveled in half circles, crisscrossing paths, stopping occasionally to listen for the slightest noise. He felt the first sting of rain, and knew she must be freezing. Her clothes afforded less protection than his. He swore a long bitter oath that echoed in the night.

He didn't know how long he had been riding. He only knew that despair and anguish had settled deep in his soul, when he first heard the weak cry. He dug his heels into Demon's sides and horse and rider made their way through the thick brush, following the cries, which seemed to become fainter. The bog. He was familiar with it, and the quicksand that could scoop someone into its depths.

His worry grew, and he prayed for a break in the rain, which was steadier now. The cries came closer, and sounded more desperate.

"Elsbeth?" he yelled frantically.

Her answer came swiftly, a haunting echo of his name, and he shouted for her to keep screaming so he could find her. The rain was pelting now, blinding him, and he could only go by her voice—which now seemed to be growing weaker. Afraid that his horse would stumble into the bog he knew was near, he dismounted, hoping Demon would stay as ordered.

He tested each step before putting a foot squarely down, making his way until finally he could see Elsbeth. She was mired in the bog to the waist, her hands clinging frantically to a branch that appeared ready to break.

"Elsbeth!" he called, and through the rain he could see her head turn toward him, although her expression was not visible. But her terror-filled screams still echoed in his head.

"It will be all right. You're safe now," he assured with a confident voice, and she nodded. He tested the ground, seeking the place where the hard ground gave way to the bog. She was just two feet inside, but had sunk deep enough that she couldn't help herself.

He anchored one arm to a slender tree and stretched out the other, almost reaching her. If she let go of the branch she could grab his hand.

But her hands remained fixed on the branch, terrified to let go of the only anchor she had.

"You must," he said softly, his voice taking on that persuasive magic she had heard before, so that she was compelled to believe him.

She let go and frantically grabbed for his hand, feeling it take her wrist and pull her with a strength she could scarcely comprehend. He was so close to the edge, she feared he would lose his grip on the tree and join her in this bottomless grave. She felt the muck drag at her legs, her dress, as he pulled her until she felt torn apart. Then slowly, very slowly, the bog surrendered its claim and inch by inch she gained sound earth.

When she was all the way out she collapsed into his arms.

"Thank God," he whispered.

She was too breathless, too frightened, too grateful to answer. His arms were immensely comforting, and she wanted nothing so much as to stay in them. She had not let herself relax in his hold during the long journey on horseback the night earlier, but now he represented safety and warmth; she had come so close to dying. She shivered as her body was racked with great heaving sobs, both from the cold and from the aftermath of overwhelming terror.

"It's all right," he crooned, as one might to a baby, his hands caressing her arms, her hands, as he held her tightly to him. "You're safe now. Thank God, I heard you."

She snuggled against him, all her resentment, all her anger lost in enormous gratitude, in the need to feel the human warmth of him. Once again her whole body shook with uncontrollable shivers. His arms moved tighter around her, trying to transfer some of his body heat, some of his strength, to her. Her arms went around his neck, and she clung to him, mindless now of all that had gone on between them earlier. She felt his lips touch her forehead with unfathomable tenderness.

Elsbeth wanted to stay there forever, even as the cold wrapped around her. Where he had been a threat hours earlier, he now represented all that was safe.

"I have to get you warm," he said as he gently disengaged himself from her and stood, holding her hand, guiding her upward on unsteady legs. In one swift movement, he swept her up in his arms, indifferent to the layers of mud that cloaked her.

Closing her eyes, she laid her head against his chest, and she heard the fast beat of his heart. More shivers racked her body, and she felt his arms tighten on her, her body pressed closer to his own.

All too soon, she was being set back on her feet, but his hand, the strong calloused hand, kept her from collapsing on legs no stronger than march weeds. She opened her eyes and saw the black stallion that had carried them the night before.

"Can you stand alone?" Lord Huntington said.

She nodded her head, barely noticing the rain that continued to fall. She would, she could, stand, if it took every last ounce of determination in her. Elsbeth noticed her rescuer looking at her with glinting approval, and despite her lingering fear she felt her heart leap.

But then he was on the horse, in a movement so graceful and quick that her eyes barely caught it. She saw him lean down, and she felt his hands under her shoulders as his strong arms lifted her and placed her in front of him, one arm holding her firmly in place while the other caught in the stallion's mane and assumed control.

Elsbeth leaned back against Alex as she had refused to do earlier. She was too tired to think. He was the only reality now.

Even in her spent state, she realized she had apparently gone around in circles. Soon they were back at the hut, and she felt herself lifted down, then once more gathered in strong arms and carried inside. Sometime while she was asleep during the afternoon, he had replaced the rushes and now he set her down gently on them. Wood was near the fireplace, and he used a flint to ignite it. Soon the hut was filled with warming flames, and she moved closer to the hearth.

Elsbeth looked up at the Englishman who had caused such havoc in her life and heart. His face was outlined against the flames, the strength of every feature like a stone carving. His jaw was set, and his mouth grim as he stared into the fire as if mesmerized by it.

Elsbeth looked down at her wet, mud-caked gown and knew her face must be similarly painted. Her hand went to her hair, and it, too, was thick with drying dirt. She must look disgusting. He, also, was dripping wet from the hard rain, and she knew neither of them had any other clothes.

Dear God, what had she done?

She wanted to disappear into nothingness as she watched—much like an insect drawn to fire before being consumed in it—the man who had become the center of her world. She saw a muscle move in his hard sculpted cheek, and knew he was exercising masterful control of some violent emotion.

Rage against her? She wondered why she felt no fear, only a terrible hollow place where her heart was. He would not hurt her, she knew, but her mind told her he must despise her. She had kidnapped and imprisoned him under harsh conditions. She had reviled him and run from him.

And in return, he had saved her life at the risk of his own. He had offered a Carey's life for that of a Ker. If he had made one mistake, if his wrist had lost its hold, they would both now be dead in the bog.

Shame washed through her. Deep and profound. She had sensed from the beginning that there was something inherently decent about this Englishman, this Carey, yet she had not let herself believe it. She had wanted to hold on to her hate.

A tear made a muddy trail through the dirt on her face just as he turned to her, and she thought to brush it away. But before she could move her arm, he was kneeling next to her, his finger trailing the path the tear had taken, his mouth working jaggedly, and his own eyes suspiciously wet.

But he said nothing. Instead he moved to where a blanket lay on the rushes, and picked it up, handing it to her. Elsbeth wondered where it had come from, perhaps the back of the horse from the smell of it. The warmth was welcome nonetheless as she wrapped it around her.

He shook his head. "Take off your gown," he said shortly, his mouth growing grimmer as he saw her eyes open wide. "Don't worry, Lady Elsbeth," he added. "I'll wait outside. But you'll catch a fever if you don't rid yourself of those wet garments."

Without another word, he turned and opened the door. Elsbeth could see the rain fall in great large drops.

"Don't go," she cried out, the words coming without thought.

He stopped, his back straightening, his hand hesitating on the door. "I have to see to Demon," he said, then disappeared into the rain, leaving Elsbeth to stare miserably after him.

She did, however, as he told her. Her hands fumbled on the ties, but she eventually undid them, and stepped from the now ruined gown. She wrapped herself in the blanket, huddling near the fire in abject misery. She worried desperately about him in the rain, even as she wondered how deeply she had come to care about the man she had abducted. She recalled that first interview, his brash arrogance despite his bound hands, and later the deep wounds to his spirit revealed in his ravings during his illness.

He had called for Nadine. Who was Nadine? The thought that he might love another woman was an agonizing one. When did it become so?

Almost from the beginning, she realized. He had touched her in some way since that first meeting, since those enigmatic gray eyes had examined her so thoroughly, since his mouth had first curved in that curious half smile.

Dear God, I love him. It was a shattering observation.

She could not let him know it. She would not. She huddled into the blanket near the fire, and willed herself to sleep, knowing that her slumber would be filled with the sound and sight of the one man in the world she wanted and could never have.

She woke to the sound of voices, but she kept her eyes closed. They were near...those voices. Probably just outside the door. One was the deep, husky seductive voice that had become so familiar. The other belonged to the English borderer, David Garrick.

"I brought quill and parchment, some fur robes and blankets. Judith sent bread, cheese and meat."

"My brother?"

"In a rage, although no one guesses why. He must have had word from his man in the Ker clan."

"He does not suspect you?"

"Nay. He warned us all of bandits, said to kill at the slightest movement in the woods. Simon is gone most of the time, looking for you, I suspect."

"And where did you say you were going?"

"Hunting. I'll need to find a deer on the way back."

Elsbeth listened with interest as she continued to feign sleep.

"How is your lady?" Garrick asked Huntington.

There was a hesitation before she heard Alex's voice. "She tried to run away last eve and almost died in the bog."

"Can you keep her here?" There was concern in Garrick's voice.

"I can, but I will not. She will try again to escape. I will not have her death on my conscience."

She listened to the sound of restless boots against leaves, then the voices resumed, lower than before.

Elsbeth quickly got to her feet and moved to the door, placing her ear near the crack.

She heard David Garrick's voice again. "She's very comely... for a Scot."

Elsbeth waited for Lord Huntington's answer. "Aye," he said mildly.

"What are you going to do?"

"See that she gets back safely."

There was another long pause. "Are you sure, m'lord? You agreed we need her to trap your brother."

The softness in Elsbeth grew hard, then shattered. She was being used again.

"No," she heard Lord Huntington say. "I will not ask her, not now. She thinks only ill of me, and I'll not put her in any more danger. The Careys have done enough to her clan. I've done enough to her." Elsbeth could hear the pain in his voice, and her heart started beating again.

"There is no other way."

"I'll find one."

"What will you do with her?"

"See her safely to someone who can return her."

"M'lord—"

"Alex," she heard the earl insist, as he had with her.

"Alex, are you sure—"

"I'll not stand behind a woman, Davey."

The English borderer's voice came slow and lazy. "Too bad she's a Scot. And a Ker."

There was a long silence before she heard Lord Huntington's voice again. "Mayhap there is still some way we can end all this."

"M'lord . . ."

"I know, Davey. 'Tis doubtful. And first I have to deal with my brother."

"And the Ker mischief maker?"

"She'll believe nothing against a Ker now, especially from me."

"If you let her go, she will never know."

"I won't hold her against her will, Davey," Elsbeth heard Lord Huntington repeat. "I know how terrible it can be. I'll not subject her to it."

"How much longer will you stay here?"

"I don't know. Long enough to give my brother apoplexy, perhaps. Lead him to make a mistake. He will have to continue meeting with the Ker traitor—he has too much at stake now. They both do."

"Why not take a trip to London?"

"'Tis possible." Alexander's voice was low, thoughtful. "I cannot charge my brother without proof, but it might be wise to let Northumberland know what mischief is brewing on the border. And I want to prevent John from using me as an excuse to invade Scotland. I'll not have anything happen to the Kers."

"They would have killed you easily enough."

"And with reason. I can fault them not for wanting payment for Carey sins." He laughed, and there was so much bitterness in his voice that Elsbeth ached for him. "At least the Ker hatred is honest. Not like my brother's."

"They don't know you, m'lord."

"Nor do they want to. I'm a Carey and nothing else matters."

"It's been that way for generations," David said gently. "No one man can change it."

"I'm just so bloody tired of it all. Hate begets hate and violence more violence." All the arrogance was gone from his voice, and Elsbeth heard the deep weariness in it. If she hadn't believed his intentions before, she did now.

She heard the voices grow louder as the men moved nearer the door, and she quickly ran back to the rushes and lay down. She could almost feel their eyes on her, and it was all she could do to remain motionless. Her thoughts were in turmoil, and she could scarcely believe what she had heard. Her arrogant Englishman, her detested Carey, worried more about her family than about himself.

She heard them say farewell, and noted the affection in each voice. When the hoofbeats faded away, she let her eyes open slowly and found the Carey sitting opposite her, his eyes intent on her face. He smiled, as if taking pleasure in the very act of watching her wake.

She kept the blanket wrapped tightly around her. Her dress had been spread on the floor, but it was black with mud and still looked damp.

Lord Huntington, on the other hand, was dressed in dark leather trousers and the rough wool shirt of a woodsman. He looked rugged and dangerous, nothing like the lord he was.

"I'm hungry, my lord. Do you intend to starve me, too?" she asked dryly.

His somber gray eyes lightened, and it was as if someone had added flecks of dancing silver to them.

"Nay. But I think you might wish to dress first."

She looked at her dress with distaste.

He grinned. "Davey brought one of his wife's gowns for you. He thought you might need one after that all-night ride. He did not know how much."

Alex disappeared out the door, returning in a moment with a simple but clean gown. "Thank you," she said, a little shyly, wishing something could be done about her hair and face. Perhaps later.

"Do you need help?"

She flushed at the thought of his assistance. To feel his fingers on her skin, to know his touch. The intensity of her want was frightening. "No," she finally managed.

He regarded her gravely for a moment, then stepped outside without another word.

When she was finally clothed, she tore a piece of material from her ruined gown and wiped her face, hoping she was scraping off at least some of the muddy layers. She could hear her stomach rumbling and she couldn't remember when she had last eaten. She slowly opened the door and went out into a day honored by cloudless blue skies and a warm sun that was already heading downward and spreading a cinnamon glow over the west. She had slept well into the afternoon, then.

She basked in warmth for a moment before moving to where Lord Huntington had made a bench out of a fallen tree and spread food over a blanket on the ground.

With a slight smile, he bowed royally and offered her a hand to help her sit. "I fear it's not quite what you're accustomed to."

She felt awkward under his light apology. "I fed you none too well myself."

"Better, mayhap, than you believed."

Her eyes questioned him.

"It was a banquet compared to other meals I've been provided." The question grew deeper on her face, and he knew he had said more than he intended.

Suddenly it was as if a curtain had fallen over his eyes and his face looked lined and tired. She wondered if he had slept at all last night. And where?

She looked down at the food he had placed in front of her. There were two loaves of bread, some cheese and cold venison. She took a hunk of bread and ate greedily.

Alex also fingered a portion of bread but merely played with it. Instead he watched her eat with pleasure, and wondered what had made her suddenly so pliable. There was still a combative air about her, but her eyes had gentled and her mouth was relaxed.

He put up one knee and rested his arm on it, watching her every move, every flicker of expression in her eyes. Had she heard anything?

Of course not. She had been in the same place where she'd slept, with the same peaceful expression, when he returned to the hut after David left. Mayhap her rest, or the previous night's ordeal had mellowed her. Mayhap, even, his meager offering of food had softened her opinion of him. He was sure, however, the truce would not last long.

She stopped eating and looked up at him. "Why didn't you take me to Huntington?"

"I thought you would be far safer here, my lady," he said, resorting to formality for his own protection. "I didn't know you would head for the nearest bog." There was a wry inflection in his voice.

She shuddered, just thinking about the horror of the night before.

"Why don't you just have your brother arrested?"

"I have no proof against him."

"Do you need it?" Her eyes were grave.

"England is now a land of laws."

"Not for your brother, apparently," she said bitingly.

"I'm not—"

"Your brother," she finished for him, having heard the statement before. "But you are the earl and a friend of the most important man in England."

"The most important man today is often the man in the tower tomorrow," Alex observed dryly. "Look at Somerset, once the Lord Protector, now a prisoner in the Tower of London. Warwick is my friend, aye, and would help where he can, but there is little to do unless John shows himself. Warwick would not twist the law for me. It would be far too dangerous. For himself and for England."

She changed the subject, lifting her chin ever so slightly. "What will you do with me?"

"We seem irretrievably destined to copy each other." He grinned unexpectedly. "You kidnapped me and then helped me escape. I kidnapped you, and now I will help you escape. That way your clan will be none the wiser that you were the one who assisted me."

"That's not what you planned?"

"No," he said slowly. His hand moved to hers and touched it lightly. "But I find I cannot involve you in this dirty business."

"I have a debt of my own," she said quietly.

He raised an eyebrow in question.

"I have my traitor, too."

He nodded, relieved. It was the first time she had admitted it to him, although he knew she had considered the possibility before now.

"I must discover him," she continued.

Alex looked at her in surprise, and his lips tightened. All of a sudden, it appeared a very poor idea. He had just become resigned to the notion of being noble and honorable and letting her go.

"I'll not allow it," he grated.

She looked at him, stunned, then a giggle started deep in her throat as she considered the absurdity of the situation. She had never giggled in her life, but now she couldn't help it. They both had changed positions so completely that it was hard to know who wanted what.

His tight lips grew tighter, then started to crack around the edges. A chuckle escaped, then a full laugh, and she joined him. Somehow they had clasped each other's fingers and now they held tighter, doing what they had wanted to do for days.

The birds stopped their singing to listen to the laughter, the happy, gay, slightly mad laughter of two people who realized something brilliant was happening between them.

And each realized they didn't know how to stop it . . . even if they wanted to. And neither did.

Chapter Fourteen

The laughter died slowly.

Eyes met eyes, and wariness was gone.

His were clearer than she had ever seen them and glittering with feelings that both terrified and elated her.

Hers were golden with emotion and longing and warmth.

The magic that had always been there between the two of them exploded into feelings of want and need.

Elsbeth longed for his caress, his gentleness, the laughter in his eyes; she wanted to see his mouth curve into a smile more true than the one that so often hid his feelings.

He needed her trust, her understanding, her tenderness.

Her touch.

And yet neither could move. The feelings were too strong, too shattering in their consequences.

Her hand moved on his, as she wondered at its hard calloused strength that disguised so much gentleness. She traced images of love on it, of need, her eyes never leaving his, drowning in the whirling depths she saw there, watching as each movement of her hand created new silvery lights in them.

A muscle stood out in his jaw, and throbbed with the effort not to grab her and hold her tight to him. Part of him cautioned. Part of him rejoiced. He ached with need for her...yet he feared frightening her. He needed her to come to him.

And she did.

Like two lodestones, they drew near and their breath became intermingled, the sound of their heartbeats melding as they pounded in quickened rhythm. Elsbeth's hands moved to his face, to the lines so deep for one his age, and her fingertips sought to ease the pain engraved there. She could feel the compulsive movement of his muscles flexing in response to every soft caress, and then she knew his touch as a finger came to her lips and played seductively with them.

"Elsbeth." His voice was a soft groan, a desperate cry she could no longer resist. Her lips sought his, and met them, first in infinite tenderness as each explored the other's essence, their mouths asking and answering in age-old language, each reply more than satisfying to hungry hearts.

Her blood turned to warm honey, slow and languorous, as the kiss deepened, his lips still gentle but more demanding. Her arms went around his neck, her fingers catching and fondling a thick lock of slightly curling hair. Then her hands tightened around magnificent shoulders as Alex's caution flew and his arms pulled her to him.

His embrace, like his kiss, was at first careful, even hesitating, as if he feared rejection. His arms tightened and held her close to him, as if she were a precious object that would shatter if pressed too tightly.

It was his restraint, the barely leashed passion she sensed underlying it, that broke any reserve she had left. She needed his nearness as the earth needed sun and rain, or a bairn needed nurturing. She needed his energy and passion as well as his gentleness, the suppressed but simmering savagery as much as tenderness.

Alex recognized her need in the growing pressure of her hands, in her eyes, and everything within him exploded with desire long held in check. His mouth pressed harder, his tongue urging her lips to open to him. As she readily acquiesced she felt his tongue probe tentatively inside her mouth, and all the sensations she had felt before in his presence were beggared by the new ones, by the incessant clamoring of every sensitive part of her.

Nothing had prepared her for this . . . the sweet explosions, the overwhelming hunger, the excruciating tingling that reached to her toes. She could have fought anything but the aching sweetness of his mouth, of his tongue that ever so subtly aroused feelings in the core of her.

She felt the touch of his calloused fingers, yet they were not rough as she expected, and she wondered if it was because of the feather lightness with which he traced the outline of her ear and made whirling movements along the nape of her neck.

How could anything so hard, so strong, be so tender?

But she had little time to consider the puzzle, for now those same fingers were traveling down her back, leaving a trail of fever wherever they moved, and she had found that she liked the taste of his mouth very much, very much indeed.

Learning the delight of his hands on her body, her own experimented on his. As he had touched her earlobe, she now touched his, delighting in the gentle tremors that suddenly seemed to rack that so carefully controlled body. As he had, so did she then move to his neck, wondering if he was experiencing the same exquisite pain as she. A soft groan told her he was.

But still his touch remained gentle, cautious, restrained.

And she didn't want him gentle, cautious and restrained.

He withdrew his lips from hers and gazed at her as if in torment. His hand seized her chin and the other traced her cheekbone. "You are so lovely."

"You are so wary."

He smiled ruefully. "I have learned to be wary."

"Why?" She leaned against his chest and looked up at him, her great golden eyes gleaming with desire.

"Must you ask, little Scot? Last time I was careless I ended up slung over the back of a horse."

She flushed as she remembered.

His hand captured an auburn lock and twisted it, watching the gold catch in the sun.

He wanted her. More than he had ever wanted anything in his life. Yet there was too much between them to take her now. He could not stand the probability that she would eventually hate him for it.

He knew, at this moment, he could have her. Her eyes told him, her tense body told him. The thought was torment as he watched the changes in her mobile face: the caring, the wanting, the needing.

Most of all . . . the caring.

It was the one thing he craved most.

The one thing he could not reject.

His hand told her what his words could not. Once more it moved, not seductively this time, but with wonder, and that wonder was more paralyzing, more miraculous, than desire could ever be.

Everything in Elsbeth melted at his expression. It was grave, unlike any she had seen before. It was devoid of mockery, of secrets, but the sadness was still there, the sadness he usually hid under the sardonic mask. She had sensed it several times, but this was the first time he had allowed her a glimpse inside his soul.

She took his hand and put it to her mouth, her lips touching the hard calluses, the tough leathery skin, her eyes never leaving him as she felt the waves of emotion passing between them.

How could anyone feel this way... and go on existing? The world stopped for Elsbeth, held in a moment that was perfect.

She didn't care if he was English.

Or a Carey.

Or her captor.

He didn't care she was Scottish.

Or a Ker.

Or his captive.

They were captives of each other now, of the magic that bound them in tight cords, more unbreakable than any either had felt before.

Neither of them could say it at the moment, afraid they would break the spell, speed away something that was infinitely precious.

Instead he drew his arms around her, and she rested her head against his heart, one hand on his, the other resting on the oak-hard leg that bent lazily at the knee.

She wanted him desperately, wanted him to become a part of her in the most intimate, most tender way possible. And yet she understood his hesitation, and as much as her body and fragile heart ached for him now, it made him more dear to her. A scoundrel would have taken her. From whispers of other women, she knew most men would.

What kind of a man was he?

Exactly the opposite of what she had once thought. But she wondered if she would ever really know him.

Cradled in his arms, she watched the last golden hue of the sun disappear. "The sun in his splendor" as the Ker crest proclaimed, and never had she seen it quite as splendid. It was richer this evening, full of promise and an aching beauty that hurt while it pleasured.

The first dim stars of dusk appeared as the blue of the sky changed subtly to darker, more royal colors. A slice of moon hung as if on a string, and the evening stilled until she could hear his quiet breathing.

Finally, she shifted against him and looked up at his face. "What are you going to do?"

His hands tightened where they held her. "I've been caught in enough traps . . . it's time I set one myself."

"Your brother?"

"And others."

Elsbeth shivered at the hint of coldness in his voice. "My clansman?"

"Aye," he replied, "for neither of us is safe until we know his identity."

"He would not hurt me, whoever he is."

"He could well have aided in your father's death." There was tension in his voice as he waited for her response.

"I don't want to believe that," she admitted miserably.

His hand came up and touched her cheek. "But you do, don't you, love?" There was an inexorable note that told her he wouldn't accept any answer but her concession that such was true.

Her eyes cloudy, she nodded slowly.

He sighed, seeing the misery in her face. It was going to be hard for her, so very hard. He had never really loved his brother, but still the betrayal had stung him deeply. How much more it would hurt if he had believed in John, had loved him and trusted him.

That she had made the admission required a great deal of courage, and he hurt for her.

He gathered her even closer to him, feeling her shiver ever so slightly. "I'm going to send you home," he said again. He had avoided insisting upon it, hoping he could devise a way to keep her safe, but he could not. Just as dangerous, he knew, were his feelings for her; he could no longer control them. But the words were among the most difficult he had ever uttered. He didn't want to let her out of his sight, out of his touch, away from his protection. But she was in danger with him. If his brother discovered them, she would as readily be killed as himself. John would leave no witnesses, especially a Ker.

"No," she said simply.

He smiled at the adamant tone of her voice. There was so much determination in it.

"I would dearly love to keep you with me, my lady, but 'twould be safer for you on Ker land."

"It's a fine time for you to consider that, my lord," she retorted saucily, and was rewarded by a rich chuckle. Her hands itched to touch him again, to run fingers up and down his bare arms, and so she did, feeling him tense once more.

"Still..."

"I won't go," she said softly. "It's my duty, as well. It's my clan that's being betrayed."

"You will go," he insisted stubbornly.

"How?" she retorted. "You can't near the border without risk, and I won't go on my own."

"You would stay here with me? Willingly?" Despite their harmony of the past few hours, there was a note of bafflement in his voice. As if he couldn't believe she really wanted this, really wanted him.

"Odd, isn't it?" She grinned.

"Most," he agreed, but something in him sang at her words. He looked over at the rough hut. It was no place for a lady, no place for Elsbeth, but the warmth of her voice, his need for her presence was overwhelming. He did not want to send her back, not to a traitor who might be dangerous to her. Yet it was not safe here, either.

The roots of an idea took hold. The longer the two of them were missing, the more desperate their two traitors would become...and the more likely to make a mistake. As long as the Kers weren't certain of Elsbeth's whereabouts or safety, they wouldn't attack Huntington. Nor, he believed, could his brother make a move against the Kers as long as he, Alex, was missing.

"How would you like to go to London?" he said suddenly.

Elsbeth hesitated. The thought of London, of being in the midst of Englishmen, was not an appealing one. She had been raised to distrust them, to hate them, and even this most unusual Englishman did little to change her overall view of his countrymen. Yet as she looked up at him, at the face that was becoming increasingly important to her, she knew she would do almost anything to stay with him.

It no longer struck her as strange or disloyal that she trusted him more at the moment than she trusted her own clan. He had saved her life last night. He wanted to protect her people as well as his own. He was a strange, puzzling man, full of contradictions and mystery, but now she knew there were few better men.

"Why?" she asked. "Why can't we stay here?"

"You are not safe here," he said slowly. "And I think I can best ensure the safety of your clan in London. If anything happens to me, he'll know it lies at my brother's door, not yours. He can provide protection that I can't."

"Northumberland?"

"Aye," he said. "He should know the whole tale."

"Why can't David Garrick go?"

He sighed. In addition to the danger here for her, for them both, he knew he could never keep away from her in this isolation. At least on the road, and at Northumberland's properties, there would be people, distractions. Dear God, he needed some distractions.

"It's London or back to your land," he said, the gentle touch of his hand belying the sternness of his voice and eyes.

Slowly she nodded her head, her hazel eyes grave and trusting.

Alex closed his eyes against the waves of feeling assaulting him. There was no more question whether he loved her. He did. So much so the pain was agonizing. He wondered if he could ever make things right, make it possible for them to live and love in peace. If she *did* love him . . .

She needed him now, needed him to find the traitor to her clan. When that was over, could she overcome the centuries of hate between their countries and families? It seemed too much to hope for, particularly since his expectations in past years had been narrowed considerably. He was afraid to hope anymore, to plan, for fate had a way of intervening.

Nadine. The picture in his mind was fuzzy now, and he despised himself for it. Elsbeth and Nadine had much in common: courage, determination, great loyalty to their people.

Remember what happened to Nadine! The image of flames clouded his mind, and he was filled with terrible fear for Elsbeth. He couldn't let anything happen to her, too.

He moved away from her, as if his touch condemned her. He saw the surprised hurt in her eyes as she sought to understand his quick change of mood.

"My lord?" she said tentatively, but her chin jutted upward in a touching gesture that was becoming increasingly engaging to him. He loved her spirit.

He looked down at her, his grim expression softening ever so slightly. He knelt and touched her cheek. "I don't ever want to see you hurt."

There was such wistful intensity, such loneliness in his face and voice, that Elsbeth knew he had suffered great hurt in the past, that he was desperately afraid it would happen again. If only she knew what . . . and why.

"Who is Nadine?" she asked, unable to bite back the question.

His brow furrowed at the question, his eyes darkening almost to black.

"When you had the fever, you cried out for Nadine," she continued slowly, feeling her heart twisting inside at his forbidding glare. But she had to know before she could give any more of her soul to him.

"Alex?"

It was the first time she had said his given name, and some of the terrible coldness in him seeped out.

"She was French," he said haltingly. "A very beautiful, very brave lady."

Was. That much registered in Elsbeth's consciousness, which was filling with pain of its own at his words. That he had loved

Nadine was obvious. She knew she was intruding on a private
grief, but now she could not stop. She had to know.

"What happened to her?"

His eyes turned to her, but she knew they were not seeing her.
There was something else in them, something terrible and faraway that he was seeing. "They burned her," he said. "They
burned her at the stake." His jaw worked compulsively, and
then he sprang to his feet and with great long strides disappeared into the woods.

Elsbeth stared after him, horror filling her, both for the unknown woman and for him. And for herself. Why had she insisted on knowing? Why had it happened? And where had Alex
been at the time? He had been gone for years, but no one had
known why or where. It had been assumed he was dead, and
the Kers had had no more interest, not until he so mysteriously
reappeared. All the questions pounded at her, yet she knew she
could ask no more. His agony was too deep for her to poke at
it again.

She felt a decided distaste for herself, for the questions she
had asked, for the hurt she had caused. And she felt her own
deep despair. He so obviously had loved the Frenchwoman. He
had called her beautiful and brave. How could she, Elsbeth,
ever compete with a memory as raw as the one she had just
glimpsed?

Elsbeth slowly wrapped up the remaining food. He had eaten
little, and she wondered if the reason were to save more for her.
Nothing would surprise her now. He was a man unlike any
other. Strength radiated from him, even as he showed tenderness and vulnerability, and grief.

But could he ever love her? Or would ghosts forever haunt
him?

Darkness fell, and still he didn't return. A cold wind once
more swept the hills, and she went inside the hut. It was dark
and gloomy, a fine setting for her own mood, but she thought
about Alex, and the need for a warm fire. She piled up the
wood and used the flint he had left to light it. But once the
flames caught and danced among the wood, she remembered
his words and had to look away from it. Did every fire remind

him of her, of Nadine? She wondered if she would ever look upon one again with quiet appreciative pleasure. She huddled in a corner, uncertain whether she had done the right thing in lighting it. Please come back, Alex. Please.

Alex prowled the woods restlessly, unable to force himself back to the cabin, to Elsbeth whom he wanted so badly, yet was afraid to claim for fear that she, too, might be taken from him.

And he didn't know, quite simply, if he could stay away from her.

It had been a strange relief, telling her about Nadine, as though release of the words also released some of the deep guilt and grief. He had told Warwick what had happened, but no one else, and had pledged the earl to silence. That part of his life had been too painful to share. If it had not been for John Knox, he doubted if he'd have endured.

What would Elsbeth Ker think if she knew he had spent years chained like a dog to oars, branded and beaten? It had taken months for the scars on his wrists and ankles to thin to the small, nearly invisible lines that still reminded him of those years. There were similar lines on his back.

He had believed many times that Henri and Nadine were the lucky ones.

"Condemned to life in the galleys." It had seemed a reprieve at the time, but he quickly had learned the harshness of the sentence. Not to see the sun, or know the simple pleasure of being clean or stretching out in sleep. He could still smell the stench of bodies, of sweat, and of fear and death. He could still hear the sizzle of his own skin as a branding iron marked him forever a criminal. And all the time the image of Nadine's calm face had been with him.

A surgeon of Warwick's had removed the brand, had cut away the mark from his chest. But it still remained in his soul, in his mind. Just as had Nadine's face.

Until recently. Until the stubborn, proud face of a Scotswoman started to cause it to blur. And he didn't know if he was ready for it, whether he was ready to risk himself . . . or her.

He leaned against a tree, still damp with last night's rain, and wondered whether this was another chance . . . or another hell.

Elsbeth didn't know how long he had been gone. She only heard the creak of the door and the soft sound of boots on rushes. The fire had died to a few embers, and from her corner she watched as he heaped wood upon it until it blazed brightly once more. He turned, looking for her, his eyes moving through the dim light until they fastened on her.

He smiled crookedly, that half smile that said so little, when he found her awake. He went over to her and sat beside her, noticing the blankets unused beside her.

Without a word, he held his arms open and she slipped inside them, knowing a quiet, almost boundless joy that was new to her. He had come back to her, and she could live with his mysteries and his ghosts as long as he was near. Her body fit into his, not with passion now, but with a sweet need to have him next to her, to give him comfort as well as take it. Her heart swelled to near explosion as she reveled in his embrace... strong, tender, aching. She could feel his need.

Her lips bent to his, and told him in so many ways that he was no longer alone.

It was the two of them now. The two of them against the others.

Neither could sleep. Neither wanted to. This feeling was too rare, too precious to lose in oblivion. Nor at the moment was consummation important. Only this unity, this purity of understanding, knowledge and needs.

"I love you," Elsbeth whispered, needing to tell him of the great soaring feeling in her.

"Hmm," he murmured. "My love."

And the differences between them were no more.

Chapter Fifteen

❧❧❧

They rode side by side, on two ancient nags Alex was sure no one would wish to steal. His was swaybacked, and the ride anything but comfortable. He looked at his traveling companion, the urchin with the dirty face, and they exchanged soft smiles.

It had been this way, these two days on the road, mixing with merchants and soldiers and farmers, as they made their way toward London. The meeting of eyes, the touch of hands, the brief exchange of smiles made all the discomforts more than bearable.

They had left Huntington with humble clothing and enough coin to purchase the horses. David had brought the clothes and some food, and accompanied them near a small town. They had then walked until they found a horse for sale, then another. Neither of them was recognized.

Alex had been gone from England too long, and no one would suspect the roughly garbed peasant was a gentleman, much less an earl.

Elsbeth had left much of her hair on the floor of the hut, with some regret, but not enough to deter her. The most important things in her life now were Alexander Carey and bringing an end to the old feud between their families. Then and only then could she and Alex hope to have a future.

Neither had discussed such a possibility. It was as if each were afraid to do so, as if by mentioning it they would in some way destroy the sweet bond between them.

Garrick had not questioned Alex's decision to go to London. John Carey's fury had noticeably grown in the past several days, and Garrick thought it would not be long before the man threw caution to the winds and ordered all his troops to comb the woods.

So this was a brief respite for Elsbeth, an adventure made many times more wonderful by the presence of the man she had once thought she hated. She looked at him now, and her heart sang, for his mouth was relaxed and his eyes merry, and he was even humming a funny little song. He had appeared to throw off at least some of his devils that night after her rescue, and though a curtain still sometimes fell over his face, he was more free than she had ever seen him.

Each night they had found some crude shelter, usually in the barn of an inn, and went to sleep in each other's arms after a meal of dubious origin. But they, or rather Alex, carefully held back from more than that. Until things were settled, he would not risk leaving her with child.

She loved him more each minute, each hour, each day. As always, she wished he would say more about himself, how he had come to be so different from the other Careys she had reviled all her life. She loved the possessive look of his eyes on her, and even the brief flashes of arrogance that brought back those first meetings. It appeared, she realized now, when he was cornered, or felt powerless over a situation. The little twisted half smile was more a real one now, full and somehow touchingly wonderful because she had come to realize how rare it was.

Sometimes she even wished he were her captive again, so she could lock them both in, and lock the world out, so that there would be no reminders of duty and responsibilities and debts to be paid.

They begged shelter that night at a poor farm and gave a small coin for bread and cheese. He gave her a wry grin as they settled for the night in some hay.

"I promise better fare tomorrow," he said.

"We will be at Northumberland's then?"

"By noon."

Elsbeth couldn't help a small shiver. Everything depended so much on the English duke. Perhaps the future of her clan. And she didn't trust the English; she wondered if she ever would—with the possible exception of Alex Carey, earl of Huntington.

As always he sensed her thoughts. "Many don't like him," he said. "He's powerful and he's made his share of enemies, but he brought me back to life. I have no better friend."

Her eyes opened wide. "How?"

There was a long silence, one that she now recognized well. It came whenever she sought entrance into his past. Once more she felt the tension in him and thought he would not answer. She wasn't quite sure he was ready, yet she needed reassurance. His hand played with one of her curls, now shortened but still as lovely to him.

"I was a galley slave in France," he finally said, each word carrying a burden of its own. He ignored her soft gasp, and continued. "When Warwick found out, he arranged for my release. I was more dead than alive, I'm afraid, and would have died shortly were it not for him. He saw that I was nursed back to health."

She knew little about the galleys, and could only imagine the horrors of slavery, especially for a man as proud as Huntington. Dear merciful God but what she had done to him! Only now did she realize how terrible her imprisonment of him must have been. Her hand reached for his hand and held it tightly.

"How long?"

"Nearly four years. Four years of the worst hell anyone could endure," he added. "If Warwick hadn't . . ." He didn't finish the sentence but she could in her mind.

"I would think you would have hated me," she said softly.

"Mayhap I did for a while," he replied thoughtfully. His voice suddenly lightened. "But you're very difficult to hate. You were so angry with me that your eyes glowed, and your chin jutted admirably."

"I was not as fearsome as I thought?" she asked regretfully.

"You could never be fearsome, little love," he said with a great deal of tenderness.

"That's most disappointing," Elsbeth observed. "I was put out with you. You did not act as a captive should."

"Nor did you, running straight into a bog."

She winced at the reminder. "I fear neither of us make good prisoners."

"Nay," he agreed, but so quietly she knew he was thinking of the other time.

She looked up at him, her eyes accustomed to the darkness, and saw the strained muscles in his face. "Will you tell me about it?"

"There's naught to tell, love. Endless days, empty stomachs, aching bodies." He couldn't tell her about the countless humiliations, the branding, the chains, the beatings. "It's over now and I prefer not to think of it."

His tone of voice closed the subject, but it was another piece of her puzzle. Nadine. The galleys. How many more secrets were there? She was sure she hadn't heard them all. He had been gone many more than four years.

She lifted her head and nibbled his lips, thinking to take his mind from the past...and even the future. There was only these moments, these glorious moments of sharing that she would fix in her own mind. She feared tomorrow. She didn't want the intrusion of an outsider, particularly an English outsider. He would not approve, she knew that. Neither the English nor Scots approved of intermarriage. And Alex was an earl, while she was naught but a lesser laird's daughter. This was all a dream and she would awake on the morrow to find it so.

She could feel his body hardening, feel the passion grow and equal her own as his lips clamped down on hers with hard honest need. He had been careful these past few days, but she sensed he felt as she did, that the wonder of these days might explode in harsh reality on the morrow.

His tongue entered her mouth, and put her to the torch, the slightest movement firing new blazes until the burning agonizing want in her was unbearable. She cried out and stiffened in his arms, her whole body moving toward his with a purpose she still didn't quite understand.

"Ah, love," he murmured, the words a love song as his lips moved from her mouth to her ears, and resumed the soft sweet seduction of her senses. The memories, the reminder of hell, made her softness heaven, and he reveled in it, unable to take his hands from the silk of her skin and the fine suppleness of her body.

Her great golden eyes beseeched him, though he realized she wasn't yet fully aware of the goal she sought. Principle, honor and good sense warred with his unendurable need for her, for her softness and the glow of love that made even this dark shelter a paradise.

How could he live without her now?

And yet the fear was there, always there, that she would be taken from him, brutally, and he knew he could not bear a loss like the other, the guilt that lingered because he survived and Nadine did not. Was he also bringing disaster to Elsbeth?

His life, currently, was not worth much, not until he solved the problem of John. And he realized, mayhap better than Elsbeth, the trouble he would bring her if she were to bear a Carey bastard.

He would not, could not, do that to her.

She saw the worried frown, the furrowed brow, and her hand went against his cheek, soothing it, teasing it, loving it. His mouth turned back to hers and kissed it lightly, meaning to do no more than that, but she would not let it go that way. Her tongue played with his lips until they opened and then it darted inside his mouth. He had only a second to appreciate what an apt pupil she was until flames made ashes of his conscience. The kiss deepened, need sharpening until they were both shaking with the intensity of the passion that streaked between them like lightning on a warm summer night.

Their bodies met and strained against the clothes as the kiss became an inferno of madness, of emotional as well as physical want. Alex felt he was on top of a precipice, ready to dive off into deceptively soft clouds.

"Dear God, you don't know what you're doing...."

Elsbeth was beyond caring about consequences, or the future, or even tomorrow. Her heart was pounding altogether too loudly to hear naught but its incessant demanding beat.

"I know I love you," she whispered.

"I'm a Carey...."

His voice, part bitter, part wry, made her look up at him. "A Carey, an Englishman," she reaffirmed slowly, each word torn from her soul.

"But your clan will not be so forgiving."

She wanted to say she didn't care, but she did. Since a small bairn, she had always been taught that the clan came first ... first ... first.

He smiled, the old enigmatic smile that she now knew he used to hide his deepest emotions. "We can't run from it, either of us. Not you from your clan, nor me from Huntington."

She felt fear nibbling at her, not for herself but for him. "Don't go back," she suddenly pleaded.

"And where would I go, little Scot? Certainly not to Ker land."

"We can marry—" she started desperately.

"And I to be your consort, among people who hate me? You also would grow to hate me, my love."

"Never."

"It is of no matter. I have had enough taken from me. I'll not give up my birthright, nor the people who deserve more than they've received from my family."

"Do you think they care?" Her cry was desperate now.

"Not now. They've been given no reason for dreams or hopes."

"Then why?"

"Because I have some of my own, Elsbeth, lovely Elsbeth. I truly will have nothing if I let them go."

"You would have me," she replied in a stubborn voice.

"No. You would have me." There was a quiet pain in his voice. "When I was a slave, I could only hope for enough bread to give me strength to work. There was no more expectation than that, no more future. Yet something drove me on, something more than the whip. I didn't know what it was, Elsbeth, until I reached England and learned I was heir to Huntington. And I knew I could do things I'd only dreamed of since a lad. I cannot forget it now."

Elsbeth was caught up in his intensity, in the force of his words. Her hand clutched his, knowing that his dream might take him from her.

He looked down, and his face softened. "When this is over...could you leave your clan?"

It was a question she had asked herself over and over again. "I—I—don't know."

His hard hand, infinitely more dear to her now that she knew the reasons why it was so, rubbed her chin thoughtfully. Her hazel eyes were flecked with gold and her mouth swollen and berry red from his kiss. "You are so lovely, my lady," he said.

"You are so bonny, my lord," she returned wistfully, thinking he was in so many ways. How could she have ever thought otherwise?

A chuckle rose from deep in his chest. "I've been called many things, my lady, but never bonny."

She wished she could laugh with him, but just looking at him hurt too much. She wanted him so very, very badly and he had never seemed so distant. Instead, she smiled weakly, and buried her head against his chest, finally pretending a sleep that wouldn't come.

As Elsbeth had expected, the estate of John Dudley, earl of Warwick and duke of Northumberland, was grander than anything she had ever seen. She felt like a beggar riding to the massive stone house on a swaybacked horse.

Yet from the moment they sighted the grand edifice, Alex had shed his guise. Despite his near rags, his back had straightened and his carriage was as proud as any noble's. He led the way to the stable where a groom grinned when he looked beyond the worn leather jerkin and rough cap.

"Milord." He looked with dismay at Alex's mount. "Demon?"

"Well cared for, Richie." He turned to Elsbeth, who now as much as ever looked the urchin lad. "Richie helped me train Demon. A finer groom you'll never meet."

Elsbeth ducked her head, but couldn't miss the broad proud smile of the man. Evidently, Alex Carey had worked his peculiar form of magic on him also.

"Will you do a boon, Richie?" he asked now.

"Aye, milord, anything."

"Do not spread word of my arrival—"

"Not even—" There was a sparkle in the groom's eye that Elsbeth did not like at all.

"Not even anyone," Alex said with a small grin that was undeniably mischievous.

Elsbeth felt a pull at her heart. Could it be a woman? She thought of how she must appear, and felt a coldness run through her.

"Is the duke in residence?"

"Aye, but he's at court now."

Alex grinned again. "Do you believe Smithwyck will allow me entrance?"

Richie eyed him dubiously. "Ye might be givin' 'im apoplexy," the groom said with a wry grin.

"We might soon be back then and beg a foot of hay."

Richie eyed the earl's companion with a practiced eye. "'E seems not brawn enough to be of worth."

"Oh, he's of unquestioned worth," Alex said, his mouth lapsing into its familiar half smile. "See that those nags are fed well."

Richie's mouth turned down, censure entering his eyes as he considered the sacrilege of these animals mingling with the duke's fine horseflesh. "Aye, milord," he said reluctantly.

Alex's half smile became a whole grin, full and as charming as any Elsbeth had seen, and she saw the groom melt under it before they turned to the great house.

She hesitated, and felt his arm go around her in assurance. "He only bites Catholics," Alex said.

"How do you know I'm not Catholic?"

Few Scots on the border were still Catholic, although most of the highlanders were. "Are you?" he asked simply.

"Does it matter?"

"Only if it matters to you," he said. "I believe everyone has a right to think as he wishes."

It was a unique sentiment to her. Both Protestants and Catholics had been burned in Scotland and England for their beliefs. Then she remembered nights earlier when he had told her about the mysterious Nadine. She had died at the stake. In

France. Which meant she must have been a Protestant. A martyred one.

She bit her lip. How could she compete with a dead woman? When she found the courage to look back up at him, he was staring at a horseman riding in, his mouth once more curved into a smile.

Elsbeth knew from the richness of the man's clothes that he must be Northumberland, and she felt shivers as he rode closer and she could make out his features. She had rarely seen such coldness in a face. She felt chilled at its icy composure as the horseman neared and regarded both of them haughtily. But then a slow smile developed, warming a face that Elsbeth thought seconds earlier could never be warm.

"Huntington? What in the devil . . ."

The duke's eyes went to Elsbeth, weighing her carefully and obviously finding her wanting. His eyebrows arched in question.

"Lady Elsbeth Ker," Alex said with a bow that would have done a practiced court dandy justice. Somehow she had not expected it of Alex.

She blushed as the duke's eyes rapidly returned to her, this time regarding her more carefully.

"Ker, you said?" Northumberland finally asked. "The Scottish Kers?"

"Aye, your grace"

The eyebrows rose higher. "I see a story here."

"And a problem, your grace."

"And what else, my dear Alex, do you ever bring here?"

"A challenge, your grace. Always a challenge."

For the second time, Northumberland granted them a brief smile. "Always," he agreed. His gaze once more wandered over the pair of them, taking in the rough clothes, the dirt smudges, the tired faces.

"But first, a bath. And some clothes."

"They would be most welcome, your grace," Alex replied, "but we'd rather no one knew we are here."

"Richie?"

"He will be silent."

"My hunting lodge, then," Northumberland said. "The servants there can be trusted."

Alex had been there. It was perfect. He bowed again. "I'm grateful."

The duke ignored the thanks and was once more studying Elsbeth carefully. He waved his hand, finally, in dismissal. "Tell Richie to give you two decent horses. I'll be there in the morning. There's a meeting tonight."

Alex merely nodded, and Elsbeth realized the two men understood each other completely.

The travelers climbed into their saddles again, this time on much more respectable horses, and Alex, now with a grim look fastened in place, pushed his mount into a fast trot.

Alex knew the hunting lodge well. He had recuperated there much of the time after his release. It was comfortable, well but simply staffed and isolated.

He looked over at Elsbeth. He had been barely able to keep even the smallest vestige of control in the past few days. He wanted her so, and the duke's hunting lodge was the ideal place for a tryst. It was a place meant for secrets and plots.

Alex wondered briefly if Mary was still there. Mary, a maid-servant, who had nursed him and then ... But the memory of Nadine had interfered, and he had found himself incapable of making love.

It was a problem, he knew, that no longer existed, not the way his blood had surged in the past days each time he looked at the Lady Ker. Four years ... five. He couldn't remember the last time he had buried himself in a woman. Nadine had been a virgin, and for some reason, mayhap because there had not been the urgency that existed between him and Elsbeth, he had never tried to seduce Nadine.

Why then could he think of little else with Elsbeth?

Because Nadine had seemed more like a saint to him, an untouchable figure to be admired, even worshiped. But not loved in human ways ...

And Elsbeth was fully and completely a woman—with all a woman's passions.

Because he loved Elsbeth.

And suddenly he knew. Although he had loved Nadine, it had never been in the soul-shattering way he was coming to love his Scottish neighbor.

He stopped his horse, watching her do the same, then he leaned over, his hand drawing her face close to his, and he kissed her with passion that had been stored for years and stoked nearly to explosion in the past weeks.

His eyes went from looking puzzled to joyful, and Elsbeth realized that part of him was finally released from chains that had still held him in some mysterious grip.

They reached the lodge, hidden in a forest, in late afternoon, and Elsbeth thought it was much more wonderful than the grand manor they had left. It was of wood and stone, warm and welcoming.

Their horses were taken from them and they mounted the steps as the door was thrown open. A tall thin man, dressed in Northumberland's livery, welcomed them.

"My lord." He bowed with supreme dignity, ignoring Alex's and Elsbeth's bedraggled appearance as if seeing Alex thus were an everyday occurrence.

"Stanson." Alex grinned in that charming manner that seemed to overwhelm everyone it touched. "This is Lady Elsbeth Ker. I think we both need baths, and perhaps you can find some more . . . suitable clothes for her."

The servant nodded. "It will be done. I shall put you in your old room." It was part statement, part question, and Alex nodded.

"And Lady Ker?"

"A room of her own, Stanson."

Nothing in Stanson's face indicated curiosity or even interest other than apparent affection for Lord Huntington. He nodded and called a maid. Alex was relieved to note it was not Mary but another girl, young and smiling.

"Take my lady to the blue chamber."

The girl curtsied before Elsbeth, again no curiosity evident. The staff was indeed well trained, Alex thought with amusement.

But he had little time to think about it, for he was being led to his previous chamber on the second floor and he knew a bath would be ready quickly. In disgust, he fingered his week's growth of beard and noted the layers of dirt on his hands. How good it would feel to be clean again!

He walked to the window and looked out over the woods. How many times he had stood thus in the three months he had stayed here, trying to make sense of all that had happened, slowly feeling the life seep back into his body and mind. He would forever be grateful to Northumberland, although he recognized the man's ruthlessness to all but those who claimed close friendship.

Alex had never known why they became friends. Mayhap because Alex was the one person who had never asked anything of the earl of Warwick, who later became the duke of Northumberland. They had met at court and shared an interest in horses. Warwick had mentioned he had a horse no one could tame, and Alex accepted the challenge. He spent weeks at Warwick's London estate, gradually breaking the horse, and Warwick and he grew close during long nights of conversation and drink. Perhaps Warwick had become a surrogate father to him. He recognized in the man an obsession with both ambition and power, and he knew that his own lack of both made him one of the few men Warwick felt he could trust.

There was a further binding when Nadine and her father came to Warwick. Warwick had a deep distrust and dislike of the Catholic church, and the task of rescuing persecuted Protestants from its clutches was an intriguing one to him. Alex had not shared that distrust and dislike, but the adventure, the excitement and the romance of spiriting Protestants away from their oppressors had appealed to a nature hungry to accomplish something. That Nadine was quite beautiful was, he admitted, a contributing factor. So then he and Warwick had shared something more.

It hadn't been until his release from the galleys that he learned Warwick had become the most important man in England, duke of Northumberland and Lord President of the Council—that he alone had personally arranged Alex's release as part of a bargain that returned the port of Boulogne to France. Warwick, who had thought Alex dead, had been told by John Knox of Alex's whereabouts.

It was one of Warwick's ships that brought Alex home to England and it was Warwick who helped heal his mental as well as physical wounds. Warwick had found Demon and challenged Alex once more to tame the untamable, and in doing so he had revived a spirit nearly dead. Alex owed Warwick much.

Warwick. He had difficulty thinking of his friend as anything else—as, for instance, the duke of Northumberland. The man's position was a precarious one that he did not envy. Being powerful in the English court usually guaranteed a short life span....

Water was brought, pail upon pail of steaming water, and Alex stripped gratefully, slipped into the tub, felt the hot water soothe and cleanse him. He leaned back to his head, and thought of Elsbeth in a similar tub... just steps away. Beautiful, lively, loving Elsbeth.

His Elsbeth.

Elsbeth spent nearly an hour in the tub, washing and scrubbing and scraping days of dirt from her. When her skin was once more white and glowing, she washed her hair with the help of Sylvie, the young maid, who seemed childishly grateful to assist in any way. Then she sat happily as Sylvie brushed her hair dry.

"Your hair has wonderful color, my lady," the girl said, tactfully, ignoring its unfashionable collar length. Elsbeth had only briefly regretted the loss of her long tresses. There was no question that it had been necessary, and her head felt immeasurably lighter. She allowed Sylvie to play with her hair, and then, when given a mirror, she exclaimed with pleasure. The girl had pulled up the curly locks, giving Elsbeth's hair a look of fullness as ringlets twisted becomingly around her face.

She had already been supplied with a night robe and mantle, and now several dresses rested on her bed. She decided not to wonder where they came from. She finally selected a topaz velvet that she thought would complement her eyes. It was as rich a gown as she had ever worn.

Sylvie helped her into it, and fastened the hooks in the back, sighing with approval as the rich cloth gracefully draped the slender frame. "You are beautiful, my lady."

And Elsbeth felt beautiful. She knew she would sup with Alex tonight, and she felt an unaccustomed shyness. He had seen her only once in a fine gown, and that was not nearly as grand as the one she wore now. She wondered once more about the dead Nadine, and hoped that she herself, if not as beautiful as the French woman, was, at least, not woefully plain in comparison.

She thanked Sylvie, who bobbed eagerly, then she went to the window. The forest was much like that around the Ker holding, but lacking the hills she loved so well. A pang of homesickness struck her as she wondered about the clan, about Patrick and Ian, and Hugh. Had she been wrong in coming here? Should she have accepted Alex's offer to return her?

But those concerns, though they lay troubling at the back of her mind, paled as she heard the knock on her door, and the low sensuous sound of Alex Carey's voice.

Chapter Sixteen

"Elsbeth." His voice was low and questioning. There was a note of uncertainty in it.

She moved quickly to the door, her eyes catching his magnificence and locking on it.

Since her clan had taken him prisoner, she had seen him in many ways, but never quite like this.

His hair was, like hers, still damp from washing. Its dark tendrils curled only slightly despite an obvious attempt to tame their disarray. Clean shaven, each feature seemed more distinct, more marbled: the strong cheekbones, the firm mouth, the arrogant chin, the straight Roman nose.

He was wearing rich clothes, and they suited him well. The dark blue velvet doublet showed a hint of a light blue linen shirt, both shades giving an added cast to those fathomless gray eyes. Silver-blue hose revealed strongly muscled legs. A dagger, tucked into a leather belt, served to enhance the image of strength and power that seemed such an inherent part of him.

His eyes were ravishing her with the same intensity with which hers adored him. "I knew you were beautiful, madam," he said with a lazy sensual sweetness that made her blood turn to honey, "but not quite how much."

She flushed with pleasure, then teased, "You did not admire the boy with whom you rode?"

"Aye, very much, but the woman is even more entrancing. The color suits you well." He bowed, as she had seen him do before in mockery at the time he was captured, but this time it was in obvious tribute. Her heart trembled.

"'Tis time for supper," he said slowly, "although my eyes have feast enough."

She laughed merrily at his extravagant compliment. "Perhaps for you, my lord, but I am most hungry."

His eyes twinkled for a moment before he adopted a much abashed look. She had once thought his features harsh and sardonic, but now they seemed incredibly mobile and sensitive—now that he was hiding much less of himself.

"You wound me, my lady," he said with a curious quirk to his lips. "I thought I looked the fine lord."

"And you are," she said. "My stomach, however, is complaining that the sight of a bonny lord is not very satisfactory fodder."

"You have a most undiscerning stomach," Alex teased her. He offered her his arm. "His grace is well-known for his love of food. He has incurred the enmity of several nobles by stealing their cooks."

They were the only guests at the lodge and were seated with great courtesy at the end of a long table. It was covered with a rich cloth, and set with silver-rimmed wooden bowls, silver cups, silver spoons and steel knives. Within a wink of Alex and Elsbeth's arrival, a trencher was set in front of them.

Course after course appeared, and Elsbeth could only wonder if such abundance was always kept on hand for unexpected guests. Quail, roast mutton, crab and oysters were served. There was blankmanger, a paste of chicken blended with rice boiled in almond milk and seasoned with sugar, and montrews, a dish of meat pounded, mixed with bread crumbs, stock and eggs, then poached. There was a bowl of honey, and platters of fresh wild fruits and nuts.

One wine came, and then another, until Elsbeth felt warm and mellow and quite sated. When she thought she could eat and drink no more, the butler brought a spiced and sweetened wine and, with a discreet air, he left Alex and Elsbeth alone in contented silence.

She didn't know whether it was the wine, or the food, or the nearness of Alex, but here, in an English hunting lodge, in a country she had learned to hate, she felt unconscionably happy and protected. She tipped up her head to look at Alex and found him staring intently at her, a heat of a particularly sensuous nature making his eyes charcoal in color.

His arm went around her, and she leaned back in it, wondering at how natural the position seemed. They fitted together nicely, she thought, as she cuddled into an angle of his body and said quiet thanks to the butler for providing them a bench rather than two separate chairs.

Alex took a sugar wafer and tempted her mouth open with it, watching with amusement as little crumbs of pastry and sugar sprinkled her lips. He leaned down and tasted them.

His lips played on hers with a slow sensuality; he licked every vestige of crumbs before indulging an appetite of an entirely different nature. He could taste the sweet wine on her lips, and then her tongue as her mouth opened to his teasing, probing assault.

Her hand went up to his neck and played with the still-damp dark locks that curled boyishly there. She savored the rich essence of him, drinking in the clean spicy scent and feeling the velvet quality of his newly scraped cheeks. His breathing was erratic, and once more she felt his body tense and shiver in its iron control.

But she wasn't going to allow it, not any more. Her hand found its way to his ear, and traced tiny patterns around the lobe as her tongue trapped his and danced a dangerously daring game with it.

The wine, the warmth and beauty of a crackling fire, the rich smell of wood smoke mixed with the fervent taste of each other, came together in a wanton call that made them both powerless. She felt herself being lifted, and she knew his resistance, like hers days ago, had finally been breached. Her head went against his heart as strong powerful arms held her tightly against him. Together they mounted the stairs, unaware, uncaring of anyone else in the world.

He took her to his chamber, carefully shut the heavy door and set her on the fine feather mattress of the mammoth carved-oak bed. He hesitated as he stared down at her, at the glowing red fire in her hair, the smooth ivory perfection of her skin, the great golden eyes now glowing with love.

Alex felt the instantaneous reaction of his manhood to her, the swirling eddies of desire that did battle against his more sober judgment. Years of loneliness, of bitter pain and heartache, welled within, and he reached out to grab a piece of joy, of happiness, of a belonging that had always eluded him.

When he held out his hand to her, Elsbeth sensed the battle fought and the decision reached, but the agonized look on his face told her the judgment was not made without consequences or suffering.

Aching to erase the lingering doubts in his dark stormy eyes, she took his hand and with great gentleness guided him down to her, every touch, every look its own avowal of love and trust. And when their lips touched, both felt no little wonder at how tenderness and hunger could combine so sweetly and so passionately, as slow exquisite fires exploded into raging need.

Elsbeth felt the hooks of her gown being unfastened with deliciously agonizing deliberateness, as if wariness and caution still held Alex slightly at bay. She felt his breath, warm and tasting of wine, come faster, and she buried her head against his shoulder, drinking in the clean male scent of him. The tight clutches of her dress fell away, and then the corset and other undergarments, until she felt gloriously free.

The freedom lasted only seconds. His lips found her breasts and nuzzled first one and then the other until her nipples seemed as hard and hot as stones in the hearth. They tingled and ached, seeming to take on a life of their own, wanting to draw every acute sensation from the mouth that awakened so much.

When she thought she could stand no more, his mouth moved upward, kissing her throat, her mouth, the lobes of her ears until every nerve in her body was tingling and alive with wanting.

The velvet of his doublet rubbed against her bare skin, tickling and teasing and adding fuel to an already burning surface. She closed her eyes, drinking in all the new feelings, wondering how one body could feel so much pleasure, so much agony at once.

His hands ceased their movement with one last teasing stroke. She slowly opened her eyes, reluctant to leave the sensation-filled world he had created.

He was standing, his hands slowly releasing his own clothes while his eyes stayed on her. She couldn't quite read his expression. He so frequently seemed the observer, keeping all his thoughts thoroughly locked inside him. The doublet was gone, and then the linen shirt, and her eyes fastened on the chest that had become so familiar to her. Dark hair made an arrow downward, and his scar stood out vividly against his skin.

She watched, mesmerized by the grace of each movement, the slow deliberate progress of his hands as he continued disrobing, his mouth turned in the slight smile that defied interpretation. Although his shoulders and chest were heavily muscled, his waist and stomach were painfully lean. She remembered now how little he had actually eaten this evening, and she wished she had coaxed him into taking more.

His silver-blue hose made a mound on the floor and he stood there before her, everything about him tentative…as if he were hesitant how, if at all, he should proceed. Dark hair tumbled over his forehead and curled around the side of his face, and he looked much like a lad about to receive his first lesson in weaponry. The slight smile had disappeared, and his lips had firmed into a tight line as he let her see all there was to see of him.

Perhaps hoping, she thought sadly, that she would turn away. He did not want this. She knew it from their previous conversations. He did not think it wise or prudent or safe. Yet, like her, he could no more stay away than the moon could stop rising.

To the devil with prudence.

Elsbeth held out her hand, and his lopsided half smile appeared; this time she could identify it. Surrender. He accepted her invitation and lay down next to her, his hand tracing patterns on her skin, rekindling the flames that had roared so wildly moments earlier. He kissed her, and no longer was he tentative or hesitant; his lips were hungry and demanding, and she felt his body grow even harder next to her. She answered caress with caress, need with need and hunger with hunger until they were both mad with wanting, their bodies arching and straining against each other.

He slid on top of her, resting his strength on one elbow. His maleness teased and played with the tenderest part of her until she whimpered, as her body reached toward the sun, toward the splendor she knew was there. She felt him enter, and she quivered with uncontrollable need for him to reach deeper and deeper until their bodies fused into one.

She felt him hesitate, and there was a pressure, a straining inside her. "My love, I need..." she whispered desperately, wanting to tell him she was not afraid, that he shouldn't stop. She felt his body tremble, and then a stabbing pain seemed to tear her body in two. She couldn't stop the cry, but even as she made it, she was already feeling something else.

Waves of sensation washed through her. They were small at first, because of the pain, but they grew with each passing second, with each of his carefully controlled movements, until she felt part of a tidal surge moving with growing strength and fury toward some irresistible destination.

She knew when he lost that infuriating control. He groaned and his movements came rapidly, compulsively, as he joined her in a ride to the stars and beyond. Billows of pleasure kept her asking for more, and her legs instinctively wrapped around him, bringing him deeper and deeper inside her until she didn't know how she could stand the delights flooding her body, stretching from the core of her to the fingers pressed tightly against his corded back.

There was one last plunge and she realized exactly how much pleasure she could stand as shivers and aftershocks racked her body. She felt his own compulsive movements, and she held him tightly against her, wanting never to let him go, never to sever the glory of their joining.

"Dear God," he murmured. Then she knew joyously that this intense pleasure was also new to him. He might have bedded women before but, she knew, never like this.

He rolled over on his side, keeping her melded to him but taking his weight from her, his arms cradling her as if she were the most precious of objects.

Love welled in her, joining the remarkable waves of delights still running haphazardly through her. She had never felt so protected, so contented, so... wanted.

She hoped with all her soul that he was feeling the same extraordinary feelings. She risked a look at his face, afraid to find the reserved mask there, but it held an open look of wonder, of a quiet profound happiness that made her heart swell to bursting.

More than anything in the world she wanted to make him happy. It was a startling conclusion, when she considered it. Her own happiness seemed minor now. Nothing was as important as Alex Carey, earl of Huntington. Enemy of the Kers.

Enemy.

Love.

She wanted never to see the tender smile leave his face, nor the brightness fade from his eyes. She, Elsbeth Ker, had put it there. She would never take it away.

Her lips nuzzled his bare chest, nibbling at the tufts of dark hair that decorated the firm skin. He made a small rumbling noise, like the purr of a lion, she thought whimsically, after an especially tasty meal. Her hand went to his lips and traced their outline, then teased them as they tried to remain still before twisting with withheld laughter.

"You, my love, are a temptress without equal."

"And how would you know, my lord?" she asked with mock ferocity, "unless you've tried all the others."

He grinned wolfishly, yet there was a sweet tenderness in his eyes that inspired songs in her heart. "I would not dare answer that, my lady."

"Beast," she said lovingly.

"Witch," he replied affectionately.

"Knave," she challenged.

"Sorceress."

"Rogue," she accused.

"Circe," he rebutted.

She smiled contentedly as she thought of the sorceress who turned men into swine.

He grinned crookedly as he read her thought. "I think I just misspoke."

"Aye, my lord, but you'll find no dispute from me."

"An educated woman is like a viper's tongue."

"You would rather have me otherwise?"

"I would rather have you just as you are . . . every lovely, enchanting, tempting—"

But he could say no more, because her lips were on his, once more eager and wanting and loving.

Alex's blood quickened, and he wondered how his chest could hold the pounding of his heart. He had carefully restrained himself the first time, wanting desperately not to give her more pain than necessary. He had no such fear this time. He felt his manhood grow and harden, and this time he plunged into her warmth, knowing that their first joining was only a prelude to what awaited them.

Together they climbed, leaped and flew to worlds beyond any they had known, worlds full of fire, dreams, ecstasy and sharing, of sweetness and pain, of giving and taking, until rapture, grand and glorious and bold, exploded in one supreme heartstopping moment of time.

Morning came all too early for Elsbeth, who was fitted perfectly into Alex's hard curves and angles, her head resting on his arm.

But the shaft of light angling through the deep-set window told her it was much too late to get back to her room and preserve what reputation she had.

At the moment, the thought was a fleeting one. More important was the joy of his arms around her. She moved slightly and felt the touch of his lips on her hair. So he, too, was awake. She could only hope he had no regrets. She didn't know if she could face masked, emotionless eyes this morning.

She felt his arms tighten around her, his hands slipping almost reverently across her naked body under the thick featherfilled covering. Immediately, every sense revived, coming to life with tingling force as she recalled each wonderful sensation he had awakened last night.

Her body arched in response, wanting to experience them again, but while she could feel his body tense once more, he moved away, the rejection eased slightly by a gentle hand pushing back a wayward curl.

"His grace is an early riser," he said with a hint of regret. "He will be here soon."

She didn't want to let him go. She felt a streak of instinctive terror that if he left her now he would not return, that he would change back into the reserved, slightly mocking Englishman who was most adept at placing distances between them.

Once again, he seemed to read her mind. "I love you, Elsbeth. I won't let you go."

Her eyes begged for even more assurance, and he smiled slowly. "Will you become the wife of a Carey?"

"A most unusual Carey," she said, her face breaking into a smile that could seduce the devil into godliness.

"And a most unusual Ker," he replied.

"We will make a most unusual husband and wife."

"Aye," he agreed with a twinkle in those usually serious gray eyes. He tipped up her chin. "That is an answer?"

"Aye," she echoed with a smile, which was only barely shaded by sudden apprehension.

He noticed it, however, and the smile left his face. "It will not be easily accepted."

"No," she said, "but my clan—"

"You will have to leave your clan," Alex said gently.

She stared at him, a small seed of doubt taking root and growing even as she lay in his arms. Huntington was only a few miles across the border from her home, yet it was a nation away, an enemy nation for much of her life. She had associated Alex with her own land. It was where she had come to love him, and somehow she had pushed aside the thought that loving him meant leaving everything she knew and loved. Not to mention her responsibilities.

Dear God, her responsibilities. She had pushed them aside in the past days, dismissed them in her obsession with the one man in the world she should not want. Shame, guilt, self-accusation filled her, slowly replacing the joy. But not the love.

Never the love, she knew, as she looked at him and saw his own eyes change as he so clearly understood her doubts.

The brightness slowly seeped from his face, and his mouth twisted with a bittersweet knowledge. She knew instantly he would not try to persuade her, entreat her. He was making it her decision completely, and the look on his face told her he thought he already knew what that decision would be.

It was obvious he expected little. She was reminded of his expression when her men first took him in the dale. Part defiance, part anger, part self-mockery. They were there now, all three emotions just barely visible through the facade he had so well perfected.

"Alex . . ."

"I'll help you with your gown," he said, not wanting to hear her words.

Elsbeth nodded miserably, knowing she had just been effectively locked out. Yet she didn't know whether she could accept England, and Huntington, much less make them her home. It was Huntington men, Huntington soldiers, who had killed her father and many of her clan.

Silently she allowed him to fasten her gown, knowing she could not do it herself. She wondered if her young maid had already been to her room, and knew she must have been and had probably guessed where Elsbeth was.

She and Alex said not another word as he completed his maid's duties and turned to his own clothes lying across a chair. Unlike the ones he had worn last night, they were plain in cut and color, though of fine material. But they suited him as well, she thought wistfully. His strong masculine looks needed no gay adornment. She knew she should go, but she couldn't force herself to leave as she watched him turn from her and quickly dress with a minimum of movement. Every action of his was so efficient.

His eyes were blank when he looked at her. "Still here, my lady?" he asked although she knew he was only too aware she hadn't left. It was a brief flash of cruelty she had never seen in him before.

She flushed and turned to leave, but there was a loud demanding knock on his door, and it flew open. His grace, the duke of Northumberland, strode in, eyebrows arching in surprise as his gaze went from Alex's stiff form to Elsbeth, who was dressed in attire obviously more suitable for evening than morning.

The corner of the duke's mouth turned upward as he bowed formally. "I am sorry, madam...I thought Alex would be alone."

Elsbeth knew her face was turning even more scarlet as she caught the amusement—and speculation—in his voice. She curtsied, trying to think of an excuse for being where she was, but none came to her.

Pride suddenly stiffened her. She need make no excuses or explanations to this Englishman. Setting her jaw, she regarded him as curiously as he had observed her. "With your permission, your grace?" She looked at the door.

"Of course, Lady...Ker, is it?"

She wanted to slap him. Or better still, run a sword through him.

Alex saw the dangerous light in her eyes. "My lady," he said softly, "merely stopped to inquire when she might be sent home."

"Home?" inquired Northumberland, his brow now furrowed in confusion.

"I did not have time to explain yesterday. Lady Ker is my...prisoner. My hostage."

That was most surely not the impression the duke had received, but he heeded the plea in Alex's eyes, his mouth curling up at the edges. He nodded at Elsbeth, giving her permission to leave. This was a story he badly wanted to hear.

The men watched as she turned, her head high, pride and dignity in the set of her shoulders. It was only slightly spoiled by the disarray of curling red-flecked hair.

"She's a beauty," Northumberland said when she'd gone. "I never would have suspected as much yesterday. Now what is this about prisoners and hostages?"

"I need some fresh air," Alex said, trying to set his thoughts in some order. "I know you've just come from London, but..."

The duke eyed him with interest. He nodded. "I have several new horses in the stable. I would not be averse to trying them."

Alex smiled his gratitude. Perhaps he could ride out some of his frustration before he tried to explain to Northumberland what he could not explain to himself.

Once they were in the saddle and walking their horses in the woods, the duke once more turned to Alex. "Now about prisoners and hostages?" he queried. "You know, of course, we want peace on the border."

"No more than I, your grace."

"Then . . ."

"I was her prisoner just two weeks ago."

Northumberland stared at him. A corner of his mouth turned up. "She does not appear a fearsome Scot."

Alex tried to smile, but the conversation earlier that morning with Elsbeth had left a residue of hopelessness, of deep aching despair. "She can be that, your grace. Especially from the top of a horse when I'm next to naked."

"Do you wish to continue," the duke asked with amusement after a brief hesitation on Alex's part, "or prefer me to guess?"

"I was going for a morning swim at Huntington when I was ambushed by Kers," Alex said, his mouth drawn tight now. "No one knew of that particular habit except John, my brother. I was held for ransom. None was forthcoming."

Northumberland no longer looked amused. "I knew your brother was greedy, but I didn't think he would go to those lengths. What do you plan to do?"

"I have no proof, and he has friends along the English border. He has done well in establishing the guilt of the Ker family—and keeping any from himself."

Northumberland's face held a perplexed expression as he regarded the man who was almost like a son to him. "How did you get away? And take the Ker heiress with you?"

"John couldn't have done this without the help of one of the Ker clan, who probably has his own reasons for igniting the border. She must find out who."

"So you joined forces," Northumberland mused, a new grin working at his face. "'Tis a most novel approach—one only you would consider, Alex. How did you get the lady to agree?"

"She didn't at first, your grace, but I was wounded when I attempted to escape. I think she realized my death could mean an invasion by you, the destruction of her clan. She had considered ransom, nothing more, and when no word came from my brother, her clansmen started to get blood-hungry."

Northumberland stared at him with fascination. "Wounded? How?"

"I was in a sword fight. My wound became poisoned."

"You never tire of adventures, do you, Alex?"

"Aye, my grace. I'm most weary of them, but I've had little choice lately."

"And the lady. You said she was your prisoner, your hostage? She did not come willingly?"

"No," Alex said with all honesty. "She helped me to escape, but she then wanted to stay. I—well...I had to knock her out."

Northumberland stared at his companion. He would have believed almost anything of him but that. He had never known a man to whom honor meant as much as it did to Alex Carey. It was a quality that intrigued him, since he himself often bent the rules for expediency's sake. Nonetheless, while he recognized his own ethics were not always above reproach, he respected Alex's unflinching integrity and loyalty, even though it seemed to lead him from one boiling pot to another.

He smiled sympathetically. Alex must indeed have strong reasons to have done what he did. He wondered how much they had to do with the lady's obvious charms. "And now?"

"And now I need her help to expose her traitor and my brother."

"Nothing more?"

"Aye, much more, your grace," Alex admitted, "but she cannot forget our clans have been enemies."

"And what can I do?"

"First of all, know that this is my brother's doing. If anything happens to me, I do not want the Kers to suffer for it."

Northumberland's jaw set. "They did kidnap you, a lord of our realm."

"With much provocation, your grace. My father and brothers killed her father in cowardly ambush."

Northumberland stiffened. At times, Alex's honesty could be daunting.

"I ask your pledge, your grace, that you will stay the hand of the English warden in any action against the Kers."

"In this matter, aye," Northumberland said, keeping other options open.

Alex let the reservation pass. It was more than he had expected.

Northumberland nodded slowly. "What else?"

"I wanted you to be aware of my brother's treachery if all does not go according to plan."

"And what is your plan?"

"To force the hand of the Ker who is working with my brother, and trap them together in sight of both families. Only then will each family see the blame lies not solely with the other. Only then can there be any kind of peace."

Northumberland let out a long breath of air. "An ambitious plan, Alex. And a dangerous one."

Alex shrugged. "It's the only way."

"And the fierce lady Scot who seems not so fierce?" Northumberland probed.

Alex's eyes darkened and his mouth tightened. "She apparently wishes to stay with her clan."

"Yet she aided you against them," Northumberland said thoughtfully. "I would not oppose a marriage uniting the border."

"I fear she would," Alex said shortly.

"Hmm," Northumberland murmured. But he said no more as Alex, his eyes darkening, spurred his mount into a trot, forcing the duke to follow.

Chapter Seventeen

Dinner, in the late morning, was even more extravagant than supper the evening before.

Elsbeth observed the dishes of food without appetite. She could not look at Alex without a sick emptiness in her stomach, and she did not like the duke of Northumberland.

He tried to be pleasant, but there was an inherent coldness about the man that warned her. His eyes warmed only when they settled on Alex, and she wondered why.

She tried to tell herself that she felt only her long-standing suspicion of Englishmen, that Alex would not like someone who was untrustworthy. But she did not care for Northumberland's knowing looks, or his slightly amused eyes, or the smile that always seemed false.

Perhaps, she thought, her discomfiture came from her feeling that Alex himself had seemed changed since this morning, although she suspected the change came from their earlier conversation and her instinctive reluctance to desert her clan.

That was what he had been asking.

She ducked her head in misery as she pushed a piece of meat across the trencher she shared with Alex. Their hands touched and quickly moved away, each tingling with the heat of the other.

Elsbeth fastened her eyes on the venison in front of her. Despite its tender perfection, few meals had ever appealed less to her. She tried to concentrate on the words of the duke of Northumberland. "Alex says you'll be leaving us soon."

She looked quickly at Alex. Alex had said little to her since this morning, and nothing about when they might leave, or how.

"It apparently is up to Lord Huntington," she said coldly. "He has not favored me with his plans."

"Because you're his prisoner?" the duke said with a slight challenge.

"It would seem so."

He chuckled. "I wonder who is prisoner of whom?"

"I would not be in England otherwise, your grace," Elsbeth said nastily.

"Yes," he said. "I've heard all about it."

All? Elsbeth blushed and turned to Alex in question.

"That you helped me," Alex said, his eyes steady on her, "and in return I kidnapped you. That now I've asked you for help in return for mine to settle the dispute between our people."

A simple account of a very unsimple affair, she mused. Was that really all there was to it in his mind?

It had to be. But her eyes couldn't leave his, not when they were so dark and probing and troubled. She gathered all her strength of will and cloaked her vulnerable heart with it. "And when do I return, then, my lord?"

"Are you so impatient?"

"Aye, my lord." Liar! *I want to stay with you always.*

"Tomorrow, then," he said in a calm dispassionate voice that belied the desperation he felt. *I want you to be with me forever.*

Afraid that his feelings would reveal themselves and make things even more difficult, Alex abruptly stood. "I need some air, my lord. With your permission?"

Don't go, Elsbeth wanted to say. Please don't go. But pride wouldn't allow her. Not in front of the English duke. Instead, she watched Alex stride out, and she was alone with the most powerful man in England. She could almost feel his eyes boring into her.

"My lady." His voice was a purr, a dangerous one like that of a cat ready to pounce on a mouse.

She looked up, almost against her will.

"I wouldn't like to see Huntington hurt." Despite the soft words, there was a hard threat in them.

Anger born of confusion, hurt and conflicting loyalties filled her. Who was this man to threaten her? "What is your interest?" she asked recklessly. "I've heard you care for naught other than power."

One side of his mouth turned upward in wry appreciation of her courage. "You've heard right, my lady. There is little I care about other than keeping the right person on the English throne, and the right religion in place."

"Then why..."

"Alex is the one exception. Partly because of me, he suffered through years of hell. And he bore it well, far better than many a man might have done."

"Because of you?"

"What has he told you, Lady Ker?"

"Only that he was in the galleys."

"Not why?"

"No."

Northumberland was silent for a moment. Did he have the right to say more? Yet he had not missed the quiet desperate looks between his two guests. He pitied them. He envied them.

"I wonder how much you really care about him," he said, almost to himself. Elsbeth was barely able to catch the words.

The misery in her eyes told him what she could not say.

"He was in France eight years, my lady. He spent the first four of those years rescuing Huguenots, Protestants, from persecution and death, and the second four paying for that passionate quest of justice."

There was cynicism in the last sentence, and she wondered why. "You said you were partly at fault."

"I wanted him there, my lady, not to right wrongs but to seed trouble between France and Scotland."

At her puzzled look, he continued softly. "Are you Protestant?"

"Aye. Many Scots on the border are," she said. She knew many were not, including another branch of Kers, which still received much of its income from the Catholic church.

"But most of the highlanders who support your Queen Mary are Catholic?"

"Mayhap, but—"

"Think, Lady Ker. French persecution of the Huguenots can only deepen the bitterness between Catholics and Protestants in Scotland. Mary has a Protestant half brother."

Understanding started to dawn. He didn't have to say anything else. It was obvious that Mary's brother as Scottish king would be more acceptable to England than the Catholic queen who also held a claim to the English throne. Yet why was the duke telling her this?

"Alex was your spy?"

"No, he was never that," Northumberland said. "He wanted to go. He wanted the adventure and I think he wanted to feel useful. Still, I knew how dangerous it was, and I encouraged him for my own reasons, not for his."

"And now you feel remorse?" she asked bitterly, thinking of Alex's suffering, of his lost years.

"Remorse?" He raised an eyebrow in disbelief. "No. I did what I thought best for England. I would do it again. But in the doing, I learned tremendous respect for our border lord. He could be of great benefit to his country at Huntington—a cool, intelligent head, and God knows there are few of those around."

"And loyal," she added with a bite to her words. She knew now why she hadn't liked the man. She didn't care for the way he so ruthlessly used the loyalties of others.

"And loyal," he agreed softly. "Once he gives his pledge, his friendship or . . . his love, there's no turning back for him."

"And why shouldn't I tell him everything you've told me?"

"You could, my lady. But then I would no longer be in a position to help him. He wouldn't let me. Is that what you want?"

She was neatly trapped, and she knew it. He had judged her well.

"He will find out what you are."

"Don't mistake me, my lady. I like Alex. I've always liked him, and wish deeply my sons were more like him. He has a strength of character that is rare. I shouldn't like to lose him as my arm on the border . . . or as my friend. And I won't let anyone else hurt him."

"Only you, your grace?" she said bitterly.

His head jerked back as if she had hit him. Then he smiled. She had courage. She would be a worthy mate for Huntington.

"Only me," he agreed. "And now I must find Alex and make plans for your return." He felt a brief sense of satisfaction at the sudden desolation on Elsbeth's face. He bowed and left her alone at the table.

Elsbeth took one of the silver goblets and threw it, with all her might, into the stone fireplace.

That afternoon Elsbeth wandered through the luxurious lodge, then visited the stables, as she tried to sort out her turbulent thoughts and feelings.

She felt outraged at Northumberland's role in Alex's enslavement in France, and then wondered if Alex would welcome her anger on his behalf. He had done what he wanted to do in going to France, and probably would have gone without Northumberland's encouragement. She had seen only a fragment of his determination, but already knew it was mighty in nature. Otherwise he would have never escaped the first time from the Ker tower.

How big a part did Nadine play in his decision to go to France? Elsbeth wondered. The thought of the dead woman always hurt. He must have loved her so fiercely.

Elsbeth's lips pressed together. She had wanted to ask Northumberland about Nadine, but she had not been able to. She detested him too much to give that much of herself away.

Her mouth quirked up in a smile as she thought of Alex as knight errant, whisking fugitives from France. The role suited him. Her cynical worn-out knight who was no' so cynical after all.

Elsbeth felt her heart twisting at the thought of leaving him, at not seeing that rare breath-stealing smile of his when the shadows were gone from him.

The shadows: a loveless family, the horrible death of his beloved, the years in the galleys, betrayal by his brother, by his friend. How could she ever imagine such sorrow? She tried to. But she had no way of doing so. Suddenly her own tragedies, her own needs seemed so very small and petty. Her father had lived a long, productive life before he died, and he had loved her dearly. She had known protection and love and comfort all her years. Her heart now hurt as it never had before, and it hurt for Alex Carey, Lord Huntington, although she knew he would not appreciate or want her pity. He was too strong a man for that.

The brief remembrance of the arrogant half smile seen in her first interview with him stabbed her. How indifferent it had made him seem as he lightly mocked her and asked whimsically for wine. What kind of strength had that taken when he had just thrown aside years of slavery and imprisonment?

Elsbeth bit her lip as she recalled the quiet defeat in his eyes this morning. She vowed to herself she would never see it there again. Patrick or Ian could carry on as clan leader, better than she, although she was loath to admit it.

She admitted to herself she could not leave the clan in the hands of a traitor. But once he was unmasked, she would marry Alex, English or not, Carey or not.

Just the thought made her body sing again, renewed the aching physical memories of what had passed between them and the joy they had shared together.

If he still wanted her.

Dear God in Heaven, please let him still want her.

It was a prayer she wasn't sure would be answered.

Before supper, the housekeeper asked her whether she wanted the meal in her room. His Grace and Lord Huntington were closeted together, she was told.

Was it because Alex didn't want to see her?

Despite the fact that she had eaten little earlier in the day, she could eat even less this eve.

What if she were to return to Scotland tomorrow?

What if Alex would not give her a chance to say she loved him, that she would marry him? Gladly. Joyfully. Without reservation.

She put on a nightdress that had been laid out for her. It was lovely, a pale gold that shimmered with every movement. If he did not come to her, she would go to him.

Elsbeth waited, and waited ... and waited. But he did not come. When the lodge seemed silent and asleep, she slipped from her room to the door of his chamber, and opened it quietly.

Still dressed, Alex was standing by the window, one foot propped on a chest and his arm resting on his knee. He turned swiftly at the sound of the door closing.

There was no fire, only a candle sending shadows cascading against the stone wall. His face was outlined by moonlight, and its solemnity seemed carved in stone.

"Elsbeth?"

The very neutrality of his voice was a blow, and her fingers made nervous little movements. "Alex ..."

"Some men of Northumberland's will accompany you to the border tomorrow. You can say you escaped the villainous Carey rogue." Each word was flat, as if carefully rehearsed.

"The plan?"

"Ah yes, the plan. I was going to tell you tomorrow, but since you are here ..."

She waited.

He moved from the window and sat in one of the velvet chairs, sprawling in it. He was careful not to go near her. He finally looked up. "You still want to go through with this?"

"Aye," she said slowly, wretchedly wanting more from him than what she was receiving.

He told her then what he wanted her to do, watching her face carefully. So much depended on her.

When he finished, he asked, "Can you do it?"

"Aye," she said carefully.

He ached to hold her. Her hair shone in the candlelight, and her eyes were grave, the determined face infinitely dear. He could still remember the fit of her body, the softness of her touch. Yet for her, as much as for himself, he dared not. It would just make things worse in the coming months.

But she had no such restraints, and her hand went to him beseechingly. She lowered her chin in surrender, but her eyes gazed at him with undisguised love.

"If you still want to marry a Ker, she would be most honored," she said shyly and with heartbreaking hope in her face.

If she had to give up everything in her past and in her future, it was all, that moment, worth it.

Something broke in his face . . . all the reserve, all the wariness. Slowly his lips turned upward in a hauntingly dear smile, a quiet exultation reaching up into the swirling gray of eyes that probed deep inside her. But still he didn't move toward her. "Are you sure, Elsbeth?" His voice was steady but there was a certain lilt to it.

She had never been quite so sure of anything in her life, particularly at this instant, when emotion flowed so strongly between them, like a river after a wild Scottish storm. The currents pushed at the banks, raging against ordinary boundaries, overflowing in their eagerness to reach their destination.

Each other.

Elsbeth trembled with the need, the wild fiery outreach of everything within her. She needed him in so many ways.

Gentle ways.

Passionate wanton ways.

Spiritual ways.

They were all part of a whole, she knew. She wanted his soul, his heart. She wanted him deep inside her until they merged so completely they became one in all ways.

She didn't have to answer him. He saw it all in her face, and knew that this battle, at least, had ended.

If only there weren't so many more before them.

His arms went around her, possessively, fearfully tender.

She felt the contradiction, the hard strength of his arms, the tender touch of his mouth. "I love you," she whispered. "I'll love you to eternity and beyond."

She felt his mouth falter, saw his eyes cloud slightly. "That is a very long time, my love." A trace of the old self-mockery was back and it pierced Elsbeth like a knife blade. Would he ever trust completely?

Her hand went up to his mouth. "You need promise nothing, my lord," she said, but a challenge was softly issued.

Alex looked at her face. He was being given so much, he didn't know if he could accept it. He wanted to. Jesus, God, but he wanted to. Yet he was hesitant to believe in this miracle of good fortune, for fear it might disappear like a night mist in the first intrusive glow of morning sun.

Might his love sentence her to death, to unhappiness, to regret?

"Are you taking back your offer?" Elsbeth finally asked after a long silence.

"No," he said, a muscle working compulsively in his cheek. "I just don't want you ever to regret this moment. That is the one thing I could not bear."

She took one of his hands and brought it to her mouth. "The only thing I will ever regret is the days and hours and moments we've lost together."

Some of the tension in his face relaxed. "Dear God, I love you so much, Elsbeth. I don't want you to return to Scotland." He had a sudden fear he would lose her if she did.

"I must," she said softly. "Otherwise we will never have peace."

He closed his eyes. Tomorrow she would be gone. For days, for weeks, perhaps even longer. His only consolation was his belief there was no danger for her.

His lips touched her forehead, then her cheeks, as he made soft strokes with his tongue; then he reached her mouth and he took it possessively, delighting in the passionate response, the hunger that equaled his own raging need.

He picked her up in one easy sweeping movement and carried her to the bed, his mouth keeping its hold on hers. Once he saw her securely settled in the bed's soft folds, he stepped back and quickly undressed, watching her every second as if she might dissolve into the air. The pale gold of her nightdress brought forth the gold in her eyes and the ivory of her skin. How totally lovely she was, this fierce little Scot of his.

He was more a captive of her tonight than he had been weeks ago. His hand went under the soft silk of her gown and teased the nipples of her breasts as his other hand deftly untied the ribbons that held the garment to her. As it fell in silken folds around her, he leaned down, his lips trailing fire from her neck to her waist, dwelling on her breasts until they were full and throbbing. She moaned as his mouth traveled farther down, reaching the triangle of silken hair, and his hand went to the most private part of her, caressing and teasing until her body arched and convulsed with a series of exquisite explosions.

And then he straightened and entered her . . . slowly, creating an aching agonizing need that made her move against him in instinctive circular motions, drawing him farther and farther inside. His strokes increased in rhythm and power until the two were riding the crest of an incredible wave, a giant force that swept them along with unthinking madness, drowning them in depths of pleasure until they thought they could endure no more.

There was one last drive, and Elsbeth felt an explosion rock her entire being with bursting sensations she would never be able to identify. She felt his warmth flood her, and she knew a completeness as he collapsed on her, his breath coming in rapid gasps as both their bodies quivered in exquisite reaction.

He rolled over, bringing her on top of him, holding her close and treasuring her nearness as his body sought to recover from its magnificent invasion.

"Hmm," she murmured.

"Hmm," he agreed.

Her lips found his, and kissed them hard, her body, by necessity, slid up and down on his in the most sensuous way. He found himself reacting, although minutes ago he would have thought it impossible.

She held still, feeling him fill her again with the most pleasurable warmth, and then she moved slowly, instinctively, riding him, first experimentally and then with growing need that erased her shyness, her awkwardness. His hand urged her to sit up, and she did, as she felt him go deeper than he ever had before, reaching the core of her soul, as she moved ever so slowly, watching his eyes darken with passion, the muscles in his cheek strain against the skin.

Spasms of pleasure ripped through her as she rode him harder and harder, moving toward a nirvana she knew was there, that she knew lay just beyond the next stroke, the next response. They moved in tandem now, rejoicing in the joint voyage, in the billows of feeling that swept them as they reached for the farthest star in the sky.

Neither was prepared when it was reached. She cried out as her whole being seemed to explode in rainbows of color, in tremors of pure ecstasy. Alex could only whisper a reverent exclamation as his body erupted and ran with rivers of hot honey that flowed through every empty part of him.

They said no more. There was nothing to say. They merely clasped each other tightly and held the past moments close to them. It was hours later before sleep separated them. But even then, they held tightly to each other as if to lose touch was to lose each other.

Alex was the last to sleep as he cradled her in his arms. He had filled her several times with his seed this night.

He touched her stomach and thought of a child. How much he would love that . . . particularly with Elsbeth. And not just one. A dozen. All with that stubborn red streak in their hair.

He swallowed the hard lump that settled in his throat. What if something were to go wrong? If he were killed? The child would be a bastard.

For already he knew they had made a child this night. It could not be otherwise, not in all the love they had shared, had given and taken.

He knew it. Dear God in heaven he knew it.

Alex smiled slightly. They would marry tomorrow. Northumberland could arrange it. He could arrange anything.

The smile broadened, and Alex's arms tightened around Elsbeth as she sleepily moved closer to his warmth. He nuzzled her ear, then contentedly closed his eyes.

Chapter Eighteen

What small civility there had been between the two conspirators existed no longer.

"English bastard!"

"Scottish dog!"

"Blundering fool."

"Coward."

Faces red, even in the moonlight, hands clutching swords, the two glared at each other. Both were facing exposure and ruin. One feared that more than death. The other did not.

The Scotsman, now fully aware of the consequences of his actions, halfway courted death, almost daring the Englishman to use his sword.

Elsbeth was gone, stolen by the Englishman he had helped bring to the Ker tower. After all that had transpired in the past months, he expected little mercy for her. The fact that she had so thoroughly disappeared did not bode well. There had been only one message, warning against any retaliatory raid on the Careys, but no demand for ransom. Only silence. Only ominous continuing silence.

What had he done?

Everything thus far he had justified as being for the good of the clan. The old laird had wanted peace, but peace, the conspirator feared, would mean the gradual decline of the clan. Its members would become victims for every raider on both sides of the border. War would come again, with England, and today's raiding kept the clan strong.

He despised weakness and passionately felt he could be the leader his clan needed. With Elsbeth at his side, anything would be possible.

Where was she? Was she even alive? Had the Englishman raped her, or worse?

A deep sense of despair settled in the pit of his stomach. He loved Elsbeth. There had been other women, but he had never considered another as wife. He had loved her since they were children, and he had sought every way he knew to win her.

And in doing so, he had put her in terrible danger.

Devil take both the Englishmen. He had underestimated, as had John Carey, the new earl of Huntington. He should have revised his opinion after the sword fight, but he had always considered the English as strutting popinjays, and he had attributed Huntington's near victory then to luck.

Now he wondered. And he wondered even more what Huntington was up to.

So did John Carey. Frustration was eating at both of them. They had scoured the surrounding forests—the Scot around Ker land, John around Huntington. Day after day. Night after night. Nothing. No sign.

John Carey had secretly hired men to watch the London roads, but neither Elsbeth nor Alexander had been sighted there.

"What do you plan to do now?" the Englishman growled.

The Scot looked at him suspiciously. He feared more day by day that if Carey found the fugitives first, he would not hesitate to kill both of them.

"If she is harmed," the Scot said slowly, "I will kill ye both."

"She can cause you trouble, too. If she has been influenced by my brother..."

"A Carey?" The Scot snorted. "She hates Careys more than I." He didn't have to say how much that was. They both knew.

"My brother can have a great deal of charm when he tries."

"Elsbeth is not easily swayed by charm. You needna worry about that."

"Yet someone must have helped him escape."

The Scot was not entirely convinced of that. Huntington, after all, had escaped once before on his own. His apparent docility had misled them all.

"He is no' a fool," the Scot said.

"He's lucky," John said flatly.

"Where has he been these years past?"

John shrugged. "The Continent . . . he has said nothing more."

"Ye underestimated him. Wha' do ye plan to do now?"

"Keep looking. Someone must be helping him."

"Look to *your* men, no' the Kers."

"I'll find them if I have to comb every piece of wood on the border."

"Remember well what I said. She's no' to meet harm."

John looked at the Scot contemptuously. "I'll do what has to be done. And I expect word from you if any message comes." He saw the Scot's rebellious look. "If anything happens to me, Ker, your role in all this will be revealed. I'll make sure of that. Then what will your whey-faced Scot think of you?"

The Scot went for his sword, but John was too quick. His pistol was out. "I still need you—now," he said, emphasizing the last word.

"When this is over, I'll take pleasure in splitting your gullet."

John laughed. "Don't wager on it."

"I am, English. I am," the Scot said before mounting his horse in one quick leap. Without looking back, he rode as if the devil were chasing him.

If nothing else, Northumberland did have a knack for getting his way, Elsbeth thought resentfully as she and Alex stood in front of a Protestant minister.

It was certainly not the marriage ceremony she would have wished for. There were only five people present: the minister; Northumberland; the butler, Stanson, who served as a second witness; and her and Alex.

An English cleric for a minister, and obviously one not above taking bribes for forgetting such things as banns and notices;

an English duke for a witness. It was enough to dampen even the happiest of occasions.

Nonetheless, when she looked up at Alex's face and watched the silver lights dance merrily in his eyes, she didn't regret her ready agreement to his proposal.

He squeezed her hand, their eyes met and it no longer mattered who was present, or who was conducting the ceremony. The only thing that mattered was Alex, and the eyes that adored her and invited her into a deep place she knew he had held private for so long.

She smiled, and his questioning half smile broadened, his hand tightened even more. She didn't hear the minister's words until they were said a second time, and she responded in a firm sure tone.

When the vows were made, Alex turned to her, and she whispered, "I love you," before his mouth touched hers and declared his love in yet another way.

When he released her, both partially numb from the rapid events, they signed the wedding papers and watched as Northumberland and Stanson did the same.

When they were through, Northumberland leaned over and kissed Elsbeth's cheek, and he felt her all but flinch at his touch. His eyes clouded slightly; he knew she had not forgiven him, nor would she, for what he said yesterday. She was a fierce one, unimpressed by his rank and obviously more than ready to do battle on her husband's behalf.

He couldn't help but envy Alex, envy them both at the moment for the feelings that vibrated in the air.

He turned to Alex. "I have ordered a wedding supper. I don't think my presence is needed any longer. I'll keep that wedding certificate safe."

Alex gave his hand to Northumberland. "Thank you, your grace."

"I wish you would let me do more . . . send some men to the border to help."

"This is something I have to do alone," Alex said. "The presence of your men would only incite the Kers further, and make my brother more cautious. It would settle nothing, only prolong the danger."

Northumberland nodded. He had argued much of the morning, but he knew Alex was right. He could only swear to protect Elsbeth if anything went wrong and, if there was issue from the marriage, ensure that the child would inherit Huntington.

"Good fortune, then. I shall have two men here in the morning to escort you and your lady wife to the border. They will be most trustworthy."

Alex nodded, all his attention on Elsbeth and the fear on her face as the discussion reminded her only too well of the dangers that lay ahead for Alex.

Beloved Alex. Husband. Her hand went to his sleeve.

Northumberland grinned. "I think I've already overworn my welcome." With a brief bow, he took his leave.

Elsbeth watched him go, her eyes softening only a trifle. Then she took Alex's arms and stared up at her new husband. They had decided to delay their departure by a day in light of the marriage, and she was greedy for every moment alone with him.

Could it have been just this morning that he had again asked her to be his wife, to marry him this very day?

She had awakened in his arms and stretched out lazily like a contented cat, comforted by his nearness. His lips were soon nuzzling her neck, and she had purred with pleasure at his very touch.

And then he had raised himself above her, his eyes boring into hers, and she thought that once more she would feel the wonder of the hard body. But words came instead.

"Will you marry me?"

It had taken a moment for the words to penetrate the sense of well-being that had dulled her brain. She had already said she would. She looked up at him, confused.

"Today, Elsbeth."

The words were said quietly, but they sounded like hammer strokes to her. She had made peace within herself about him. She knew she wanted him, to live with him, to love him. But today?

She felt him tense as she hesitated, and knew he was readying himself for a blow. Perhaps he had never really believed she meant what she said. She felt love curling around inside her, swelling to overcome any objections that still lingered there. "Aye," she smiled softly. "Today."

Elsbeth didn't ask how. She was beginning to learn that Alex usually accomplished what he set out to do. She put her heart in those words and gave to him everything she could possibly give: her faith, her trust, her love, her life. And she did it without reservation. Regardless of what the future held, she wanted him to know she loved him totally, and nothing could change that.

"My fierce little Scot," he whispered, his eyes devouring every nuance of her expression, every glowing part of her as he realized he had from her what he wanted most: absolute trust.

"My arrogant English lord," she said lovingly, thinking him anything but arrogant.

"You make me arrogant, my love. I can do anything with you beside me."

"Anything?" There was a wanton tone to her voice.

He grinned and proved it.

An hour later he had left the room, leaving Elsbeth half-drugged with contentment. Only the tiniest of voices in her head told her everything was too wonderful, too perfect to last. Once she was alone, it was joined by yet another, a painful warning of days to come. Alex had a brother who wanted to kill him. She had a kinsman who wanted to discredit her. Their families were happiest when killing each other.

Could Alex's scheme work? And would it really make a difference? Could it truly bring peace among peoples who had been warring for hundreds of years?

Or were they both hiding from the truth—that their people would never reconcile themselves to such a marriage, that it would result only in more violence and treachery.

She knew from their journey together that Alex had many plans, many hopes to enrich not only Huntington but the lot of the tenants and serfs who lived there. He had so many dreams, so many hopes, this lord of hers.

This lord of hers.

She wondered how so many things could change so quickly. How hate could turn into love. Rage into trust. Distrust into such complete faith.

And now they were man and wife. She looked up at Alex, grateful that the duke had left. Northumberland created a chill in her heart that she didn't want to dampen the love threatening to burst from her body's confines. "Alone at last, my lord husband."

His gray eyes were like the darkest charcoal, burning with an intensity that reached out and wrapped her in warmth. "Aye, my lady wife."

"There's a wedding supper...."

"A succulent first course," he ventured mischievously, leaving no question as to the second one.

Looking at the tender, expectant expression on his face, she was willing to forgo even the first course. But he grinned, understanding her thoughts only too well, as he usually did. "We may need our strength," he said with a wee boy's impishness that drove straight into her heart.

She bit her lip. Was it always to be like this . . . this glorious meeting of mind and body? Would she always start trembling at his barest look?

"Yes, my lady," he said quietly, the laughter gone. "My sweet Scot . . ."

Elsbeth tasted little of the food although it was even grander than before, and she didn't even try to wonder where it came from so quickly. The servants, after leaving the platters of food, had discreetly disappeared. She and Alex nibbled on pheasant and partridge, luscious oysters and roasted meats. He fed her, and she him, and they laughed when wine dribbled from cups held shakily. He leaned over and licked a small trail of red liquid from her chin, and her lips tasted his wine-flavored ones.

There was no yesterday, no tomorrow, only the lovely present. Forgotten for the moment was the fact that they would separate tomorrow, a separation postponed from today because of the wedding.

Or perhaps, Elsbeth thought giddily, it wasn't forgotten. It only made every moment that much more precious. They lingered over the table, each loath to move from the spell of the other, from teasing eyes and tender touches.

It was not until the fire died in the great fireplace that Alex rose and picked up Elsbeth as easily as he had before, as if she were no more than an autumn leaf. She nuzzled his neck as he carried her to his rooms, and he chuckled lightly, pressing her even closer to his heart.

Hours later, they held each other tightly, willing the dawn to hold back. There had been a bittersweet agony this time in their love, a desperation born of not knowing when they would share another night together. Every kiss, every touch held special meaning that they knew would be stored in their hearts.

Her fingers smoothed the lines at the corners of his eyes, went down to the scar on his chest, and then her lips kissed it. Her eyes filled with tears as she thought of the pain that once must have been there. "What happened?" she asked. She did not want to renew old hurts, but she wanted to know everything about him. Everything. He had said so little.

He took a wisp of her hair and twisted it around his finger before answering. "I was branded," he said finally in a toneless voice. "The French do it to their galley slaves. They mark them forever in the unusual event they escape. They can always recognize a French criminal."

Elsbeth met his gaze steadily. The answer was worse than she had imagined, but she owed it to him not to flinch, to accept his past as he apparently still had not.

His hand tightened on her, and she saw his jaw set. "They take away every vestige of dignity, do everything they can to turn you into the lowest of beasts. You fight your fellow prisoners for a crust of bread, but you can't fight too hard because you're chained to a bench, your hands to the oars."

Elsbeth could only look at him with horror, not able to comprehend fully what he was saying.

"For one year, I went without seeing the sky," he continued, unable to stop now. He wanted her to understand, to know his fear and loneliness and pain. He didn't understand why, but he knew it was important. He couldn't tell her all of it . . . the intimate searches, the head shaving, the parading down French streets in chains, the countless humiliations that humans often inflict on those weaker than themselves.

He had almost surrendered to it, had wanted to die, until John Knox was chained next to him. The minister's fury and passion had kept him going. And then Knox was gone, and he was alone once more. His fellow prisoners were all French and hated someone of Alex's obvious breeding and station, despite the fact they were all in the same desperate position.

Alex felt Elsbeth's comforting, accepting strokes, and he tried to banish the memories. She needed to know, because they were part of him, and he wanted nothing held back, not by either of them.

He felt her lips once more on the scar and knew she was trying to erase the pain of it. "When I returned from France," he continued slowly, "I asked Northumberland to find a surgeon to remove the brand. I would not bear the mark of France, or slavery, the rest of my life."

Alex felt the wetness on his chest and knew she was crying, soundlessly so he would not know. He lifted her face to look into his.

"Don't cry, love. It's over, and it taught me a great deal. Most of all not to waste life..."

But the tears wouldn't stop coming. She thought about the small room in which she had confined him, almost gleefully. She had wanted him to hurt, to suffer, because of her father. And he must have suffered much more than she could imagine. He most certainly must have been reminded of the hell he had so recently left.

But now his eyes were clear in the candlelight, clear and worried as his lips brushed aside wet tears. He didn't want this night spent in recriminations or blame or regrets. "The moment I saw you in that glade," he whispered softly, "I knew I wanted you, and when you could barely hold back a smile that first time in your tower I knew I would marry you."

Her head snapped back. "Oh you did, did you?" she said, partially offended. She had not thought she had been so transparent.

"Aye," he mocked her playfully. "And there was absolutely no doubt when I woke in Patrick's room and you were nursing me."

"I would have done that for a dog," she said, a little resentfully.

"Not with that look in your eye, I hope," he said, grinning lazily. "In any event I consider my kidnapping the luckiest thing that ever disrupted my . . . rather oft-interrupted life."

"Alex?"

"Say that again," he demanded.

"Alex," she said, happily obedient.

"No one has ever said it like that before."

"Like what?"

"Soft and . . . loving."

It was a matter-of-fact observation that struck her to the core. Had no one really loved him before? Nadine? She could not hold back the question any longer. It was pounding in her head. "Not even . . . Nadine?"

His hand took her chin and made her look directly at him. "No, love, not even Nadine."

"But—" She wished she could be silent, but she couldn't. She had to know. There had been so much pain in his voice the first time he had mentioned her.

"At first, I think, I thought myself in love with her," Alex said slowly. "But it was a pure admiring form of love, I suppose. Over the years we shared dangers and victories together, and she and her father became the family I never truly had. But she cared for me as a sister would . . . she had no time for anything more. She was totally swept up in her cause and the people who needed her." His fingers caressed Elsbeth's face softly. "I cared for Nadine deeply. Part of her will always be with me . . . I hope it will, because she was bright and shining, and her memory should not be lost or forgotten." He hesitated as he sought the right words. It was so important that he do so. So very important as he watched the intense golden eyes reflect a multitude of emotions.

"But I love you, Elsbeth, in so many ways I can never explain. You have gifted me with a joy I never knew existed. You make me ache with loving you, and wanting you, and yet it is such a fine aching . . . such an exquisite thing. You've brought life to me, Elsbeth, and I have never loved anyone, nor will I, the way I love you.''

He was so painfully honest that Elsbeth wanted to shed even more tears. She wanted to smile. She wanted to press him close. She wanted to sprinkle him with kisses. She wanted to give him so much joy that the boundaries of earth would no longer hold them.

But his eyes were begging her to understand, and she suddenly knew the best way to let him know she did. Her mouth nibbled on his fingers then slowly, sensuously moved to his nipples. Her tongue played with them wickedly, as he had done to her just hours earlier, and she felt his swift pleased reaction. Minutes later, the ghost of Nadine was gone, locked in both their hearts, but never more to intrude.

Alex's face was grim the next morning, all the quiet exultation gone. Elsbeth did not have to wonder why.

He was going home, to a place that was really no home at all but where deadly danger lay. And there were only two outcomes: his death or the death of his brother.

And no matter what his brother had done, Elsbeth could only shudder at the prospect of Alex's shedding blood he shared, or holding the responsibility for it.

Her task, she knew, was no easier. She was going back to try to trap a traitor, one who was probably a lifelong friend. The thought was a terrible one.

Alex helped Elsbeth dress, needing this time with her rather than calling the maidservant. She wore a fresh pair of rough boy's clothes, and she looked so very young and forlorn in them. His hands lingered on her shoulders when he finished.

"We could always just disappear."

She turned to him. "Run away?"

His eyes banked, became emotionless as he watched her. They had been words he hadn't wanted to say, but he felt he owed her the choice. He nodded.

"And let *them* have what they want?"

He gave her the old half grin that was part question, part cynicism. "It's an idea."

"One of your worst ones, my lord." But her smile softened the words.

His hands tightened on her shoulders. "I couldn't bear the thought of you in danger."

"It's you, Alex, who is at risk. I would gladly flee in a moment if I thought you could be content to do so. But you couldn't be . . . and I want *you,* not a shadow who surrendered his responsibilities for me."

He rested his head on her auburn one. He loved her so much.

There was a knock at the door, and Stanson came in with breakfast. "His grace's men are here, my lord," he said and quickly withdrew.

Neither of them could eat much. It had already been decided they would travel separately. It would be safer that way. As soon as she arrived she would send Hugh to David Garrick and tell him the plan.

"The marriage certificate?" she said.

"Northumberland will keep it," Alex said. "If anyone found it on you or me, and something went wrong . . ."

"Alex?"

He looked at her questioningly.

"I don't trust him."

Alex grinned for the first time that morning. "You have good instincts, my love. I have never underestimated Northumberland's talent for intrigue. He would do anything to accomplish his aims. However, I stand in the way of none of them and hold the key to one—the pacification of at least part of the border."

She looked at him, startled. "But—"

"I like him, Elsbeth. Don't ask me why, but I do. And he, in his own way, likes me. He will keep his word on this. If anything happens to me, he will look after you. Promise me you will go to him."

Elsbeth's expression was stubborn. Alex was one thing, the rarest of rare honorable Englishmen. Lord Northumberland was an entirely different matter.

"If anything happens to you," she finally replied, "I would not want to live."

He took her in his arms. "Don't say that, Elsbeth. Don't ever say that."

"It's true," she insisted, leaning her head against his heart.

"Then I cannot let anything happen." There was a defeated wryness in his voice that tugged at her heart. But then everything about him tugged at her heart, or her head, or her emotions, or her. . . .

Blast or bless that uncommon thread that ran between them so very strongly, for she heard his loving chuckle. He still read her so very well. She lifted her face toward him, only to find her lips caught securely by his mouth, his lips. It was a hard kiss as he put his hands around her waist and lifted her to his height. It held a promise, all the promises she yearned for.

There was a knock on the door.

Her husband slowly put her down, his lips still melded to hers, and only reluctantly leaving them.

"Your promise?" he demanded, reminding her of his distasteful request that she go to Northumberland.

At the moment, she could deny him nothing. "Aye," she said, and was gratified with his quick dazzling smile. But she couldn't resist a brief rebellion. "But not happily."

"I know," he said soothingly. "Thank you." The last was so solemnly said that she knew he realized what the promise had cost her.

"Don't go down with me," she said achingly. "I couldn't bear to leave if I saw you standing there."

He didn't think he could let her leave. He nodded.

"It won't be long," she pleaded for reassurance.

"Nay, my love. And then we will have a lifetime."

"And many black-haired children."

"Red-haired children," he retorted.

She grinned. "Half-and-half."

"I love you, Elsbeth."

A tear slid out of her eye. "Be careful, my lord."

He nodded, afraid to say anything more, afraid he would snatch her up and never let her go.

Her golden eyes, now mist covered, memorized every part of him before she turned and ran out the door and down the steps.

Chapter Nineteen

Elsbeth was silently grateful that Northumberland's men traveled so quickly. After the second day, she was so numb with weariness and her backside so sore that her mind had little space to mourn the absence of Alex. When they stopped at night, she was asleep when her head met the blanket on the forest floor.

It was not that her two escorts were discourteous. They often asked during the first few days whether she would like to stop more often than for the brief rests needed by the horses. After her several refusals, respect took the place of resentment in their eyes, and they merely asked that she tell them if she grew too weary. She never did.

Her two escorts were William and Tate, and she knew from their careful speech that they were professional soldiers, and officers. They did not wear the duke's colors but were dressed as unemployed mercenaries, in light armor to dissuade any outlaws. She was dressed as their servant, and at brief stops at inns for food she took care of their horses and ate in the stable.

There were profuse apologies from the two in the beginning for the mean meals and lodging, but she had merely grinned and said she preferred the company of honest English folk to that of thieving English gentry. She said the words with mischief and a twinkle in her eye, and no offense was taken; her easy acceptance of the situation ended some of the awkwardness.

Both men were scrupulously polite, except in the presence of others; at one such time Tate affectionately cuffed her when she was not fast enough. That he could do so was a sign, she knew, that she was playing her role very well indeed.

At first Elsbeth had detected they resented the assignment—escorting a Scotswoman to the border seemed to them far beneath their skills and rank—but as several days passed they succumbed to her charm. Her uncomplaining nature and quick smile won their admiration, and the few times she allowed her sadness to show they tried in any number of ways to cheer her.

If detained, they had only been told to say they had found her, alone and confused, on the border and were escorting her to the Ker stronghold as a matter of chivalry.

As the party neared the border, they were more cautious, avoiding the inns. On the morning of the day they believed they would reach the Ker peel tower, Elsbeth replaced her boy's clothes with the dress and cloak she had worn when kidnapped. It had been cleaned at Northumberland's lodge, and now they creatively tore holes in her dress and rubbed dirt on both garments as well as on her face and arms.

Tate looked at her with narrowed eyes. She indeed looked as if she had been captive for a month or more, and little like the saucy attractive lady with whom they had started the journey. He did not like the idea of taking her to a place where such playacting was necessary. He did not want to see her in danger.

He looked at William and saw the same wariness reflected in his face.

"Perhaps," Tate said slowly, "you might put up two wandering soldiers for several nights."

"Or even hire us?" William said.

Elsbeth looked at them both. They had become more than mere escorts. They were friends. Mayhap most of the English weren't so bad after all.

"The Kers hire English mercenaries?" Her pert question was stated with a small smile. "How could I explain that? And what would your duke say?"

"That we should give you all the protection you require," Tate said readily.

"Employment is impossible," she said, "but...mayhap you can rest a few days...." Her mind was whirling with possibilities. It would be another diversion for whoever was the traitor. A cause of more confusion and, hopefully, more panic. And it was possible these two men could see more than she, who was so close to her clan. She certainly had an excuse to allow them to stay a few days, even if they were obviously English. They had, after all, rescued her.

The decision arrived at, the three of them made a most spectacular entrance beyond the walls of the Ker tower.

"Dear God be praised!" yelled one Ker clansman, guarding a trail to the tower. "Lady Elsbeth!"

The cry was taken up by sentries farther down the path until noise was ringing in Elsbeth's ears as she neared the gates. A growing throng of her clan—men, women and children—gathered and followed her and her escorts into the courtyard.

Ian was coming out the door of the tower, summoned by the shouts, and his face became wreathed in a broad smile as he recognized Elsbeth. In a gait more like a trot than a walk, he reached her side and raised his hands to help her down from her horse, squeezing her tightly as he held her.

"Are ye all right, Elsbeth?" There was no question about the sincerity in his voice. His face was drawn and weary looking.

"I'm tired, Ian," Elsbeth replied honestly enough. She wanted to escape to her room as soon as possible and rest before putting Alex's plan in motion. She needed to have all her wits about her.

"What happened? Where did ye come from? Who are these men?"

"I...escaped," she said in a trembling voice that was only half pretense. So much depended on her now.

"And these men?"

"They found me on the road. If they had not..." She shuddered, leaving Ian to swallow his dislike of the English and adopt at least a semblance of gratitude toward the two mounted mercenaries.

"It's grateful we are to ye," he said, "for bringing our lady home." It was an obvious dismissal.

"I promised them they could rest here," Elsbeth said, some part of her weary mind noting her cousin's mouth tighten.

Ian turned to the two men. "Ye are welcome," he said in a tone that indicated anything but welcome. He ordered a clansman to take the horses and another to show the two men to the barracks.

He then turned his entire attention to Elsbeth, noticing all the dishevelment. His gaze stopped and fastened on her shorn hair. His hand went up to finger a curl. "Your hair, Elsbeth..." There was both sympathy and pain in his voice.

"He—he cut it."

"Huntington?"

She bent her head. "He thought I wouldn't be recognized so readily if anyone saw me."

Ian took her arm and led her inside the tower. He didn't want anyone to hear his other questions. In the withdrawing room, he turned again to face her. "What else did he do, Elsbeth?"

Elsbeth looked at a face contorted by grief and fear. Fear for her. She felt suddenly guilty at the deception. Very, very guilty.

"Nothing," she said, "except keep me prisoner."

"He didn't—"

"He said he wanted no Scottish..." She stopped, letting him imagine the word.

"The English dog!" The words that followed were among the most colorful and profane she had ever heard from her usually good-natured cousin.

Ian stopped midway through his string of oaths to notice how tired she looked. He took her hand. "I'm sorry, little cousin. Ye need some rest. But first...can ye tell me where he took you, where he is?"

She shook her head. "He blindfolded me. Please, Ian, a bath...and some sleep."

"We will talk later, Elsbeth. Try to remember something, anything."

She nodded and started for the door when suddenly it burst open, and Patrick was there. He looked at her with disbelief, then bounded over to her and gave her a bear hug, unlike any display of affection he had ever shown her before.

He pulled back, almost as if embarrassed. "God's blood, but we've been looking everywhere for ye." Then, like Ian, he studied her carefully. "The English bastard. He'll pay for this!"

She wanted to cry out in protest, but she couldn't, not now. "He did not hurt me, Patrick, except perhaps my pride." Again, it was a true enough statement. Her pride *had* been hurt immediately after the kidnapping.

"Your hair, your bonny hair..."

"It will grow back," she said, growing impatient with their concentration on a detail she considered unimportant, considering all that had happened, all that was at stake.

"Tell me everything tha' happened," he commanded in a tone far more insistent that Ian's. "Where is he? I'll call out all the men."

"I don't know," she said. "He blindfolded me."

"But was it a castle? A cottage? How far did ye ride?"

Elsbeth widened her great golden eyes. "Patrick, I'm too tired to think. Please, I need a bath and some sleep, then you can ask all you want."

His voice gentled. "Of course, Elsbeth. I'm sorry, but I want to teach tha' whoreson a lesson."

"Both of us do," Ian broke in, his voice irritated. "Every member of the clan is aching to get their hands on Huntington."

Elsbeth felt like a ball being batted back and forth. She wanted to be alone. She wanted to think of Alex, wanted to remember his touch and the wonderful honeyed feelings he created in her. She stared at her two would-be champions vacantly.

"Please...I must go," she said unexpectedly in a voice harsher than she had ever used with them. As she saw the shock in their faces, her expression softened. "Please. I will go mad if I don't have some rest. I will talk to you both tomorrow."

Ian looked sheepish. "I'm sorry, Elsbeth. Come, Patrick."

Patrick threw him a disdainful look, but didn't argue after noticing an unusual hardness in Elsbeth's face. He didn't even want to think of the ordeal she had endured, but it was essential they go after the Englishman as soon as possible. And they needed information to do it. At last he nodded grudgingly. "In the morning, then, Elsbeth?"

"Aye," she agreed.

Patrick and Ian started to leave, and Annie, who apparently had been hovering outside, entered. "I've ordered a bath, my lady."

"Heaven," Elsbeth sighed, thinking of her tired muscles and backside...and privacy. Glorious wonderful privacy to think of Alex.

"Elsbeth!" Louisa stood there, anxiety written all over her face. "Are you all right?" she asked.

Elsbeth summoned a smile. There was so much concern on the girl's face she could do naught else. "I'm tired and hungry, Louisa, but other than that...quite whole."

"They didn't—I mean he didn't—"

"No," Elsbeth said gently.

Louisa's face spread into a great smile. "I'm so glad. Is there anything I can do for you, anything at all? Please."

Her expression was so open and honest, Elsbeth felt a sudden lurch in her heart. These were her people. What was she doing? Lying to them all? Trying to trap one of them? And yet, wasn't it better for them all if the traitor was revealed and peace came to the border?

Her smile faltered, and her shoulders sagged. Ian had gone, but Patrick remained in the doorway, having stopped as Louisa appeared. Now he seemed to notice Elsbeth's sudden weakness and leaned down, picking her up. Without a word he quickly carried her into the hall and up the steps to her bedchamber, Louisa skittering close behind him. When they reached her room, he placed her gently on the bed. "I'll talk to ye in the morning," he said. "Louisa, ye stay and look after her."

Even in her weary state, Elsbeth once more noticed the way Louisa's eyes followed Patrick, and the way Patrick's voice softened when he talked to her young ward. But she didn't dwell on the thought. A tub of steaming water was sitting in the center of the room, and Elsbeth smiled faintly. She should have known that Annie would have taken care of the matter.

She rose wearily and hugged Annie, who was standing by watchfully. "I've missed you," she said. She was surprised as the hug was returned in good measure, for Annie rarely allowed her feelings to show.

The housekeeper quickly released Elsbeth from her embrace and glared at Patrick until he left. She then eyed Louisa suspiciously before deciding to relinquish her charge. Elsbeth was being well tended. "I'll get ye some food," she said with a smile.

Elsbeth allowed Louisa to help her undress and then reclined into the tub with a sigh of pleasure, feeling the warm water soothe her tired body and sore muscles. "May I help you bathe?" Louisa asked.

Elsbeth wanted to say nay. She wanted to be alone with her own thoughts, but Louisa's eyes were like those of a spaniel, begging for affection and a chance to be of comfort.

She nodded, and closed her eyes as Louisa carefully soaped her back, kneading her shoulders and neck, until Elsbeth was totally relaxed. "What has happened since I've been gone?" she asked.

"Patrick and Ian have been like madmen," Louisa said. "They've been riding out every day. There's been no pleasing either of them."

"No attacks on the Careys?"

"No, my lady."

"Elsbeth. Please call me Elsbeth," Elsbeth said. She had been surprised when Louisa had spoken her name earlier when she had burst into her room. It was the first time she had departed from her shy "my lady." It had sounded good to Elsbeth's ears.

The girl's face lit up. "Elsbeth," she said tentatively.

Elsbeth rose and took a towel. She gave Louisa a hug and said good-eve, grateful at last to be alone. She put on the nightdress that had been laid on the bed, undoubtedly by Annie, and sank gratefully into the huge feather bed. A knock came, and she bade entrance. Annie came in with a tray containing a goblet of wine and some meat pies.

But Elsbeth was too tired to eat. She took several sips of wine under Annie's watchful eyes, and forced herself to eat a few bites, but then she shook her head helplessly. "I can do no more, Annie."

"'Tis no' enough to keep a wee bird alive."

Elsbeth tried a weak smile. "I'll do better in the morn, Annie. I swear."

"Then good night, my lady." Annie hesitated before leaving. "'Tis pleased I am ye're home. And safe. I would not ha' thought it of that blackguard, that he would steal ye awa'...and ye so kind to him."

"I abducted him, Annie," Elsbeth said wearily, tired of all the abuse being heaped on her husband.

"Aye, and ye nursed him when he was ill. He's just like all the others, although I thought different for a wee bit."

"He did not hurt me, Annie. He was very...considerate."

Annie grumped. "Ha. And what of yer reputation, my lady? Did he care about that? And yer hair. Yer beautiful hair."

Elsbeth closed her eyes, unable to bear more.

"Aye," she heard Annie's voice. "You get some sleep, little lamb. I'll jest sit here awhile with ye."

It was the last thing Elsbeth wished. She wanted to scream for everyone to leave her alone. She wanted only her own thoughts of Alex, of Lord and Lady Huntington and the hours they had spent together.

She satisfied herself with images of black unruly hair and lazy gray eyes and a smile that curled in crooked little ways, enchanting her.

Where are you, Alex? The question hovered in her mind. Had he made it back to the cabin? They had planned for it to be so. He could travel faster alone. Was he safe? Had he talked to David Garrick?

Alex. My husband. Alexander.

Complex, gentle, fierce Alexander.

Across from her, Annie watched her lady's face relax in sleep, then crease in a smile. The housekeeper made altogether the wrong assumption. She's that glad to be home, Annie thought. Now she'll marry Ian or Patrick. She'll know how badly she needs a strong husband. Now she'll provide an heir for the Kers.

* * *

Alex was tortured by his own images. It had been a hellish ride across England. Unlike Elsbeth and her escort, he dared not stop at any inns, but carried a supply of bread and cheese and some oatmeal. Despite the past several days of rich food, his stomach still demanded little, and he knew exactly how long he could go without food. He drank from the streams and slept under the trees, a not altogether disagreeable necessity for he had the stars and moon, and the whisper of trees to keep him company. He would never take any of them for granted. Not ever again.

But it was infernally lonely after the days he had spent with Elsbeth. He had grown accustomed to her impish smile and impulsive touches that told him, more than words, that she loved him. Loved him. It was a miracle above all others.

Alex shook her from his thoughts, however, as he neared the Huntington estate. He needed all his wits about him. He looked wryly at his clothes, comparing them to the fine velvets he had worn just a few days ago. The garments had belonged to an itinerant woodcutter. He rode a deceptively poor-looking mount. Though a fine animal, strong of leg and lung, nothing about it really matched. It was bony and appeared to be stiff-legged until pushed into gallop, and then it nearly flew. Northumberland had suggested the mount, saying with amusement he kept it only for comparison to his other horses. But Alex had seen the gleam in his eye and knew there was much more to the animal than met the eye.

He patted the gelding now, knowing he had pushed it to near, if not beyond, its endurance.

He rubbed his hands over his cheeks. In the past five days, they had become bristly and, he knew, dark. With his hat pulled down, he doubted if any but his brother would recognize him. Still, he moved with caution. He had waited until nightfall to approach the forest around Huntington. There was only a quarter moon, and even that was dotted by clouds. As he moved into the forest, the trees made eerie shadows in what little light filtered through the heavy growth. It was cold, and he had only a rough woolen doublet for warmth.

Alex and his horse, both tired and hungry, made for the poacher's cabin, Alex praying that it had remained undiscovered. Every rustle seemed ominous for nothing now was more important than staying alive.

He was near the barely visible opening to the hut when he heard the soft thud of hoofbeats. The sound was so soft he might have dismissed it had it not been for the sudden twitching of his horse's ears. The animal, too, had heard something.

Alex stood in the stirrups and reached for a branch overhead. In one swift movement, his hands grabbed it and his arms propelled him up and over the limb. One heel touched the horse's back, urging the animal forward. The confused but obedient gelding obeyed. Alex stretched along the branch, carefully balancing himself as he waited for whoever was coming.

The sound of hoofbeats came louder, and a lone rider appeared. Alex waited for several minutes, watching to see if anyone was with him. He grunted softly with satisfaction when no one appeared. He couldn't make out the rider in the dim light, until a cloud skittered from under the quarter moon, and a shaft of light penetrated the forest.

David.

Alex grinned. As quickly as he had ascended the tree, he now descended, landing on slightly bent knees before David's horse.

David Garrick fought to control his horse while he reached for his sword. And then he heard Alex's soft laughter. His hand released the hilt, and he shook his head.

"You can get killed that way, m'lord. Startling poor woodsmen," he said testily.

"I trust your reflexes, Davey."

It was the "Davey" that wiped away the frown and replaced it with a smile. "I'm glad to see you m'lord. Was it a profitable trip?"

"I thought we had eliminated 'my lord,' Davey."

David shrugged. "'Tis a hard habit to break. Did all go to plan?"

"Partially," Alex replied with a grin.

David's heavy brows furrowed together.

"I hadn't exactly planned on getting wed," Alex continued with an even wider smile, one that David had never seen before.

David stared at him. "It wouldn't be anyone I helped kidnap, would it?" It was asked suspiciously and not altogether happily.

"Aye."

"And with her own free will?"

"Most certainly."

David digested the information. A Carey to a Ker? Had the world come to an end?

He couldn't help but wonder about the reaction of both families. And he thought Alex Carey was completely out of his mind. But Alex Carey was, nonetheless, his friend, his lord. So he merely nodded without comment.

"No good wishes, Davey?"

"May I speak my mind?"

Alex smiled. "Please do."

"She's very pretty, but..."

"But?" Alex prompted.

David shrugged. The deed was done, and it was really none of his business. His lord knew, more than most, the possible consequences of his action. It was not David's place to gainsay him.

The smile left Alex's face. "No one else knows, Davey, other than Northumberland, who has the marriage certificate." All of the laughter was gone from Alex's voice now, and it was deadly serious. "I wanted you to know in case my plans go...awry. Take care of her, Davey. Take her, if necessary, to Northumberland. There could be a child. I want him or her protected, as well as Elsbeth."

David could only stare at him.

"Your word, David."

"You have it, of course, but—"

"If all goes as planned, we will marry again...here at Huntington with Careys and Kers invited."

"It would be war, my lord."

"Not if we approach it properly. They will know then that we both have traitors, who have plotted to continue to feud for their own purpose."

"Aye," David conceded, "but still there's much hatred. You can't erase it in a day."

"Perhaps not, but mayhap we can make a beginning."

David's doubt showed on his face.

"You and Hugh fared well enough together," Alex observed.

"Until I knocked him flat and stole his lady," David said wryly. "I no' think he'll be in much mind for friendship."

Alex couldn't stop a smile. It seemed he was smiling a lot lately, even if this were deadly business. "You will know soon enough. As soon as Lady Elsbeth returns to the Ker tower, she'll be sending Hugh to you."

David winced and lifted his eyes to the sky in supplication.

Alex chuckled. "Come with me, Davey. We have much to talk about tonight, and I don't think this is the best place to do it."

David dismounted and, after Alex had retrieved his horse, they both led their animals through the thickets to the hut. They tied their mounts to trees and went inside for protection against the growing wind.

"How has my brother been?"

For the first time, David smiled. "He's been doing a lot of riding. And each day he becomes more unreasonable. There will be many who will not be sad to see him gone."

"Has he said anything to you?"

"Only that there are outlaws and Kers in the woods, and we're to shoot at any movement."

"Nothing of me?"

"Only that the Kers must have murdered you. There are those who now wonder why he hasn't ordered a retaliatory raid."

Alex let out a long breath. It was going as planned. Yet seeing his brother revealed as a traitor gave him little joy. His life, by necessity, probably meant his brother's death. But there was no turning back now.

"Stay as close to my brother as possible from now on. Elsbeth will be giving the two men whom we suspect conflicting directions on how to get to me. The guilty one will rush to meet John and they will try to get rid of me quietly. Neither can afford to take a chance on my capture. The innocent one will wait and gather up enough men not only to take me but to exact revenge on Huntington. You must find out who the traitor is, and let Hugh know. He'll know what to do then. So do you."

"What if the Kers don't care if one of their own is involved? What if the two clans start fighting?"

"I'm hoping they will be too stunned to do that, too humiliated by their own betrayer."

David shook his head. "You're giving them credit for sense I've not yet seen."

"It's the only hope we have, David, if Elsbeth and I are to live in peace."

"Are you sure she's worth it?"

"If I'm not sure of another thing, Davey, I'm sure of that."

"Love," David said disgustedly. "It's the downfall of many a good man."

"You don't include yourself in that?"

"Aye, I do. That's exactly what I mean."

With a sympathetic but wry smile, David took his leave.

Chapter Twenty

The first morning back at the Ker tower was every bit as miserable as Elsbeth had thought it would be.

She was still sleeping when she woke to a harsh demanding pounding on her door. It wouldn't be either Patrick or Ian, she knew, for no matter how much they wanted information, neither would invade her sleeping chamber—although they might send someone else to do it.

When she finally pulled her wits together, she rose and put on a mantle lined with fur and fastened it at the neck with a brooch. Reluctantly she went to the door, hesitant to begin a day that almost certainly would be one of the worst in her life—a day of lies and treachery.

Joan was standing at the door. Elsbeth wondered why. Patrick's mother was usually the last person to wake and bestir herself, but now she was fully dressed, a frown further distorting a face made plain and tight by dissatisfaction.

There were no pleasantries as Joan pushed her way in. "I tried to see ye last night, but Annie would not allow me in. She takes too much upon herself."

"I gave her orders, Joan. She merely obeyed them."

"I can't believe ye didn't want to see your own family after such an ordeal."

Ordeal? This was the ordeal, Elsbeth wanted to yell. She was silent, however.

"Ye must go ahead with your marriage to Patrick," Joan continued heedlessly.

"Marriage?"

"Your reputation, Lady Elsbeth. After spending a month with that...that creature, ye're quite fortunate Patrick still wishes to marry ye."

Rage rose in Elsbeth, threatening to break down her cool pose. "Is that what Patrick said?"

Joan saw the flush rise in Elsbeth's face, and knew she had gone too far. "No, no, of course not," she hastened to add, "but I thought it was up to me—as your friend—to point out what everyone will be saying."

"I'm grateful you are so generous," Elsbeth said in a deceptively gentle voice. "But I think Patrick should speak for himself. Mayhap he is not quite as duty conscious as you are. Mayhap he believes me too sullied."

"Patrick would never..." There was an edge of desperation to Joan's voice.

"And I'm quite well, thank you for asking," Elsbeth said sarcastically.

Joan turned white at the implication of the words. "Of course, I asked Annie if ye had been hurt—"

"Then why do you believe I must marry?"

"No one will believe—"

"Do you think I lie?"

"No... but a month!"

"I would not saddle Patrick with such a burden," Elsbeth said sweetly.

"But he loves you..."

"Does he, Joan? Does he really? It appears he has an eye for Louisa."

"Of course he's kind to her," Joan said desperately. "But she means nothing to him. He has always loved ye."

Elsbeth wanted to say more, to ask about the other women she had oft heard about, but she had other battles to wage today. "Then let him tell me, Joan," she said in dismissal.

She was saved then by Annie, who entered with a tray of food. The housekeeper cast a disapproving look at Joan after spying Elsbeth's slightly flushed face. "My lady needs rest," she said abruptly.

Joan turned around angrily. "I was only trying to help."

"My thanks," Elsbeth said with a tinge of irony that completely escaped Joan, who was slightly mollified as she left.

"And what did that one want?" Annie asked.

"To save my sullied reputation by marriage to her son."

Annie studied her mistress's face. There was something different about it, something glowing behind the worry that also lay there. "'Twould not be a bad thing for ye to marry, my lady."

"And whom would you have me take? Ian or Patrick?" Elsbeth asked curiously.

Annie hesitated, but she had been with Elsbeth many years and was used to speaking her mind. "Patrick," she said finally.

"Why?"

Annie shrugged. She herself didn't know why. Perhaps because he seemed the stronger of the two, the more able to cope with what surely must come now. Since Elsbeth's return yestereve, there had been naught but talk of revenge for Elsbeth's kidnapping. It was a matter of clan honor. Blood would be running across the border like water.

"Why not Ian?" Elsbeth probed.

Annie smiled. Mayhap her lady was finally coming to her senses about the need for marriage. "He'd make a good husband, too," she allowed.

"You're no help at all, Annie," Elsbeth said wryly, wondering why she had bothered, why she thought Annie might have seen something she hadn't.

"Now eat," Annie scolded. "Ye look much too peaked."

Elsbeth eyed the hot oatmeal, ale and bread and thought of the courses upon courses at Northumberland's hunting lodge. And, consequently of Alex. She sat quickly and lowered her head, hoping the flush in her cheeks didn't betray her.

"Tell Patrick I would like to see him alone right after I break fast," she told Annie, who beamed in complete misunderstanding.

"Aye, my lady," she said and left quickly.

* * *

Patrick looked grim when he faced Elsbeth in the withdrawing room. "I'm gathering the clan," he said abruptly. "I would like your approval to attack Huntington."

Elsbeth's eyes widened. It was not what she had expected. "When?"

"No more than four days' time."

"I don't think Lord Huntington will be there," she said slowly. "He knows his brother didn't pay the ransom."

"He has no place else to go," Patrick said, eyeing her speculatively. "Unless ye heard something different."

"He isn't sure of the loyalty of his tenants or men at war after so long an absence," Elsbeth said. "He has some plan. I don't know what it is."

"Can ye remember anything about where you were held?"

"It was by a stream," she said. "I know that because he let me wash there."

"How far?" The question was curt as Patrick weighed the information.

"I—don't know. He blindfolded me. It seemed we rode forever."

"Remember, Elsbeth. Try to remember anything. How many streams did ye pass on the way? And when ye escaped, which direction did ye go in?"

"Two," she said slowly. "I think we passed over two streams."

"And returning?"

"I don't know. I got lost and went in circles. There was a bog. I know that."

"Was he alone, Elsbeth, or did he have someone helping him?"

"Alone, I think. I never saw anyone."

"Where did he keep ye?"

"It was a small hut...no windows and a stout door. He often left me there alone several days in a row. But he always made sure I had enough food and water."

Patrick's face tightened. "Where did he sleep?"

"I don't know," Elsbeth said. "He never stayed in the hut."

Patrick looked into her face, and was finally satisfied. There was no shame there . . . or guilt.

"How close were the two streams?" he asked, returning to his previous line of questions.

"Not far, I think," she said. She could almost see the calculations in his mind—the convergence of the two streams, an old hunting cabin. It was not the one she and Alex had stayed at, but another Alex knew about.

Patrick changed the subject. "The two Englishmen—they've been fed and sheltered. 'Tis time, I think, they left. They could be spies."

Elsbeth shook her head. "They were very kind, Patrick, and they are tired. I promised them several days' rest."

Patrick stood silently for a moment. "Ye are too soft-hearted, Elsbeth, but it will be as ye say." His hand came down on her shoulder, and his mouth softened in a way she had never seen before. "We'll make the bastard pay, Elsbeth. Aye, we'll make all the Careys pay. This I swear to ye."

He leaned down, and his lips touched her cheek, before he swept out of the room with great purpose.

Ian was next. He had been waiting impatiently, his hand on his sword, wearing a path in the stone floor outside the withdrawing room. He had greatly resented the fact that Patrick had been summoned first, but then, he allowed, he had been outside earlier, practicing his swordsmanship. Perhaps Patrick had been available first.

He only slightly wondered why Elsbeth wanted to see them separately. It was a tactic she had used before, seeking their opinions individually before making a decision. Together, he and Patrick often started arguing. They could, he realized ruefully, be overbearing in combination. But why Patrick first?

If Patrick had received any favoritism, Ian couldn't tell from the bright welcoming smile on Elsbeth's face. He grinned back and took her hand to his lips.

"God's tooth, but 'tis good to have ye back. Now for a bit of Carey bloodletting," he said with enthusiasm. "Patrick has already called in the clan."

"I want you to get word to the Rutherford clan," Elsbeth said. "If we go on Huntington land, I want sufficient strength."

"Aye," Ian said. "But do ye know where to find the Carey?"

"I told Patrick I don't think he will go to Huntington... not yet. He had something afoot, perhaps summoning help from London. We must strike before he does so."

Ian unrolled something in his hand, and Elsbeth saw it was a map of the border area, one she hadn't seen before. "I thought if ye looked at the map, ye might be able to guess where he is."

Elsbeth studied it carefully and found the second site Alex had selected. There was a waterfall nearby.

"I think... I remember hearing a waterfall," she said hesitantly. She hated herself as she looked at Ian's open face.

It's for the good of everyone, of every Ker, she told herself. Everyone but the traitor.

But how could it be Ian?

Or Patrick?

Dear God, let it be someone else.

She had four days. The traitor had four days. Four days before the clan would be called out. Both she and Alex had gambled that she could put a stop to any raid on Huntington in the event Alex's brother and the Ker traitor didn't show their hands. Today she wasn't quite so sure, not now that she had seen the deep anger of her people.

But Alex had been positive that their plan would work, that their two targets would be so well trapped that they would have no choice but to act together.

"I'll go now," Ian was saying, his blue eyes fixed piercingly on Elsbeth. "I love ye," he said, and the corner of his mouth trembled with emotion. "Dear God, I would like to tear tha' Carey to pieces."

Elsbeth tried to smile as she held out a hand to him in farewell.

There was one more person for Elsbeth to see.

Hugh.

She didn't know exactly how he would respond to her request. The last time she had seen him, he was on the floor of the stable, his head bleeding on the straw. She didn't think he would have much fondness for the Careys.

But he was still the same Hugh, rugged and profane and hearty.

She had ridden over to his cottage, not wanting anyone in the tower to hear her words. It was obvious he was expecting her. He was sitting in front of the cottage, his eyes bemused as she rode up, and he hobbled over to help her down from the saddle.

"Ye look no' the worse for wear, lassie," he observed dryly as he studied her carefully.

She smiled slightly. "Neither do you."

"I should ha' known ye can never trust a Carey."

"Do you trust *me,* Hugh?"

His eyes opened wide at the meaning, the implication of her words. . . .

"Ye didna, lass?"

Her smile deepened. She and Alex had agreed they would tell no one yet. It was too dangerous and could ruin all their plans, but she could tell Hugh that she planned to wed Alex. It should help rein in his anger.

"You would disapprove?"

"I would ha' to ponder it, lass," he said, his hand rubbing the back of his neck.

"I love him, Hugh," Elsbeth said, her smile disappearing.

"Aye, I thought ye did even then, tho' you didna know it."

"You're not angry with me then?"

"Not when I see that sparkle in yer eye, Lady Elsbeth. Now, I know ye ha' something on yer mind. We'll go for a wee walk."

It was done!

Everything had been set in place, Elsbeth thought as she dressed for dinner.

She had asked both Patrick and Ian to delay their journeys until the morn. She had to be sure that Hugh had time to reach David Garrick.

The meal was a nightmare, she thought, instead of the celebration Ian and Patrick had planned. She looked at the dear faces—and even the not so dear ones—and wondered again if what she was doing was right. Ian and Patrick were on either side of her, both looking relaxed and pleased she was back with them. Louisa was next to Ian, and Joan to Patrick, and she saw Louisa look longingly across the table. Farther down sat the other clansmen in order of rank and importance.

She shared a trencher with Ian, and food was heaped upon it as if everyone feared she had been starved near to death. Once more she felt not a little traitorous.

No questions about her captivity were forthcoming, and she was grateful. It was as if there had been common agreement that unpleasant things would not be mentioned at dinner. Even Joan was pleasant.

Wine was poured in plentiful amounts until she thought she could swim in it. It dulled some of the pain. Pain of betrayal, pain of aloneness, pain of missing Alex. She could only remember another dinner...a wedding dinner when fingers touched and souls met, and promises were exchanged.

Several fiddlers and a harp player were called upon to provide entertainment, and Elsbeth studiously kept her eyes on the performers rather than Ian, whose leg touched hers more often than needed, and whose hand continued to pour wine. When she looked at him, his blue eyes were intense with passion, and she felt still another sickening stab of guilt. What was she doing?

She finally pleaded fatigue, and both her cousins insisted on accompanying her to her bedchamber, despite her protestations. She was grateful for Ian's strong arm as the floor seemed to move beneath her, and she felt her smile grow silly. But she had needed the wine, the liquid courage, to survive this night.

She had three more to survive.

Annie was still busy in the kitchen, and had asked one of the other women servants to build a fire in Elsbeth's chamber and help her prepare for bed. Uncharacteristically, Elsbeth accepted the assistance, knowing she had drunk far more than was wise.

When the girl had snuffed out the candles and gone, Elsbeth lay in the great bed, half awake, half asleep. Crowds of people filled her mind. Careys and Kers. Ian and Patrick, whose handsome faces turned ugly, and Hugh, who was splashed with blood. Then there was Alex, sitting on a tall black horse, looking out over it all. Until an arrow found his chest and pierced it.

"Here, lamb. Poor little lamb." Annie's familiar soothing voice broke into the nightmare. Elsbeth grasped her hands and held on to them as she had held onto Alex's the night she almost sank in the bog. Alex! her mind cried. *I need you.* Alex.

Alex woke up in the hut. The blankets there still smelled slightly of Elsbeth, and he pulled them closer than necessary for the warmth. In his sleep, he had thought he heard her cry out. The sound still hovered in the small hut.

She should have reached the Ker holding sometime in the past two days. He had no way to determine how fast she and Northumberland's men had traveled. But he knew she was there now.

He lay looking up at the thatch roof, his mind crowded with worry about her. Should he have sent her back?

Alex knew his part of the plan was much easier than hers, and even his role hurt part of his soul. Hers must be terrible, indeed, since she was so close to those she had to deceive.

He smiled bleakly in the darkness. She had so much courage, so much spirit. He had been fortunate in his life to know two such women, and miraculously lucky to have had the friendship of one and the love of the other.

But still, it ate like poison into his spirit that Elsbeth was alone now, and needed him . . . for her call had come to him as surely as if she were in this room.

A few days. That should be all that was required. And then he would never let her out of his sight again.

He toyed with the idea of disguising himself and going to the Ker castle, but it was a mad idea, and he knew it instantly.

He also considered returning to Huntington and commandeering the troops, fetching her forcibly from among the Kers. But he would only be increasing her danger. If she were with child, John would do anything to eliminate all three of them. And only God knew the amount of blood that would then be shed between the families.

God's blood, he swore to himself, his fingers moving with frustration. It had to work. Dear Jesus in heaven, it had to work!

In the meantime, he could only wait. Wait and fear and hope, for he was as chained to this hut now as he ever had been to the galley benches.

Elsbeth. I love you, Elsbeth.

Miles away, Elsbeth relaxed and finally fell into a peaceful sleep.

David Garrick leaned against the thick stone outer wall of Huntington. He had checked the guards, trading several ribald jokes as his eyes carefully scanned the courtyard. He accepted a cup of ale and sat cross-legged, trading tales of battle.

The great gates would be closed for the night within minutes. He was waiting to see whether any strangers approached with the crowd of humanity moving in and out of the gates: servants from the castle returning to their cottages, soldiers relieved of duty returning to their barracks. There was another way out of the castle grounds, but few knew of it. Those few included John and Alexander Carey, and David, who had once been shown the tortuous tunnel by Alex. It was an escape route that ran under the castle walls to a cave in the woods.

It was the way John Carey had left the castle several times, but David knew no messenger would be given the secret. He would have to come through the front gates.

He wondered whether this were not a worthless vigil. The Lady Elsbeth would probably not have had time to reach Scotland yet. But he would take no chances.

His eyes caught a new face. More noticeable than the strangeness of the features was the way the man tried to blend in with the others. He leaned over to another man and said something quietly, and listened intently as the man he had queried pointed to the barracks.

David lazily rose, saying he must complete his inspection, and followed the stranger. Once at the door of the barracks, the man asked one of the mercenaries for a man named Simon. He had news of the man's family, he said. A death to report.

David allowed himself a grim satisfaction. So the lady had returned to the tower, and the plan was under way. Now to watch the secret exit in the woods.

With a hearty word for the guards at the gate, he slipped out. It would take time for the message to get to John. David could get something to eat. It would be a long night.

And it was. His horse well hidden, David spent a chilled night just beyond the secret exit. The hours passed painfully slowly as nothing stirred except a cold wind. By dawn, he knew that John had not met his counterpart that night, and he didn't think John would dare a meeting during daylight.

David would get some sleep, some warm food and perhaps even some comfort from a lonely wife.

Tomorrow night. It had to be tomorrow night.

Chapter Twenty-one

David's sleep did not last long. A peddler's wagon, bells tinkling, drew up to his cottage, and he was awake at the first faint sound of its coming.

His wife, Judith, was out the door immediately. The arrival of a peddler was a major event. In seconds she was exclaiming over a selection of needles, always a wanted item.

The peddler, a cap pulled down over his fleshy face and a cane giving him support, glowered at David.

David felt a discomfort new to him. He had done this man a disservice during a truce, and he did not like the guilt he was feeling. But he spoke pleasantly enough. "You look well, peddler."

"No thanks to certain blackguards," the peddler replied with a baleful eye. "Ye canna trust anyone in these hard days."

David nearly choked at the open insult. "Aye," he said slowly, regaining his composure. "'Tis hard to know who is friend and who is enemy."

Judith looked up, almost feeling the palpable hostility in the air. "David?"

"Is there something you need, Judith?"

Her face lit with sudden joy.

"Fetch some coins from the pouch," he said, "and select as you will." The wariness in his eyes left for a second as he watched her move quickly into the cottage.

"She's a bonny lass," Hugh said reluctantly.

David stood there awkwardly. He had never apologized to anyone in his life, particularly an enemy. It galled him that

honor dictate he do it now. "I—am sorry it was necessary to..."
He couldn't force any more words from his throat.

Unbelievably, the peddler grinned. He could tell each word
was wrenched from the Englishman's soul, and he understood. Duty was oft unpleasant. "'Tis apparent no real harm
was done." His grin disappeared. "But if one hair of my lady's
head had been hurt—"

"Or my lord's," David said, and the truce was back in place,
their positions firmly stated.

"Aye," the peddler said. "Your lord should be back."

"I know," David said. "I've seen him. And Lady Elsbeth?"

"She is well."

"She has courage," David conceded.

"Aye...and Lord Huntington's a braw and canny man for
all he's English and a Carey. He must have Scot in him."

David couldn't stop a low chuckle at the observation, then his
tone turned serious. "A stranger arrived last night with a message for a man name Simon, a personal servant to John."

"You think it came from the traitor?"

David nodded. "With news of your lady's return."

"And mayhap plans for a meeting?"

"Almost certainly."

"When?"

"Tonight, I wager. That's when they've met before—at night
like two craven dogs."

"Dogs, mayhap," Hugh said softly. "But not craven. Do not
underestimate either Ian or Patrick Ker—if one of them is
guilty."

"I should know tonight."

"I'll go wi' ye."

"Nay. 'Tis better if you wait. If I'm discovered..."

There was sense in the Englishman's words. Hugh also knew
he could no longer dart silently about the woods as he once
could. He cursed his leg, and himself as a useless old man.

David Garrick offered his hand. Hugh took it, firmed his
shoulders and turned back to the wagon as Judith Garrick returned, clutching a gold piece.

* * *

David had no difficulty following John that night. Alex's brother had emerged from the cave and was met there by Simon, who had left with a horse before the gates closed. Now John took the horse, and ordered Simon to trot alongside him.

Although he had brought a mount with him, David decided to follow on foot. Since Simon was also on foot, it was doubtful that John would travel too fast for him to follow. And it was much quieter and safer to walk than to ride. He moved quietly, his shadow blending in with those of the trees.

He did not know how long he followed, only that it seemed a very long time. Finally John Carey stopped, and David dropped to the ground and carefully inched forward. He did not forget about Simon, who stood off to one side, holding the horse, while Carey paced impatiently. Soon there was the rustle of leaves as another horseman emerged from the woods, dressed as before in a flowing black cloak that made him all but invisible.

There were no greetings this time.

"I know where he is," the cloaked man said after dismounting.

"Can we get to him tonight?"

"Nay. He's on the other side of your holding, and I have to get back."

"Tomorrow night, then."

"Aye. I want him dead now as badly as ye. And I want to make it slow."

"Don't be a fool! Give him a chance and he'll have you, not the other way. He's to be ambushed."

"I want to face him, man to man, after what he's done to Elsbeth."

"Christ!" John swore. "Another bloody fool."

"It will be my way, or I won't tell ye where he is."

John hesitated, and David could almost hear him thinking. "Done," Carey said finally. "Where is he?"

The Ker used a flint to light a torch, then knelt on the ground, using a branch to make a map. He didn't worry about Carey going earlier than agreed. The Englishman couldn't afford to take any of his men, other than Simon, and the Scot knew John Carey needed him.

"Elsbeth described a hut there...."

David could hear John's indrawn breath. "I know it. An old hunting cabin. There're several scattered throughout these woods. But I looked there. There was no trace."

"He's no fool. He kept her moving, but that was the last location. She remembers the waterfall."

David leaned against the tree. The waterfall. He now knew which cousin was involved.

Quietly, very quietly, he stole away and took another trail through the forest to Huntington. He must get back as soon as possible and tell Hugh of the meeting. The Scot would have a long ride tonight, and much convincing to do tomorrow.

Hugh arrived by horse. Elsbeth didn't ask where the wagon was, not when she saw the grim expression on his face. "You know," she said.

"Aye, and it gi' me little pleasure."

Elsbeth's face went white, and she led the way into the withdrawing room and closed the doors. It was late midday. Ian had left this morning for the Rutherfords, and Patrick was training a group of clansmen in the courtyard.

Several tears spilled from her eyes as she heard Hugh out. There had always been a hope, buried deep inside, that there was another explanation. Now she had to accept the truth.

"How could he, Hugh?"

Hugh shrugged. He had little sympathy for a traitor, yet he sought to soften the blow. "I think mayhap he thought he was the rightful leader," he comforted her as he saw the suffering in her eyes.

"Do you think he could have had a hand in my father's death?"

"Garrick says so, that he heard 'em speaking of it."

"Do you believe him?"

"It hurts me to believe an Englishman against my own kind, my lady, but aye, I do. I always wondered about that ambush, how they knew where your fa was going that day."

Elsbeth let the tears come and felt Hugh's warm awkward embrace. "Cry, my lass. Cry 'em out."

It was like the night she sat with Alex after he was wounded and she feared he might die. For weeks she had bottled up such strong emotions that once they started to leak, tears came in torrents. She cried for her lost innocence, and for three children who had played together. She cried for her father, and she cried for Alex. She cried for the centuries of hatred that had brought this tragedy about.

When there were no more tears left, she straightened her shoulders. "Call Patrick."

David carefully recruited five men. He had fought with them all and knew them to be courageous and reasonably honorable—as honorable as mercenaries could be. He was fairly sure they would not countenance the death of the rightful earl of Huntington. Once John Carey was killed or taken, all the other men at arms would follow the five.

David was thankful the captain was on patrol, for he did not trust that man's honor. He had been employed by John and was involved in the ambush death of the old laird of Ker. If John went, the captain would know his days in a lucrative post would soon be ended.

David explained to his small group that he had been told of some outlaws near the waterfall on the eastern side of Huntington. He emphasized several times over that no action was to be taken without his approval. He wanted the leader alive.

David knew his small party had time to reach the clearing at the waterfall. Although John had left earlier on horseback to meet, David presumed, the Ker clansman, it would take the two conspirators several hours to reach the setting of the trap.

He could only pray now that Hugh and Elsbeth had been able to convince a number of Kers to be there also.

And he particularly prayed that the bands would not start fighting and destroy each other before the main players of their very dangerous game appeared.

He knew Alex was waiting at the clearing beside the waterfall. Earlier in the day, David had used the excuse of trailing the outlaws to visit Alex and tell him what had happened the pre-

vious night. David and Alex had debated the wisdom of the
earl's being the bait, but Alex insisted on being there.

"God's blood," David had told him. "You're determined to
get killed one way or another."

"Not now," the earl said softly. "Not with Elsbeth waiting."

With a snort of disgust, David had left.

Now David worried, as he had worried all day, that something would go wrong. So many things, in fact, could go
wrong. The plan had seemed logical at first under Alex's
coaxing tongue, but now he saw any number of problems in it.
Not the least of which was the stark, blood-red hatred between
the two clans, the two families, the two enemies.

He had kissed Judith with more than usual passion this evening, wondering whether he would see her again.

The night was pitch-black, yet each of the men was used to
night riding and night raiding. Their eyes adjusted until they
could make out shapes and forms, and instinct did the rest.

Elsbeth shifted in her saddle as she looked at the stiff backs
of her comrades. There were six of them, no more. It had taken
all her persuasion, and that of Hugh, to convince Patrick, and
still she saw from his savage expression he didn't like the situation one bit.

He hadn't believed her at first. He and Ian had never been
close friends, but they had fought together for years and respected each other's abilities.

"It's a Carey trick to divide us," he had said when Elsbeth
slowly, sadly, told him what had happened.

"Then how did a Carey know where I told Ian that the earl
of Huntington could be found?"

Patrick's eyes narrowed. "Ye also told me."

Elsbeth hesitated. This was the hardest part. He would know
she had not trusted him, either.

"I told you different places," she said finally.

"And waited to find out which popped out of a Carey's
mouth?" His tone was bitter as he realized exactly what had
happened. He turned around and stared at a wall.

"And your kidnapping?" he finally asked. "Was that a trick too?"

She heard the pain in his voice, and she wondered if she had ever really known Patrick. She certainly hadn't known Ian. "No," she replied softly. "It was very real."

"But you helped him escape? A Carey?"

"Aye," she admitted softly.

"And ye call Ian a traitor?"

The accusation, bitter and damning, was like a knife thrust into her heart.

Hugh, seeing her face whiten, spoke for the first time. "I aided him, too, Patrick. He's no' like the other Careys. He wants peace on the border. It wouldna done us any good to kill him, and tha' was what it was coming to."

Patrick spun around on him. Everything he had known, had trusted, was coming apart. Ian. Elsbeth. Hugh. The Careys had been his enemy, his clan's enemies, all his life. "Damn ye to hell," he whispered, his hands clenching and unclenching in an effort to keep from striking out.

Elsbeth took a step toward him. "Patrick . . . it's time for it to end, for the killing to end. Please. We need you."

"And what about Huntington? Do ye need him, too?"

Elsbeth flinched at the deep bitterness in his voice, and she was trying to form an answer as he continued.

"What happened in that month ye were gone?" There was accusation in his voice, condemnation.

I married him, she wanted to say. But she had promised Alex, and, looking at Patrick's furious face, she knew this was not the time.

"I learned what kind of man he is," she said quietly.

"God's blood, Elsbeth, he kidnapped ye!"

"And what did we do to him?"

"That was war. He's a man, an enemy, not a helpless—"

"Am I helpless, Patrick? Is that what you believe? Was I not there when we took him? Did I not give the orders?"

" 'Tis different," he said stubbornly.

"It's no' so different," she replied gently, lapsing into the border speech. "He wanted to stop the killing, to get me to listen to him. I wouldna when he was here, a prisoner. Why should I have? I knew he would do anything, say anything, to get free."

At least Patrick was listening, she thought as she noticed his face set in a deep frown.

"He knew his brother wanted him dead," Elsbeth continued, pleading with him to understand. "He knew someone from here had helped John Carey. No one but his brother knew he swam in that pool in the morning. And despite our sending three messengers with ransom demands, not one arrived at Huntington. That meant one of our men had to kill them before they reached Huntington. John couldna afford to have anyone know he refused his brother's ransom and caused his death."

"And wha' is a Carey's life to us?"

"It's much to me," Elsbeth said softly. "It could be much to us all. Think, Patrick, if we can graze our sheep and cattle in peace, if the crofters can farm without knowing 'tis likely the harvest will be stolen or burned."

"Ye canna trust a Carey," Patrick said stubbornly.

"You trust me, don't you?"

She saw the doubt in his face, and once again she felt mortally wounded. She wondered if some of the wounds could ever be healed.

"I canna believe Ian is a traitor," he said.

"If I can prove it . . ." Even as she said the words, they hurt. Dear God in heaven, but she needed Alex. She thought of Ian's laughter, his smiling mouth, his teasing way. . . .

"How?" The one word was like a pistol shot in the room, full of challenge.

Hugh answered this time, afraid that his lady was near the end of her strength. Her mouth was trembling and he could tell she was barely withholding tears.

"John Carey and Ian met last night, and Ian told Carey where he could find his brother—in a hunter's cottage near a waterfall. They plan to go there tonight to slay him."

"Ian's gone to the Rutherfords," Patrick protested.

Neither Hugh nor Elsbeth said anything.

"It's naught but another Carey trick," Patrick said. "They probably intend to ambush all of us."

"I will go with you, Patrick," Elsbeth said.

"He has ye bewitched."

"He is my husband," Elsbeth said. At some point—she didn't know when—she had realized she would have to tell him. She could convince him no other way.

Patrick stood there stunned. Hugh was also struck silent.

When Patrick finally found his tongue, he said furiously, "Ye've just given me another reason to kill him."

"Then you might as well kill me. Now."

She saw from Patrick's face that he knew she meant it. It went white. She moved to him.

"Patrick...I love him. There's so much you don't know about him, or how good a man he truly is. Forget for a moment he's a Carey. Remember when he could have killed you, and he did not?"

"I canna forget he's a Carey," Patrick said. "What in God's name have ye done?"

"Help me, Patrick," she pleaded, knowing that if she didn't have his support she would have none at all. Not now. She had risked all in telling him.

He stared at her, at her intense golden eyes that pleaded with him, at the trembling mouth that betrayed the fear she was trying so hard to hide. He remembered her as a girl, crying when an animal died in a trap, or when one of the men was hurt in training. He had teased her then, telling her she had too soft a heart. He had said it again only recently.

"D'ye really love him, Elsbeth?" His voice was softer than she had ever heard it.

"Aye."

"Ye truly have a soft heart, but usually a good head."

For the first time, she felt hope rising in her.

"I'm no' convinced," he warned, "but if Ian has betrayed us..." He stopped as if he could not bear to consider the possibility. "I'll raise the men we need."

Elsbeth prayed. This was the second hurdle. "We can take no more than six."

Patrick stared at her as if she were mad. "On Carey land?"

"Any more, and we'll scare them away. Alex will have no more Careys there."

"Ye're daft, lass. Alex. *Alex!* He's a Carey. Remember your father."

Elsbeth's back stiffened. "I'll go alone with Hugh, if need be . . . if you're afraid."

Patrick's face flushed. She had neatly trapped him.

"I pick the men," he said.

"Hugh and I go."

He had given her one last bitter look before striding out. "God help ye, Elsbeth. Ye best be right."

Patrick had said no further words to her. They had saddled and mounted in silence after she had explained the location they were headed for. The other men had been equally silent. They hadn't been told where they were going, but the tension between Patrick and Elsbeth was only too evident. There was a grimness, a terrible sense of purpose that seemed to affect them all.

Emotions rushed through Elsbeth like water through a cracked vessel. Several times she felt her stomach would reject the few bites of food she had forced down. She would soon see Alex, be with him forever, she hoped. But before that could happen, there would probably be at least one death tonight. She had no illusions about the outcome. If Ian were caught, her clan would never let him leave alive. Nor, she thought, would the Careys let John go free.

She had already shed her tears for Ian, but that didn't make her grief any less. And she knew Alex well enough now to know he would grieve even over a brother who had betrayed him.

And that, she knew, was probably the least that could happen.

Elsbeth couldn't help but note the wariness of her clansmen as they approached Carey land, and the way they kept their hands close to their swords. All carried the two-handed swords, and Patrick also had a pistol strapped to his side.

A terrible clawing fear took hold inside her, and she clasped the pommel of her saddle. Something she didn't understand, something dark and deadly, flooded her. At the same moment a cloud passed over the half moon, and an ominous blackness quenched what little light there was. The forest seemed impossibly still and silent. Leather had been tied to the horses' hooves to muffle their sound, and there was only their very soft thuds to pierce the quiet.

She trembled. Something terrible was going to happen, something more than had been planned. She knew it. Her head felt smothered in the closeness of the air, and her breath came unevenly.

Alex, she cried silently in the night. *Alex, be careful, my love. Be careful.*

Moments later, Hugh moved up next to Patrick. The soft hoot of an owl came across the forest, and Hugh answered it with one of his own. He signaled the riders to stop and wait, and soon two dark-clothed horsemen emerged from the trees; Elsbeth recognized Alex and David Garrick.

If there was tension before, it was doubly so now. Hands were on weapons. Lips were tight and grim, and faces were etched with suspicion.

Alex and Garrick made sure their own hands were nowhere near their weapons as they cautiously approached Patrick and Hugh in the deep shadows. Elsbeth moved forward to join them.

The clouds passed from over the moon, and she could see the harsh, guarded expressions on the faces of the men. They gave no greetings, but merely studied one another for several moments. There was so much dislike in the exchange that Elsbeth knew the slightest wrong movement could end in wholesale battle.

"Lord Huntington?" she said anxiously, breaking the stalemate, and she saw Alex's quick flashing smile in the moonlight. Yet it was not the easy smile she had discovered in London, but one filled with warning.

Patrick looked from one to another, disliking intensely the unspoken but very clear familiarity between the two. His back arched in displeasure and resentment. "Ye say a Ker man will be along?"

Alex looked at Elsbeth. "It will be a hard night for all of us. I think Lady Elsbeth should wait here."

"No," Elsbeth said. "I am part of it. I stand with you."

Patrick's hands clenched tightly on the pommel of his saddle as he felt the strength of feeling flowing between his cousin and the man he considered his enemy. He did not want to agree with Lord Huntington. He was still convinced this was a trap, even while two Careys were neatly surrounded by his own six men.

"Elsbeth—" her cousin started.

"No," she said, anticipating his agreement with Alex. It was, she thought wryly, the one time they had seemed to agree about anything. She pulled herself straight in the saddle. "I am still leader of the clan."

Patrick eyed her balefully as the other riders shifted uncomfortably in their saddles. He knew they would follow his orders to hold her here. But he needed each one of them in case of a Carey trick.

He nodded, noticing the way Alex's lips thinned. "Ye can try to keep her here if ye think ye can," Patrick said with a brief trace of amusement, the first indication of anything but complete hostility toward Alex. But then his countenance turned forbidding again. "What d'ye think to show us?" It was a challenge.

Alex eyed the man he had fought not long previously. It was clear the Scot was unconvinced either of Alex's intentions or of the accusation against Ian Ker. Elsbeth must have had one devil of a time getting him here.

"We have five men-at-arms hidden in the trees," Alex said. "I'd suggest you tie your horses here and follow me." He was careful to make it a suggestion.

Patrick glowered at him. "Wi' my pistol at your back, my lord."

Alex looked at him and shrugged. It was all he could do to keep his eyes from Elsbeth, but he knew it was the better part of wisdom. The Scots were dangerously hot-tempered at the moment. He wanted to do nothing to spark an explosion.

They dismounted, Patrick reluctantly leaving one man to keep the horses quiet, although Garrick said they were some distance from the clearing.

True to his word, Patrick kept his pistol aimed at Alex's back, and Alex could only pray he didn't stumble and discharge the weapon by mistake. It was obvious no ready trust was being offered. But then he had suspected it would not be.

He glanced to one side where Garrick walked, and to the other where Elsbeth hurried to keep pace with the long-legged Scots. She turned and smiled, uncertainly, even fearfully, and he badly wanted to take her hand and reassure her. His hand ached to do so, but he looked at the fury-filled faces of his reluctant companions and resisted, his fingers knotting in a tight fist.

They reached the clearing, and Alex could see the Huntington men emerging from the trees. The pistol pressed harder into his back. He could see Garrick's men go for their weapons as they saw the Scots, and he heard surprised exclamations as they caught sight of their long-missing lord.

Again came the soft hoot of an owl, and David Garrick waved his hands to signal them all to move back into the trees. Alex, disregarding whispered questions, nodded for the men to obey.

Patrick, his weapon still pressed firmly against Alex's back, ordered his men to move back also, and the eight of them stepped quietly into the thick band of trees.

The clearing itself was only dimly lit by moonlight. The shadow of the hunter's shelter looked haunting, as a wisp of pale gray smoke from its chimney invaded the deep blue velvet of the night. A second hoot came, and Elsbeth knew, as did the others, that it heralded the arrival of more riders. She leaned closer to Alex, taking strength from him.

One man came first on horseback to the edge of the trees. He studied the clearing as both the Scots and English stayed hidden behind the foliage. Within a few minutes, two more men appeared.

Alex felt the pistol against his back waver as the moonlight caught the figure of one of the two men and shone on the rider's bright gold hair. A grunt that was something like raw pain reached his ears as they watched the two newcomers join the third. Alex recognized his brother and the man named Simon, as well as Ian, and he, too, felt a certain agony although unlike Patrick, he had known whom he would see.

Alex could also hear, just barely, the gasps of several other Scots. Huntington's men were quiet. Garrick had already prepared them.

Pistols drawn, the three men approached the door of the shelter. Alex watched as they entered, and he heard the discharge of a pistol, then a second. The blankets he had rolled to look like a sleeping body had worked. No man among them could doubt either John Carey's or Ian Ker's intentions. The listeners heard loud muttered curses, and then saw the three men emerge from the rough shelter.

Alex turned around and stared at Patrick, as he slowly lowered the gun that had been aimed at Alex. Alex's hand touched the man's sleeve in something like understanding, and he did not take offense when Patrick's arm was jerked away. "I'm sorry," he whispered, seeing the stricken disbelieving face of Patrick Ker.

He stood and moved from the trees into the clearing, not waiting to see whether the others accompanied him.

"Are you looking for me, John?" he said clearly in the night.

All three men whirled around. John Carey stood still for a moment, then he reached for his sword. He did not have time to reload his pistol.

"Aye," he said. "You've led me a merry chase."

"Not so merry, I think, brother."

Ian's hand came up, and there was a pistol in it. All three conspirators had pistols, and Alex remembered only two had been discharged.

"I wouldna, Ian." Patrick's words were softly spoken but deadly in intent. "Drop it to the ground."

Ian moved forward, his eyes searching the woods around him. He saw Patrick emerge from the trees, then several other of his kinsmen. A slight smile came to his lips as his eyes found Elsbeth. He dropped the gun as ordered and bowed as if there were no one else there. "My lovely cousin." And Elsbeth knew he understood exactly what had happened.

Elsbeth stood transfixed. Huntington's men had also come from the trees and they all stood there, like an audience, she thought, to some terrible scene in a Greek tragedy.

John Carey was the first to move. "To me," he ordered the Huntington men, taking the gamble they would support him since he had hired and paid them. But each stood in place with Alex.

"To me," the younger Carey said again, desperately.

"You'll have to fight your own battles now, brother," Alex said, holding his sword as he approached John.

With a roar of rage, John Carey drew his sword from the heavy leather belt around his waist. "A pleasure," he rasped.

The two swords met in air, each testing the strength of the other, before Alex stepped back, and lowered his sword. Then he lunged forward with a thrust met by John.

Both had fought together as boys, but that was years ago, and it was not with the deadly purpose now evident between them. John knew his only chance was to kill Alex and try to regain the loyalty of his men. Even so, he realized his life was probably forfeit because of this trap. That knowledge gave him a recklessness that made him a better swordsman than he generally was.

The clash of heavy steel against steel rang in the night air. Elsbeth felt the presence of Hugh behind her, felt his hand on her shoulder as she watched the deadly duel. Her eyes darted to Patrick, whose gun was now leveled at his cousin. Two other Scots were guarding the third conspirator.

Everyone else was watching the fight between brother and brother. Despite the chilled air, Alex was already dripping with sweat. The earlier sword injury to his arm slowed his movement, and a particularly powerful blow caused waves of agony to travel up his arm and into his shoulder.

Alex moved back awkwardly, seeming to lose his balance, and John drove in, seeking his brother's heart. Elsbeth cried out and started toward Alex but in that one second everything changed. John, thinking himself victorious, left an opening.

Alex's sword caught the point of John's sword in a sudden shattering blow that knocked it from his brother's hand. Alex drove his sword on, catching his brother's arm and opening it to the bone. As John fell, Alex's sword followed him, and its point touched his brother's throat, hesitating there.

"Yield," Alex said.

"Never, whoreson," his brother said.

Alex knew he should kill him, but something inside would not let him. The sword trembled in his hands, but he could not press it deeper. "You will leave England," he finally grated through his teeth. "And God help you if you ever return. There's enough evidence now to see you drawn and quartered."

He turned to two of Huntington's men. "Watch him."

Alex turned to Elsbeth, who flung herself into his arms, uncaring of the stares of the Scots and English. He took her in his arms and held her tight.

"A charming scene." Through her relief that Alex had survived, Elsbeth heard Ian's sarcastic remark. She started to move, but Alex held her head pressed close to his heart.

"Traitor!" It was Patrick's voice, full of anguish and anger.

Elsbeth heard Ian's voice—defeated, tired. Yet still there was a lilt to it, a lilt that had always charmed her. "I gambled," he said with a shrug. "I thought the clan needed a stronger leader."

"By killing your own laird?" Patrick's tone was, even now, incredulous. "By making the devil's bargains with our enemies?"

"Ye always said, cousin, the objective justified the means."

"God's blood, Ian, not by such means!" Patrick replied.

Elsbeth wriggled, seeking escape from Alex's embrace. She knew what was coming. She had to stop it. Perhaps Ian could go away...far away.

But Alex's arms were like steel, and he whispered into her ear. "There's no going back now." He could spare his own brother, for he had been the one wronged. It was his choice. But he knew he could not stop this battle. This was between the Kers, and he had no right to interfere.

Elsbeth once more heard the icy bone-chilling sound of steel clashing, but it lasted only seconds, before she heard the sickening sound of steel in flesh, and a small groan. She wrenched away from Alex and saw Ian kneeling on the ground, a hand covering a spreading splotch of red on his jack. His eyes found her. "I'm sorry, Elsbeth. I...I...love you." Then he slowly fell to the ground.

Elsbeth ran to him, kneeling beside him, watching the bright blue of his eyes glaze over. "Oh, Ian. Ian."

"Almost," he whispered. "You...almost loved me." The light went from his eyes, and they became blank as his hand fell from his chest to the ground.

Patrick had also knelt next to Ian. "He let me win. He didn't even try." There was a strange huskiness in his voice as he leaned over and closed Ian's eyes. He rose slowly, looking away from the still form, and his eyes caught a sudden movement.

"Huntington!" he shouted as his hand went for the pistol he had laid on the ground when he took up the sword.

Elsbeth whirled in time to see Simon, whom everyone had forgotten while Patrick and Ian fought, kick the pistol, which Ian had dropped earlier, to John Carey. She saw John grab the weapon, raise it and aim at Alex.

"Alex!" Elsbeth screamed and threw herself at him as John Carey's and Patrick's guns discharged simultaneously.

John Carey fell back, a bullet hole through his forehead.

Then the English and Scots stood in stunned horrified silence as they watched their two leaders, the border lord and his Scottish lady, their arms around each other, fall slowly to the ground as their blood mingled and shone bright in the moonlight.

Chapter Twenty-two

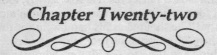

Alex woke with a blinding ache in his head. Flashes of scenes darted in and out of his mind—John, Ian, pistols firing, Elsbeth hurling herself at him.

"Elsbeth!" He called out her name, his eyes opening against hurtful light as they searched for her.

But his gaze found only a dour Scotsman with dark hair and a plaid slung over his shoulder. At the sound of Alex's voice, he had turned from the window he'd been staring out of.

"My lord," the Scot said with obviously feigned humility. "Ye've a mighty constitution. I'll say tha' for ye."

"Elsbeth?" Alex repeated.

"In the next room," Patrick replied with a slight smile. "Sleeping off one of Magdalene's potions. 'Twas the only way we could keep her from ye."

"Was she injured?"

"Not as badly as ye, Huntington. A crease, nothing more, but it might have slowed the bullet that nearly split your hard skull."

"I want to see her."

Patrick sighed. "Ye're in no shape...."

Alex ignored him and tried to sit. Waves of pain flooded him, but still he struggled up. He steadied himself with one hand on the bed as the world spun around him.

He reached out toward Patrick. "Your arm." It was more an order than a request, and Patrick was surprised to find himself offering his aid, half lifting the English earl and supporting him as they stumbled toward the door that led to the adjoining room.

Alex just barely noted they had placed him in Huntington's master chamber, John's chamber, and Elsbeth in the room usually reserved for the master's wife. But the pain in his head was too great to make much of the fact.

Patrick opened the door, and Alex peered in. Magdalene was sitting beside Elsbeth and looked up with concern at Alex. "Ye should be abed, m'lord," she said.

Alex ignored her and looked intently at the still form on the bed. A bandage was wrapped neatly around her head, her hair peaking out beneath the edges. Alex took another step, compelling Patrick to move with him, then another until he could lean down and hear her soft breathing and touch her cheek.

"Satisfied, Huntington?" Patrick finally said. "Ye've almost broken my sword arm."

Alex turned painfully and gave him a wry look. "'Twas partly my intention," he said, but then his face blanched, and he stumbled as weakness overtook him.

Magdalene gave Patrick a baleful look. "Lackwit," she pronounced without deference as she nodded at Alex. "He should never ha' left the bed."

"He would ha' crawled ha' I not given an arm," Patrick replied. Looking only slightly chastened, he maneuvered his charge back to the other room and into bed.

Alex fell into the soft folds, cursing his weakness. There was so much he wanted to know.

"John?"

"Dead. Ye're too bloody softhearted, just like Elsbeth. 'Twill be no sport fighting ye." Patrick glared at him as if he'd just committed a mortal sin.

Alex grinned weakly. "I don't wish to match you again. You're too skilled with that sword."

Patrick dropped his eyes a moment as he recalled the fight in the courtyard at the Ker tower and last night's match between Huntington and his brother. "'Tis a bad habit ye have, not killing your opponent when ye ha' the chance."

"I was right at least one time," Alex observed wryly.

"I would have killed ye had it not been for Elsbeth."

"I know," Alex replied.

"Ye keep doing that and ye'll make Elsbeth a widow."

Alex stared at the Scot.

"Aye," Patrick said. "I know. Elsbeth had to tell me to make me listen. Even then, I believed it a Carey trick."

"And now?" Alex asked softly.

"I still think it's a bloody Carey trick," Patrick said dourly, but the side of his mouth twitched. "The only thing that will convince me otherwise is a proper wedding."

Alex's stare grew even more disbelieving. The pain in his head was obviously making him hear fanciful things.

"Don't ye think I am happy about it," Patrick said. "I would ha' much preferred a fine Scotsman such as myself." His mouth twitched a little more. "But I ken my cousin well. She can be as stubborn and one-minded as a wounded boar."

"Patrick . . ."

But the Scot stared him into silence. "When she tried to gi' her life for yours, I kenned ye must be worth something, Carey or no'. I donna like it, but there it be."

They both stopped talking as Magdalene entered the room. Alex frowned, her appearance finally registering in his whirling head. "Magdalene?" Alex said.

Patrick frowned at him. "Ye donna think I would trust Elsbeth with a Carey, do ye? I sent for Magdalene."

Alex couldn't stop a crooked grin. "What do all the Careys think of this invasion?"

"I donna think they like it a bit more than we," Patrick admitted wryly. "Your Garrick ha' some fine talking to do, and my Kers feel a wee bit outnumbered."

A wee bit, Alex thought with another smile, which ended abruptly as pain rolled through him like thunder. A wee bit. More than three hundred against six.

It was as if Patrick read his mind. "We Kers would just ha' to fight a bit harder."

Alex's mouth twisted at the Scot bravado. "Where is Davey?"

"Keeping peace, I'd wager." Patrick started to say something more, but Magdalene pushed him aside without ceremony and leaned over Alex, her hands gently unwinding the bandage at his head.

"How do ye feel, m'lord?"

Alex considered the question at length. His head felt as if it had been trampled by horses, he was as weak as a babe, and the dizziness unnerved him. But a sense of relief, a sense of freedom were surging inside him. It was over, and the fact that Patrick Ker stood here meant that the larger battle, the objective of peace, had not been lost.

"Thanks to the Kers," Alex said with just a touch of charming mischief, "I believe I'll live."

"'Tis the hard Carey head," Patrick replied acidly. "I'll take no' the blame."

"Out," Magdalene scolded, although her lips, too, were twitching. She watched as Patrick gave her a blistering look before ungraciously disappearing out the door.

She carefully undid Alex's bandage, and took from it a foul-smelling poultice. There was a deep ridge carved by the bullet along his forehead and the side of his head. The whole area was swollen but there were none of the red streaks she had dreaded, nor did he have the brain fever she had thought possible.

"Ye'll have a handsome scar, m'lord."

"Elsbeth?"

Magdalene's severe face broke into a small smile. "She'll have one, m'lord, but barely noticeable."

"She *is* all right?"

"Aye, except for her fretting ov'r ye. She wouldna leave yer side all night until I put something in her wine. Ye both are uncommonly stubborn. Now ye lie still," she ordered, and Alex suffered under her quick hands as she placed a fresh poultice on his wound and gave him a cup of some malodorous substance.

He held it dubiously.

"Ye need yer strength, m'lord," she said quietly. "For Lady Elsbeth. She will need it."

Alex met her eyes directly. "You approve?"

"Anyone with half an eye could see the love ye ha' for each other. But there are some who will not."

Alex's fist knotted. It had taken many years to develop and strengthen the hatred on the border. He could not think to erase it in a night. At least they had made a beginning. He sipped the liquid, the bright red of pain dulling, fading into gray and then blackness.

Elsbeth sat beside Alex, watching him sleep. The bright white of the bandage contrasted with the black of his hair and the tan of his face. Long black lashes covered those deep gray eyes, and he looked more peaceful than she had ever seen him.

Magdalene had warned her there would be a deep scar on his face, but now his mouth was relaxed in a way she had seen rarely, even in sleep, and she knew instinctively some of the uglier hidden wounds within him had been healed. She took his hand and held it, loving him with every fiber of her being.

After the loud report of the shot in the woods, she had felt a sudden pain and had fallen with him. She didn't know how long she lay there, stunned, before she felt the blood pouring from a deep wound on his head and knew the uncommon stillness of his body.

She had screamed, and screamed, and screamed. He was dead, and she didn't want to live without him. She felt hands around her, but she wouldn't let go of Alex. And then Patrick had lifted her and handed her to someone else, and David Garrick was kneeling beside Alex.

"Don't let him die," she had pleaded. "Don't let him die."

There was not one of the twelve men standing in the small clearing who did not recognize the love and desperation in her voice. Kers had looked at Careys and Careys had looked back, confusion and wariness in every exchange.

"He's not dead," David said. "We must get him back to the house."

Elsbeth struggled to free herself and ran to his side, her fingers touching his mouth, wanting to feel his breath. "Alex . . . you have to live. For me. You have to live."

She felt an arm, gentle but insistent, and she heard Patrick's voice. "Ye're bleeding, Elsbeth. We ha' to get it tended."

"I'm going with him," she said, barely listening to his words. There was blood on her, but she had thought it Alex's. Now pain—throbbing insistent pain—pierced the shock that had temporarily dulled her senses.

"Elsbeth."

"I'm going with him."

There was so much agonized determination in her voice that Patrick surrendered. "We'll go wi' ye. I'll not leave ye alone wi' the Careys."

She reached for his hand. "Patrick . . ."

He took her hand with his big one, and pulled her to him with supreme gentleness. "He'll be all right, lass. He ha' more lives than a cat."

She suddenly thought of what he was offering . . . a Ker going to Huntington. "Is it safe?" Her eyes went to Ian on the ground, and she struggled to keep back the tears. "I couldn't bear—"

David Garrick looked up. "I guarantee safe conduct." He looked at the men of arms with him, and they nodded.

Patrick glanced at him dryly. One Carey was dead, and the missing lord, suspected kidnapped by the Kers, was near death. He wondered exactly how much control this Englishman had. If circumstances had been reversed, he doubted if his men would have permitted much explanation. Still, he could not leave Elsbeth alone, nor did he want to drag her away bodily and fight her all the way home. Even then, he suspected she would find a way back to Huntington.

"I go," he told his Kers. "Ye can make yer own decision." All of them nodded their intent to accompany him. Patrick started to turn back to Elsbeth, hesitated, then ordered one of his men to go and bring Magdalene to Huntington.

David had torn a piece of material from his shirt and wrapped it around Alex's head. He asked for help in getting Alex mounted, and hands, both Scot and English, reached out to help, lifting him gently on a horse that had been fetched from the woods.

David mounted behind his lord, cradling him in his arms, while Elsbeth, blood still streaming down her face, mounted her horse and moved next to David, her eyes never leaving Alex's still form. They didn't leave him during the long torturous ride . . .

* * *

Alex moved slightly, and Elsbeth tightened her fingers on his hand. Slowly, his eyes opened and he saw her sitting there. His lips curved in a slow lazy smile.

He brought her hand to his mouth and kissed it slowly, first her palm and then each of her fingers. He opened his arms and she went into them, and he knew a sudden blinding happiness. She had come here with him, to him, and Patrick Ker, in his own stoic way, had given consent.

"Your cousin thinks we should have a proper marriage."

Elsbeth took her head from Alex's heart, and looked at him with surprise. She had not talked to Patrick since they arrived, although she knew from Magdalene that everything was miraculously calm between the Kers and Careys—though a wee bit tense.

"He does?"

"Reluctantly, I think. He said he would have preferred a 'fine Scotsman such as myself.'" He imitated Patrick's Scots border accent.

She grinned at him. "'Tis Patrick's way of teasing. I don't think he ever loved me—not that way."

"I love you, my bonny little Scotswoman."

Elsbeth self-consciously put her hand to her head, and the bandage there, and her eyes clouded.

"Magdalene said your scar will be scarcely visible, though I would care not were it otherwise. But you, my love, you will have to look at this great ugly face."

"It's a beautiful face," she protested. "It will always be a beautiful face." To prove it, she showered the unbandaged parts with kisses, light feathery loving tender kisses that speeded his heart and made it ache with joy.

"You will marry me again, then?"

"Oh yes, my love! Again and again and again and . . ."

She could have gone forever, but her words were caught in his lips while her eyes kept telling him.

The wedding was three weeks later on a clear crisp autumn day. Colorful tents were spread throughout Huntington since nearly the entire population of the border had been invited.

The two Englishmen, William and Tate, who had accompanied Elsbeth across England, surveyed the scene from the ramparts of the castle with no small amount of satisfaction. This was exactly what their lord, Northumberland, had wanted.

For a while they had thought they had failed. They had followed the Scots to the confrontation with the conspirators three weeks ago, and had arrived as Elsbeth and Huntington fell to the ground. Their unlikely presence was barely noted by the two opposing groups who rushed to aid their fallen leaders.

Tate and William had returned to Huntington with the others and had waited outside, as had a growing number of Huntington tenants and servants, for word of the earl. News of what had transpired spread rapidly from one group to another, and there was a vast uncertainty and dread about the future.

When word came that Huntington would live, and later that there would be a formal marriage, William and Tate left to report to Northumberland. They had arrived back only yesterday, bringing with them a magnificent black mare as a wedding present for Elsbeth. The duke was pleased. This part of the border, at least, would be pacified.

Tate watched as the Ker banners mixed with those of the Rutherfords and Gordons and Turnbulls and Douglases. English colors were also scattered throughout the grounds. There were jousts and games, and the Scots and English mingled peaceably enough for the moment. Most of the families were grateful the blood feud between two of the strongest families on the border had ended. The feud had threatened to bring them all into wholesale war, and while an occasional raid was expected and good sport, the war between the Careys and Kers was another matter altogether.

The two Englishmen knew that few besides themselves and the Ker and Carey families were aware of what had really happened that night in the forest. Neither wanted their traitor, or the dishonor, exposed, and there was a conspiracy of silence. It had been announced that John Carey and Ian Ker had been killed by border outlaws, and that the two families had finally joined to rid themselves of the threat to both.

Whether the tale was altogether believed was unimportant. It was accepted by the English and Scottish wardens, who merely wanted the peace established. Tate suspected the real story was bound to leak out and would merely become another legend in a place rife with such tales.

He turned to William, who had a strangely sad smile on his face. William had been much taken with Lady Elsbeth on the trip from London, and still harbored a wistful longing for her. "We must be off," Tate said with understanding. The lady had also laid claim to part of his heart.

"We will not stay for the wedding?"

"Our business is finished."

"Aye," William said, looking with some awe at the mixture of Scottish and English colors. "I wouldn't have believed it had I not seen with my own two eyes."

"The power of love," Tate observed with a trace of cynicism. He wondered how long it would last, this uncommon, even unnatural, harmony between the Scot and English borderers. Then he shrugged. It was no longer his affair.

"Should we say farewell to Lady Elsbeth?" William said wistfully.

"I think she has other things on her mind," Tate said.

Two hours later they were on their way to London.

Elsbeth indeed had other things on her mind. Tomorrow she would be wed. Again.

And she thought she had the most glorious wedding present for her husband.

It could be, she warned herself, the tension, the terror of the past few weeks. Perhaps that was why the blood had not flowed from her this month, or why her body seemed different in some way.

Yet she thought not. She remembered when they were parting in London, and they had disagreed about the color of their children's hair. She smiled to herself. The issue would be settled soon.

Joy filled her, crowding out the last shadows that remained from that dreadful night. She would not think of the past, only the future . . . and that was so very beautiful.

She was interrupted by Annie, whom she had brought to Huntington for the wedding. Annie took one look at her mistress's glowing face and the hand on her abdomen.

"Ye're not..."

"I believe so, Annie. Isn't it wonderful?" Elsbeth almost laughed at Annie's warring emotions. The housekeeper had not been overly pleased by the marriage, yet she had wanted a new baby in the family for so long.

Annie's mouth pinched. "A Carey baby?" she snorted.

"My baby," Elsbeth corrected. "Mine and Alex's, and you're not to tell anyone. Not yet."

"A Carey baby," Annie said again, but some of the disgust was gone as she looked at Elsbeth's face—soft and tender and so full of love. She had never thought to see such a look on her mistress's face, and if the Carey lord could do that, mayhap he was not so wicked as she had thought. Mayhap she should give him a chance.

Mayhap...

It was as if the heavens blessed the union, Elsbeth thought as she looked up at skies uncommonly clear for this time of year on the border. The sun was bright and warm, the sky a rich blue embroidered by lacy wisps of cloud.

Patrick, his countenance slightly grim and his eyes unsmiling, led her across the courtyard to the small chapel where the actual ceremony would be performed. Although he had suggested this ceremony, she knew he was taking no pleasure in it. Louisa was behind Elsbeth, holding the train of her dress, and Elsbeth had seen Patrick's eyes return repeatedly to her ward. She smiled to herself. She suspected Patrick was soon to learn the true impact of love.

Her hand tightened around his arm. He had been a tower of strength in the past weeks. It was he who had persuaded the Kers to accept the marriage, to attend the ceremony. It was he who had broken the news of Ian's betrayal, and later had convinced Elsbeth and Alex that their marriage would be better accepted were it not known there had been an earlier English ceremony. It was he who had found a Scottish minister, who, with an English one, would bind the two families.

Yet she knew he had not entirely accepted the marriage himself, not because *he* wanted her, but because he still couldn't wholly accept the union with a hated enemy. That, too, Elsbeth thought sadly, would take time.

She and Patrick entered the small chapel and walked down the aisle toward Alex, who stood straight and magnificent in blue velvet trimmed in gold. Her legs trembled as she passed the leaders of various clans and the English border lords and their ladies. It seemed a never-ending walk...a walk bridging centuries.

She felt Alex's hand take hers from Patrick's. She looked up at him, at the once fathomless eyes now filled with love and tenderness, at the inquisitive half smile she loved so much, at the scar, still red and angry, which bespoke his rare honor and compassion. She loved him so much. So very much.

She smiled at him, sure and confident, and the half smile widened as his hand tightened on hers. They were alone together for endless seconds as love flowed between them like a mighty unconquerable river.

The words of the Scottish minister brought them back to the present, and Elsbeth listened as if in a daze. The only reality was Alex's strong hand. She was surprised when she heard her own voice respond in a clear loud tone, and Alex's in his distinctive lazy border brogue.

And then it was over. She felt his lips on hers and once more they were alone among their guests. His kiss deepened, and she responded with a passion that had been simmering during his long recuperative period. They had not made love since coming to Huntington, and now her body felt like melting wax, warm and trembling and expectant.

Somewhere at the back of her senses, she heard the clearing of a throat, and then a louder one, and finally a few chuckles. Reluctantly, Alex released her lips but kept a steely hold on her arm. Together they retreated down the aisle, accepting amused congratulations along the way.

The next hours were a nightmare. They ate, they danced, they talked, they accepted good wishes, but they wanted nothing more than privacy. They were unaware of the exchanges between the Kers and Careys—the lingering looks of vigilance and curiosity and dislike. It was all David Garrick, now named captain of the men-at-arms, and Patrick could do to maintain some semblance of harmony.

Alex and Elsbeth suffered through the great wedding banquet, each remembering the one at London, which they had shared alone. Now their guests were noisy and quarrelsome; one veiled insult erupted into battle. As Patrick and Garrick once more stepped in, Alex and Elsbeth slipped away.

Once up in the master chamber, Elsbeth regarded her husband worriedly. "You don't think they will kill one another?"

"I have great faith in my David and your Patrick," he answered, rubbing his face against hers.

There was a great crash downstairs, and Elsbeth winced.

Alex kissed her long and lingeringly.

There was another crash, and Elsbeth trembled. Alex's kiss deepened.

There were voices, loud and harsh, and more sounds as if tables were being overturned.

"Hmm," Alex said, moving his lips to her neck.

A roar came up from the great banquet room.

"Alex!"

"Hmm," he replied, his hands moving to the fastenings on the back of her dress.

"Don't you think . . . ?"

He sighed and slowly withdrew his hands. "I will see that all is well."

Alex straightened his clothes and went out, closing the door behind him. He descended the steps and passed through the huge entrance area to the great hall. There he looked balefully over the scene in front of him.

One of the great long tables was overturned and two men were fighting on top of it, while members of the Ker family watched from one side, and his men-at-arms from another. The men on the table were Patrick and David, battered and bruised. As the fighters noted the sudden silence they turned to Alex and gave him great happy grins.

"'Tis a draw," yelled one of the men near the table.

"David!" Alex's voice was uncommonly sharp, his mouth in a deep frown. He had expected David to hold the peace.

Patrick answered with his usual air of insolence. "'Twas a fight tha' was needed," he observed as blood dripped from the side of the mouth. "And better between twa than all." Patrick's hand reached out and clasped David's. "A good fight it was, too, for all ye be English."

Alex couldn't help holding back a smile. So David and Patrick had reduced the hostility in their own unique way. The simmering tension had been replaced by good-natured goading. But he tried to look severe as he gave the required disciplinary speech. "The lady must needs be convinced of your peaceful intentions," Alex commented wryly to the sound of laughter as each man there realized they had delayed the most important part of today's event.

Patrick jumped down from the table. "Come, Garrick. We'll take your lord back upstairs and convince my lady we're naught but happy lambs." To another burst of laughter, David joined him and they lifted Alex onto their shoulders, totally disregarding his protests as he swayed back and forth.

Up they went, Alex expecting to go sprawling any second, until they reached the master chamber. Patrick released his hold on one of Alex's legs and pounded on the door. When Elsbeth opened it, her face white and anxious, she saw the discomfited Alex supported by the grinning Patrick and David, followed by scores of both Kers and Careys behind them in the wide hall.

Patrick and David lowered Alex, none too carefully, and he almost went down as Elsbeth reached out a hand and steadied him. Patrick and David bowed drunkenly, trying to remove the leers from their faces.

"We bring your lord," Patrick said, "and a truce." He turned around. "To the ale."

"To the ale!" rang out supporting cries, and hurriedly, awkwardly, drunkenly, the Careys and Kers turned as one and headed back down to the great hall, leaving Elsbeth and Alex to stare at each other in wonder, before their expressions turned ardent and wanting.

Together, devouring each other with their eyes, they closed the door to the revelry below.

Epilogue

They came together again, eight months later, the Careys and the Kers. This time there was no question of hostility.

There was fighting, of course. Competitive matches and games. Good-natured wrestling. Sly but harmless insults.

Such was the way of the border, Elsbeth thought on this clear lovely May morning as she watched a rough game of bowls. As a roar went up from onlookers, a loud complaining wail came from the bundle in her arms.

She lifted young Alexander Patrick Carey and soothed the angry red face with kisses. He would be baptized this afternoon in view of both clans. Patrick was to be godfather, and his wife, Louisa, godmother.

Elsbeth glanced over at Patrick, who was leading the Kers in the game. His eyes were brighter than she had ever seen them, the onyx gleaming with competitive fervor and his mouth in an intense determined frown. It was only when he saw Louisa, who was also swelling now with child, that his face relaxed and his mouth gentled.

He was, Elsbeth thought with no little amazement, a besotted husband. She wondered if he had only been awaiting a little gentleness in his life.

Patrick was now the acknowledged laird of the Kers. Elsbeth had surrendered all claim to the Ker holdings and asked Queen Mary to acknowledge Patrick, the next in line, as heir. It had given Patrick a confidence that brought forth the qualities, the leadership, that Elsbeth suspected had lain untapped under the hated burden of being labeled a bastard.

Since her wedding, there had been no more raids. Cattle and sheep were growing fat. Fields had been plowed and planted with expectations of large crops. Alex had paid Patrick a huge sum in reparation for past Carey raids, and cottages had been rebuilt and livestock replenished.

The baby gurgled, and Elsbeth felt such contentment, such joy, that she thought she would burst. She felt Alex's hand on her shoulder and looked up.

The scar on the right side of his face had left his mouth perpetually turned up in a slight smile. She thought it did nothing to mar the handsomeness of his face, but merely instilled it with the character she knew was so deep within him. She leaned over and kissed the top of his hand and then looked up, mouthing the silent words of love that were always so strong between them.

And then they both turned back to watch the play, her hand touching his, as their child's pleased cries spurred first one, then the other team on until two exhausted groups of Kers and Careys fell laughing and sated on the ground.

*   *   *   *   *

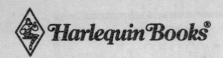

GREAT NEWS...

HARLEQUIN UNVEILS NEW SHIPPING PLANS

For the convenience of customers, Harlequin has announced that Harlequin romances will now be available in stores at these convenient times each month*:

Harlequin Presents, American Romance, Historical, Intrigue:

> May titles: April 10
> June titles: May 8
> July titles: June 5
> August titles: July 10

Harlequin Romance, Superromance, Temptation, Regency Romance:

> May titles: April 24
> June titles: May 22
> July titles: June 19
> August titles: July 24

We hope this new schedule is convenient for you.

With only two trips each month to your local bookseller, you'll never miss any of your favorite authors!

*Please note: There may be slight variations in on-sale dates in your area due to differences in shipping and handling.   HDATES-RR

*Applicable to U.S. only.

```
┌─────────────────────────────────┐
│          A CENTURY OF           │
│    1890s AMERICAN 1990s         │
│          ROMANCE                │
└─────────────────────────────────┘
```

A CENTURY OF AMERICAN ROMANCE has taken you on a nostalgic journey through time—from the turn of the century to the dawn of the year 2000.

Relive all the memories . . . the passions . . . of
A CENTURY OF AMERICAN ROMANCE.

1890s #345 AMERICAN PIE by Margaret St. George
1900s #349 SATURDAY'S CHILD by Dallas Schulze
1910s #353 THE GOLDEN RAINTREE by Suzanne Simmons Guntrum
1920s #357 THE SENSATION by Rebecca Flanders
1930s #361 ANGELS WINGS by Anne Stuart
1940s #365 SENTIMENTAL JOURNEY by Barbara Bretton
1950s #369 STRANGER IN PARADISE by Barbara Bretton
1960s #373 HEARTS AT RISK by Libby Hall
1960s #377 TILL THE END OF TIME by Elise Title
1970s #381 HONORBOUND by Tracy Hughes
1980s #385 MY ONLY ONE by Eileen Nauman
1990s #389 A ＞ LOVERBOY by Judith Arnold

Back by Popular Demand

Janet Dailey
Americana

A romantic tour of America through fifty favorite Harlequin Presents® novels, each set in a different state researched by Janet and her husband, Bill. A journey of a lifetime in one cherished collection.

In June, don't miss the sultry states featured in:

Title # 9 - FLORIDA
       Southern Nights
  #10 - GEORGIA
       Night of the Cotillion

Available wherever Harlequin books are sold.

JD-JR

THIS JULY, HARLEQUIN OFFERS YOU THE PERFECT SUMMER READ!

Sunsational

**EMMA DARCY
EMMA GOLDRICK
PENNY JORDAN
CAROLE MORTIMER**

From top authors of Harlequin Presents comes HARLEQUIN SUNSATIONAL, a four-stories-in-one book with 768 pages of romantic reading.

Written by such prolific Harlequin authors as Emma Darcy, Emma Goldrick, Penny Jordan and Carole Mortimer, HARLEQUIN SUNSATIONAL is the perfect summer companion to take along to the beach, cottage, on your dream destination or just for reading at home in the warm sunshine!

Don't miss this unique reading opportunity.

Available wherever Harlequin books are sold.

SUN